SEDUCED BY THE NET

"X'GBris have two choices to consider now," LLna said to them. "You can be part of the Net, or you can be left out of it."

"We can *not* choose to be left out of the Net," snapped a matriarch. "The Net will still eat members of our families!"

"That is true," said LLna. "You would have to forbid all contact with GodHeads and other races who are connected to it. Ultimately, you would be left far behind in technology, science, and commerce."

"That is no choice," said another matriarch. "You're telling us we must be corrupted or we must die."

"No," said LLna, "I'm telling you that you must change or you will fade away."

GODHEADS

Emily Devenport

A ROC BOOK

ROC
Published by the Penguin Group
Penguin Putnam Inc., 375 Hudson Street,
New York, New York 10014, U.S.A.
Penguin Books Ltd, 27 Wrights Lane,
London W8 5TZ, England
Penguin Books Australia Ltd, Ringwood,
Victoria, Australia
Penguin Books Canada Ltd, 10 Alcorn Avenue,
Toronto, Ontario, Canada M4V 3B2
Penguin Books (N.Z.) Ltd, 182–190 Wairau Road,
Auckland 10, New Zealand

Penguin Books Ltd, Registered Offices:
Harmondsworth, Middlesex, England

First published by Roc, an imprint of Dutton Signet,
a member of Penguin Putnam Inc.

First Printing, April, 1998
10 9 8 7 6 5 4 3 2 1

 REGISTERED TRADEMARK—MARCA REGISTRADA

Printed in the United States of America

For my grandmother and grandfather
Bunny and Lester Devenport

ACKNOWLEDGMENTS

I would like to thank the usual suspects, Ernest Hogan, Rick Cook, and Gia DeSimone, for brainstorming and for reading the whole damned thing when it was finished. I fed them tamales, rice, beans, and homemade tortillas from El Bravo, the best Mexican restaurant in the known universe (located at 7th Street and Butler, in case you're ever in Phoenix). The owner of El Bravo, Carmen Tafoya, made the tortillas for us on a busy Saturday, and somehow "thank you" doesn't seem sufficient; but I offer it anyway.

PRONUNCIATION GUIDE

Aten	AH-ten
Bomarigala	boh-mah-ree-GAHL-AH
Kirito	Kih-ree-TOH
X'GBri	ex-GIB-ree
WWul	WUH-wul
KLse	KEHL-see
JKre	JACK-ree
STra	SUHT-rah
MRnu	MUHR-new
GDro	GEED-roh
TGri	TIG-ree
O'KHro	OH-koh-roh
Voxi	VAHK-see
LLna	LEHL-nah
KRni	KUHR-nee
SSka	SUHS-kah

I felt a cleaving in my Mind
As if my Brain had split
I tried to match it—Seam by Seam
But could not make them fit.

The thought behind, I strove to join
Unto the thought before
But Sequence ravelled out of Sound
Like Balls—upon a Floor

—Emily Dickinson
Poem 937

THE EGG

I keep having that dream.

It always starts out so well. I'm barefoot, and the warm ground feels so good under my feet. The day is very hot, and I'm very thirsty; but these problems seem eclipsed by this Great Good Feeling. The Feeling is hard to put into words, but you might understand what I mean if you think about the way you felt on the last day of school, or the last day of a job you really hated. It's a feeling completely uncomplicated by guilt or regrets. I wonder if that's important. I'll bet it is.

I'm walking down a long, dusty road. No pavement. The houses that I'm passing aren't shacks; some of them even have neat little rock gardens, or statuettes, or bridges over non-existent streams. But they are the houses of people who are one step away from poverty, from death. They are the houses of the working poor.

And I'm leaving them. I'll never see them again; and because of that I'm fond of them. People are standing in those yards; some are even passing me in the road, but none of them look at me. They are pretending not to see me. This is important, too.

And now I'm passing through the desert. This desert stretches over the entire world; I'm just walking through a small part of it, yet even that small part is so huge. I have a sense of single-minded purpose. If I didn't, I'd sit down in the road, overwhelmed by the heat and my thirst. But these things are happening for the last time, I won't have to feel them again. So I can stand them a little longer.

And now I'm in the city. I've had the dream so many

times that I've begun to recognize this as the part where things start to go wrong. Lately I've tried to make myself wake up at this point, while I still have the Great Good Feeling, but before I see the terrible eyes. So far, I haven't succeeded.

So on I go to a particular building and up some steps, through a door and into an office that's so cool it almost hurts. I can smell water in here. They keep it in coolers, with little water spouts in the side and little paper cups for drinks; but only office people are allowed to drink it. If ordinary people try to get some, they yell at you. They stop you.

Wake up! Wake up! Take deep breaths, get some oxygen into your blood, wake up!

I'm small in this dream. I'm so short, people don't see me going through the office, through doors that ordinary people aren't supposed to go through. And now I've got something in my hands. Daddy's gun.

There's a man in one of the back offices. He wears a good, clean suit, and he's talking to a secretary. His name is Mr. Kyl. He's holding one of those cups of precious water in his hands, sipping it like he doesn't care whether he drinks it or not. Mr. Kyl is tall, and he has this wry smile on his face. He always has that smile, and lately I wonder if it isn't more superior than wry. But my heart always leaps at the sight of him. I always raise my gun.

"Don't shoot! Edna, please don't shoot!" a dreadful voice begs me, and that Great Good Feeling I mentioned before goes right out the window. But I raise that gun and I shoot Mr. Kyl, who has turned to look at me.

I was aiming for his heart, but I'm too short. I hit him in the groin instead.

He folds up like a piece of paper and drifts to the floor. His face is such a mixture of pain and surprise, it's almost comical. But I'm too shocked to laugh. People come flocking about like birds; and there I am with that gun, but they still don't notice me. I get pushed to the back of the room by the crowd.

This is another place where I want to bail out of the dream, while no one's looking. But then someone else comes into the room, and this guy *does* see me. He looks right at me. He takes the gun from my hands.

"Can I have a drink of water?" I ask him.

He leads me to a chair and sets me on his lap. Someone else fetches the water, someone who stands behind me so I can't see her, except for the slender lady-hand that gives me the cup. And now I hear myself telling the man things, but I don't know what I'm saying. All kinds of things, all jumbled up; but the actual words elude me. I sort of think I might be telling him that something bad was done to me. The dream is almost good again now. It feels good to tell him what I've suffered.

But then I hear a cry. It isn't a sound a human voice would make, yet it seems that I know it as well as I (should) know my own face. I turn my head, thinking Mr. Kyl has made that sound. I see the knot of people clustered around his body, but he's not there. Something else is there. Something with huge, black wings that are spread out across the floor, stretching wider than Mr. Kyl was tall. Whatever it is, it cries out again, and I feel the first bolt of pain.

I shot it. *I* did.

"What have I done?" I hear myself saying. "What have I done?"

A hand grabs me by the chin, and the fellow on whose lap I was sitting forces my head around to look at him. But it's not him anymore, it's the old man. The old man I should know from—somewhere. His eyes are full of pain.

"I should never have tamed you," he says. "I should never have helped you. It's all my fault. Why couldn't I just leave you alone?"

He lets go of my face, so I can look around again at the knot of people; but though I don't want to look at him anymore, I can't help but wonder what he's talking about. His words seem like they should be *my* words, and I can't remember why.

Now the knot of people is moving, and I can glimpse the thing they're hiding, the thing with the black wings. It's black all over, so I can't see it very well. And someone is still in the way. But then that someone moves

over a few inches, and I see the eyes. They're looking for
me, looking right *at* me, and they seem to be asking . . .

Asking . . .

Those eyes! Those terrible eyes. They're an arrow
straight to my heart. It hurts so much that it wakes me
every time; and I sit up, gasping, choking on all that
feeling.

This time Aten woke and said, "That dream again?"

I could only nod.

"Are you going to cry?"

"Not this time."

She watched me, not believing it until she saw it with
her own eyes. But I had already lost the need to cry.
The pain had receded; it does that more quickly every
time. Yet something of it always remains behind. It's
changing me, making me more serious, more melan-
choly.

That's funny. Changing me from what? Everyone said
my brain wipe was pretty comprehensive. I've still got a
personality, but the doctors say I'm filling that in as I
go along. They say the human brain is resilient, it likes
patterns, it'll make them if they don't already exist.

I twisted around in our tiny habitat to check our location. Two of us were crammed into an egg ship meant
for one, but they were afraid to send us in anything
bigger. They were afraid we'd attract too much
attention.

"Still bound for GodWorld?" Aten asked, humoring
me.

"Yes," I said. It's true that I get a big kick out of
playing pilot. They taught me how to do that with an
RNA drip, and I still can't get over how much I learned
in just a few weeks. With a chemical brain implant!
Ready-made memories, just add glucose and stir. I think
I like the future. Aten says that people who pilot egg
ships are called EggHeads. If I want to, I can call myself that.

I can't believe all this is happening to plain old me.
In fact, sometimes I *really* can't believe it. Like last
night, when it suddenly occurred to me that we were
about to do something so scary I didn't even want to
think about it.

"Aten," I said, "is it really possible?"

"Of course," she said, stretching her beautiful legs as far as she could in the zero-gravity webbing.

"But is it *probable*?"

"That's up to us."

She's so confident. She's completely the opposite of me. Sometimes I wish they hadn't teamed me up with someone so gorgeous. But most of the time I don't know what I would do without her.

And anyway, they're going to pay me lots of money. I might not remember much about my past, but I sure must have been poor, because I really like the sound of that. And even better—if the GodHeads don't want me, I get paid anyway. Not as much, but enough to make me anyone's definition of rich.

I really hope they don't want me.

"I bet they will," said Aten, proving that the synthetic GodWeed really has linked us. Usually I have to think a deliberate message at her, but sometimes stuff leaks through that I didn't mean to send. If we had been infected with *real* GodWeed, we would have become God-Heads, which I guess means that we would have shared the mental space they call the Net. Guessing is all I can do, because I can't imagine why eating a plant would let you read the mind of someone else who had eaten the same plant.

It's even harder to believe some of the other stuff they told me on OMSK. For instance, they said that GodWeed can think. It's intelligent, self-aware. It can talk to you, like a person, once you've eaten it. Sounds like some kind of drug hallucination to me.

But it must be true, because the synthetic has linked Aten and me.

Aten says it's not telepathy. She says no one has ever discovered a telepath among any of the intelligent races in the known galaxy. She says the synthetic isn't intelligent, it only works because it's so close in chemical structure to GodWeed, and somehow that lets it ride piggyback on the GodHead Net. If the Net wasn't in place, our synthetic would be completely useless.

But then when I press her for specifics about how the

GodHead Net works, she's as much in the dark as I am. And that's what makes me nervous.

"Don't be such a scaredy-cat," Aten said. "You're a good candidate. You might even like the Net. I'm curious to enter it myself. It must be a profound experience."

I stared into her cool, green eyes, hoping to find comfort. "You'll bail me out if I get stuck there. Right?"

"That's what I'm here for, Edna," she said, meaning it. I know she meant it. I'm not the only one who leaks.

"The GodHeads are pretty weird, aren't they?" I said, trying to imagine them, trying to comprehend the monopoly on communications they've contrived.

"Weird," agreed Aten. "At least. Our sponsors would like to bust up their monopoly. That's the situation in a nutshell. Of course"—she turned her head and pierced me with that gaze—"situations don't really fit very well in nutshells, do they?"

"I don't know if they do or not," I said. "I'll have to take your word for it."

Aten sighed and tried to make herself comfortable on our shared couch. I knew she didn't like being crammed in there with me. It bugged me, too, but I had to admit I liked having someone to talk to. I settled back, trying not to disturb her. We still had a few hours left in our sleep cycle, that simulated night that wasn't anywhere near as dark as the perpetual night outside our egg.

I looked at a tactical screen, watching simulated stars slide and stop, slide and stop as we made our hundreds of jumps from OMSK to GodWorld. Aten went back to sleep, but I lay awake for hours, wondering.

Was it all really true? The drips, the jumps, the Net? I was like a newborn, finding things out for the first time. But if it was for the first time, why did it all surprise me so much? As if I was expecting something else.

Thinking back to when I woke up on OMSK, I was embarrassed by how eager I was to please, how eager I was just to *be*. I was scared to leave, then; but now I hoped I would never have to go back.

Where did that feeling come from? Would I ever find out?

Just then I was glad to be going somewhere. It was

almost like the Great Good Feeling. I hoped it would last.

Because those jumps were speeding us toward God-World, that place where plants were intelligent and the sun could kill you if you stood under its naked light. That place where the GodHeads knew each other's thoughts and maybe would know ours, too, if the synthetic worked as well as OMSK was hoping. We would be there within a couple more cycles, and when we got there I knew I would be scared.

I just knew I would.

I knew I was in for trouble as soon as I was ushered into Bomarigala's office. He had on his poker face. His very beautiful, very expensive poker face, I might add. It always took my breath away with its satanic lines, its arched brows and chiseled mouth. I used to think he was vain, buying himself a face like that; but now I realize his beauty was just another way to deceive people, to manipulate them.

As you can see, I wasn't in a charitable mood.

"Aten," he said, pronouncing the name carefully, reminding me how much lower I was in status and syllables than he. "I have an important assignment for you. Probably the most important assignment you will ever have in your life."

"Yes, sir," I said, as neutrally as I could, but he laughed, showing me most of his white teeth.

"Yes, you're going to hate it. But you are uniquely qualified for this job. You are the only agent I have whose personality is strong enough to survive the Net intact."

"Now wait a minute!" I cried, losing my cool like I had sworn I wouldn't. "Who do you think you're kidding? Is that what you said to Rena? Is that what you said to Andera and Kori? Now they're all GodHeads. I guess you *like* giving all your best agents to the enemy."

Bomarigala let me get all the way through that speech without interrupting. That should have told me something right there. He would have cut me off at the knees if he hadn't been amused by what I was saying.

"None of those esteemed individuals would ever have

dared to speak to me with that tone," he said. "You have only proven my point."

I nailed my cool back down. "At your service, sir."

"Yes," he said. "You are." He got up, moving as lithely as a big cat, and walked around his desk. I tried not to flinch; that only amuses him. I kept still until he had walked past me. Then I got up and followed him. I kept one step behind him, my eyes on the curtain of hair that fell down his back, as long as mine, but black, so dark it was nearly blue. It was almost a feminine touch.

But there was nothing feminine about Bomarigala. Nothing soft.

I had no idea where we were going. I never did; not until it was too late, anyway. I had known from the beginning that there would be sacrifices to make. Sacrifices for enormous gain. That's the exchange when you sign on at OMSK.

We got into a lift and moved in toward the center of the complex, toward the medical levels. The conditioned air was a little too dry, as usual. It made my nose itch. I didn't scratch. Bomarigala watched me to see if I was afraid, but I wasn't particularly. I had been in there before, mostly to my benefit.

"*You* aren't the one who's going into the Net," he said. "We found a woman in deep stasis who's perfect for the job."

"Just how many stiffs have you got in deep stasis anyway?"

"Frankly, I don't know," he said. "There are some levels even I haven't been to. She was in an unmarked casket, and there's no record of her in the files. But we do know one thing about her. Her name. It was on her wrist band. *Edna.*"

I frowned. I had never heard that particular combination of syllables before. She was a person of better than average status, though, to have two syllables like that.

"Exotic, isn't it?" he asked. "We did a name search, trying to find anything remotely like it. We found out it's an Old Empire name. From back before the status system."

"Old Empire?" I said, wondering who would look that

far back to find a name for their kid. He watched me, amused, waiting for me to figure it out. I finally did.

"How long, then?" I asked.

"We estimate she's been in stasis for one thousand years."

"And there was something left of her?"

"There was a great deal left of her."

The door opened and we entered forbidden territory. You didn't walk those spotless corridors unless you were a top-level tech, a special agent, or Bomarigala.

You might be wheeled in, of course, blind, sedated, and strapped down.

Bomarigala took me into an observation room. One entire wall was blanked (from our side) to reveal a training session. A woman was sitting with her back to me; I assumed she was Edna. Her trainer sat facing her across the table. He never glanced in our direction, though he certainly must have known that the wall was false.

He was a pleasant-looking fellow, with a kind and watchful face. I don't think he was faking the approval he was showing Edna as she answered various questions (obviously to his satisfaction). Periodically he flashed things into her eyes from his stimulator. I tried not to look at the flashes.

"Did you tell her the truth about how long she was in stasis?" I asked.

"Yes," he said. "Why not? She wanted to know about herself, and it was the only thing we could tell her—other than her name."

I wished I could see Edna's face. She looked like she was almost as tall as me, six feet. Her shoulders were wider than usual for a woman. She was slimly muscled, her build almost athletic. Probably she would have looked more fit if she hadn't been in stasis for one thousand years. One thing surprised me right off the bat. Her hair was red, like mine. *Really* red.

"Her eyes are green, too," said Bomarigala. "I thought that would tickle you."

It didn't tickle me exactly, but it did intrigue me. I'm accustomed to being exotic, people are always teasing me that I need to get out in the sun and get some healthy color. We all read in the history books that the human race used to be more diverse; Edna was physical proof of that. So maybe I'm a throwback instead of an oddball.

I felt Bomarigala's eyes on me. I glanced at him, caught him checking me out. I don't mind being looked at that way, except with him. I never know if he's going to show me the common courtesy of lifting his eyes to my face when I'm looking at him. He's my superior. He has the power of life and death over me.

He looked into my eyes as if he had been looking there all along and said, "We've perfected the synthetic."

"Hmmn," I said, not really believing it.

"Believe it," he warned me. "We're moving forward with this."

"I believe *that*," I said, and looked at Edna again. Her instructor was smiling at her. Her back was straight, her shoulders squared; she leaned forward eagerly. I felt a terrible pity, and squelched it.

I wondered what the synthetic would do to her. To *us,* actually, because I had no doubt that Bomarigala intended to infect me, too. The buzz around OMSK was that it would allow people to achieve something pretty close to telepathy. I'm sure he thought Edna and I would work better together if we had that kind of link.

And of course, I would then be OMSK's link to the Net, once Edna was in. I would be their outside line, as it were.

"Our collaborators deserve most of the credit on this one," he said. "They sacrificed three people to the Net getting this last sample."

"Three for three," I said, thinking of Rena, et al. Then I thought some more. "Collaborators," I said. "X'GBri collaborators? Did they kidnap some GodHeads and taste them?" That was the only theory that made sense to me. X'GBris could copy any compound as long as they were able to taste it first.

Bomarigala shook his head. "You can't kidnap a GodHead."

"So they got friendly and the X'GBris licked them all over."

"Yes," he said. I could feel his eyes on me again, but this time I didn't look. "Some people find X'GBris attractive, you know."

I wondered what Edna would think of X'GBris. Not to mention Vorns, Earlies, and a half dozen other races who had been encountered since she had gone to sleep. I was pretty sure that one thousand years ago was precontact. Uninvited, a mental image of an X'GBri licking Edna popped into my head, followed by a distressing thought.

"Those three who were lost," I said, "wouldn't they have exposed your entire plan to the GodHeads?"

"No," he said. "They only knew they had to obtain a sample. They didn't know why, or for whom."

"Well Jeez, figure it out. Someone wants to know what GodWeed does in a person's bloodstream. Now, who could that be? And why?"

"Any number of interested parties would like to know," he said, unruffled. "For a thousand reasons."

I had my doubts about that. There may have been many parties who would have liked to grab the power and autonomy the Net had given to the Outer Worlds and take it back again for the Inner Worlds, the tyrants and businessmen who had been so fat in the old days. But all of those parties went one place to get things done.

OMSK, where my tender self was now.

"You and Edna will travel to GodWorld in an egg," said Bomarigala, and watched me cringe at the thought. "There you will meet with six of our collaborators, WWul and her husbands. From there, they have made arrangements for Edna to be presented as a candidate in TradeTown. If she's accepted, we're in."

"These collaborators," I said. "Have any of them been infected with the synthetic?"

"One of the husbands. KLse, I believe his name is."

"Did you say *Kelsy*?"

"Close enough."

"So they've got their own piggyback in mind. Strange bedfellows we've found ourselves with."

"Really, Aten," he said, his tone a shade cooler, "is it so unpleasant to be in bed with someone who wants to lick you from head to toe?"

I didn't answer. He might not have been making the reference I thought he was.

Two years before, when I was sleeping on OMSK before another assignment, someone slipped into my quarters in the pitch dark and made love to me. I mean really hot, wild stuff. Someone with a great build, someone who knew what he was doing. And of course, there had been all that hair to run my hands through in the dark. It hadn't been a rape, but I couldn't see who it was; that was part of the thrill. Bomarigala wasn't the only man on OMSK who liked to wear his hair long.

But now, the memory made me uncomfortable. I wasn't sure what the person I had made love to thought about what I had done with him. I wasn't sure if he though it meant he could do whatever he wanted to me, or that I was a whore, or that I was lonely, or . . .

And I couldn't bring it up to Bomarigala. If it hadn't been him that night after all, he would learn one more piece of information about me that was none of his business.

"You're so sure they won't kill me and use Edna themselves," I said.

"No. I'm not sure. That's the hard part, Aten. That's what you get paid for." He cupped my elbow like a gentleman escorting a lady into a ballroom. "Time to go to the doctor," he said.

"I haven't said *yes* yet."

"Yes you have."

I walked willingly down the hall with him, to the synthetic GodWeed that was waiting to infect me.

GodWorld used to be called Storm. It said so on tactical. At first I got really worried and confused that it was called one thing some places and another thing in others. But Aten told me not to worry about it. She was completely unconcerned, even in the face of all my fidgeting, and we got there okay anyway.

It was a red and yellow world. We couldn't see any water from orbit. In fact, we couldn't see much of anything, because we came down in the middle of a planetwide superstorm. We had to; we would have had to wait in orbit another week otherwise, and we didn't have the supplies for that. I wanted to pilot the egg down myself, but that's apparently against the rules in storm conditions. They put us on auto, guided us down, and then tugged us into a storm shelter. So I didn't even get to see what GodWorld looked like when we popped the egg open.

I wasn't scared, like I thought I was going to be, but I was nervous. Shy. The gravity was hard on me, even though Aten said it was close to earth normal. I was clumsy and tangled myself up in my shoulder-bag strap when we were climbing out of the egg. I almost fell on top of Aten. She laughed about it. She wasn't weak at all. She wasn't even nervous.

The shelter was huge. There were people everywhere, with all sorts of small ships and machinery crowded together, and even animals. I saw a chicken perched on top of someone's egg ship. I laughed at that and people looked at me like I was mentally ill or something. Aten was plowing a straight line through the chaos; I just kept following her.

We went up some ramps and into a hallway filled with strange, tumultuous light. There were view windows all along its length; the light was coming from outside. I had to stop and stare in awe at the superstorm. The colored sand mixed with the wind and obscured the sun, making GodWorld hell red in some places, burning yellow in others.

"They should have called this place Wrath of God-World," I said to Aten.

She didn't answer. I looked around and realized she was gone.

"Aten!" I cried, like a lost kitten crying for its mother. People stared at me as they passed me. I didn't care. I was near panic. Then I remembered our link.

I felt for it, found it. *Aten,* I sent, along with a picture of me standing next to the view windows. Then I clamped down on my panic and waited.

In another moment, she appeared through the crowd. I ran to join her.

"I thought you would look," I said, indicating the storm outside.

She did look, then. Our link was still strong; she was thinking that there had been a time when she had been interested in the sights and the people around her. She was glad I had reminded her of that time.

"Where are we going?" I asked her.

"To find a com," she said. "I hope our associates have left a message for us. I also hope that they've arranged for accommodations."

I fervently hoped that, too. The thought of reclining on a hotel bed and sipping a cool drink was very tantalizing. We rushed off to look for that com.

Now that I had some idea what we were doing, I wasn't as nervous. I even indulged in a little people-watching. I noticed that most people were like the techs back on OMSK. They had skin that was either golden brown or red brown. Eyes varied from amber all the way to black. Hair did, too. Aten and I were oddities with our pale skin and red hair. But occasionally I caught glimpses of people who were odder. They had

what looked like grey skin; though that may have been
their clothing. They were extremely tall, maybe eight
feet, and their hair was almost blue black. I wondered
who they were and why they looked that way.

And then we found the coms.

Aten looked in the directory under messages, first, and
found something for us. I tried to read it over her shoulder, but the letters weren't from a human alphabet. My
heart thudded at the thought of that. The people we
were going to meet weren't human. Suddenly I felt shy
again.

Aten sent them a written message of her own, in the
same characters. We waited a minute, and another message scrolled across the screen.

"Okay," Aten said, "I have directions. Let's call a
cab."

The cab took us out into the superstorm. We could
hear the wind out there, howling like a monster. My
eyes were dazzled by the wild, turbulent light coming
through the cab windows.

"Want me to dim the filters?" asked the driver, who
wasn't driving. He just monitored readouts.

"No," I said, thinking that the darkness might be
worse.

The cab must have had a guidance system, because
we didn't hit anything. It let us off inside a basement
garage and we got onto an elevator.

My heart had been pounding all along. Now it was
ready to leap out of my chest.

"Relax," Aten said. "You're valuable. You're important, remember?"

"What if the GodHeads reject me?" I said, and was
ashamed when my voice shook.

"I thought you wanted them to do that."

Now I didn't know what I wanted. I didn't even know
what I was doing there.

"I'm here," said Aten. "I'm on your side."

"What are they like?" I asked, meaning the X'GBris.

"Big," said Aten. "Intimidating. Don't feel bad if
you're scared of them. It takes a while to get used to
them."

The elevator was speeding us up to their floor. I wished it could slow down. I wished Aten and I could turn around and go . . .

Home? I didn't have a home. So we kept going up, until we were there. The doors opened and we stepped out onto plush carpet. The ceilings were so high, the doors so tall, we were like a couple of children standing there. We walked down a grand hallway and looked at numbers on massive doors.

"These are suites," Aten said, pleased.

As my feet sank into the soft carpeting, I had a brief flashback of the feeling of my bare feet on a dirt road. And then Aten was sounding a doorbell.

"Who is it?" someone snarled from the wall com.

"Aten," she replied.

The door opened by itself. We walked in.

I hate walking into rooms with Aten. She's so gorgeous that every eye immediately turns to her, every man in the room stares at *her* and I end up feeling ten times plainer than I already am.

On the other hand, maybe this time it was for the best. They were looking at her, so I got a chance to look at them. They were positioned as if they had been waiting for us, as if they had intended to make a startling impression. They were akin to those grey people I had seen earlier. They weren't human at all, I could see that now that I was in the same room with them.

There were five men standing around one woman, who was seated. They were all giants. Their hair was inky black, thicker than it should have been. Their faces were—maybe dramatic is the best word. Every expression seemed exaggerated, almost masklike. Some of them were scowling and some smiling. I wasn't sure which I preferred. Their clothing was the same grey shade as their skin, and covered them from head to toe so that it was hard to see where flesh began and cloth ended.

Two of the men came forward, prowling toward Aten like a couple of predators. I thought they were going to grab her, but when they got close, they stopped and just glared at her.

I clutched my shoulder bag as though it was a life

preserver and moved back until I bumped into the wall, but Aten stayed where she was. "This is the candidate," she said, indicating me. "Edna."

Suddenly all eyes turned in my direction.

I didn't know whom to look at. Every one of them seemed to be demanding my attention. And their eyes . . .

Their eyes . . .

Different shades of purple. Startling. Unblinking. They reminded me of birds, of . . .

Raptors.

"What's wrong with you?" snapped the woman. I tried to focus on her face alone. She was interesting; at least some remote part of my mind told me so, noting how feminine she looked even though she was so large and so un-human. But her eyes . . .

What is a raptor? someone asked me. It was one of the men, the one standing behind her right shoulder. I looked at him, and his eyes were the worst of all. They were very pale, and they pierced me right to the heart.

What is a raptor? he asked me again, in my head.

He must be the one, Aten told me. *He's infected with the synthetic, too.*

I was shocked, only used to thought messages from Aten. Is this what it would be like with the GodHeads? Could they hear us *right now*? Was our synthetic GodWeed sending echos of us back through the Net whose energy we were stealing?

He looked at me, took a firm hold of our link and touched me through it. Now I could feel the emotions behind his expressions, and that just made it worse. He reacted to my feelings, and his face started to twist in anguish.

"Stop," I told him, but he couldn't. He was caught up. *I* was caught up. I was back inside my dream, sitting on the old man's lap, looking at the knot of people around the black thing, the thing with the huge wings.

"Stop," I said again, but he still couldn't. The others were speaking to him now, in low X'GBri voices that made my breastbone vibrate. I couldn't understand them, he couldn't hear them, he was looking through my eyes at the thing on the floor, and then the people moved and we could see the eyes, the terrible eyes.

"Stop," I said, one last time, and then it was over and I was on the floor. Aten was bending over me.

He was trying to reach me, too, but they wouldn't let him. They kept him from me like they thought I had a contagious disease.

Is it over? he asked me through our link.

I didn't answer because I wasn't sure.

My name is KLse. . . .

I know, I told him. *My name is Edna.*

Is it over? he asked again, sounding worried, but I couldn't stand the emotions any longer, so I shut the link down.

"What happened?" Aten was asking me. She shielded me from them with her body.

I thought about it. I focused on her green eyes and tried to forget the other ones, the terrible ones.

"Their eyes are . . ." I started to say. "They reminded me of . . ."

"The raptor," she said. "I know, I heard that. Is it something from your past?"

I shrugged. "Maybe. Or maybe it's some kind of"—I reached for the lingo the techs had thrown at me after the drips and the training—"artifact," I said.

"Are we so ugly?" said the X'GBri woman. I couldn't tell from her tone if she was insulted or amused.

"No," I said, "you're beautiful." Then I saw the expression on Aten's face and wished I hadn't said it. *Careful,* she warned me through our link. I could feel KLse trying to get back in, too. Aten blocked him as tactfully as she could. He didn't like it, but he relented.

"I'm glad you find us so aesthetically pleasing," said the woman. "Perhaps you should go into your rooms and rest. We'll send for food, if you like."

"That's a good idea," said Aten. She helped me to my feet. I felt exposed, now that I was standing again; I felt their eyes on me as I picked up my bag. I didn't look directly at them. Instead, I focused on their hands. The hands gestured toward a door.

Aten nudged me in that direction. I was glad to go.

The thought of lying on the bed and sipping a cool drink almost made me want to weep.

"Perhaps an alcoholic drink is in order," said the X'GBri woman.

"Something light," suggested Aten.

"Yes, of course."

I put one foot in front of the other until we had left that room and entered our own. I was intensely aware of my own clumsiness, and of Aten's grace as she moved beside me. She closed the door behind us and guided me to the large, soft bed.

"Just one bed in here," I said, dropping my bag like a ton of bricks.

She shrugged. "It's huge. Four people could sleep in this bed and never touch each other. Besides"—she grinned—"it's bigger than the egg."

It was. I tried to crawl onto it, but she made me stop and take off my safety suit and my boots. When I was dressed in just my shorts and T-shirt, she let me get onto the bed.

The soft, cool, clean bed. I laid my head on the pillow and took a long, deep breath.

"Sleep if you want," said Aten. "I'll wake you when the food gets here." She was wandering about the room, admiring the pretty furniture. She was impressed. She was thinking that most expensive hotels aren't worth the money they charge, but this one had real class. The furnishings were tasteful and elegant. Some things even appeared to be real antiques.

"X'GBri or human?" I asked her.

"Both," she said, unflustered by my intrusion into her thoughts. "Their decorator has a good eye." And then she was thinking that it would be nice if she and I could find the same sort of harmony with our X'GBri collaborators.

I began to relax. I delighted in the feeling of the cool air being pushed around the room by the ventilators. The gauzy drapes transformed the turbulent light of the superstorm into something almost whimsical, almost restful.

Those curtains have a UV filter woven into them, Aten

said. *This solar system has a type-F sun. You'll under-stand once the superstorm is over.*

I know, I said. *They told me on OMSK.*

We'll have to wear protective clothing, even in the shaded parts of the streets.

I tried to imagine the monster burning behind the storm. It wasn't too hard. I could feel it, even when I couldn't see it. But that was probably just my imagination.

Aten was enjoying her explorations. She went into our adjoining sitting room, the dressing room, the lavish bathroom.

When I felt calmer, I let myself think about what had happened in the sitting room. I wondered why it had been so easy to lose control. Just because of their eyes? I wondered if I should avoid looking into people's eyes in the future. I should certainly avoid blurting things out.

You're beautiful.

I must have sounded like I was making romantic over-tures or something. Or even if I hadn't, they would cer-tainly get the idea that romantic overtures were possible. Did they think I was being foolish? After all, Aten was the beautiful one. I must have looked desperate to them, lonely.

Not to mention crazy.

Someone touched me.

I reacted as if to a physical touch, but it was KLse, in the next room. He didn't say anything, he just held the touch, waiting for me to accept him.

It wasn't as shocking, this time. In fact, it wasn't shocking at all. I was getting used to him. I felt a brief impulse to giggle; he certainly was persistent. A human would have waited much longer before trying to reestab-lish the link. But he thought he had already waited a long time. I knew that, even though he wasn't directly telling me so. That was interesting.

What now? I asked him.

He considered how he should answer. He didn't want to upset me. *Food has been ordered,* he said, *and a drink. Something light.*

Thank you, I said.

He held on, letting me know that he intended to be

a permanent part of our link. I let him. It was odd; it was almost as if he and I were bride and groom in an arranged marriage. For him it was an advantageous marriage, one that had bestowed great status on him, and he intended to keep that status.

Soon, he said, cautiously, *there is something I must do. Yes?*

I must taste you. I will do it quickly. Perhaps before you eat?

Get it over with, you mean? I asked, almost giggling again.

It is something we do. I must determine that you are fit.

I felt a pang. This was what I got for acting so crazy. What else could I expect?

Do what you think is right, I said. *I trust you.*

That pleased him enormously. I wondered what Aten would think if she knew I had acted so impulsively. Again.

She was still occupied with her exploration. I left her out of it. I needed to make friends with KLse. I needed him to like me. If we were going to be this intimate, I couldn't stand it any other way.

Right now he didn't like me or dislike me. He thought I was odd. But he did have a capacity for empathy. That was probably why they had chosen him for the mission. He was a junior husband; it would have taken him years to fight his way up the status ladder if WWul hadn't recognized his special talent and granted him the opportunity to please her.

Stop it, he said. He was growing angry with me. He didn't like that I could see into his heart.

My life is open to you, too, I said, sorry that I had embarrassed him.

It's not the same.

He clamped down on the link. He didn't sever it; he wasn't about to do that, no matter how much he disliked my peeking into my feelings. I resisted the urge to nudge him, to try to get those friendly feelings I wanted. I was human; I couldn't help being afraid of the rejection.

He had said it wasn't the same. I knew what he meant. I was still so incomplete; my personality was still forming. If he wanted to know everything there was to know about me, there wouldn't be much for him to find out.

His, on the other hand, was a long and fascinating story. I was sorely tempted to move close again, find out more about him. In the short time we had been linked, I was more than used to him. I was beginning to like the contact.

I didn't remember ever being involved with a man before. But I had a feeling I was asking for trouble.

Impulsive, Aten sent, chiding me.

I sighed, and tried to work up some enthusiasm about supper.

Edna was dozing when they knocked on the door with the food. KLse and another one of the junior husbands brought it in. The other fellow threw us a suspicious look and left immediately, but KLse stayed. We shut the door again for privacy.

I knew what he needed to do. I hoped Edna wouldn't panic.

She sat up on the bed and looked inquisitively at the tray of food. But she didn't make a move for it. KLse set her drink down on the bedside table.

"Don't drink it yet," he said. "It will confuse matters."

"All right," she agreed, looking anywhere but his face. "Where shall we . . . I mean, would it be better if we sat on the edge of the bed?"

"Lie down," he said.

She looked a little panicked about that, but she reclined again. I watched as she tried to relax her body.

"Go easy," I warned KLse.

I thought he looked a little uncertain. But he moved with confidence. Perhaps a little too much confidence: Edna tensed when he got onto the bed. But she didn't try to pull away.

Poor Edna. She was embarrassed. She wasn't used to being that close to a man. I wondered if she had ever made love to anyone in her life. She looked so young; she looked like she was barely out of her teens, if that.

KLse leaned over her. She turned her face away from him. He put his face against her neck and she shut her eyes.

I felt a tug on our link. He was trying to calm her. It was really almost sweet, almost like watching a young couple on their wedding night. He started to lick her neck, and she became calmer as she got used to the feeling.

He was careful not to touch her in any other way. He was trying to avoid the appearance of sexual impropriety. I gave him credit for that. When he had finished, he sat up and gave Edna her drink.

"Drink it slowly," he said.

She nodded, still avoiding his eyes.

He looked at me then. I kept my face neutral, and I could see that he was trying to do the same. Hard work, for an X'GBri. He thought I was attractive. I probably would have known that even without the synthetic link.

He had been pleased when Edna had said she thought they were beautiful. And I don't think he had been the only one. I wished I had been able to stop her from saying that; it would complicate our situation. But she had been so shaken, she had just blurted out what she thought.

Strange girl.

"She'll be all right," I told him. "She needs food and rest. She went straight from training to an egg."

"Yes," he said. "Tomorrow we will show you the city. We will go slowly. Our work is too important to rush." He was so pleased, his hair was standing out from his scalp. X'GBri hair isn't dead, like human hair. It's alive, and it acts like it.

Enjoying your new status, are you? I thought, but was careful to keep the thought to myself. It was true: He wanted to savor his new position before his world changed again. In his own way, he was as nervous about linking up with the Net as Edna was.

I probably should have been, too. But I had always been reckless.

"She is very—" he began, then remembered that Edna was still in the room. He glanced at her, but she refused to look back. He had been about to say *incomplete,* a reference to her brain wipe. His face twisted in dismay at his own rudeness.

But Edna didn't blame him for it. She knew it was

true, and there wasn't enough of her original self left to be angry about it. She continued to drink as if he had said nothing about it.

"I am concerned," he continued, "that the GodHeads will not accept someone who has been so comprehensively wiped."

I didn't tell him that Edna was hoping that he was right. And I didn't tell Edna that I had a feeling she was right up their alley.

"Relax," I told them both. "Who knows what the GodHeads want or think? We have no way of knowing until we try."

Edna accepted that. KLse's feelings were more complicated. But he didn't spare even a moment of regret that he had chosen the path he was on. As far as I was concerned, that was another admirable quality.

"If you need anything, let me know through our link," he said. "We should practice with that as much as we can."

And you want us to yourself, for now, I thought, once again keeping the thought to myself. I was happy to know that I *could* keep the thought to myself, if I concentrated. I had worried that the "leaks" we were always experiencing would make privacy impossible. "We'll practice," I promised, and smiled at him. He gave me a grin in return that would make most other humans flinch. Every one of his sharp teeth showed.

Abruptly he turned and left the room. Edna sighed, when he had closed the door.

"All right?" I asked her.

"Better," she said, meaning everything.

"Mind if I take the first shower?"

"Nope," she said. "I'm too sleepy to be that ambitious."

So I left her to her meal and went to explore the pleasures of the bathroom.

We had been in the egg for three weeks. Not long, when you consider how long it used to take people to travel between stars, back when just one jump was the norm and you had to make lots of stopovers. That had been the state of things for centuries, at least for most people. Races who traded and/or were friendly with each other cooperated to some extent, all trying to find a way to push the jumps farther, get to places faster. They made some small advances. But it took a mysterious race called the Earlies to change the universe for the rest of us.

The Earlies, with their superior technology and their mania for sharing information.

It was funny how I took that technology for granted now. It had all happened before I was born, but it almost didn't happen at all. The Earlies had disappeared from our side of the galaxy, leaving nothing but ruins behind. Those ruins had been covered in Early glyphs, and that had been what started it all. Those glyphs were so densely packed with information, it had taken people years just to decipher a few of them. But it was worth it, all that hard work. The information was about technology so far in advance of ours, it was almost incomprehensible.

Edna had been so tickled when I had said she could call herself an EggHead, because the EggHeads had been the prospectors who had tracked down those Early glyphs. And the most famous EggHead had been Ankere, who had found the most important glyphs of all, the ones that had told her where the Earlies were still living.

The ones that had infected her mind with an Early personality. Who was the ancient philosopher who had said language is a virus? Apparently some languages are more viral than others.

Ankere had *become* an Early, mentally at least; and then she had gone to find the people who had infected her. And once she had found them, she had brought them back to meet the GodHeads, because after all, wasn't GodWeed a sort of infection, too? Didn't the GodHeads and the Earlies have something in common? Not that that really explained why she had done it. The history books were all pretty vague about that part. The only clue I could find was that the GodHeads were from Ankere's home planet, Storm, now called GodWorld. Maybe she owed them a favor.

Must have been one heck of a favor. The Earlies had helped make the Net, and that was why Edna and I were on GodWorld in the first place. Because the Earlies had changed the universe.

But one thing they hadn't shown us how to do was how to fit a nice, hot-water shower facility into an egg. My last good scrub was on OMSK, and my skin was crying out for another one.

The hotel bathroom had a tub and a sauna, too, but if I had one vanity, it was my hair. I wanted to scrub it until it shone. I pulled off my clothing and hopped into the shower.

The water pressure was fabulous. The cleansing bar was my favorite brand. I scrubbed myself from head to toe with it. My muscles unwound.

What's wrong with her? someone was asking.

Things were leaking through our link with KLse. It was WWul who had asked. In their language, not ours. I could speak the main dialect, but it was interesting to hear it from the inside out, as it were.

She is not psychotic, KLse was saying. *She is not mentally ill, and she is in good health.*

Then why that mad little scene? one of the senior husbands asked.

She has been wiped.

We know that, said WWul. *They promised us she wasn't a criminal.*

She is not a sociopath, KLse assured her.

How do you know? asked the senior husband. *This is something you could taste?*

KLse regarded this one with an interesting blend of resentment and respect.

My link, he reminded him, proudly.

I didn't get KLse's reading of what the others thought of that. But I assumed it was a complicated mix of reactions.

She has the agent, said KLse, trying to reassure them. *The agent is her lifeline.*

The conversation broke up then. I assumed the conflict had been resolved, for the time being.

I opened the complimentary shampoo. My hair is long, so it takes a while to get it all lathered up. I was about halfway through it when I felt a gust of cool air, behind me.

Someone had gotten into the shower with me.

I turned my head, saw naked grey skin and lots of muscles. He had wrapped his arms around me before I could see anything more.

"Who are you?" he said.

He didn't know. From behind, Edna and I must have looked exactly alike.

"Aten," I answered.

He touched my face, as if he could see with his fingertips. "I think *you* are beautiful," he said.

How I wished Edna hadn't blurted that out.

He reached for the soap with one hand, holding me still with the other. He began to lather my back.

"I've already done that," I said.

"I want to touch you."

"Shampoo is getting in my eyes."

He let me lean back and wash the shampoo out of my face and off the top of my head. If I had opened my eyes, I could have looked up into his face. But I didn't have to do that. I knew he wasn't KLse. I could feel KLse was still in his own room. This was one of the senior husbands.

If KLse found out he was in there with me, there would be a fight. I didn't want that. I felt for Edna, to make sure she was all right. She was asleep.

Once the soap was out of my eyes, he began to lather my skin again. He did it very carefully, as if I were a baby. I didn't resist. He didn't linger unduly in private areas. And he was so much taller than me, there was no way he could have penetrated me from a standing position. There was no room for other positions in that shower.

Assuming penetration was what he had in mind. I wasn't sure it was. You never know with X'GBris. Sometimes they're just plain curious about you. He finished soaping me from my back all the way down to my ankles. Then he turned me around.

Now I looked at his face. I expected to see him grinning at me, but instead he was scowling. I wondered what the heck that meant.

"I could break your neck with one hand," he said.

"I know."

Edna had been right about their eyes. They really were like the eyes of predatory birds.

He began to soap me from the front. He was fascinated with my breasts, but he didn't pinch them or try to stimulate my nipples. I glanced down, got a very interesting view of X'GBri male anatomy. It was notably similar to that of human males. He was only half erect, so it could go either way. I stayed neutral.

I was glad, at least, for the soap and water. He wouldn't be able to taste or smell my emotions.

When he had finished with me, he handed me the soap.

"Do me now," he said.

So now it was my turn to satisfy my curiosity. Maybe that was what he had in mind in the first place. He watched me while I worked.

"So much hair," he said, pulling it out of my face.

I, in the meantime, was finding out that X'GBri pubic hair was as alive as the stuff on their heads. It was a little unnerving.

"What's your name?" I asked him, trying to think of other things.

"Didn't you read our file?"

Touchy area. I knew KLse's name, but not his.

"I know you're one of the seniors. I could see that just by looking at you."

Oops. That remark had improved the erection.

"My name is JKre," he said, making it sound sort of like *Jackry*. "I suggest you memorize it. It will be important for your continued survival."

I glanced up the long length of him to that scowling face. He wasn't happy with KLse's unprecedented advantage over his senior self. That I could guess at. But there was more going on here.

"Am I in danger?" I asked.

"Yes. I am your advocate."

Indeed? I hadn't heard him say so in the other room. But that didn't mean he was lying. After all, he was saying so now. And now was probably a wiser time and place, anyway.

He pushed me against the wall, out of reach of the shower head, and rinsed himself off, watching me for any sign of movement. I was perfectly still. When he was free of soap, he said, "Get on your knees."

"No," I said. I had anticipated he might say something like that, and I had already thought out my reply.

"Do as I say," he said, meaning business, but I knew I had the right to say no. I knew he couldn't force me to do that. After all, you can lead a horse to water, but you can't make her give you a blow job. The question was, what would he do now that I had refused? Was he really my advocate?

"I didn't come here to be your little plaything," I said. "I'm here for a good reason. I'm the only one who can get Edna back if she gets lost. Do you really want KLse to risk himself doing *my* job?"

He grinned. This one was dangerous. His face always did the opposite of what I thought he was feeling.

"You're my plaything if I say you are," he informed me.

I didn't let that upset me, though I had every right to be outraged at what he had done, so far. But outrage would get me absolutely nowhere. I hadn't been a successful agent all these years by giving in to useless emotions.

"Or if you want," he continued, "I could be your plaything. It's your choice."

To be honest, it wasn't the worst offer I'd ever had. He was a fine male, by anyone's standards. His teeth were a little spooky; especially the way they slanted inward, so that anything he sank them into couldn't get away from him.

But KLse would be furious if I made love to JKre. JKre was a senior husband. That meant that he received WWul's favors far more often that KLse did. So the synthetic link KLse had with us meant a lot more to him than it would have meant to a human male. We were his, in a way. He might be willing to die to keep us that way.

And he was no good dead.

"I understand why WWul favors you," I said. "But you can't bully me. I won't do as you say. Don't try to force me." That had to be said. I couldn't have stalled him with diplomacy or false promises.

But sometimes it doesn't help to say the right things.

He stayed very still for a few, painful moments, and then he moved like lightning. In half a second he had one arm hooked under my right knee and the other around the small of my back. He picked me up and shoved me against the wall, holding me there without the slightest effort.

I had been overconfident when I had thought that penetration would not be possible from a standing position. All he had to do was let me slide down another few inches, and he would be inside me. He let me down a couple of inches, just to prove his point. So to speak.

"Don't," I said. "You're jeopardizing our mission with your behavior."

"How so?" he said, and let me slide another inch.

He knew perfectly well that I couldn't come right out and say that it would make KLse jealous. If I said that, I would be impaled in a flash. And he knew how I felt about that without even having to taste me. He could feel my heart pounding against his chest.

"I don't want you to do this," I said. "If you continue, you will be a rapist."

He was still grinning, but it was beginning to look more like a grimace. He didn't like that word. Most rapes perpetrated by X'GBri males on human females were the result of miscommunication. I wanted to let him know exactly what I thought was happening.

"Fight me, then," he said. And that was an option, of course. But despite how the fantasy vids liked to show female secret agents throwing big men all over the landscape, the truth was that I was no match for him. I could seduce him into letting me give him that aforementioned blow job and then take a healthy bite out of him, if I was desperate. But he might have just enough fight left afterward to kill me.

And if he didn't, WWul would do it for him. I hadn't been flattering him when I mentioned her favor for him. I could see how proud she was of her husbands when we had met them. She would never forgive me if I did that kind of damage to him.

"I'm not interested in being beaten or raped," I said. "If you're my advocate, prove it."

"I could prove it very nicely, if you'd stop being so stubborn."

With sudden inspiration, I said, "I'm not lovers with KLse either. I'm not here to be lovers with anyone. I'm here to be Edna's lifeline. That's all."

That had been risky, implying that he considered KLse his rival. But it was right on target. He stopped me before I could slide that last, vital inch.

"You seem educated," he said. "You must understand the concept of status."

I didn't remind him that I only had two syllables in my name, and that I was trying to earn a third.

"It's not wise to disregard the pecking order," he continued. "I warn you."

"I understand."

"I wonder if you really do," he said. But he let me down, unimpaled. We had another uncomfortable silence while he stared at me and I did my best to look unmovable. I wasn't entirely successful. He leaned down and kissed me, and I couldn't stop him. I struggled a little, but stopped when I saw that it just got him more excited. Instead, I settled for being unenthusiastic.

Finally he backed off and opened the door.

"Thank you for the shower," he said, scowling again. And he left.

I waited a few minutes before I went to the door joining our sitting room with theirs. I jammed a chair under the knob. I still had to get my hair properly washed and rinsed, and I didn't want to go through the same scene with every single damned husband in the joint.

In the middle of the night, there was a fight.

Edna woke up frightened. I could feel her shivering. "It's just a challenge," I told her. "You know, a status thing."

But I was worried, too, until I checked our link with KLse and realized it wasn't him.

Who is it? I asked him through the link.

He almost didn't answer me. He was absorbed in the fight, a little more excited than he normally would have been, because he knew that in a way he had provoked this unrest.

The seniors, he sent back. *JKre and STra.*

Are you all right? I asked, for Edna's sake. She was worried about him. I let him see that.

He was surprised, but swift in his reply.

Fine, he sent us both. *This is to be expected.*

He wasn't even afraid, just excited. Strict ritual was the only thing that kept him from joining in the fight. He controlled himself perfectly, like all adult X'GBris are expected to do. The ones who can't do it are eliminated. A harsh rule, but it works for them.

And what do you do with ones who can't control themselves? KLse asked me. Apparently what I had been thinking was interesting enough to shake him loose from the drama, just a little.

I thought about OMSK, about the drips and the wipes. The reprogramming, the behavior modification.

This is effective? he asked. But there was something he was holding back. I even knew what it was. X'GBris were no strangers to wipes or drips. There was probably a lot they could teach *us* about them. But his question got me thinking.

It works well for some people, not so well for others. I didn't go on to add that there were just too many criminals to process, even if it worked properly.

There are too many humans, KLse said, picking up on my train of thought.

We heard the sound of furniture breaking. All of those antiques jeopardized. I hoped they were just good reproductions.

What about the heavy-world prisons? KLse asked, as long as he had me on the line.

But that was one I wasn't prepared to answer. I had my opinions about the heavy-world prisons. I also had the sense not to express them. I didn't want to end up on one.

Edna is worried, I told him. *Is it almost resolved?*

He was sorry that she was scared. That was interesting. He was concerned about her. He was starting to feel downright protective. My Edna was more of a charmer than she had thought.

They are both strong, he said, *and both angry. They are good at this. It may take another half hour or so.*

In that case, it looks like we'll be sleeping late.

I'll make arrangements, he promised. Then he sent Edna a message of reassurance: *No one will hurt you. I am here.*

She sighed. She wasn't shivering anymore.

"They changed the dream," she whispered.

"Huh?" I whispered back.

"I was having the dream. But I never got to town, I was still on the dirt road. I heard them fighting—JKre and STra—and I looked up, into the sky. I've never done that before. In the dream, I mean."

My first impulse was to brush the matter off. Not because it was the right thing to do, but because I had a feeling a new complication was about to develop. It was the middle of the night, and I wasn't in the mood for it.

But sleeping was not what I got paid for. "What happened that was different?" I asked her.

"Just as I looked up, a shadow passed over me. It was huge, but I wasn't scared. I was—thrilled."

"Did you see what was casting the shadow?"

I felt her move. She was shaking her head.

"Then what happened?"

"I got disoriented. I still heard the noise, the fighting, but I couldn't see who was making it. They always seemed to be just out of sight. I thought they were human men. I thought I heard them speaking Standard, and I wasn't even sure if they were fighting or if they were just . . . just mean."

"Just mean?"

"You know. How some men are always ready to do something bad even when they're in a good mood."

I hadn't met many men who were like that. As far as I knew, Edna hadn't met *any* men who were like that. Not since her wipe.

I tried to look at her in the darkness. I could see her face dimly silhouetted by the light coming through the window. The storm light, still turbulent, two-moons' worth. She came and went in my sight. It was a little uncanny.

"Are you remembering something, Edna?" I ventured.

"I don't know," she said. "Maybe I'm just making it

all up because there isn't anything there, and I want there to be . . . something."

"Maybe," I answered. "I've heard that before."

There were more thumps and bumps from the other room. JKre and STra were still going strong. I checked KLse to make sure he was all right, found him close and listening. He wasn't embarrassed that I had caught him. And I supposed he had a right to know what we were talking about, since his own mind was on the line.

Edna sighed again. She was starting to fall asleep. I hoped she wouldn't have the dream. She usually didn't have it more than once a night. But she usually didn't get interrupted.

Will I be able to hear her dream? KLse asked me.

I never have, I answered. *Yet.*

His curiosity was piqued. But I didn't want to think about it. I didn't want to think about anything, I was too tired. He let me go and turned his attention back to his two superiors, who he suspected were starting to regard him as a serious rival.

The idea filled him with triumph. I left him to enjoy himself.

I didn't think I should mention this to Aten, but I thought I knew why I had had the dream. It was because of KLse's eyes. They were like those other eyes, the ones I couldn't stand to see.

Actually, they weren't *exactly* like them. But they shared some very similar qualities. The unblinking stare and an odd, savage innocence.

I was getting all poetic. KLse wasn't innocent, he just wasn't human. From his point of view, I might have been innocent, too. In fact, I'm fairly sure I was.

In the morning, he rapped on our door, with breakfast. We were both up and dressed by then. Aten was stretching. She didn't stop when he came in. But I was feeling clumsy, dizzy. I wondered if I had some kind of bug.

Aten said I couldn't; we had been thoroughly inoculated before we got into the egg.

"Who won last night?" she asked KLse as she flexed her beautiful legs. He was transfixed for a moment before he remembered to answer.

"Neither." He put the tray down on our table. "WWul called a draw. She always has to do that; if she didn't, one would kill the other."

"They hate each other that much?" I asked. He looked at me, and I averted my eyes just in time.

"Hate?" he asked. "Why should they?"

"Because of jealousy?"

That, he understood. But maybe not exactly the same way I did. "Status," he said, and shrugged. He watched

Aten finish her stretches, staring without shame. It didn't seem to bother her.

I looked at the food on the tray. It didn't look appetizing to me, but it didn't turn my stomach, either. I picked up a piece of fruit and started to nibble it. I didn't know what it was, but it had a lovely, light taste.

"Edna," said KLse, cautiously.

I knew what he was going to say next. It didn't scare me as much, this time.

"Do I have to lie down again?"

"You are so small. It would be awkward, if we tried to do it sitting."

Small! I was six feet tall. But he and his co-husbands were all over eight feet tall.

"Do your spouses think I went crazy overnight?" I teased.

"They will ask me how you are. I want to tell them you are fine."

I finished the fruit and licked my fingers. Then I pushed myself back on the bed. He knelt on the edge and leaned over me.

His shadow fell across me.

I looked up, startled. I looked right into those eyes.

"No!" he said, as I started to fall.

I jammed my eyes shut. I felt his body press down on mine. He was heavy; I couldn't breathe.

"You're crushing her!" I heard Aten saying.

I felt his weight lessen; he was propping himself up, trying to give me room to breathe. I dragged in some air, and immediately felt better.

I opened my eyes again, slowly. I didn't want to look directly into his. Instead, I focused on his mouth. His lips were pressed tightly together until he saw that I was all right. They parted, and his tongue made a brief appearance, darting between sharp teeth.

They really were extraordinary teeth.

"You're not dreaming," he said. "You're awake." His hair fell over my face, tickling me.

"I'm all right," I told him. He had withdrawn as far as he could from the link, afraid of falling into that pit with me again. But it didn't look like we were going there, today. He had just startled me, that was all.

I turned my head, giving him access to my neck. He hesitated to do it; he was wondering if he should wait until after breakfast. But then the others would accuse him of going too easy on me, letting sympathy cancel out his common sense. For an X'GBri, that might have been a serious charge.

While he thought about it, his breath came warm on my neck. It felt good. An uncomfortable thing happened. I started to get excited.

He licked me, and I gasped. He pressed down on me a little harder, and I felt his lips brushing my skin, wet and slippery from his tongue.

I was embarrassed. I scolded myself. *Calm!* I commanded my body. *This is a job, act like a professional!* It didn't do much good, but at least I knew what I was *supposed* to be doing.

I didn't know if he took longer that time or not. I did know that when he pulled away again, I didn't want him to. I wanted Aten to go away, wanted WWul and the other husbands to go away. I wanted KLse.

I felt like an idiot.

Don't be so hard on yourself, Aten told me. *It's nature. You'll calm down once you get some food in you.*

That was probably so, but I didn't dare look KLse in the face again. I didn't even feel for him along our link. He was close, I knew that. But I didn't want to know anything else, anything that might hurt me. Or encourage me.

So Aten and I sat down to breakfast. KLse sat, too. He didn't eat, though. He just watched us.

"Aren't you hungry?" Aten asked him.

"I've eaten," he said.

"You could eat with us, if you'd like."

"You would find it disturbing."

That piqued her interest. I could tell that she wouldn't have been disturbed at all, only fascinated. I wondered how I would feel. Maybe I would be fascinated, too. I hoped I would.

Aten had been right; I cooled down during breakfast. I was very aware of KLse, but in a different way. It was finally sinking in with me that I was sitting down to eat with an alien. From the corner of my eye I could see him there, his back so straight. He was capable of moving faster than my eye could follow; yet at the moment his hands were relaxed, his arms folded on the table.

He had a distinctive smell, sort of spicy but also recognizably male. I rather wished that it wasn't so pleasant. If he had smelled bad, maybe I wouldn't have gotten excited, earlier.

"The superstorm is diminishing," he said. "They predict it will end within the next few days."

I almost said *good,* but then it occurred to me that they were going to present me to the GodHeads when the storm was over. I honestly wouldn't have minded if the winds had blown for another couple of weeks. KLse felt the same way, but for different reasons.

At least, I thought they were different. There was no whisper in the link of his thoughts about the GodHeads. It was as if he didn't *want* to think about them. Or maybe those thoughts were hidden, kept out of my reach.

"Where are we going today?" I asked him.

"WWul thought you might like to shop."

WWul was entirely correct. Aten and I had only safety suits to wear. I wanted to see what else the future had to offer, what kind of clothes people wore when they weren't working or flying around in eggs. Aten grinned at me, pleased that we were going to get to have some fun before we got down to the serious stuff.

"Done?" KLse asked, when both of us had finished eating and were simply dallying over our coffee.

"Yes," said Aten, and we stood. KLse went to the door and ushered us out into the main sitting room where the others were waiting, as if they had been waiting for us the whole time. I hoped they hadn't. I couldn't tell if they were impatient or not, because I wouldn't let myself look directly at their faces. But I saw enough of them to notice that two of those faces were cut and bruised from the night before.

"You've eaten well?" WWul asked with formal courtesy.

"Yes," Aten and I said together.

"Good. We'll go downstairs and call a cab."

WWul preceded everyone to the door. She moved as

if she was accustomed to that authority. That was okay with me; I was feeling awkward again. I was willing to go along for the ride. As I fell in behind her with the others, one of the battle-scarred husbands came so close to me that we were bumping as we walked. I tried to move away, but he moved with me. I felt him staring hard at me, but I didn't want to look back.

KLse touched me through our link. Then he grabbed my arm from behind and gently moved me back to where he was. *That is JKre,* he said, *a senior husband. You can't walk with him unless he invites you.*

Oh, I said. *Sorry.*

He might have invited you, if you had looked at him, said KLse, but he wasn't trying to give me instructions about how to get friendly with JKre. He was glad that I hadn't taken the senior husband up on his challenge. It was another triumph for him, and there wasn't anything JKre could do about it. Not anything direct, anyway, like fight with KLse. If he picked a fight with KLse, that would either move KLse up or him down, no matter who won.

Complicated, I said.

Natural, he replied.

I wouldn't want to see your face scarred up like that.

We heal rapidly. We do not scar.

When we got into the elevator together, we had to go through a complicated and almost comical shuffle so the high-status people could be up front again. It probably wouldn't have been comical if Aten and I hadn't been there: The X'GBris moved like dancers who all knew their choreography perfectly. We messed them up. But they took it in stride, apparently expecting that we would.

The elevator let us out into an austere but expensively furnished lobby. I felt an invisible hand squeeze my heart, and I suddenly wished I could run back up to the room. It seemed like everyone was looking at me, thinking, *what's she doing here? She doesn't belong.* It got worse when we approached the office people working behind the main desk. They were human. They were so poised and polished, so cool when they answered WWul's questions. They treated her with the respect she commanded, but I knew they wouldn't have talked to me that way. They wouldn't have talked to me at all.

The woman in charge was giving WWul a printout of likely stores, places that would be accessible from underground entrances. Aten nudged me and whispered, "Look at her temple, just under the hair."

I looked, hoping the woman wouldn't catch me at it. I saw a faint rainbow glitter.

"She's augmented," Aten whispered. "She's plugged into the Net."

I remembered then. Augmented people could get instant information from the Net, just by thinking about it. They weren't GodHeads, they weren't "Plugged in" the same way GodHeads were. They were mechanically connected to special GodHeads who were also mechanically augmented. Without those special GodHeads, they would have to crawl along with the rest of us at a snail's pace.

And without the GodHeads, the Net would just be a net.

It was too complicated to follow, even after my drips and my training sessions. I didn't really know what I was in for. I didn't really know how the whole thing worked. But then, who did? Except for the GodHeads. And maybe even they couldn't grasp the whole picture.

The Earlies understand, Aten said through the link. *You can bet on that. The Earlies helped the GodHeads set up their Net. Maybe someday we'll talk to an Early. . . . Wouldn't that be great?*

Theoretically I thought it might. But I didn't really know how I would feel meeting people who were so different, both physically and mentally. In all of the video footage I had seen of Earlies, they had resembled big salamanders more than anything else, just a little shorter in stature than humans. I didn't know if I really wanted to meet a big salamander. Especially one that was so much smarter than me.

WWul thanked the woman behind the desk with the strict formality required between persons of vastly different status and walked away, leaving the rest of us to trail after her in our descending ranks. I was glad to be going. As the desk woman had turned away from us, I had glimpsed a water cooler in the corner next to an inner door. A man had been getting a drink, pressing the button and watching cool water pour into a little paper cup. Just thinking about it gave me a headache.

You are thirsty? KLse asked me through the link, amazed that I could want more than the coffee and juice I had drunk at breakfast.

Not thirsty, I assured him. I couldn't explain about the dream, about the office people and their water privileges.

They are merely paid servants, he said, trying to reassure me.

No, they aren't, Aten said. *They're* employees. *There's a big difference.*

KLse almost disagreed; but this was a subject about which he felt less confident. Human relationships. Human status. He was young, and he was still amazed when he interacted with humans and we didn't seem to have a sense of our own place. He was intrigued by our friendliness, our strange notions of equality that seemed to depend more on what we thought of ourselves than on what others thought of us. To him this was backward, chaotic, yet attractive, too.

We did the elevator shuffle again, this time more gracefully, and rode down into the underground parking garage, where our cab was already waiting for us. I was amazed to see that it wasn't any bigger than the cab Aten and I had taken the day before. The eight of us crammed in there together, crowding the driver who seemed to take it all in stride. He was apparently used to X'GBris and their ways.

KLse sat between Aten and me, with another junior husband between me and the window. Just to be polite, I asked his name.

"MRnu," he replied, scowling.

"*Muhr-new,*" I said, hoping I was pronouncing it right. His scowl deepened, so I don't know if I was or not.

The cab shifted into drive, and our combined weight pressed us back into the seat. It was a silly moment, made more so by the fact that MRnu was now staring intently at my face. I wondered what the heck I was supposed to do now. I hoped I had remembered to clean

my right ear properly, since he had such a close view
of it.

KLse, I asked. *Have I offended him?*

No, he said, but didn't seem inclined to enlighten me
any further. Currents were running swift and deep under
the surface of our link. I tried to gain an impression of
what was there without intruding too much. He didn't
chase me away, and eventually I got the impression that
not all of WWul's husbands approved of the venture we
were undertaking. That didn't mean MRnu didn't. But
apparently it *did* mean that he was inclined to scrutinize
me closely.

It was a long ride, with one man staring at me nonstop
the whole way and another touching me so deeply.
MRnu made me so uncomfortable that I found myself
leaning into KLse, turning my face in his direction, un-
consciously looking to him for comfort. I became aware
that our hands were resting against each other.

KLse said something to WWul; I didn't understand
the X'GBri dialect, but I thought I could hear intimacy
in his tone. Perhaps some of his passion for her was
leaking through our link. It seemed to me that he sa-
vored the syllables of her name as he spoke them, turning it into a thing of beauty. She answered him in a
similar tone, and he basked in it.

My heart felt like it was being stabbed.

Don't be silly, I scolded myself. *Would you really want
to interfere in their marriage, even if you could?* I looked
at the back of her beautifully coifed head, her hair so
thick and lustrous, the delicate grey skin on the back of
her neck fading up into the blue-black coils. One of her
husbands must have fixed her hair like that. Perhaps it
was KLse's job.

Aten had beautiful hair, but mine was full of snarls
and flyaway strands. Aten's was lustrous, with gold high-
lights shining inside the red. Mine was dull and mousy.

KLse's fingers tickled my hand. I didn't jump, but my
breath caught in my throat. I would have looked into
his eyes then, if I could have. I would have touched him
through the link, but he had carefully withdrawn, slowly
so I wouldn't feel him go. His fingertips slipped gently
under my hand, then tickled my palm.

KLse, I called. *Don't.*

You want me to stop? he asked, his words crisp little jabs along a taut line.

I didn't know what to answer. I thought he must be enjoying himself. Usually he had to share one woman with the other husbands, but here was another woman who had a crush on him. It must have pleased him.

It was hurting me. I wanted it, but I didn't want it. I was afraid to get it and then lose it, and I couldn't tell him that without humiliating myself.

"Your skin is turning the same color as your hair," MRnu announced in a loud voice. I felt the heat move farther up my neck, into my face, and then finally burning all the way up to my scalp. I needed to take a few deep breaths to get my equilibrium back, but I was afraid they would sound like sobs. MRnu began to fan my face with his hand, as if he were trying to put out a forest fire.

I couldn't help it. I started to laugh.

I tried not to sound hysterical, but it was just too funny, too crazy. KLse and Aten were both trying to calm me through the link. But the laughter was just what I needed: I was able to take nice big gulps of air. In a few moments I felt better, and I stopped laughing. I leaned back against the seat, spent and relieved.

There was a dead, icy quiet from the front seat.

But in the backseat, the ice had been broken. We had shared an inside joke, a bit of absurdity, and now we could relax. Even MRnu seemed friendlier. He turned his eyes away from me long enough to look out his window.

"The storm is losing power," he announced.

We all looked out our windows. He was right. You could see glimpses of the city through the blowing sand, illuminated by a fierce, white light. Those glimpses were tantalizing, and startled me out of my self-absorption.

This is real. This isn't just a bunch of pictures of a make-believe place.

I had seen pictures of TradeTown, on OMSK during my training. It had seemed grand, but the pictures had not been able to do it justice. I was only catching glimpses of it now, yet its scale and symmetry awed me.

Could this really be a human city? Were we really capable of this?

"This is all new," Aten said. "Less than a hundred years old. I hear they had to demolish most of the old city and start over again. They used Early technology to build this new stuff."

"How wonderful," I said.

I felt so good, suddenly. I felt the way I had in the egg when I had lain there in the dark, thinking about the future that I was living in, what an amazing place it was, full of such wonders. And here I was, right in the middle of it! With Aten and KLse at my side.

Without thinking about it, I grasped KLse's hand. I let him know what I thought about him, about this thing that was happening to us. He listened through the link. He absorbed my feelings, and he was amazed. He wasn't disturbed with the rapid shift from sorrow to joy; X'GBris were capable of more violent shifts than that. What startled him was that my feelings were *alien,* and I was touching him in that impossible way. He began to feel his own version of wonder.

And then the taxi took us underground again. In the darkness, I realized that I was holding KLse's hand. He gently disengaged. I didn't mind so much, not with that good feeling still singing inside me.

Let's go spend some money, Aten said. *Let's have fun.*

We pried ourselves out of the taxi. The parking structure was full of people going to and from the shops. Apparently a superstorm was no excuse for business to shut down in TradeTown. WWul cut a swath through the crowd with her entourage, but people didn't seem to mind. These people were cosmopolitan; they just went with the flow.

We rode up in the elevator with strangers, and this time there was no status shuffle. I took note of that. Crowd situations called for a temporary suspension of rank. There was more of a feeling of solidarity. The men positioned themselves so that they could see everything that was happening, and could protect WWul, and even us, from hostility.

We got off the elevator and joined a throng walking down a huge hallway. Shops opened up on both sides of us, and something in the back of my mind said *mall*. That was an odd feeling. The mall was familiar in a particular kind of way, as basic as the concepts of *house, people, food*. Yet I couldn't remember ever having been in one, ever having heard the word. I was pretty sure it hadn't been mentioned to me on OMSK. No one had said, *When you get to TradeTown you can go shopping at the mall*.

It must have been a concept from before. Something from my old life. That got me thinking. When they wipe a brain, what are they trying to get rid of? Memories, yes, but at what place do memories end and important functions like language begin? Are they all mixed up? How do they sort through them? How come I can still talk if I was that thoroughly wiped? I remember I said something just as soon as they woke me up. I said, "What time is it?" I can even remember thinking I must be late for something, though I had no idea what.

"Wake up." Aten nudged me. "You're supposed to be looking. What kind of clothes do you want?"

"What kind of clothes?" I said, stupidly, still half dreaming.

"Maybe we should start with basics," she said. "Bras and underwear."

"Good idea," I said, brightening. Start simple and work up to the harder choices.

"WWul," she called, "let's head for a department store."

WWul actually let Aten take the lead then. She relinquished it gracefully, as if she could take it back at any moment. Aten stepped into the role with equal grace. I was glad she was there. Again.

Aten led us into a very large shop, through a perfume and cosmetic department. As soon as we entered, I knew I was remembering another place/concept from before, but this time it made me uncomfortable. I felt the same way I had back at the lobby, with the office people. The sales people should be looking down on me. But instead they were gazing at WWul and her husbands with respect and a little apprehension. That made me feel better.

We rode up an escalator; another group of X'GBris

were riding past us on the down side. Their group and ours looked at each other in a way that made the hair on the back of my neck prickle. I realized that the problem was that this other group had no woman in it. These were four men by themselves.

WWul's group had *three* women in it.

But they weren't going to fight. I picked that up from KLse. They were among aliens, and they were strictly controlling themselves. They were simply exchanging stares, promising each other that if circumstances were different, they would act accordingly. I couldn't help shivering when they passed, though it wasn't really a bad feeling. In another moment they were gone and we were ascending into a frilly heaven.

Aten walked confidently through the rows of undergarments. WWul also looked comfortable there. But what really surprised me was that her husbands did, too. They didn't seem embarrassed. They didn't suggest that they should meet us downstairs in the sporting goods department. They inspected the merchandise with expert eyes, their faces surprisingly neutral. Frankly, if I had been a lady shopper trying to find a bra and I had seen an X'GBri male looking at the intimate merchandise with a really big, sharp-toothed grin on his face, I would have been just the least bit discomfited.

No, they didn't start grinning until they found the teddies.

"Here," Aten said, steering me toward a rack of panties. "Do you know what size you are?"

I went blank.

"I'll bet you're the same size as me," she guessed. "Five in the underwear. Maybe a 34-C in bras. You get to try the bras on, but you can't do the same for the underwear."

I hadn't known that. I was glad she had warned me. She was picking out several different bikini styles in bright colors for herself. But I didn't like bikinis. I went for hipsters in pastels.

"Don't let them con you into getting the matching sets," Aten warned.

We had picked out everything we needed within half

an hour. But when Aten tried to pay, WWul wouldn't let her.

"I have Company credit," Aten said.

"You won't need it as long as you're with us," WWul insisted. Aten stepped out of the way and let her pay.

My face began to burn again. I turned away and pretended to look at a rack of garter belts. I didn't feel comfortable spending someone else's money. I wished Aten had insisted we use our own credit. KLse picked up on my feelings. He came over and pretended to look with me.

"This is a small matter," he said softly.

But I had been looking forward to buying things just because I wanted them, regardless of cost. I felt I had earned the right to dip into the Company coffers. After all, wasn't I their hope for the future, their personal connection into the Net?

You are, Aten said, *but they would have deducted it from our pay anyway.*

We could have afforded it, I said, stubbornly.

I know. Don't worry, I'll make sure we aren't stepping over the lines of courtesy with the X'GBris. And if you're in doubt, we can always ask KLse's advice.

I nodded, forgetting how odd that gesture would look to anyone who wasn't tuned in to our conversation. KLse understood it, though. He smiled at me, presenting me with a toned-down version of his usual face-stretching grin.

So down the escalator we all rode again, this time laden with dainty packages. The husbands carried them, and in that respect they fit right in with all of the other husbands in that store. I sneaked peeks at the bags JKre was carrying. They were for WWul, and I wondered what sorts of things had been purchased for her. Were they all in shades of grey? That was all I had ever seen X'GBris wear. Yet I thought I had seen JKre looking at a red teddy earlier. Maybe colors like that were only worn in private.

I watched KLse while he was people-watching. He was doing it for the purpose of entertainment as much as for the purpose of security. He enjoyed seeing different kinds of people, their interactions, their clothing. But it seemed to me that he was a little disturbed by certain colors, though he didn't let himself become too disoriented by it. I made a mental note to ask him about it in the future. I would hate to send a message I didn't mean to just by wearing the wrong color.

We left the department store and joined the crowds in the mall. My spirits had climbed high again, I was enjoying myself as much as KLse and Aten were. I gazed at the shops along the mall. At least half of them were clothing stores. They displayed a bewildering array of styles, most of which looked either too young or too harsh for me.

"Aten," I said, "somewhere there's got to be something that's . . . you know, clean and simple but . . . *elegant*. . . ."

"There is," she said. "You just have to plow through the junk to find it."

She was running a well-trained eye over everything, disregarding most of it, moving us along at a fast pace. We reached a point were our corridor converged with five others into a huge central court. The ceiling of this court must have been made entirely of prismatic diamond glass, because light from the superstorm was pouring through it onto the crowd below. It was a fantastical sight. The people walking through that storm of light were transformed by it.

We slowed our pace. WWul's husbands were disturbed by all that illusory movement. It triggered attack\defense instincts that were best left undisturbed in crowd situations. Some people were passing around the perimeter of the court; others were walking right through the center, only veering off toward the corridor of their choice at the last moment. WWul's husbands couldn't decide which path was the safest.

Aten made the choice for them. She charged right down the middle. The rest of us followed with almost military precision. Some people stared at us as we passed, fascinated by our spectacle. Others averted their eyes, wishing only to pass through with a minimum of confusion.

Still others were staring at someone else.

At first I couldn't figure out who they were looking

at in all that wild light. Then Aten suddenly stopped dead. Shock passed down her link to me, numbing me. WWul and her husbands stopped, too, and the feelings that came down the link from KLse stung me into alertness again.

I crept out from behind them and had a look myself. Benches were placed around the inner circle of the court, so that people could enjoy the scenery or watch passersby. People were seated there now, but they were looking at only one person. He was standing in the very middle with his profile to us. He was impossibly tall, his black hair wild and almost prehensile, his features a hatchet cutting into space.

KLse was shocked by the color of the man's clothing—I had been right about that particular sensitivity— because the man was an X'GBri, and he was wearing all black. His black leggings were tucked into black boots, and he wore a long tunic that was split at the hips and the groin. The tunic had a high collar, almost like a priest's, and the man's hands were covered in black gloves. The tunic also had a hood that was pulled back for indoors.

As the storm light played over him I noticed something else. Red flashes moved across the fabric of the tunic, dancing like living things.

Early glyphs, said Aten, with awe. *He's covered in them.*

Her mental voice sounded brittle along our link. I felt something outside it, something like static. I investigated the feeling, Aten and KLse behind me, but not with me. I was aware that the man was outside us, pressing against our space with his disturbing presence, and beyond him . . .

Beyond him was the Net. He was a GodHead. An X'GBri GodHead.

"Don't go near him," WWul commanded, her voice almost dead. She veered away from the court and her husbands followed, sweeping Aten and me along in their midst; and we all hurried down the corridor that was directly in line with the GodHead's back. I tried to glance over my shoulder to see if he had felt us and/or seen us, but MRnu and the other junior husband blocked my view.

I had felt the Net through the GodHead. The synthetic was reacting to it. Up until that point I had thought the Net would be like my link with KLse and Aten, only with more people involved. I hadn't had a clue. It was like our link, all right, the same way that a candle flame is like a type-F sun.

Who was he looking for? I asked Aten.

I don't know, she replied, cautiously.

Were those people who were watching him augmented?

I couldn't see if they were or not.

They were looking at him as if he were some sort of display screen, I said.

They wouldn't have to look at him to have access to the Net.

I almost said, *Maybe they were just curious.* But they hadn't looked that way, either. They had looked attentive. Not worshipful or anything, just watching.

They were looking at the glyphs! Aten said, suddenly. *There were Early glyphs on his tunic. Early glyphs are loaded with information. They say that if you know how to interpret them, even one glyph contains volumes.*

I remembered how the tunic had looked in the storm light, how the red figures had writhed. Were they really moving?

Yes, said Aten.

How do they do that?

Beats me.

I wished I could have gotten a better look at them, but Aten didn't agree. *You have to be careful with Early glyphs,* she told me. *Some of them are designed to reorganize neural nets. That kind of glyph is called an infection glyph, and that's what happened to Ankere. She looked at a bunch of those infection glyphs and they programmed her with an artificial personality. An Early personality.*

Now I remembered, from the history lessons I had gotten on OMSK. Ankere was the one who had rediscovered the Earlies and brought them back to this side of the galaxy. Most people thought of her as a hero, but that's not what they thought of her on OMSK.

The GodHeads wouldn't run around infecting people with Early viruses, would they? I wondered. *What would be the point?*

I don't know, said Aten. She still didn't quite trust the GodHeads. I hadn't known that. But now that I had really seen one, I could understand how they had gotten their names. That man had looked like one of those wild-eyed people who had found God, who could see Him standing right before him and could hear His voice every moment of his life.

Well, actually, he hadn't quite looked like that, but there was something similar about his intensity. During my orientation sessions I had heard something about the discovery of GodWeed, how people had thought it might make a good narcotic for recreational use until they actually tried it out. It wasn't a hallucinogen, it wasn't a narcotic, it didn't speed you up, slow you down, or make you paranoid. The guys at OMSK couldn't really describe to me what GodWeed did to people back then, before the Earlies came into the picture. But they said that GodHeads had left their lives behind for GodWeed, had gone wandering out into the desert in small, starved groups, only talking to people in a cryptic, raving fashion. That must have been how they had earned the name GodHeads.

Which had turned out to be strangely appropriate, after all.

The GodHead had dwindled behind us until he was swallowed by the crowd. We were walking so fast now, we had passed many shops without seeing them. I wondered if the whole expedition would be aborted now. But Aten suddenly stopped again.

"This looks like a good shop," she announced, and turned into it. The rest of us followed.

Aten was right. I saw many things that interested me as we walked through the racks. Aten was headed for the back of the store, though. *The sales are back here,* she said.

I felt a twinge of disappointment.

Don't fret, she said. *The stuff on sale is every bit as good. Sometimes it's even better. Just look, okay?*

So I looked, and she was right. The sales racks actually

had more variety. Within fifteen minutes I had picked several items to try on, including slacks, blouses, dresses, and a one-piece catsuit that looked particularly hot. I wondered if I would dare to wear it. But why not? If I had one thing going for me, it was that I was slim and tall.

But the catsuit was black. KLse looked at it oddly.

Would it bother you if I wore this color? I asked him.

He didn't answer immediately. He looked at me, as if he were trying to envision how I would look in the suit. I held my breath.

Black is the color of secret paths, he said. *Of clever trickery.*

He didn't necessarily disapprove of those things, but he was thinking about the GodHead again.

You have the right to wear it, he said.

That's not what I asked you. I asked you if it would bother you.

It might, he admitted. *But it is also appropriate, don't you think?*

I almost put it back, but he stopped me.

It is *hot. Try it on.*

So Aten and I went into the dressing rooms together. WWul came with us, to supervise and give her opinion. She seemed to enjoy this, and I was tempted to think that maybe having time "with the girls" was something she liked, even needed. But that would have been a human value judgment, and WWul was not human. Not in the least.

She did have a good eye for what was flattering and what was not. She pointed out flaws in some of the things that I at first thought were okay. Following her advice, and Aten's, I picked two pairs of slacks, two blouses, two dresses, and the catsuit.

If they both hadn't given their unequivocal approval of the latter, I wouldn't have dared. But they did.

"Wear it for now," Aten suggested. "Why not? We'll take the tag up to the register. It even looks good with your safety boots."

"Should we look for shoes, too?" I wondered.

"Not much point in that," said WWul. "This is God-World. You must wear boots."

I had forgotten about that. GodWorld had flora and fauna that could do people considerable harm if they weren't wearing the right kind of shoes. Or in this case, boots.

After all, GodWorld had GodWeed, possibly the most dangerous plant of all. Radiation from GodWorld's type-F sun had blended with terraforming viruses to render a native plant into a self-aware, infectious intelligence. I had to wonder if people had discovered the infectious nature of that intelligence by eating the plant or by stepping on it in the wrong shoes.

I gave my purchases to Aten and WWul, including the tags for the catsuit, and stayed behind to brush my hair while they went to pay. When they were gone, I could look at myself without shyness. When my hair was brushed, I looked very nice. In fact, I even looked sort of attractive. I couldn't believe it. If I had had Aten's confidence, I might have even tricked *other* people into thinking that I was attractive.

I took a deep breath and walked out of the dressing rooms. KLse was waiting for me; the others had gone up front with Aten and WWul. He looked at me, hard. He looked at me the way he had looked at Aten that morning.

"Good," he said. "Turn around."

I did, trying not to be clumsy. When I was facing him again, he was smiling.

"Even better," he said.

I knew I was blushing again, but I didn't care. The two of us walked up front together, almost as if we were a couple. But I didn't let myself really believe that. KLse was married. It didn't matter that he was one of five husbands, he still thought of WWul as his wife.

Still, it was fun when he looked at me that way.

As we passed up our row, I saw someone else coming down another. He was tall and dressed in black. *Another X'GBri,* I thought, then felt a jolt when I realized which one. He turned his head in my direction and saw me.

KLse grabbed my elbow. We had both stopped, and the GodHead was coming toward us. His eyes looked directly into mine. I tried to look away, but it was impossible. He walked up to me as if KLse weren't even there and gazed down at me for—I don't know how long.

This is what GodWeed does to you, I thought. His eyes were even paler than KLse's, almost like the eyes of a blind man, except that they saw me and a million things beyond me. In a way, they were worse than the terrible eyes from my dream. But I couldn't fall away from them, they held me tight. When he put his gloved hands on my face, I didn't even think of resisting.

"You are a candidate," he said.

I heard nothing but his voice. Dead quiet reigned in the rest of the store. Even the human customers were watching, not daring to make a sound. KLse was a ringing silence at the end of our link, and I couldn't feel Aten at all.

"Come to me at Red Springs," he said. "Tell them at the monastery. Tell them TGri wants you to walk in the desert."

I didn't answer for the longest time. I didn't know he wanted me to. But then I kind of got the feeling that he was worried I would say no.

"Yes," I agreed, wondering just what the hell I was promising. But after all, wasn't that what I was there for? I had assured them at OMSK that I would give it my best try. And now I was promising TGri the same.

I thought he was pleased, but I wasn't sure. His eyes looked mad, as if a superstorm raged behind them. His smell was slightly odd, my nose didn't know what to make of it. I couldn't tell if it was a good smell or a bad one, and the harder I tried, the more I began to wonder if the question wasn't completely irrelevant.

"I'll see you there," he said. It was a prophesy, not a departing courtesy. Then he turned and walked purposefully out of the shop.

I found that I was short of breath. KLse's hand was still gripping my arm, I could feel it again. "He was looking for *me,*" I gasped. "Out there in the courtyard, he was waiting for *me.*"

"You looked right into his eyes," KLse said, sounding surprised. After all, I avoided KLse's eyes so carefully. Or at least, I had before; because now I *was* looking into them, just as steadily as I had looked into the God-

Head's. I had done it without thinking. I blinked, bracing myself for the fall. We both held our breath.

But I didn't fall. I still felt funny, but I could stand it. *A victory,* he said through the link. *Perhaps . . .*

He didn't have to say the rest of it. *Perhaps the Net will be good for you.* It was an odd thought, but I was thinking it, too.

"The GodHead touched you," said WWul. Suddenly she was standing next to us and her voice was cold, possibly dangerous. I could tell through KLse's link that WWul was shocked, as if she thought that a single touch was enough to infect me with the Net. And more: She hadn't realized just how deeply she and her husbands were going to be pulled into this situation, or just how much it would bother her.

I didn't answer. We were at a crossroads. WWul was on the verge of calling the whole thing off. She must have had at least as much of a financial stake in our success as OMSK's backers did, but at that moment she wanted to take KLse and flee GodWorld. I could feel KLse's worry, his shame at the prospect of going into deep hiding. Though there would be many sympathizers who would gladly hide them, yes; many X'GBris who were horrified by how deeply their race had become entwined with the Net, with alien races and alien ways.

But KLse . . .

KLse thought it was a good thing. He would obey WWul's decision, but it would crush him.

The other four husbands had pressed close. They spoke to WWul in that deep, deep tone, the one I could feel but not really hear. The scowl never left WWul's face, but it did change slowly, softening a bit and becoming something more like anguish.

"We have shopped enough for one day," she said finally. "Back to the hotel."

She turned and led the way out of the store. KLse, Aten, and I exchanged several glances on the way down to meet the taxi. The plan was still on. WWul wasn't happy, and she wasn't the only one who felt that way, but they still mostly thought it was the right thing to do.

As we rode out into the superstorm, it began to diminish. By the time we were back at the hotel it had died and fierce light was shining down, biting even through the protective screens that had opened up between the buildings. Sand was everywhere, lying in drifts against the colossal buildings, pouring in gritty waterfalls down sloping surfaces. We got out of the taxi and stood in the dead air, stunned by the change in temperature. Even when filtered, GodWorld's sun was like a hammer.

"We can go to the monastery tomorrow morning," said WWul, without looking at any of us.

"The sooner the better, I think," said Aten.

"Tomorrow morning," WWul said, sounding sure of it.

But she was wrong.

I wasn't inclined to think it had been a bad day. An eventful one, yes; but not bad. I wasn't the least bit surprised that Edna had impressed the GodHead at the mall. It was better that WWul was struggling with her doubts now than that she should be overwhelmed by them unexpectedly at the monastery.

KLse was inclined to agree. He had supper with us, despite trepidations that he would upset us with his eating habits. But we weren't upset. Even Edna was fascinated.

X'GBris don't chew. They work food back into their throats with their inward slanting teeth and swallow it whole. Their throats expand and special muscles contract to push the food down a canal that leads to the first in a series of stomachs that pulverize the food with powerful acids. I've heard that X'GBri bile can give you a third-degree burn, but I didn't ask KLse if that was true.

He and I were both watching Edna from the corners of our eyes, not to mention our link. She had been strangely calm since her encounter with the GodHead. She seemed at peace. That worried me. In her place, I would have had painful thoughts about the loss of my old life, fears about the shape of the new one.

But Edna didn't have an old life. And as for the new one . . . she couldn't imagine it. I had trouble with that, myself. I was looking forward to dipping into the Net, but I wasn't the one who was going to become part of it.

It's a nice place to visit, but you wouldn't want to live there, said KLse, picking up on my thoughts. *I feel the same.* He didn't add that he was even more worried

about Edna than I was. Not to mention his other feelings, which were beginning to confuse him and complicate his life. I didn't know what to say about that, what
advice to offer. I had never been married, and I had
thought that X'GBri marriages were usually rock solid,
based on a husband's absolute unwillingness to give up
a woman once he's become connected to her.

But the Net was changing that. X'GBri spouses were
being lost to it. That was what WWul was afraid of. She
didn't think she would lose KLse to Edna, she thought
the GodHeads were going to get him.

*Humans have broken up our marriages before, without
the help of the Net,* said KLse, surprising me with his
honesty, surprising even himself. But he knew his life
was on the verge of a huge change, no matter which
way we jumped now. He was inclined to examine things.
Even himself.

I didn't know that, I said, lamely.

*It's not common, but it's always a threat. You have
as many females as you do males; we don't. And you
are—affectionate.*

I glanced at Edna, worried that she might have heard
that. But she was lost in her own world, a quiet place
that I didn't want to disturb.

Are you falling in love with Edna? I asked KLse
bluntly.

I have feelings, he replied, ambiguously. At least, it
seemed so to me; *he* thought he had just said everything.

We finished supper quietly, dragging it out as long as
we could. The three of us were becoming close, and I
wondered how much that bothered WWul. And JKre.
He couldn't be happy about the fact that KLse had *three*
women in his life. I wished that I could talk it over with
WWul; but the more upset she was, the more she drew
her husbands close to her, insulating herself from
outsiders.

"I'm going to take a shower," I told them. I caught a
look from KLse, and added, "Then I think I'll go into
the sitting room for a while. See you in a couple of
hours."

He wanted to be alone with Edna, and I didn't have
the heart to talk them out of it. Edna would be part of

the Net soon—he might never get to be alone with her again. JKre wouldn't like it, but that was just too bad.

(Needless to say, I jammed a chair under the drawing room door again, so I wouldn't have to find out just how much JKre wouldn't like it.)

I really had every intention of minding my own business. I needed the shower and I was looking forward to a peaceful hour in the sitting room, perhaps looking at the news vids. But something had happened when that GodHead had touched Edna. Even through his gloves, something had reached her, changing her. Our link was stronger than it had ever been, and I was getting it from both sides, from Edna and KLse.

I tried to concentrate on soaping myself up.

I must taste you again, KLse was saying. *They are concerned about what may have happened when the GodHead touched you.*

That was not true. But it was a very subtle lie, and I wondered if I would have caught it before.

The GodHeads are going to touch me tomorrow, when we go to the monastery, Edna replied. *And then I'm supposed to actually eat some buds. I'm going to be about as subverted as I can get.*

But now, he insisted, *you must be clear minded, not influenced by any outside source.*

Clear minded. Hah.

Whatever you want, she said, possibly meaning more than even she knew.

There was a stab of excitement from him. Did Edna feel it? Or was she still in that happy place where peace reigned?

I tried to scrub myself. I forgot what I had already done and had to start over. I got distracted by the tender places of my own body and had guilty thoughts about turning into a voyeur.

But they were so sweet. Yes, Edna knew what he wanted. She had known even before I had offered to stay away for a couple of hours. She lay on the bed for him, playing along. He leaned over her and she bared her neck. He began to lick her.

But this time he did it differently. This time he did it to please. And he succeeded. With both of us.

I had to sit down in the shower. I couldn't think straight with that going on. I should have gotten up and gotten dressed, should have gone into the sitting room and turned the news up loud.

But I didn't. I stayed there and let myself be drawn in.

KLse licked every inch of Edna's neck. He licked his way up her chin and found her mouth. He kissed her, then his tongue slid between her lips. No more pretense then. She kissed him back. She shed a few tears, and he licked them up.

He tasted her earlobes for a while, then gently lifted her shoulders. The catsuit she was still wearing zipped in the back. He pulled the zipper down and peeled it off her shoulders. She was wearing a modest cotton bra; he unhooked it and exposed her breasts.

They both became so excited at that point that if I hadn't already been sitting, I would have lost my footing.

KLse licked and tasted every inch of her, stopping only to peel her clothing down further. She was passive, except in the feelings she was broadcasting down the link. I almost lost my cool, almost joined them in bed at one point; but I knew those feelings were just for the two of them. It was their time, I didn't want to spoil or complicate it.

But my god, he even did her toes. That wasn't my favorite part, of course, or his, but it was certainly a delightful appetizer. When he was through tasting, he took off his own clothing and made love to her.

It wasn't her first time, but I'll bet it was only her second. She enjoyed it. In fact, *enjoy* doesn't even begin to describe the pleasure she felt. And he, for his part, felt a triumph and passion that would have disturbed WWul and JKre very much if they could have known.

Well, I certainly wasn't going to tell them.

Afterward, he lay beside her and held her for a little while. *I must go,* he said. *I've been here too long, and there will be questions.*

I love you, Edna replied.

Hah, I thought when he couldn't find a reply, *I wouldn't try that line about your feelings, if I were you.*

But he didn't. He surprised me with his tenderness.

You are my concern, he told her. She could feel how significant that was to him.

He got up and dressed himself. She did the same. She couldn't help but be curious about his clothes, how they came on and off. She couldn't help but wish he would stay the night. But he turned without a word and left.

Aten, called Edna.

Yes?

Aren't your toes getting kind of wrinkled in that shower?

Sorry. I got up and turned off the water.

Don't apologize. After all, when GodHeads make love, the whole damned Net must listen in.

I laughed. Then I stopped and thought about it. It must be an incredible experience. . . .

Don't get started! laughed Edna. *We can't make up an excuse to call KLse back.*

JKre would be willing, I said. *But WWul would strangle us if we dallied with two of her husbands!*

She laughed again. She was feeling good, and I was glad. Making love is supposed to be that way. Afterglow is supposed to be warm.

I guess I won't be needing a shower. She giggled. *I've been licked clean.*

Don't remind me, I said, toweling myself off. *But believe it or not, I still want to watch the news for a while. Don't wait up for me.*

I won't, she promised. She was already slowing down; sleep was creeping up on her. She took off the catsuit and put on her pajamas.

In the bathroom, I was doing the same. I brushed my teeth and combed out my hair. Edna was getting into bed, turning off the light. Now that the excitement was over, she was deliciously weary. I felt her drift off to sleep.

I dressed myself in my brand-new lounging clothes and sauntered into the sitting room, feeling as happy as if *I* had been KLse's lover. I was thinking that this wasn't turning out to be such a bad job after all.

A man was sitting on the couch. A human.

I stopped dead. The ridiculous notion passed through

my mind that I had accidentally wandered into someone else's suite; but this man seemed to be expecting me.

"Don't be alarmed," he said.

Of course I was. How had he gotten there? He couldn't have slipped past WWul and her husbands; he must have broken in while we were all out shopping. He had a very clever face—it wouldn't have surprised me if he had finessed the locks.

"I'm here to warn you," he said. "You don't know me, but I know you. My name is Peterhamil. I'm from OMSK."

Before that moment I had been debating whether I should call for help with my voice or contact KLse through the link. I canceled both plans, stood taller, and waited respectfully for him to continue.

"I'm the technician who wiped your memories," he said.

"I haven't—" I began, but stopped when I saw the expression of pity on his face. It horrified me. The supper I had just eaten turned to lead in my stomach.

"You were about to say you've never had a wipe," he said. When I couldn't answer him, he continued: "Forgive me. I've been trying to find a way to talk to you since before you left OMSK. Your memories are in great danger."

"My—memories?"

"Things are not as they seem. You have been very badly used, and you have been lied to. I can help you recover what was lost, but your current mission jeopardizes the work I've already done."

I studied him. He was a pleasant-looking man; trim, with a tennis player's build. His skin was almost as pale as mine, and his hair was an odd sandy color. His eyes were blue, but they could have been engineered. His face would not have been attractive if there hadn't been such a lively intelligence behind it. I found myself wanting to take him at his word.

But I don't give in to feelings like that.

"I would like to hear the rest," I said.

"You don't believe me."

I didn't move a muscle, I simply waited for him to

continue. He didn't seem offended by my skepticism. In fact, he seemed intrigued by it.

"Where were you born?" he asked.

"Celestine."

"What was your mother's name?"

"Kirito." I gave her the last status syllable she had earned, even though she had earned it posthumously. I would tell him how she had died, too, if he asked, and what medals she had earned in the service.

But instead he said, "How old are you?"

"Twenty-five."

"What is your favorite color?"

"I have several favorites. I don't think I can pick one. How long are you going to ask silly questions?"

"We plant clues on you, did you know that?" he said, looking ashamed. "Just in case we need to know who made you and why. If you had been one of mine, you would have answered those questions exactly the way I had programmed you to. You didn't."

That made me feel good. "So you *didn't* wipe me."

"I wiped the old you. But I didn't make the new you. I had a different you planned for you."

I dearly hoped he was full of shit. His implications were not just confusing and frightening. They were devastating. I was fond of my past, of my *self*.

"Why?" I asked, as if I were only mildly interested.

"Because that's what we do on OMSK. We can make you. We can unmake you. We can cure your illness and save your life; we can change you from a monster into an angel; or we can turn you into a useful tool and set you loose on the universe. The first two things are supposed to justify the last."

Obviously he didn't think they did. He couldn't look at me for several moments while he composed himself. I used the time to try to get myself in order. Edna was still asleep; that was a mercy. I focused on some mantras and on my breathing until I felt my old self again. I didn't try to ask myself just who that was.

Peterhamil. He had as many syllables as Bomarigala. It didn't sound like it when you were saying the name aloud, but there was that sneaky *rh* in the middle of it all. Unless you were really on your toes, you wouldn't know exactly where he stood, and that was not good. Not when he stood that high.

"You're having doubts about the ethics of your job," I said, cautiously.

He looked at me sharply, but not because he was offended. "It's that sort of job," he said. "You can't have that sort of power without stepping into some nebulous areas. Even if you mean well, as I like to think I did. Believe me, there are enough of them at OMSK who *don't* mean well."

"Yes," I agreed.

"You touched me," he said. "Your plight moved me as I never dreamed I could be moved. I couldn't let them do what they planned to you, despite your crimes."

Crimes. That was not a word I had wanted to hear, or even think. He saw through my mask to the turmoil underneath, and his own face became grim.

"This is going to be hard," he said. "But I think it's time we got started on the path back to you."

I didn't want to get started on any new paths. I thought the one I was on was complicated enough. And then, as if to prove my point, the door behind me exploded, sending my ineffectual chair prop flying right at my head.

I ducked, saw Peterhamil do the same, and then turned to see JKre breaking through the door as if the wood were little more than cardboard. He brushed the pieces from himself and fixed me with a stare that made me want to run as fast and as far away from him as I could. But there was no time to run.

In two steps he was close enough to grab me. He picked me up and threw me onto the couch. I thought I would fly into Peterhamil, but he wasn't there anymore. I thought he must have jumped up and hidden behind something.

And now JKre was standing over me with that damned grin, the one that meant exactly the opposite of what it should. His hands were flexing at his sides like they longed to be around my throat.

"You lied to me!" he hissed.

I had no idea what he meant, and now didn't seem a good time to ask.

"You lied!" he accused again, seeming to get angrier every moment he looked at me. "You said you wouldn't be lovers with KLse! A *junior* husband, Aten; you *dared* to do that to me!"

"I didn't!" I squeaked. "Edna slept with him, JKre! Not me!"

He seized me and threw me back on the couch again. My head banged into the arm and I saw stars.

"I smelled you on him!" he screamed.

I blinked, and in another moment he had seized me again. But this time he didn't throw me. He was pulling me off my feet. He was baring his teeth and dipping his head. He was going for my throat.

I put my arms up, tried to push his head away. He dropped me and instantly picked me up again, this time pinning my arms to my sides. Again, he dipped his head toward my throat. I strained backward as far as I could.

"JKre," I cried, "I didn't lie to you! I didn't!"

He was squeezing me so hard I thought my back would break. He didn't let go when I pleaded with him; he didn't stop trying to get at my throat. There was absolutely nothing I could do about it except keep bending in that impossible, painful position.

Suddenly I felt him shift his weight. Two more pairs of arms were pulling at him, KLse's and STra's. They, at least, had proper frowns on their faces as they fought with him. But they couldn't budge him.

I heard WWul screaming at him. She was speaking their dialect, and in my fear it took me a little more time to translate than usual.

"She doesn't know!" she was saying. "Stop, JKre! She doesn't know!"

But he didn't stop. He just tried harder. MRnu joined the struggle, and they managed to at least pull him away from my throat. But he wouldn't let go of me. I was amazed at the depth of his feelings. If I had known he would react that way, I never would have stood back and let KLse make love to Edna.

His eyes glared into mine. They were as dark as a storm, but I burned under the intensity of that glare. KLse and STra were using every ounce of their strength against him, pinching pressure points and trying to lever his arms away from me; MRnu had his forearm locked around JKre's throat, yet he couldn't be moved.

Suddenly the fifth husband popped up between KLse and MRnu. He stuck something into JKre's arm. JKre stiffened. I cried out as his hands clutched me tighter for a moment, then began (too slowly) to relax.

"You don't understand," he said, his voice strained with rage and pain. "You silly bitch."

I was shaking as they pulled him away from me. "Don't you call me names," I said, sobbing most of it. "Don't you *ever* call me names."

I glared back at him, even though I was still crying. His face slowly twisted, and then he hung his head. He let MRnu and STra lead him away.

The others stayed, their faces like tragedy masks. I let myself fall back on the couch. I wiped my eyes and waited for the shaking to subside. I wondered where the hell Peterhamil was. They should have discovered him by now. Did he have an X'GBri-invisible suit? I hadn't heard that the OMSK techs had worked that one out yet.

Whatever the reason was, I hoped Peterhamil would remain out of sight. The appearance of another man in my room would have blown up what was left of the fragile peace.

KLse's weight bent the cushions beside me until I almost fell into his lap. His arm came around me and held me upright.

I regret what happened he sent along a link that was now stretched tight as a sore muscle. *It was my fault.*

I didn't tell him that I agreed. Not that I didn't share some of the blame myself. Only Edna was blameless, and I was glad that it hadn't been she who was in this room when JKre came bursting in.

Aten? he asked. There was something odd about the way he asked it, almost as if he wasn't sure I was really me. After the conversation I had had with Peterhamil, I wasn't sure I liked the implication.

He didn't hurt me, I said. *Not my body, anyway.*

He patted me, awkwardly. He was doing it because he thought it was the sort of thing a human female needed. He was doing it too roughly. I almost laughed. But I didn't, because I could feel that he was deeply disturbed

by what had happened. He had thought he could protect
us from the other husbands. He had never seen JKre
react so violently. He had thought he knew the man.

"He was your advocate," said WWul. "I'm not sure
where this puts us now."

I sighed. I was growing tired of this back and forth
nonsense.

"Edna is still a candidate," I said wearily. "The God-
Heads have her now, whether we like it or not. If you
and your troop want to pull out, that's your right. But
I'm staying with her. I'm going to do my job."

KLse stopped patting me. His hand tightened subtly
on my shoulder, as if he was claiming it.

Or asking for it.

"I know you don't want to risk your family," I said.

"I . . . love them," she said, with great difficulty. It
was not a word she would normally use; she was trying
to make me understand.

"I know," I said. "Think about it tonight. I'll respect
whatever decision you make tomorrow. If we part, no
hard feelings."

"No hard feelings," she said tonelessly, and she
walked out of the room. MRnu followed her, with the
fifth husband—what was his name . . . ?

GDro, said KLse.

I was alone with him now. I felt along our link for
Edna; she was still astonishingly, blessedly asleep.

I won't be able to sleep tonight, he said.

I didn't think I would either. My muscles were sore
and twitchy. I wished there was a gym I could use. I
supposed the one in the hotel was closed by now.

Do you think we could take a walk? I asked.

He hesitated. He felt that things had been strained
pretty far already. But he liked the idea of a walk. *Wait,*
he said, and disappeared for a few moments.

He was back again more quickly than I had thought he
would be.

"JKre won't wake for a few more hours," he said.
"We'll be back long before that."

I nodded, and followed him out of the room. The others had disappeared into their bedrooms, so I didn't see
them as we left. I was glad.

*   *   *

KLse and I didn't look at each other as we rode down in the elevator. We were careful not to touch. You would have thought that I had been the one to jump into bed with him, I was feeling so guilty. But I tried to get rid of those feelings. Even if they had rightfully belonged to me, there was no use crying over spilt milk.

Good metaphor, said KLse, sending me a mental image to go with it. I laughed. It made me feel a little better.

His feelings were complicated. If I were to try to describe them, I think I would say that they were smoldering under ashes. His earlier triumph had been eclipsed by worry and regret. Yet he didn't think he had been wrong to do what he had done. He thought JKre was wrong, and he thought that it was too bad he couldn't fix that. I supposed he was right.

We walked down the beautiful streets with monolithic buildings towering on all sides of us. We weren't alone; the city was too big to go to sleep. Most lights still glared, and it was only half as noisy as usual. I rather liked that, at least for the moment.

"Who is Peterhamil?" asked KLse.

I felt him out through the link before I was willing to answer. He let me. I knew he could hide feelings and thoughts from me if he really wanted to, but I couldn't see the point in trying to kid him when he already knew so much.

"He appeared in my sitting room just before JKre blew up," I said. "He claimed to be from OMSK."

"Do you believe him?"

"I don't know." *I don't want to.*

"Did he bring a message from—*them?*"

"No. He said that they were lying to me. He said a lot of things that made me wish I had never gotten involved with this mission."

KLse went blank from his side of the link. It was as if a heavy curtain had descended. He must have thought he could hide things from me that way, but instead he was telling me that Peterhamil was at least telling part of the truth.

I slid my hand into his. He acted like he might pull

away, but then I squeezed, possessively. He squeezed back.

What are your associates hoping to accomplish by tapping into the Net? I asked him.

The corners of his mouth turned way down. He was getting angry with me, but he tried to tell me the truth anyway.

My associates want to have the benefit of the Net without losing family to it, he said. *But others . . .*

I saw where he was leading. *Others want to destroy it. Yes.*

And how would they accomplish that?

He seemed surprised that I couldn't guess. *Many ways. They could find a way to kill GodWeed. They could blow up GodWorld's sun.*

Not likely, I said. *Blow up a sun? I've never seen such a weapon with my own eyes, have you?*

It exists, he said, sure of himself.

They'd be detected before they could get their machinery close enough.

How do you know that? he challenged.

Because they already tried that from OMSK. Or at least, that was what I had heard. They had tried it a hundred years ago, when Ankere had brought the Earlies back from the other side of the galaxy. It had been an attempt by the Inner Worlds to throw their weight around, make an example of the upstarts. But the Earlies had swatted them aside like flies.

One hundred years later, Bomarigala had tried again, through sneakier means. I don't know if he had a sun-killer; that was one of those rumors that sounded more like legend than truth. But he should have been able to do them some harm. And he hadn't.

The GodHeads had even sent him a little message. He had shown it to me. It had said: *Shame on you.* That was all. I don't think he had felt ashamed, but I knew he had been embarrassed.

I remember feeling disappointed when his attempt had failed. I had been afraid of the GodHeads. Now I realized that the thought of destroying GodWorld sickened me. So maybe I wasn't quite as programmed as I was supposed to be.

They think they can exploit the Net, said KLse. *I think they can't dream of what the Net really is.*

But you can? I wondered. To me it seemed a mystery almost as great as death. In fact, that was what had drawn me to it. I don't think I ever believed that Bomarigala could do anything to disrupt it. I had been humoring him when I accepted the mission, just like I always humored them on OMSK. And now the Net was calling me, too. The idea that I could dip into such a place and emerge again was irresistible.

For me, too, said KLse. *But I have feelings. . . .*

He wasn't talking about the same sort of thing he had meant when he had been referring to Edna. He wasn't really talking about *feelings* at all. He meant something more along the line of—ideas.

No. *Premonitions.* That's what it was. He had a feeling that the Net was . . .

How could anyone say what it was? Even the God-Heads only told people bits of things. They only told what was useful, what was understandable. It was like being able to perceive ten dimensions, and then having to explain it to people who could only perceive three.

Certain forces, KLse said, *would like to think they can peek into infinity, pick out the useful bits, then use them to destroy the Net.*

Can they succeed? I asked. *What do your* feelings *say?*

We had crossed a street and walked under another hotel awning. He stopped there, in front of some huge double doors. I could feel people inside the lobby looking out at us, but KLse was lost in his musings. I was surprised. I hadn't known he had any precognistic tendencies. Those were characteristics the GodHeads looked for in their candidates.

Perhaps some of WWul's fears were justified.

Anything is possible, KLse said. *Anything. The Net is not invincible.*

I felt those eyes from the lobby boring into us. I wanted to move, but he was still half in a trance. What he was seeing was too important. I was afraid to disturb him.

We're important, Aten. You and I. And Edna. I sensed that the first time I was approached on the matter. It ex-

cited me then. It frightened me. The others don't quite see it.

He was thinking of WWul now, how much she had always meant to him, how he had leapt for the chance to rise in her regard. But he hadn't been entirely honest with himself. He hadn't let himself think about how short lived that new status would be before their relationship changed forever. Now he was thinking about it. Now that future included me. And Edna. He looked at me, shaking himself out of his trance. He touched my face.

I'm not sorry I made love to Edna, he said.

No, I agreed. *I guess I'm not, either.*

For a moment the future lay ahead of us, sparkling. For a moment we both realized that we really were important to that future. And then the lobby doors opened and the people who had been staring at us came out to get us.

Four X'GBri men surrounded us.

"Out for a walk?" one inquired pleasantly.

"We were just leaving," said KLse.

"You were just staying," corrected the man. He hadn't finished speaking before KLse hit him.

I was grabbed from behind and hauled off my feet. I curled into a ball and kicked out against the wall, managing to knock myself loose. I hit the ground and rolled, springing quite nicely to my feet again. But he was there one second before me. He stabbed a pressure point in my shoulder and my legs went out from under me. I fell to the pavement again.

Then something else struck my body, wrapping around it like snakes. Suddenly it was hard to breathe. The man picked me up and threw me over his shoulder.

I caught a glimpse of KLse fighting like JKre had fought before, like a madman. The three of them were having trouble subduing him. The man who held me turned, and I felt the kick against his body as he fired his wrap-gun.

I heard KLse cursing as he hit the ground.

"Don't struggle," the man told him. "The bonds get tighter when you do that. You want to breathe, yes?"

KLse called him a number of vile names before he

was picked up by two of the other men. The fourth
opened the lobby doors so we could be carried in.

I wondered what the humans in there would be thinking about our spectacle. Surely someone had called the
police by now. But when I craned my head, I saw that
I had been very much mistaken. This was an X'GBri
establishment. Except for me, there wasn't a human in
sight.

There were some women present, surrounded by their
various husbands. Clerks, guards, other guests. They all
wore expressions that ran the gamut from one end of the
spectrum to the other. Our captors carried us through a
forest of grimaces and grins, into an elevator.

Someone was already in there. I saw his boots. When
the doors had closed, he cupped my chin and lifted my
head until I could see his face. His expression was fairly
neutral. Or at least, that's what I thought at first. I had
been applying X'GBri standards to him, and he wasn't
an X'GBri.

Not exactly, anyway.

I'm a half-breed, he said through the link, then smiled
when he saw how that affected me. *Yes. I've been infected by the synthetic, too.*

"KLse and Aten," he said aloud. "We thought we'd
have to come get you. How lovely for you to come to
us like this. It saves so much time and blood."

I started to choke with my neck in that impossible
position. "Stand her up," the man ordered. My captor
obliged, and I swayed there on my bound feet. Now I
had a better look at the half-breed. He was as tall and
powerfully built as the other X'GBri men, and his hair
was every bit as lively. His coloring was almost human,
sort of dusky, and his features were somewhere in-
between what I thought of as human soft and X'GBri
sharp.

How the heck did you *happen?* I found myself
thinking.

It was love sweet love, he answered, grinning at me.
His teeth were definitely X'GBri. *My name is Voxi. Yes,
it's a human name. I'm your new boss.*

He cocked his head as he looked at me. He was as
amazed by my appearance as I was by his. He had never

seen anyone like me. *Did they make you on OMSK?* he asked. *You can't be natural.*

I'm natural, I said, though I was beginning to have my doubts.

I'm not. They had to fuse my father's genes into my mother's egg. It was all quite scandalous at the time. But I've recovered from those early setbacks.

He glanced at KLse, who had also been stood on his feet. KLse's eyes promised murder.

Did you think you had your own little harem, brother? Voxi asked him. *Now it's mine. I would never have waited as long to have them as you did. But I have to admit, when you finally did it, you did it well.*

Voxi looked at me again. *You enjoyed it as much as I did, Aten. I thought you'd drown in that shower.*

You need to get a life, I said.

Don't worry, I've got plenty. You'll find out.

The door opened, and I was carted out again. It felt like we had ridden up at least a hundred floors. I doubted that WWul and her spouses would be able to penetrate these defenses. But it might be enough for them just to know where we were. Edna could tell them if she would just wake up. Why wouldn't she wake up? I had been calling her for fifteen minutes now.

There's so much you don't know yet, Voxi said, with something almost like sympathy.

I felt a warning tug from KLse and quieted my mind. Whatever was going to happen, I'd better be calm and ready for it. We were taken into another beautiful suite—Voxi had taste, anyway—and were carted through several lavish rooms. I kept expecting to see a woman there, the wife who would be overseeing all of this. But she wasn't around.

The Net ate her, said Voxi, his thoughts stabbing me.

Panic and rage washed over me from KLse's side of the link. These were unattached males, the most danger-ous kind of all. Now they had *me.* KLse wanted desper-ately to free his hands and kill them.

Voxi started to laugh. *Our motives aren't that simple,* he said. *But your fears are understandable, brother. She's such an interesting thing. You won't be getting her back, one way or the other.*

KLse kept silent. He was trying to think calmly. I loaned him whatever strength I could. Sooner or later Edna was going to wake up. She would warn JKre and WWul. Then they would go through whatever channels they had to and get us back.

They opened one of the doors and the two guys carrying KLse disappeared through it. Through KLse's link I could feel them dumping him on the bed.

"Don't move around too much during the night," Voxi called to him. "The bonds will kill you if they get too tight."

KLse told him to do something painful to himself. Voxi smiled and nodded for them to shut the door.

"I have very nice quarters for you, Aten," Voxi said as they carried me farther down the hall. They opened my door and I was placed much more gently on my own bed. Then they all stood there and glared down at me. I reminded myself that with those bonds so tightly strapped around me, they would have a hard time molesting me.

We would cut them off first, said Voxi. But he didn't make a move to do so. I should have been grateful for that, but I kept thinking how uncomfortable it was going to be to have my circulation cut off for so many hours.

It will be painful, said Voxi. *I can't let KLse loose or he'll try to kill someone. I can't let you loose because you're too smart.*

What he didn't say was that he couldn't make the moves on me without inciting conflict inside his own group. They had been without their wife too long. They were under enormous strain.

You don't know the half of it, said Voxi. He was too good, cutting right through my shields. Maybe KLse could do that, too, and he just wasn't saying so.

What are you going to do with us? I asked him.

Take you where you can't do any harm.

What do you mean, harm?

I'm not going to explain it to you tonight, Aten. You'll know what I'm talking about eventually. Right now I'm going to lock you in here where we can't see you and be tempted by you. I wouldn't talk too much to KLse, either, because I can hear you and it's better if I'm not thinking about you too much. The more I think about you, the easier it is for me to rationalize coming in here and touching you. Understand?

Yes.

Good. You're a professional, say some mantras or something. That's what I always do.

I couldn't help it. That remark made me curious.

I'll tell you all about it some day, he said. *But not tonight.*

Is KLse going to be all right? I asked, worrying that he would really strangle in those bonds.

I don't know, said Voxi. He signaled his men, and they all filed out of the room. The door shut behind them and I heard them engaging the lock.

Not that I was going to try to get out of those bonds. They were tighter than anything I had ever felt in my life. I reached down our link for KLse; he met me halfway, but no words were exchanged. He just wanted me to know that he was all right. Uncomfortable, angry, worried, but all right. I sighed and tried once more to call Edna.

I got a faint answer. But it wasn't where I had thought it would be. Slowly I turned my head, not wanting to believe what I had felt. Someone else was in bed with me.

It was Edna. She was bound, like me. She was sound asleep; they must have drugged her. No wonder she hadn't responded to JKre's attack. They had probably used the diversion to kidnap her. They must have followed us home from the mall.

Edna, I called again. There was a faint answer, but she had no idea where she was. She didn't know we were in trouble.

Big trouble. And I had no idea how we were going to get out of it.

Edna and Aten, together again, said Voxi. *I would never try to separate you. Kiss her good night for me, will you sweetheart? I can't do it, myself.*

Leave her alone, I warned him.

I wish I could, he said. And he meant it.

That was what really scared me.

RAPTORS

I was stuck in the dream again. I knew I was dreaming, like I always do; but this time it was twice as frustrating, because although I had some slight control over things, I wasn't able to make the dream go the way I really wanted it to.

I started out on that same dusty road. Since that's the part of it I always enjoy, I didn't try to change that; but this time the Great Good Feeling wasn't there. I tried to pretend that it was, as if I could jump start it. But it wouldn't come. My body ached and I couldn't catch my breath. Oddly, my thirst wasn't as bad, but somehow that made it harder to bear.

Well, if this is the way it's going to be, forget it! I finally decided. Just then, the shadow passed over me. I looked up. I felt a pang of triumph as I realized that I could see a huge, dark object up there; but that quickly turned to disappointment as I realized that I was just looking at a lifeless blob. My mind had simply provided a prop for me; now it was just hanging there, shapeless and without meaning. As I continued to gaze at it, it faded into nothingness.

I heard the sounds of men fighting nearby. They were off the road somewhere, out of sight. I hated them. I would stop every time they seemed to get closer and my arms would pull an invisible bow to make an invisible arrow fly at them. My arms did that compulsively; they ached to be in those positions, to feel the resistance of the bow and string, to let that arrow fly. After it had happened a few times, I remembered to wonder why.

Why? I couldn't remember learning to shoot with a

bow and arrow. Why would anyone do that in this day
and age? Except for sport. But I hadn't done it on
OMSK. I hadn't done it on GodWorld.

I heard Aten's voice, in among the men's. That confused me. Was I misinterpreting the sounds? Maybe they
weren't fighting. It was a good thing I didn't have a real
bow and arrow. But why did they sound so agitated?
Where were they? I could see only rocks and glaring
sun. My feet were burning. That damned city was up
ahead, things were about to go wrong again.

They were already wrong. *I should just call the whole
thing off and start over,* I decided.

My feet kept going up that road. Just for laughs, I
tried to slow down. Instead, I walked faster. I tried to
veer to the right. I started to turn and congratulated
myself. But the turn became a circle. I went around
and around.

Oh great! Some improvement!

Edna, a man called.

I was embarrassed. Someone was watching me turn
circles like an obsessive nut. I tried to stop, and speeded
up, instead.

Poor, plain Edna.

I didn't recognize the voice. But suddenly I realized
that the man who was talking to me was an X'GBri.

KLse? I asked.

No.

Who are you?

You'll know soon enough.

Can you see into my dream?

I can't see.

Did he mean he was blind? Or that he could feel and
hear my dream but not see it?

Can you— I started to ask, but then someone grabbed
my elbow and stopped me cold. Another man was standing in my path; not an X'GBri, but a strange, pale
human.

"Don't listen to them," he said. "They don't have
your best interests in mind. They just want to use you."

"Who?" I asked him.

"OMSK."

"Well, yes, I already knew that."

He shook his head. It was odd, but I felt like he was really there, not just a dream phantom. "You think you know how low they can go," he said, "but you don't. You need to know your past before you do anything else. I need to help you find your past."

"You can do that?" I asked.

"Yes," he said, and I was thinking, *Why not? At least the dreams would go away, and then I would be a better lover to KLse, and . . .*

"Edna!" someone yelled, making me jump. My hands grabbed for the invisible bow again, my arms strained it apart, and I shot the invisible arrow before I could even think about who I was shooting at. But it *wasn't* an invisible arrow. It was a real one. And the person I had shot at was Aten.

The arrow went right into her throat. She fell backward, into the dusty road.

"Aten!" I screamed, and tried to run to her. But the man was holding my arm.

"I should never have tamed you," he said. "I should never have helped you. It's all my fault. Why couldn't I just leave you alone?"

"I shot Aten," I tried to yell at him. But I was gasping. I couldn't breathe, and I couldn't feel my body. Aten was mortally wounded, but I was the one who was dying. "Help Aten," I begged him. "Help Aten."

"Edna!"

"Help Aten."

"Edna!"

The dream was going away, but there was nothing to replace it but the yelling. Someone yelling at *me*. It was dark, and I couldn't figure out where I was; for a moment I was afraid that those evil men from my dream had finally found me. But then I heard X'GBris snarling at each other.

"KLse!" I cried. "Help Aten! I shot her!"

You were dreaming, someone said, through the link. But he wasn't KLse. He was the man who had talked into my dream.

Who are you? I asked him.

Voxi. I'm right here, cutting your bonds. Can you see me?

I couldn't. And I was going to pass out, too. It wasn't at all like falling asleep; it was a sick feeling.

I'm giving you a stim. Don't pass out. Look at me.

I tried. But everything looked upside down to me. I passed out anyway, for a few moments. When I came to again, someone was rubbing my arms and legs.

"What about Aten?" I asked him. "I shot her."

"You didn't shoot Aten," he said. I knew he must be Voxi. I could barely make his features out in the semidarkness. The only reason I could tell he was an X'GBri was because of his size. And his wild hair glistening in the dim light from the doorway.

"Was I dreaming?" I asked, wanting to hear it again.

"Yes."

"Then where is Aten?"

He made an oddly human sound of exasperation. "Where she always is!" he snapped. "With you."

Pins and needles were stabbing me from head to toe. It hurt enough to make me cry. I saw the glint of his teeth as he smiled.

"Poor Edna," he mocked. His tone didn't make me feel any better.

"Why am I here?" I asked. "This isn't my room."

"That's an astute observation," he said. "I'm not your lover, either. Or hadn't you figured that out, yet?"

Why was he being so mean? No, not mean, exactly. He was mad about something. I started to get scared.

"We're not going to hurt you," he said. "Calm down. Do you see Aten?"

There was motion in the bed next to me. They were untying someone there. I looked closer and found Aten. I was so relieved, it was pathetic. Voxi laughed out loud.

"You're so timid," he said. "You won't be any fun at all."

"Where's KLse?" I asked, suddenly remembering him. I felt for him down the link. He was there. But he was in pain. He could barely do more than acknowledge me.

"Untie KLse, too!" I demanded.

"No." said Voxi.

"He'll die if you don't!"

Voxi shrugged. "Then he'll die."

Suddenly I was so angry at him even I was shocked. I tried to leap up; only got halfway there. I wanted to scratch his eyes, but my hands clutched ineffectually at his clothing. "Don't you dare hurt him!" I was crying. "Don't you dare!"

He pushed my arms down and pinned them, holding me around the middle, keeping me in that awkward, halfway-up position.

"Calm down," he snarled, but that just made me madder.

"Untie him!" I demanded.

I was making him really angry. He was losing his patience, I could feel him down the link. I could feel that if he lost his temper I was going to get hurt. But I couldn't be reasonable about it; I just struggled more.

"Stop it," he said, so angry that it came out a whisper. "I won't untie him. He'll try to kill us if I do. If I were him, I would do the same thing. He's staying where he is."

"No," I insisted. "He'll die."

"So he dies. He's a man, not a child."

"I couldn't stand it if he died!"

"Then don't stand it. Suffer. Lie down and shut up, or I'll tie *you* again."

I wouldn't. He could have forced me down, but he wanted me to obey his orders. He was trying to bully me down.

"Aten wouldn't act like this," he said. "Aten is too smart."

I could feel Aten's mind stirring down the link. She was worried about KLse, too.

"Drug him," I said. "You don't have to tie him like that. Drug him and then put cuffs on his ankles and wrists."

He raised his chin and looked down his nose at me, amazed that I was being so stubborn. He wanted to punish me for it. He was sending his feelings down the link like an old pro, like a surgeon, attacking me and trying to scare me into submitting. But every time I thought about KLse lying in his room, slowly suffocating, I went crazy. I was ready to fly at Voxi, hurt him as much as I could.

If only I could move.

"You're not a very strong girl," he said. "Or very smart. Or very pretty. I don't know why I should even keep you. Aten is so much better than you."

I tried to bite him through his clothing. My teeth just slid off. I tried harder.

I felt the muscles moving under his clothing as he lifted me up like a child. He raised me until I was face-to-face with him, and then he showed me his own teeth.

So sharp.

"My turn," he said, and pulled me close.

And then he kissed me. I hung there, confused and overwhelmed. He had surprised himself as much as me, and now there was no telling what he would do.

He tossed me onto the bed. I bumped Aten, and she sent me a quick message: *Don't push any further!*

"Cuffs and drugs for you," said Voxi. "And Aten, too."

Other men were already coming forward. They swarmed over me, touching me more than they had to. One touched my breasts before he let me go again.

When they were done, Aten and I were both bound hand and foot. Voxi leaned over us with a hypo. He did Aten first. He watched her relax and drift away. Then he leaned over me. But he didn't inject me immediately.

What will you give me if I untie KLse? he asked.

I was tongue-tied. Or in this case, brain-tied.

Come on, you drab little thing, he said. *Think. What do you think I would want?*

Money? I guessed.

Think again.

He was trying to get me to come on to him, to offer myself. But I wasn't like Aten, I didn't have that kind of confidence.

You don't need confidence, he said. *You just need a tongue. And a soft little mouth to keep it in.*

He sent me an image down the link. I blushed. *I thought I was too drab for you,* I fired back, then felt guilty about it. It sounded like I was offering Aten, instead.

Maybe, he said. *Maybe not. You might look good in*

certain positions. I know you taste good. I saw what KLse did.

He still hadn't decided if he was going to untie KLse or not. He still didn't care if KLse died.

I'll do whatever you want, I promised.

Not now, you won't, he said. *Later.*

He stuck me with the hypo, then walked out of the room, his movements unhurried. He wouldn't let me see down the link to what he was planning. The other men followed him out and shut the door.

Aten, I called.

She responded, but so sleepily I couldn't make out any words in her message. I let her alone.

I felt for KLse again. Someone else was waiting for me there.

Go away, ordered Voxi.

No.

I thought he would order me away again, but he didn't. He let me feel KLse being untied, let me feel the pain as KLse's circulation returned. He let me feel the rage and frustration that KLse felt when he realized he was being drugged and cuffed.

Feel better? asked Voxi, when it was done.

Yes, I said stubbornly.

You owe me. I'll let you know when it's time to pay.

The drug was stealing over me, too. I let it. It was better than worrying. I felt Aten stir again; she put her mouth right next to my ear.

"You got him to do something he didn't want to do," she whispered. "Don't forget that, when the time comes."

"I won't," I said. But I tried not to think too hard about what that meant. I didn't want Voxi to tune in on me. It was uncanny how good he was with the link.

"How did we get here?" I whispered.

"Kidnapped," she mumbled.

"Why?"

Aten was having a hard time focusing. But she felt an urgent need to tell me what was going on. She didn't want to do it through the link any more than I did, for fear of Voxi knowing. That was funny—we had to speak aloud if we didn't want to be heard.

"Might hear us anyway," whispered Aten. "Prob'ly does. He says the Net ate his wife. Politics."

And then she fell asleep. I could have asked her a million questions.

Don't worry, Voxi's voice said in my head. *I'll tell you everything you could possibly want to know about our motives and reasons once we're away from GodWorld.*

I can't go away, I told him, sleepily. *The GodHeads want me.*

They can't have you, he insisted.

They already have me, I said, and wondered myself what I meant as I toppled over the edge into drugged sleep.

I woke in a strange place, my heart pounding with panic. There was more light, but not much more; and I was strapped into a couch. My hands and feet were still bound. I craned my neck and saw Aten lying on a similar couch nearby.

The door slid open and Voxi walked in. I knew it was him before he spoke, though I hadn't seen him clearly the night before.

"I wouldn't separate you from Aten," he said. "Not after the way you acted last night."

I quickly checked for KLse down the link. He was gone. My heart squeezed painfully.

"He's not dead," said Voxi. "We left him behind. His family has picked him up by now."

"Really?" I begged, though it was painful to think that he was gone. And then it sunk in just what he meant by *behind*. "Have we left GodWorld?"

"Yes." He strolled over to Aten's couch and gazed at her body admiringly. "You can forget about your previous plans. We won't let you join the GodHeads. You're going where you can't do any harm."

I remembered what Aten had told me about heavy-world prisons. My mouth went dry.

"Not prison," said Voxi. "You're going home with us. We'll take you into our household." He looked like he wanted to touch Aten, very badly. But he was restraining himself. I wondered why; after all, she was tied down.

She couldn't fight, and he seemed to feel she—we—belonged to him already.

"Why don't you want me to be a GodHead?" I asked him.

He tore his gaze away from Aten long enough to give me a searing glance. "If you were just going by yourself, it wouldn't matter to me at all," he said. "But you'll take the rest of us with you. KLse and me." He looked back at Aten again. "And *her*," he added. "And OMSK. You're their poison."

"How could I take you with me? I couldn't infect you through the synthetic link. If that were possible, wouldn't we all be GodHeads by now?"

"You don't even understand how the synthetic link works," he said, dismissively.

"Aten says it rides piggyback on the Net," I declared, hoping that didn't sound as lame as I thought it did. He didn't laugh, though. He seemed to be considering the comparison.

"That's pretty close to the truth," he said. "And you're right, we wouldn't become GodHeads just because you did. But I'm not going to let you become a GodHead. If you do harm, and we are still connected to you by our synthetic link, your trail will lead right back to *us*."

"If you were worried about that, why did you let yourself get infected?" I asked.

He grinned. "I was infected before you were."

I wanted to think about the ramifications of that, but his expression was distracting me. He was grinning as wide as he could, yet his grin wasn't up to par with what I had come to think of as the X'GBri grimace. His face looked softer than it ought to. For one startling moment, I thought he was human. But a moment later, I didn't know what to think.

"Do you intend to marry Aten?" I asked.

"Edna," he sighed. "You think you're buying time with that question, but the answer is more complicated than you can imagine." He brushed Aten's hair out of her face. Once he had touched her, he couldn't help lingering, exploring the texture of her skin.

"You are human," he continued. "You will never have the status of an X'GBri wife."

"What does that make us, then?" I asked.

"Playthings," he answered. "Just like my mother was."

He was warning me down the link, wordlessly, not to touch that subject. But it didn't take me long to come up with another topic. "OMSK still has the synthetic," I said. "They can find other candidates."

"You're distorting the truth," he said. "They took a long time to find someone as blank as you, someone who could be programmed. It will take them even longer to make or find another. We still have time to act."

"Act?" I said.

"Don't worry your head about it," He couldn't keep his hands off Aten. He wanted to stop, but he couldn't help himself. He was trying to provoke me in order to distract himself. But the fact was, I really *didn't* want to worry my head about it. I didn't want to think about it at all. I couldn't help feeling down the link for KLse, and every time he wasn't there, it was like a little knife going into my heart.

"You loved him," said Voxi. "You couldn't do otherwise. You would have loved any man who paid attention to you, Edna. Your personality is so full of holes that you're desperate to fill. You could love me if I wanted you to."

I tried not to disagree with him. I tried to be neutral. I averted my eyes from him and turned my attention back to my own situation. I was strapped down, but I could probably get out of the restraints with a little time and effort. My catsuit was made of a slippery material.

My catsuit. I had changed into my pajamas before I went to bed. Now I had my catsuit back on, and my underwear and bra beneath it. Who had put those things back on me? Had it been Voxi? I was in a panic trying to remember, hoping that I had dressed myself and just forgotten.

My embarrassment caught Voxi's attention. It intrigued him. He took his hands off Aten and came over to my couch, leaned over me. He started to caress me as he had caressed Aten.

"KLse's gone," Voxi said. "You'll never be allowed near him again, and I won't let him through the link if he follows us. Aten is mine, and if you want to be near her, you'll have to go along with it."

His face dipped toward mine, and I closed my eyes because I thought he was going to kiss me again. But instead, he rested his cheek against mine. His body pressed me into the couch, but he wasn't putting all of his weight on me. He was being careful. He opened up the link between us, and I got the funniest feeling. I was aware of him from the inside out. It was complete communication; but instead of blurring the differences between us, it accentuated them. It was like the male and female of yin and yang lying curled up together, touching but never blending.

He was amused when he discovered that I was upset because I was worried he had dressed me. He made me remember what it had been like to have KLse *un*-dress me. I couldn't help lingering over the memory. He stayed right with me, a constant reminder that KLse was gone. Gone.

Little pangs were stabbing my heart. He felt them too.

"My pain," he said. "Your pain. Our pain. We've both lost our loves. And now we're pressed so close together. Do you like the way my body feels? I like yours."

I didn't try to answer. I couldn't say whether the pressure of his body comforted me or not. I don't think it was supposed to.

"There is no comfort," he told me. "Not for you and me. This is what it's like to have a history, Edna. How do you like yours, so far?"

"It was all right up to a point," I said.

"No it wasn't," he accused. "Don't lie to me. Love has two edges, like a blade. Would you like to have your memories wiped again? I can arrange it."

"No."

"I can even make sure you'll be happy in your new life."

"No."

"You're fixated on KLse like a baby bird on its mother."

He got up. It wasn't that he was tired of lying on top

of me, it was that he was starting to get too excited, and
he didn't want to feel excited by me; he preferred Aten.
He undid my straps and stepped away from me. I sat
up, but I regretted it. The room spun for several seconds.
I tried blinking, but that just started the whole process
over again.

"Eye movement," offered Voxi. "Look up and down
several times, and then to both sides several times."

I tried that, though I felt silly doing it. He was right;
it worked. When I could see again, Aten was sitting up.
She looked dazed, but a lot more alert than I felt.

"What's for breakfast?" she asked. I wished I could
have been that practical.

Voxi grinned at her. Now that she was awake, he was
in a better mood. He really liked her.

"This way," he said, and walked to the door. He had
that characteristic X'GBri way of stalking, but it was
tempered with another quality, a human one. Aten and
I hopped off our couches and hurried after him.

As I passed through the door, I noticed how large and
heavy it was. It had locking mechanisms that gleamed
as I passed them, threatening me. Everything was so
huge, even more so than our hotel had been, built on
an X'GBri scale. Our cell must have been considered
tiny on that scale. I wondered about its purpose on the
ship. Were they in the habit of taking prisoners that
often?

Undoubtedly, Aten said, through our link.

I was so relieved to hear her mental voice again, I
almost cried. *Why have they kidnapped us, Aten? We
weren't hurting them!*

Maybe we were, from their point of view, she said.
After all, the Net ate their wife.

But we're . . .

Hush, she warned. *Voxi hears us better than we hear
him.*

He was walking ahead of us, seemingly unconcerned.
We had to hurry to keep up with his long legs.

If he could hear us, he would say something, I said.

We don't know him. We don't know what he'll do.

I looked at her. As always, she looked calm, in control, like she was the boss. I tried to make my face look

like hers. All that I managed to achieve was a blank expression.

We'll feel better after breakfast, Aten promised.

Voxi had led us down a long hall. He stopped in front of a closed door and played his fingers rapidly over some keys on the wall. They were marked with X'GBri symbols. I wished that they could have given me some language drips at OMSK as well as the technical ones.

The door slid open and we entered a galley. It was large even by X'GBri standards, and I could feel how impressed Aten was by that, just as she had been impressed by the suites back in the hotel.

Two very rich families are fighting over us, she said. *I've got to admit, it does something for my ego.*

The galley had an elegant utilitarianism to it, something that even I could see. It was another hint that my wipe was not as comprehensive as I had thought. I knew that a human galley would not have this sense of beauty in its design. X'GBris just seemed to have more style. Maybe it was because they were a matriarchy.

Voxi ushered us into a couple of seats and went to fetch some food for us. I was surprised that he would do that. If this was what it was going to be like to be a "plaything," maybe that wasn't such a bad thing to be. I blushed when I realized who might overhear me thinking that. Aten reached over and tweaked my earlobe, playfully.

We would probably become experts at nonverbal communication.

"Voxi," she said to his back, "you are the senior husband, yes?"

"Of course," he said.

"Why don't you have one of the juniors serve us?"

"Perhaps later," he shot back.

She quirked an eyebrow at me. Something was going on, and I wasn't sure what it was. What was I missing? What would I do without Aten?

Voxi brought us juice, coffee, fruit, and cereal. He brought some for himself, too. I tried not to look at him or Aten as I ate, hoping that eventually what was so obvious to the two of them would become obvious to me, too. Or at least less obscure. That was why it took me so long to realize that Voxi was chewing and swallowing his food just like a human. I couldn't help it, I stared at him.

"Yes?" he inquired.

Having been caught, I decided to take the Aten approach. "Your teeth don't look like chewing teeth," I said.

"They aren't exactly," he admitted. "Some of the back ones serve well enough for it. After much practice, I can manage the human style very well."

"Your throat doesn't expand?" Aten asked.

He shrugged. "It does, after a fashion. But it's a lot more work. I usually combine the two styles."

He was doing a good job of it. I hadn't even noticed. I supposed that X'GBris noticed all the time. Yet he had made it to senior husband.

Eating is a small matter, he said through the link, making me jump. *Fighting is the big one.*

"How did you get to be senior husband?" Aten asked boldly.

He continued to chew his food in a leisurely fashion, but his eyes burned at Aten. *Guess,* he said.

"Fighting, alone, would not be enough. Not for someone like you."

Someone like me?

"A hybrid."

You're still guessing.

She shrugged. She sipped her coffee and regarded him as if he were nothing more than an interesting dining companion. I watched like a spectator at a tennis match.

The GodHeads aren't going to let Edna go that easily, Aten said suddenly, her mental voice like a warning bell. It stopped Voxi dead in his tracks for a moment. He looked almost startled. But then he belched, contemptuously.

You overestimate your worth to them.

Not at all, said Aten. *Not to them, or to OMSK.*

OMSK does not dictate to us.

"So," she said aloud. "We're just a couple of cuties you picked up on a lark."

"An impulse," he suggested.

"You don't seem like the impulsive type."

He grinned at her. He couldn't achieve the full-blown X'GBri grimace, but what he did was impressive enough. "Some impulses are irresistible," he said.

"Is that why you won't let the other husbands near us?" she asked.

He didn't answer, but the grin died.

"Here's another guess," Aten said, as if she couldn't feel the thunderstorm brewing down the link. "You grabbed us because of what we were about to do to the Net. All this talk about being your *playthings* is spur of the moment. And now that you've actually got us, you're not all that anxious to install us in your family after all."

"It's hard to work up much affection for a couple of assassins," he countered.

"If that's what you think we are, why didn't you kill us?" Aten said, sipping her coffee with her pinky extended. I almost choked on mine. Voxi didn't even spare me a glance.

"You like to take chances," he said, and I was sure his tone would make Aten back off. But she didn't. She smiled, charmingly.

"What else can I do?" she asked.

He seized her wrist. Her smile didn't falter, but I could feel the pain through our link. I had to fight not to rub my own wrist in sympathy.

"Since we're being so honest with each other," said Voxi, "just what were you planning to do to the Net? What were your orders from OMSK?"

"I couldn't tell you that even if I wanted to," she said sweetly. "I've been conditioned."

"Liar," he said.

She only smiled. He squeezed harder, to no avail. Suddenly he grinned back at her.

"You won't tell," he said. "But Edna will."

"I will not!" I protested. If Aten was going to be brave, then I would, too.

He let her go. He started eating his breakfast again, as if nothing had been said. But I could tell he didn't believe I had it in me to resist the way Aten could. I felt hurt. I felt like I had to get back at him.

"If you miss your wife so much, why don't you enter the Net so you can be with her?" I asked, triumphantly.

The look he cast me was not the same sort that he had been giving Aten. It made me wish I had kept my big mouth shut. "You should keep silent," he said. "You're not good at this."

"It was a good question," Aten said. "Why don't you? Are you afraid of the Net?"

"Yeah," I said, still smarting. "*We're* not afraid of it."

He snorted. We just kept staring at him, demanding an answer.

"Why should I tell you anything?" he asked, amused.

"Why not?" countered Aten.

"I could simply beat you, instead," he said, as if he were really considering it. "Like a human male would. After all, I am half human."

"We would hate you if you did that," she replied.

That should have been a lame response. A laughable one, even. But it wasn't. He wouldn't look at her for a long time after she said that, and his side of the link went suspiciously dead. His face looked admirably neutral, I must admit. He and Aten were a couple of pros.

"I won't beat you," he said finally. "Not for fun, anyway. I don't promise you won't get hurt if you don't cooperate. It's not a happy situation for you, and I suppose I regret that; but you shouldn't have meddled in the Net. OMSK shouldn't have meddled. Their power and influence has been dwindling for a hundred years, and they haven't realized it yet."

"You'll have to explain it to them," Aten said, dryly.

He shrugged. "Have you had enough to eat?"

I had. Aten was still sipping her coffee, but I think she was buying time. She was trying to goad more information out of him, but she was realizing that it would take days to do that. Maybe even months. That was a dismal thought. Months as prisoners in this shaky situation! I didn't know if my nerves could stand it.

"We've had enough," said Aten.

"Good," said Voxi.

He finished his own coffee. And then he attacked me.

Edna was so surprised when Voxi struck her, she didn't even scream. She laughed, instead. It was an embarrassed laugh, full of pain and humiliation. The sound of it enraged me, and I lost my sense of caution. I leaped to her defense, thinking to use the tactics I had learned on OMSK.

Voxi saw me coming a mile off. He let me get in close, then jabbed me in the ribs. I felt something go *crack,* and then I was doubled over, trying to breathe.

"Don't make any more stupid moves," he warned me, and yanked Edna to her feet, pinning her arm behind her. She started to let herself fall to the ground, just like they had taught *her* on OMSK. But that move was wrong for this situation, she almost broke her own arm by letting herself fall that way. Voxi fell with her at the last moment and pinned her to the floor. He pulled something out of a hidden pocket. A hypo.

I ignored the stab in my ribs and hit him hard, on his chin. If he had been human, he would have had a bundle of nerves behind his jaw that would have knocked him out when they were pinched by the blow. But he wasn't. He just ignored me while I hit him until my fists were sore.

"Don't make me hit *you,* Aten," he warned. It was a tone of voice I knew well. Bomarigala had used it many times. I stopped hitting him.

Edna was crying with pain now. He jabbed her with the hypo and hauled her to her feet. She went sluggishly, but he didn't care. He held her tight and dragged her along with him. I staggered behind them.

"You're going to make her sick if you keep injecting her with drugs," I gasped.

"Gods forbid that I should ever make her sick," he said, mockingly.

He hauled Edna back to our cell and strapped her down to her couch. I just stood by, hoping that he wouldn't hurt her. He pulled out another hypo and gave her an appraising look.

She glared back as bravely as she could. She was trying not to look at me, trying not to talk through the link. I could feel Voxi there anyway; he would have interfered with anything we tried to tell each other.

"This is a truth drug," he said. "It isn't going to hurt. You'll just tell me everything you know."

I was so relieved to hear that I almost fell over. But poor Edna got very scared. She thought she knew a lot of things he didn't. I knew that she knew nothing of the sort. I tried to reassure her, wordlessly through the link. But I don't know if she got the message or not.

"Who are you, Edna?" Voxi asked.

Edna pressed her lips together, refusing to answer, but that was just the first of a thousand questions. Edna tried not to answer any of them, and she had to be injected two more times. In the end, she answered everything, told him as much as she knew and even as much as she guessed. I stood by and held my ribs, pitying her for some of the childish, naive dreams she revealed to him.

Sometime later, I don't know how long, he was finished with her. He let her drift into sleep. I tried to drag in a breath to let my relief out, but I couldn't quite manage it. He looked over at me, sharply, then picked me up and carried me to my own couch. He pulled open my lounging clothes—how funny, the ones I bought back on GodWorld, it seemed like a thousand years ago—and found my cracked ribs with expert hands.

Soon he had taped them as well as any doctor would have. He even gave me a painkiller. I accepted it, gratefully.

Voxi didn't try to molest me, despite the fact that he had glimpsed my body. He was too preoccupied, worried even. He went back to Edna's couch and frowned down at her. I made myself get up and join him.

"What a ridiculous, half-baked plan," he said, at last. "Didn't you stop to think about it, Aten? Sending Edna into the Net, knowing how easily she spills the beans?"

I didn't remind him that he had had to inject her *three* times to get her to do so, she had fought the drug so valiantly. I also didn't mention how glad I was that he had used that method. I couldn't have stood to watch him torture her. I probably would have spilled the beans myself if he had done that, conditioning or no conditioning.

"I don't ask questions," I told him. "That's why I'm still an agent for OMSK."

He clicked his teeth. I was startled. I had been told that X'GBris laughed by clicking their teeth, but in all the time we had spent with X'GBris, this was the first time I had heard one do it. And Voxi was only *half* X'GBri. "You know how to be a good pawn," he said. "I hope they pay you well."

"They do."

He put his hands on his hips, regarding Edna almost affectionately. At least, I hoped he felt that way. My hands were bruised and throbbing, and the painkiller wasn't making that much of a dent in my sore ribs. He didn't have a scratch on him; he hadn't even been working that hard to subdue us. He had handled us like we were a couple of children. Now I could believe that he had really fought his way to the top of the husbands' hierarchy.

"I wonder what Bomarigala's real plans are?" Voxi said. "The moment Edna dips into the Net, all she knows is right there for them to see. You and KLse and I will be there as well. If we can get into their Net, they can certainly get into ours. So what would OMSK gain, really?"

I shrugged, hurting myself.

"Perhaps I should use some truth drugs on you," he said.

"Whatever." I didn't have to fake nonchalance. Edna had already told him as much as I knew myself. I made it a habit never to think too much about the motivations of the movers on OMSK. Not unless I was pretty sure they were trying to kill me.

He didn't seem inclined to dose me anyway. He seemed more relaxed than he had before. Apparently, aggression and violence could be very soothing to X'GBris. One thing I had to say for them, though. They did it efficiently. And there didn't seem to be a whole lot of malice connected with it.

"*Edna,*" he said. "Such a plain name. No wonder it's fallen into disuse."

"Don't say that." I was surprised at how mad I was suddenly getting. I hadn't been as mad even when he had bullied and interrogated her, though I had certainly been more afraid. "Don't call Edna plain. You know she's not. In her own way, she's just as good looking as I am."

"Yes," he said, regarding her clinically. "But she doesn't know it, so it doesn't count."

Edna stirred on the couch. Her face looked so peaceful, I couldn't bear to disturb her. She missed KLse so much. I should have known that something like that would happen with someone as tender as she.

"How old is she?" Voxi asked, softly.

"I don't know. I'll bet she's not even twenty."

"And they were willing to use her? We would never do that to one of our own young ones."

"Good for you," I said, meaning it. X'GBris were the strangest combination of cruelty and kindness I had ever seen. But maybe they thought the same of us.

Voxi gave me a searching look and said, "Where is she now?"

I returned his look with a blank one. Then I understood he was talking about her mind. He must have thought I could hear her dreams, too; but I couldn't. "I suppose she's dreaming," I said. "Or maybe just drifting."

"You don't know?"

"No."

"Interesting. The two of you are so close, I should think you would know everything she's thinking."

I almost said, *I don't,* but then it occurred to me that he might think I knew what *he* was thinking, too. I wasn't sure I wanted him to think otherwise. Assuming he didn't. And assuming he didn't know what *I* was thinking, already.

He was regarding me with lively interest in his face. I didn't like being that fascinating.

"Can we leave her alone?" I asked. "She's been through too much."

"She should be in a good mood now," he said. "This particular truth drug makes humans cheerful. There's a strong black market trade for it."

But he turned away from her and led me out of the room. He went slowly, allowing for my injured gait. He had taped my ribs well, but they stabbed me every time I took a step. I thought about asking for some more painkiller; then decided against it.

I assumed we would go to the galley again, but instead he took me to another suite of rooms. These seemed too lavish and personal to be remotely utilitarian.

"My quarters," he explained.

That would have caused me some alarm if my attention hadn't been immediately grabbed by another startling sight. There was a landscape filling the enormous view window: a river and its tributaries, a vast forest, some mountains, all drifting in and out of sight under clouds. We were in orbit around a planet.

He went to stand before the view, his hands clasped behind his back. I could only follow. It was a magnificent sight. The terrain was far more varied than GodWorld's; it was more like Earth, with polar caps, a few deserts, grasslands, forests, and so on. I looked at it while trying to perform calculations in my head. Finally I asked him.

"How long were Edna and I in stasis?"

"You weren't."

"So our trip took forty-eight hours?"

"Closer to fifty-seven Earth standard hours."

Our trip in the egg had taken three weeks, and it had covered only one-quarter of the distance this ship had just traveled. At least, I think that's how far, assuming we were where I thought we were. Right at the heart of their empire.

"Early technology has done a lot for you," I said, looking down at the world slowly turning beneath us. I knew there were cities down there, but they couldn't be seen from orbit. X'GBris were careful that way.

"How do you know we didn't figure things out on our own?" he asked.

"I'm sure you did. You plundered Early ruins and their glyphs just like everyone else did before Ankere found out where the Earlies were still living. Once she brought them back to talk, everyone got an equal share of information. And god knows there was plenty of it to get."

"You underestimate us."

"No, I don't. You got further with the information than we did. OMSK has a healthy respect for you."

I felt a gentle tug on my hair. He was touching it. I shivered, and my ribs gave me another jab.

"I wish you weren't so beautiful," he said.

"Yes, that's awkward." I saw a flash of light streaking over the landscape. Sunlight had briefly betrayed an invisible ship.

"You'll generate a lot of interest," he said.

I looked at him. His face was more inscrutable than a full-blooded X'GBri's would have been, but not much. He was definitely worried.

"You'll have trouble—holding on to us?" I asked.

He frowned. "I've decided not to adopt you into our family."

"You don't like us anymore?" I teased. I thought I knew why he had made that decision. He didn't want his fellow husbands to have sexual access to us.

"You think I'm being selfish," he said, softly. "You're wrong. It's not for my sake. It's for yours. I remember what it was like for my mother."

"Oh." I almost looked away; but he didn't, so I satisfied my curiosity. His face really said everything I needed to know. He did like us. He liked us too much. My ribs jabbed me again, as if to warn me about limitations. Mine and his, both.

"So," I said, "does that mean we're up for grabs?"

"No." He let go of my hair. "It just means I have to be more truthful about what you're doing here. That's dangerous. It's almost as dangerous as releasing you to the GodHeads."

That admission made me a little dizzy. I knew OMSK business was always important, always complicated. But I was used to being a small cog, not a big one.

Apparently it didn't matter whether we were on GodWorld or at X'GBri court, Edna and I were destined to shake things up, to unravel things. We didn't even have to *do* anything; all we had to do was *be*. That didn't make sense. No one was that important.

"Is that your world?" a shaky voice asked behind us. We turned and saw Edna in the doorway. She came closer, limping a little, just like me. I wondered how she had undone her straps. I had hoped she would sleep longer.

"If you mean, was I born here," said Voxi, "the answer is yes. If you mean, is this the world where the X'GBri race originated, the answer is also yes."

"What's it called?" she asked, standing so that I was between her and Voxi.

"They called it Earth, just like your people called your world."

"What's the X'GBri word?"

He gazed down at the world beneath us; a beautiful place, but not a green one. Its forests were blue, purple, grey. Probably there was some green down there, but it was overwhelmed. "O'KHro," he said, as if he were speaking the name of a beautiful woman.

"Are all of the bigwigs down there?"

He gave her a puzzled look.

"All of the head honchos," she said. "The mucky-mucks."

You're using slang from a thousand years ago, I warned Edna. "The leaders of state," I explained out loud.

"Not all of them," he said. "But enough of them are. They'll want to have a look at you."

"What good will it do them to look at us?" She pulled at her hair, self-consciously. "It's what's inside our heads that's caused the problem."

I was wondering that, myself. Why hadn't we been killed, outright? The X'GBris were the ones who had made the synthetic and sold it to OMSK. Obviously Voxi didn't think that had been a good idea.

Or maybe not so obviously. X'GBris only resembled humans, they didn't necessarily think like us. All I knew for sure was that there was nothing we could teach them about the synthetic. So why should they keep us around at all?

"Look at all the water!" Edna said, suddenly. An ocean had come into view. She had never seen one; but her reaction to it seemed a little strange. She was thrilled and upset at the same time. "I'll bet you never run out of it!" she said.

Not a click from Voxi, though I was sure he felt like laughing. "We've run out of it on other worlds," he said. "You'd be surprised how much a space-going civilization can use. But here we've got plenty of water in-system, plenty of asteroids and comets. We wouldn't have to touch a drop of that down there if we didn't want to."

Edna was awed. I tried to feel along our link for the reason, but she didn't know herself. It was part of her wiped past. The reason was gone, but the reaction was still there.

"And we're really on a space ship," she said. "So how come we're not weightless?"

"Because this is an *expensive* space ship," said Voxi.

That was a little mean. OMSK had sent us to God-World in an egg, and eggs didn't have artificial gravity. Edna hadn't even known there was any such thing until now. She was thinking that gravity was only for rich, important people. And that she was a nobody.

That's not really true, I told her. *Lots of people travel without gravity. It isn't really necessary unless you're going to be on a long trip. Your bones would lose mass on a long trip without it.*

This wasn't a long trip, she reminded me.

I know. I told you, two important families are fighting over us. Because we're important! I don't know why, but we are, so let's make the most of it.

"This ship is creating artificial gravity by spinning?" she asked Voxi.

"No," he said. "It's a generated field."

She just looked at him.

"Early technology," I reminded her.

"Yeah, but that's pretty staggering," she said, looking doubtful.

"Keep your eyes open," said Voxi. "You'll do a lot of staggering before this is over."

That sounded just a little too prophetic for my tastes. Edna and I were already limping as it was.

"When can we go down?" Edna asked, her voice small and almost childlike. A phantom passed through my mind then, a little ragged girl stumbling through a desert. I shook her loose, then went running after her again when I realized who she must be. But she was gone, leaving me to wonder if I had imagined her from Edna's accounts of her recurring dream or if she had drifted down the link to me.

"I don't know," Voxi was saying. "They're still arguing about us."

"*Who* is?"

He cocked his head, human-style, and looked at her. "The ones who favor the Net and the ones who hate it. The ones who haven't made up their minds yet and the ones who are waiting to see on which side it will be the most comfortable to rest."

"Do they really think they can stop progress?" she asked, defiantly.

He clicked his teeth. "First they'll define it. Then they'll stop it. Just as *you* were planning to stop it."

Edna touched her own ribs. I felt a sympathetic jab. Standing was beginning to be painful. I settled on one of the couches near the window. She came and sat with me. Voxi stayed where he was, alternating his attention between us and the view. I wondered if there was something he could see that we could not. His gaze did not appear casual.

Edna was looking more and more worried. "Will we need lessons in protocol?" she asked, suddenly. "I don't want to seem rude."

"They won't help," said Voxi.

I know a little about it, I told her through the link. *Don't worry.*

I'll prompt you when you need it, the same way, Voxi added. I thought Edna might be upset to be reminded that he was part of our link, but instead it calmed her.

It was odd, but they were developing an understanding. I was much angrier with Voxi over Edna's interrogation than she was. She had already put it behind her. I hoped she wouldn't fall in love with him, now that KLse was out of the picture.

But no, she didn't seem to be responding to him the way she had to KLse. The warmth and shyness were missing. Instead, she was allowing herself to indulge in her curiosity about him, about his particular situation, about X'GBri culture in general.

This is their homeworld, isn't it! she asked me, excitedly. *I'll bet hardly any humans ever get to come here!*

I'll bet you're right, I agreed, but didn't add why this was probably so.

Have you ever heard any of their music? she asked.

No.

Have you ever seen one of their cities?

Not from the inside, I said, beginning to warm to the idea myself. She was right; there was no point in being miserable one hundred percent of the time. No point in being afraid. In my experience, fear had never proven to be an effective, long-term approach to problems. It was great for fast, autonomic-type spurts of energy, but otherwise useless.

I had worried that half my energy would be expended calming Edna, yet she was the one who had put *me* back on track. Now she was gazing earnestly at the view, trying to imagine what was really down there.

"How many people live down there?" she asked Voxi.

"Four billion or so."

She frowned. She looked at me, and I could see she was trying to grasp what the numbers really meant. *How many people usually live on a planet?* she asked.

I think Earth has about seven billion, I told her. *GodWorld has about two billion. They're both about the same size as this world.*

GodWorld is so crowded!

No, it isn't. TradeTown was a crowded city; and so are the other major cities, but the rest of the planet is pretty sparsely populated.

"It isn't crowded down there?" she asked Voxi.

"No." He seemed surprised by the question. "We don't do well in crowds."

"You didn't used to, anyway," she mused. He looked at her sharply.

But she seemed unaware that she had said something disturbing. she was gazing past him, thinking aloud. "KLse liked crowds. You do, too. The synthetic GodWeed makes you react differently than other X'GBris. You're not having to rely as much on body language to tell you whether or not you're in danger. Or maybe you can just read it better, I don't know. But it makes a difference."

He didn't answer, but he was gazing at her with something like respect. My Edna had scored a hit. "Is that an issue?" I asked. "Leaving aside the GodHeads, would a synthetic Net change your culture as drastically as I think it would?"

"Probably," he conceded.

"So no matter what you or anyone down there does about the GodHeads, things have changed forever. Your culture—"

He cut me off with a chopping motion. "Unless," he snapped, "they round up the infected ones and kill us."

Edna was horrified. "Would they do a thing like that?"

Voxi clicked his teeth. It was a brittle sound.

For a long moment, no one seemed willing to speak. Voxi was staring down at his world again, at the whorls of clouds and the jagged mountain peaks unfolding like a giant relief map beneath him. Edna was looking there, too, but she was thinking about the X'GBri alphabet, about the way the characters looked. It was an odd train of thought, but I could see what had led her to it. X'GBri characters were beautiful, yet they always looked like they were about to leap off the keys and start fighting with each other.

Raptors, she sent me down the link. *So innocent and so awful.*

Innocent? I wondered.

She struggled to find the words. *X'GBris are beautiful,* she said. *They're—you know. Magnificent. Humans are so plain and ordinary. I mean, we're nice guys, but . . .*

But you said innocent, I reminded her.

She didn't answer. She was groping after something, but not necessarily what we had just been talking about.

Are you saying that X'GBris are like raptors? I asked. *Like predatory birds? I can see why you would say that. They have the same unblinking gaze. And when they strike, they're swift and fearless.*

There's a price they pay for being the way they are, said Edna. *Strong and fierce, like the raptors. The ones who don't fit in are left to die. Nothing personal, nothing malicious, but totally ruthless.*

We're not innocent, Voxi broke in, suddenly. *Don't be fooled. We know when we're doing evil, just like you do. We know.*

Edna was startled, but she didn't totally agree with him. I knew what she was getting at. I knew why she admired them. Perfect physical specimens of their race, perfect psychological profiles. She was right, too. KLse had told me that the X'GBris who couldn't control themselves were always destroyed. The ones who still lived were strong, beautiful, smart.

And that's why I still live, said Voxi. *Yes. That much is true. Is it right or wrong, Aten? What would you do with the imperfect ones?*

Define imperfect, I said, and he clicked his teeth again. This time, at least, with genuine humor.

The raptors know, he said. *They don't have to define survival of the fittest. But civilization short-circuits nature.*

Who says nature is so smart anyway? I said. *All nature really wants you to do is reproduce and die.*

"Reproduce and die," he said aloud. "Sounds like a curse. Like *eat shit and die.*"

"I'm not cursing you."

He just looked at me then, with a face so full of longing, and sadness, and bitterness. My eardrums throbbed, and for a moment I thought he was speaking to me in X'GBri subtones, telling me something he wanted me to know but couldn't bear for anyone else to hear.

But then he was crossing the room and keying a com pad. Someone had called him, that was all. He listened for a moment, and my eardrums throbbed some more. He stiffened, then keyed something else into the pad.

Our window became a screen. A woman filled it, her image dwarfing us. Edna and Voxi both gasped.

She wore GodHead robes; Early glyphs danced a red pattern across the black fabric. Her face was serene, her eyes carried the weight of the Net behind them.

"Voxi," she said in X'GBri, "my lovely hybrid. How I've missed you."

"LLna," he choked, but that was all he could say; so she turned her gaze to us.

"Edna and Aten," she said. "You must return home."

I was astonished. In fact, I was almost scared. Edna had only talked with one GodHead; yet here was another to fetch us back again. "To GodWorld, you mean," I said.

"Yes."

I thought she would say something more. When she didn't continue, I said, "We'd like to. But we have been forbidden to do so. It seems your X'GBri sisters still have some things to work out."

"We are working for your release," she said. She looked frail for an X'GBri, almost willowy; yet she was imposing. Her promise carried weight.

"Why?" Edna blurted, suddenly. "Don't you know who sent us to GodWorld? Don't you know they'd like to destroy you?"

"They can't destroy us," LLna said. "You must return. You must eat the GodWeed, Edna. I can't tell you anything more. Come home."

"I can't come home," Edna said, stubbornly.

"I won't let them." Voxi's voice was full of ashes. LLna looked at him then, and suddenly I knew something. Maybe he knew it, too.

The GodHeads were going to get us back, no matter what. They were pulling their punches, they were trying not to upset the matriarchy too much. They didn't want bloodshed. It was all right there, behind LLna's eyes. They wanted to convince, not to conquer.

But they were going to get us back, one way or another.

"Someone here would like to speak with you," she told me. She stepped aside, and someone else stepped into view. This time, *I* was the one who gasped.

It was Bomarigala. Magnificent Bomarigala.

"Aten," he said, "are you all right?"

"Y-yes," I stammered, still unable to believe my eyes. I blushed, thinking of him there with his enemies, knowing how much harm he intended them.

"We'll see you downstairs," he promised/threatened. And then the screen turned back into a window.

I begged Voxi to let me sit on the command deck for the landing.

"Only if Aten is with you," he commanded, like Aten was my mother or something. But I didn't mind having Aten along. I would have been telling her everything over our link anyway.

The other husbands stared at us for as long as they dared while they were at their posts. Voxi ignored their behavior, though I'm sure he would have snapped at them if they had kept their eyes off the business at hand even one second longer than they did. He sat in the command chair. I wondered if that used to be LLna's chair.

Maybe not, said Aten, listening to my thoughts. *He looks like he's used to sitting there. What I wonder is if he's told the other husbands about his decision, yet.*

His decision?

You and I aren't going to be adopted into the family after all.

What's our status, then?

I couldn't tell you. I have a feeling it keeps changing, minute to minute.

That wasn't a very comforting thought. But on the other hand, LLna was going to try to take us back to GodWorld; and for some reason, that *was* a comforting thought. I didn't even mind that we would have to see Bomarigala again, even after what he had done to me on OMSK.

What? asked Aten, still listening in. *What was that about Bomarigala?*

I was only half paying attention to her. I was watching the helmsman rotate the ship. I was looking at the tactical screens, delighted that I could interpret some of the data, even though the characters were X'GBri. I was getting a great big kick out of the whole scene, and I didn't want to think about how embarrassed I had been when . . .

When what? Aten prompted, gently.

We were entering the lower atmosphere. I looked at the front viewscreen and watched the glow on the ship's nose. *Bomarigala visited me in my room once,* I told Aten. *On OMSK. In the middle of the night.*

There was a queer deadness from her end of the link for several moments. I watched as the ground seemed to accelerate beneath us. Our egg had landed on its bottom; I wondered how we were going to do it with this ship. Would there be a runway? I looked at the tacticals, trying to see where we were going. I'm glad I did that, because I saw the city on one of the grids. The helmsman was watching that, not the window, because the city was invisible to the naked eye.

Edna, Aten asked cautiously, *did Bomarigala make love to you?*

Yes, I said, looking at amber lines, and red ones, and green and blue.

Did you consent?

Yes. Well, sort of. I didn't know how. I'm not sure I knew what was going on. I was still just waking up from the wipe—I mean, from stasis. And I was a virgin.

She got mad when I told her that. Not at me, at Bomarigala. She thought he shouldn't have done it to me, that he had taken advantage. But I wasn't mad about it, just embarrassed. It hadn't gone very well, and I didn't think he had had very much fun. I had sort of enjoyed it, once the pain had stopped; but maybe I had just been grateful for the attention. I didn't even know, and I suppose I didn't want to.

The helmsman was braking, but we were still going very fast. I watched the lines and dots, admiring him for knowing where he was going. We weren't going to land on our butts, like we did in the egg. We were going to glide in, touch down like an aircraft and roll along until our brakes stopped us. It was exhilarating.

Voxi activated some other view screens so we could see where we were landing. At first I only saw forest and mountain. But we dropped lower, and suddenly the city shivered into sight. It had been underneath us all along; we had simply dropped beneath some kind of obscuring shield.

If we didn't have clearance to land, we never would have gotten this low, Aten told me. *We would have been destroyed in low orbit.*

"Yow," I said out loud, making the helmsman think I was scared of the flight. But I wasn't, not even as we headed straight between some narrow mountains. I wished I could get someone to teach me how to do what he was doing.

Aten gasped. She wasn't afraid either; she had just gotten her first real glimpse of where we were going. The city was built in and around the mountains, and it was no modest construction. It was monumental, like TradeTown, but that was where the resemblance ended. It was not a haphazard jumble of buildings grown up around business and residential areas like you would find in a human city. It was ordered in a way that probably reflected the X'GBri family unit and X'GBri society, small core groups associated with each other, all deferring ultimately to a larger, societal unit. I suppose that makes it sound like a cold, mathematical arrangement, but it wasn't.

It was a marvelous and imposing work of art. It reminded me of pictures I had seen of what ancient Egypt was supposed to have looked like, though it really wasn't quite like any human city. Its lines were angular and sharp, just like the X'GBris themselves. It spoke to us in a tongue that was foreign yet perfectly understandable. It told us that mere people were not worthy to live there. Gods lived there, or giants.

Aten laughed. "There are your giants!"

Colossi reared up before us, as if to block our way. But they couldn't move: They were stone warriors who were almost as tall as the mountains from which they surely must have been carved. We were going to fly right between them. The helmsman aimed us perfectly; we could see the giant faces on either side as we passed them, one scowling and one grinning. I wondered if their stone weapons would fire at us; but they remained cold and still.

Down we went, onto a runway that seemed far too short. Our brakes fired, and we slowed almost to the speed of a simple land vehicle. In another minute we had come to a full stop.

Voxi snapped orders at his fellow husbands. His voice was controlled, but I could feel his tension as if it were prickling across my own skin, stinging me like static electricity. I almost asked him, *What now?* But I was already learning when to keep my questions to myself. He would tell us what to do when the time came.

You're right, Aten agreed. *Play it cool for now, Edna. Just be the observer. Pretend you're watching an interesting vid or something.*

Except that I can't pause it while I run to the bathroom. She laughed, silently.

Do I look presentable? I asked her, worrying about my hair and my catsuit. We hadn't had much time to clean up, and I was beginning to have doubts that I should be walking around in such a revealing piece of clothing.

You look drop-dead gorgeous, she said, firmly. *And very elegant.*

Really? I asked, amazed. Aten didn't lie to me, and she had impeccable taste.

Really, she sent back. *You couldn't have picked a better outfit for this situation, Edna. You'll knock them off balance. Keep playing it cool, and they'll stay that way.*

Yes, ma'am, I promised. I was glad I had asked her, because now I wasn't even nervous. I should have been; I could feel how alert Voxi had become. He and his fellow husbands had already become a tight unit, reacting to cues both verbal and nonverbal, ready for whatever might come our way. It was quite impressive, quite wonderful to observe, especially knowing that it was for our benefit. I wondered what it must be like to have a group of husbands who did that for you. I found myself envying LLna and WWul.

I knew I shouldn't be enjoying myself. But I couldn't help it. They arranged themselves around us and ushered us down a hall, out a lock, down a ramp, and onto the runway, into sunshine tinged with blue.

A large group of people were waiting for us at the far end, outside a terminal. I would have liked to look around, but I was caught up in the tension of the moment. Our group stood and examined them for several moments, during which no one moved a muscle. I was trying not to touch Voxi through the link. I didn't want to distract him. But I could feel that he was startled by something.

It was the clothing in which the other group was all dressed. Voxi and his guys were wearing grey, but those others were wearing dark red, a red like congealed blood. They outnumbered us; there were twenty men and two women, all staring intently at us. Behind them the terminal was silent, not the busy, bustling place a human terminal would have been.

Finally one man separated himself from the other group. He strode across the tarmac, his eyes on Voxi's, never wavering. He came within five paces of us and stopped. He and Voxi stared some more, but they didn't seem to be struggling with each other. They weren't matching wills, like human males would have. They were watching each other for signs, clues. I had never seen X'GBri faces look so neutral before; but I don't think they were trying to be. They were just so focused that they didn't have time or thought for expression.

The man spoke to Voxi. He used the rumbling undertone. Voxi answered him, and through the link I got the impression he was making some sort of ritual acknowledgment. It was as if the two of them were trying to pilot through unknown territory, relying on rituals to guide them.

Suddenly the man looked at *me,* ignoring Aten. "You are Edna," he said.

"Yes," I confirmed.

"I am SSka."

Human etiquette would demand that I say, *Pleased to meet you* or *Glad to know you,* but those didn't seem like wise things for a female to say to an X'GBri male. So I just said, "Hello, SSka."

"They are waiting to speak with you," he said. "I will convey you to the audience chamber."

"I'm eager to meet with . . . um . . . everyone," I said, and even smiled at the end of it, to cover my uncertainty. He responded with an expression of increased alertness, as if I had said something far more significant than I thought I had. I just kept smiling. It wasn't even hard.

SSka turned his back to us, moving like an automaton. I glanced over at his group, saw the tenseness of their expressions. But Voxi's group relaxed—slightly—at the sight of SSka's back. He was making himself vulnerable to them, demonstrating good faith. He began to walk back to the other group. We followed him.

So far so good, Aten said.

They sure do like to get right down to business, I said. *No drinks, no little snacks, no "How was your trip?"*

We're prisoners, remember?

Not prisoners, Voxi put in. *Not anymore.*

Then what are we? Aten asked him.

That's what we're going to find out.

No wonder he was so tense. This place wasn't God-World, those people waiting for us weren't X'GBris adapting themselves to an alien city, trying to do like the Romans do while in Rome. They had their own Rome, and their social interaction was volatile, prone to sudden explosions. Yet they preferred order, and we were challenging that order with our ambiguous status.

Once we were closer to the other group, I could see that some of those faces looked happy to see us. Or perhaps happy wasn't the word. *Intrigued* might be more accurate. X'GBris might prefer order, but that didn't mean they didn't enjoy having a little chaos to spice things up. Some of them, anyway. Others were scowling.

Which are your foes and which are your friends, Edna? Voxi asked me suddenly.

I looked at the faces. Those weren't human smiles and frowns they were wearing. *I don't know,* I said.

Exactly.

Do you know? I challenged.

No, he admitted. But the admission didn't make me feel triumphant.

Their group surrounded ours. I didn't think I was imagining the aggressiveness of this action; yet Voxi and the others seemed to expect it. We all turned to face the terminal and began to walk toward the huge doors, which stood open for us. Aten and I followed those who were just ahead of us, Voxi and one of his fellow husbands. The group moved slowly enough to allow for our shorter legs, an act of consideration that left me absolutely breathless.

As we entered the terminal I saw the guards who were waiting inside. I knew that they were guards because of their military bearing, the professionalism of their gazes, and of course their uniforms. Their uniforms were both grey *and* black. My poor brain couldn't sort out what that might possibly mean. I couldn't see any weapons on them, yet I was sure they were carrying some.

They surrounded our larger group, and we all began to move en masse through those massive, echoing rooms. The size of the place seemed appropriate for situations like ours; the building was otherwise mostly empty. I saw some technicians standing at attention here and there. They returned my stare with lively interest, but made no sudden gestures.

As interesting as the people were, it was the terminal that fascinated me the most. I could tell that parts of it were far older than others. The technology was new, the furnishings varied from new to antique, and the structure itself seemed very old.

How old? I couldn't resist asking Voxi.

It is constantly updated and refurbished, he told me.

I'm sure it is. But how old is the building?

Some parts of it are probably ten thousand years old, he said. *As old as the brothers who guard the Gate.*

The colossi, Aten said, with awe.

And now it's an airport? I asked, trying to make the pieces of the puzzle fit.

It is not *an airport,* he said. *It is the Gate.*

I had an idea what he might mean, but I supposed I would have to know a lot more about X'GBri culture to know what the Gate really meant to *them.* If I thought of it in human terms, I could picture the gate at some-one's front walk, that place that you either let people through or you didn't. Maybe if you entered this Gate you couldn't always leave again.

Maybe not alive, agreed Aten.

The art painted on or carved into some of the walls didn't tell me too much about the building either, though in a way it was very revealing. As we passed through a succession of halls, I saw scenes that piqued my curiosity. Young men dancing or playing instruments, hunting, engaging in games and sports, even embracing female lovers. Some of these scenes were brightly colored, others were painted in subdued tones. I regretted that I lacked the background to decipher the emotional content of those colors.

Some scenes were so old they were little more than shadows on the walls. I could see a progression in complexity from the old to the new, a greater understanding of perspective and anatomy; yet somehow the overall style remained the same. The figures reminded me of the X'GBri alphabet; they contained the same sort of power and movement. The same sort of beauty.

You're right! Aten said. *I hadn't noticed that, at first.*

I was glad I was being of some use. I was feeling a lot more confident than I had on GodWorld, when I had first met KLse and the others. But how I wished KLse were here now, so I could talk to him, ask him questions, be with him. Seeing the lovers on the walls . . .

In other scenes, people were being killed. Some were dying in fights, some were being executed.

"Hhmmm," Aten mused. One of the guards glanced at her, looked away again when she did nothing that warranted his continued attention. His alertness, the tension of the people around us, the scenes of death on the wall were all combining to make me feel the gravity of the situation.

Maybe the scenes depict what the city has to offer, Aten said. *Or rather, what might befall you here. They might be saying, "This is what we do, this is what we are, this is what you will find here, and here is what will happen if you break the rules."*

I waited for Voxi to confirm or deny that, but he did

neither. He didn't seem to be interested in art discussions.

I think it's a good theory, I told Aten.

We were coming to some wide, open doors. I could feel everyone getting stiffer by the moment. What was out there? All I could see was bluish sunshine. Yet it was an act of courage for the X'GBris to keep moving forward. They didn't waver, but I needed to know something before I could step into that light.

Voxi, I demanded, *what does the red clothing mean?*

He didn't answer. But I wouldn't let it go. *What does it mean?* I insisted.

Challenge, he sent back. *Accusation. Sacrifice.*

Their sacrifice or ours? I wondered. Maybe both. We all passed through that doorway and out into the open air. A warm breeze lifted our hair, brought the scent of exotic flowers to us. My heart wanted to respond to these things; I looked for the blooms, and that's when I saw the people watching us.

We were crossing a huge, square paved area, almost a courtyard except that it was far too large to be anything so simple. We were walking on a lovely mosaic of floral and leaf patterns, subtly colored, perhaps for neutrality, toward another building. An open doorway was waiting for us on the far side. But to our right and left were a series of columns, and between those columns people were standing and studying us. At first I didn't understand why that bothered Voxi so much, until I realized how many watchers there were. There must have been a couple hundred.

And each of them had motives, hatreds, hopes, doubts, schemes, questions. Their eyes bored into Aten and me. Our guards wanted to close ranks around us. I could sense that; yet they held themselves apart so people could see us. Was that the purpose of the place? Come look at the petitioners, come look at the strangers? I could practically smell the aggression in the air, yet everyone controlled himself or herself perfectly. It must have taken every ounce of discipline the X'GBris had to ignore their natural paranoia.

The ones who can't control themselves are destroyed, Aten reminded me. Now I really was beginning to understand what that meant, and even why it was necessary.

What's the rule on the other side? I wondered, not daring to ask the question aloud.

The guards are watching, Voxi sent, though it taxed him to do so. *Once on the other side, you will be protected.*

I believed him. But I didn't dare to look into any of those eyes that watched me so avidly. I would have lost all of my new courage and confidence. I had to hold on to what I had, keep it around me like a cloak.

I'm here, Aten said. She was nervous, too, but exhilarated as well. She held her head high. I tried to do the same.

After an endless struggle, we finally climbed the stairs to the other doorway. There was no actual door to open and close for us; but I saw the others illuminated by a red glow as they passed through. When it was my turn, I felt the tingling on my skin, as if I were passing through an electric current. It almost stung. I assumed that if I had been deemed an enemy, I would have been burned or even disintegrated by it.

As Voxi had promised, the guards closed ranks around us once we had entered the grand hall. I breathed a sigh of relief. I felt Aten doing the same, but her attention had already been diverted by the luxury of this new building. I say new, though it was just as old as the other, just as sacred and marvelous.

Do you know what is sacred to us? Voxi asked, pointedly; but he didn't seem to expect an answer and I didn't try to give him one. I didn't want to say that some day I *would* know. Aten believed that, but to me it seemed presumptuous.

Presume a little, she told me. *That's how great deeds are done.*

The place was getting to her. Its decorations looked beautiful without being overblown, expensive without being lavish, utterly tasteful, yet exotic and alien. Mysterious, dangerous, wonderful.

I'm glad you like it, Voxi said dryly, though I could tell our reactions pleased him. He was proud of this place, as much as he dreaded it.

Our group moved solemnly and steadily down the long hall and into an vast audience chamber. Thirteen seats were arranged in a semicircle at the far end of the room. Elegant women sat in eleven of these chairs. Even when we were close enough to see them well, I couldn't tell how old they were; but I knew they couldn't be too young. The intimate knowledge and use of power had molded their faces. All of them were dressed in red, though the husbands who stood behind them wore the traditional grey. The two women in our group left us and sat in the empty chairs. Their husbands also left us, moving around the chairs to stand behind their wives. The guards arranged themselves at regular points around the perimeter of the room, leaving us to stand in its middle.

But not quite alone. Bomarigala and LLna were standing to one side of the matriarchs, waiting for us. I was surprised that LLna was taller than Bomarigala; compared to her fellow X'GBris she was short. As soon as everyone else stopped moving, as soon as our little group stood lonely and accused in the center of that room, LLna came forward. She walked directly up to me, past her husbands who suffered in silence at the sight of her. She didn't ignore them. She was painfully aware of them. Yet it was me who had the greatest measure of her attention.

She looked into my eyes and I felt a mental tug. It was LLna; I could almost feel her taking hold of the threads of our synthetic link with invisible fingers. Then it was as if she were casting the Net around me, yet somehow I still wasn't a part of it. It touched me through LLna, but I couldn't touch it back.

She took my hands. She wasn't wearing gloves.

I heard the shocked silence in the room. I knew how badly shaken the matriarchs were to have an X'GBri GodHead in their audience room, to see her black robes with their burden of Early information written all over them, the reminder of the source of their recent leaps in technology. I knew it because LLna knew it. Her hands burned mine, her GodWeed-tainted sweat and oils penetrating my skin. Her eyes were like the storms of GodWorld.

It's not your fault, she told me, tapping into our link as if it were already part of the Net. *Remember that, through all your lonely wanderings. You have been caught up in the storm, and someday you will come home. We want you there, Edna. And that's why the matriarchs have brought you here.*

And then she let go of my hands. My palms still burned; I wondered if she had really infected me with GodWeed through her own excretions. No one on OMSK had warned me that that could happen, but maybe they didn't know it was possible. I felt weird. My head buzzed and I was very thirsty, as if I had just walked through a desert.

Through all your lonely wanderings . . .

LLna backed away several paces, but didn't return to where Bomarigala was standing. She seemed to be indicating that she was my advocate. She must have thought I was very important. I was almost beginning to think that myself.

The matriarchs glared at me. "Who are you?" one of them demanded.

I was sure she wanted more than my name. Voxi had wanted more when he had questioned me so closely on his ship. But there wasn't much more than my name to give. "Edna," I told them. "Just Edna. I wasn't anyone before that."

I glanced at Bomarigala. He looked calm and confident, like he was exactly where he belonged. He wore X'GBri-style clothing, quite deliberately black, but with blue gloves and boots. I wondered how the blue affected the black. Keeping my eyes on his, I said, "I was supposed to be an agent for OMSK. I was supposed to infiltrate the Net. But the Net has infiltrated me, instead."

What the heck do we have to do with all of this? Aten was wondering. *They could have had this argument without us.*

Maybe they want to find out why the GodHeads want me so badly, I guessed.

I hope they're not just trying to take revenge on the GodHeads through you, Aten said.

"Edna must come home with me," LLna said.

"We'll consider it," said the eldest matriarch.

"I understand," LLna said, graciously. "But she will come home with me."

"Or what?" asked one of the matriarchs who had escorted us from the runway. "Or GodWorld will attack us?"

"We do not *have* to attack you," said LLna. "I am extending you a courtesy by allowing you to keep her as long as you have. I know you need to talk things over with each other. I know you must listen to the arguments of the petitioners in the Court of Enemies. When your honor is satisfied, and you may release her without losing face, I will take her home."

Our escort deepened her scowl. "And what if our honor can only be satisfied by executing her?"

"That would not be honorable," said LLna, "that would only be spiteful. And useless. It will not be permitted."

Just how would she stop them? Aten wondered. *They could gun us down right here.*

No, Voxi put in, emphatically. *Not here. That would be an unforgivable breach of conduct.*

I didn't tell either of them that I had a feeling it didn't matter what anyone might try to do to us. The God-Heads were looking after us now. The GodHeads had abilities they hadn't bothered to mention to anyone. Perhaps they didn't like to brag. Or they didn't want to humiliate the matriarchs by showing them how futile it had been to kidnap me, how easy it would be to take me back. Or perhaps they didn't like to tell people things that sounded impossible. I wished they would tell *me* some of those impossible things. I was in the mood to believe them.

"Voxi," said the eldest matriarch. "You have discharged your duty to us by bringing Edna here. You are released from further obligation. What, then, is your opinion of the matter?"

"I have been infected with the synthetic," he said. "My opinion is colored by self-interest."

"Of course," she said, courteously.

"I agree with LLna that we must join the Net. But that does not mean that we must become GodHeads.

The synthetic might allow us to access the Net without mechanical augmentation."

Ah hah! Aten's voice was like a great ringing bell in my mind. *Of course! What an idiot I've been!*

"Further experimentation should be conducted to determine whether the synthetic will allow us the sort of access that I suspect it would," Voxi was saying. "I offer myself. I will return to GodWorld with LLna and Edna."

"Several females have inquired after your marital status," the matriarch said, stiffly.

There was a terrible silence in the room. Aten was holding her breath, but she wasn't waiting for Voxi to answer. She was waiting for LLna. LLna was the one who was supposed to speak up and say that Voxi was married to *her,* that he belonged to *her.* LLna looked at him, but he refused to meet her storm-haunted eyes.

"It is for Voxi to say whether he is free or not," LLna said. Her answer caused a wave of shock and disapproval to pass through the room. She was not acting like an X'GBri wife by refusing to claim Voxi, to fight for him ritually, if not in fact.

"I am still married," Voxi said. It cost him dearly to get the words out.

"Will you permit him to study the Net in the fashion that he has proposed?" the eldest matriarch asked LLna.

"Yes," replied the GodHead.

"The rest of you," the matriarch addressed LLna's junior husbands. "Are you still married as well?"

"Yes," replied each of them, in order of their status. A couple of them hesitated before answering, but with LLna in the room, they couldn't bring themselves to divorce her.

The matriarchs regarded LLna with new respect. They disapproved of her break with tradition, with her un-X'GBri behavior; yet they couldn't help admiring her power over her husbands. They had not expected such a response.

"There is one other who wishes to speak at this hearing," said the eldest matriarch, nodding to the guards at the back of the room. They opened the door. Another group was waiting in the hallway, an X'GBri woman and her husbands. They entered the room in order of their rank.

WWul, JKre, and STra came first. KLse was in the middle of the group. I almost cried out when I saw him, but I felt Aten's hand on my arm.

KLse! I called.

He didn't answer me in words, but touched me through the link with reassurance. And with joy, too; he was as relieved to see me as I was to see him. It was all he could do to keep his composure.

I felt Voxi behind me like a storm, holding himself in check. At the sight of him, KLse bit back hot rage. Our link pulled taut from both sides. It was as if Aten and I were standing between the two stone colossi, the Brothers suddenly come to life, ready to crush each other and consequently all who stood between them.

But they did *not* crush us. They held on to their tempers.

Edna, Aten warned. *Tear your eyes away from KLse for one second and look at WWul.*

I didn't want to. It felt so good to look at him, to feast my eyes on the man I had been told I would never see again. But I forced myself to look at WWul, instead. What I saw in her face made me blush with embarrassment.

Her face was a mask of bitterness and sorrow. She couldn't bring herself to do more than glance at Aten and me, her eyes widening as if in horror at the sight of us.

KLse, I called, wanting to ask him what was wrong, but Aten clamped down on me like a vise.

Can't you see it? she sent on a tight beam. *She's about to lose him. Their marriage is in trouble. We're the ones that did it, Edna: you, me, and the Net.*

I supposed I should have felt triumph, but I felt ashamed, instead. I had never meant to come between KLse and his wife. I hadn't meant to make them so sad. When I looked at KLse again, I could see the anguish in his face, too. I had thought it was there because he was worried about us; but that had only been half the reason. I looked at WWul again, and waited for her to denounce us.

But she didn't.

"We have been concerned for the safety of Edna and Aten," she said, her voice low and careful. "We were not informed of your intentions until we called to tell you that they had been kidnapped. We protest this treatment, both of them and of ourselves."

"Your protest is noted," said the eldest matriarch.

"We request an explanation," said WWul. "We acted as your agents in good faith. It was not necessary to send others to interfere with us."

Her statement was met with silence. I tried to read the various faces in the room; but even the human ones baffled me. Failing at that, I tried to reach out through the link, hoping that KLse or Aten would inform me. But it was Voxi who was waiting for me.

It is only a token protest, he said. *What was done was standard procedure. And you and KLse proved its necessity, little Edna. Your ambitions didn't match the ambitions of the Court, did they? Or the ambitions of OMSK. Understand?*

He wasn't goading me. He even seemed sympathetic. But why shouldn't he? Things were going his way. He might be back with his beloved LLna soon. And I . . .

Where would I be?

With KLse and Aten? asked Voxi. *In your own group marriage. Is that your heart's desire?*

It was. God help me, it was. My face burned at the nakedness and the intensity of that desire. Still Voxi didn't laugh. He understood me perfectly.

You must have some X'GBri blood in your veins, he said, approvingly.

"Do you wish to withdraw your family from this matter?" the eldest matriarch asked WWul at last.

"I wish for things to proceed as planned," said WWul. "Edna will enter the link. The agent, Aten, will be her liaison with us. With KLse." The way she said his name betrayed how precious he was to her. It didn't matter that she had other husbands. She loved them all, wanted them all. "Our intentions are the same as they have always been, our goal is the same. We hope that you have not allowed . . . complications . . . to change your minds."

The eldest matriarch seemed almost amused. But others looked dismayed. WWul had shamed them, somehow.

"Your plans need not be mutually exclusive," said the eldest matriarch. "We will discuss them. Until we reach a decision, the humans will be confined to their quarters." She gave me a warning look that made my mouth go dry. "No communication of *any* sort will be tolerated," she said.

The guards came forward. Voxi and his fellow husbands were obliged to stand aside and let them claim Aten and me. They moved grudgingly. Voxi had wanted to keep us with him, maybe permanently. KLse and JKre didn't want to let us go, either. But none of them had any choice, and neither did we. I was surprised by how torn that made me feel.

We're together, Aten said. *You and I. We're going to stay that way.*

But Aten wasn't the only one I felt in the link as we were marched from the room. Voxi was there, his presence both a comfort and a threat. KLse was there, wishing he could speak to us. LLna was there, and probably would be forever, now that she had touched me with her naked hands. But someone else was there, too, watching, waiting.

Now that he was close, I realized that he had always been there, but he had always been silent. He wasn't silent anymore. He must have had miraculous patience to be so still all this time. It was the patience of a predator, or an assassin. He was looking at me as I passed him on the way out the door. I raised my eyes and looked back.

Bomarigala nodded and gave me the shadow of a smile.

Later, he sent.

I nodded back, and lowered my eyes again.

Do you think he can hear us now? Edna asked me as we were escorted out of the building. I felt along the link for the shadow that had been waiting there all along. He hadn't moved. He let me touch him, showing me how patient he could be.

"Looks like we can't avoid him," I said aloud. Somehow I was less disturbed by letting the guards hear us than by letting Bomarigala.

"He probably can still hear us," said Edna, wearily.

"Not as well," I guessed.

We were rushed out another gate (one that was much less grand and metaphorical), and into a waiting vehicle, which was large and plain with opaque windows. I wondered if we were really at such risk for assassination or if this was a standard design for X'GBri circles.

At least it was luxurious on the inside. Edna and I sat in the back with two large guards on either side of us. These fellows were almost expressionless, for X'GBris. I wondered if they were married. There was something solitary about each of them, though they worked as a unit.

"Excuse me," I said to the fellow sitting next to me, in his own language. "Are you allowed to speak with us?"

"It is permitted," he said, not unpleasantly, though he continued to scan everything outside the window.

"I hope you won't consider this a rude question," I began, "but are you married?"

"You wish to know if I'm available?" he asked politely.

I should have known he would construe the question

that way. But I plowed on, anyway. "I'm curious about your society. All of the X'GBri males I've encountered so far have worked in marital groups."

"While I serve in the military I am not permitted to marry," he said. "Even casual liaisons are discouraged. My duties may not be compromised by conflicting interests."

"How long must you serve?" I asked, trying not to study him too obviously.

"At least six years," he said. "Some like the military so well that they serve for life. These never marry. But most of us leave the service for marriage after the first six years."

"Oh," I said, and wondered if I dared to ask one of the other nosy questions that were buzzing inside my head.

"I have only one year left to serve," he said, with as much subtlety as an X'GBri could possibly muster. I rewarded him with a smile, but decided not to distract him any further.

I wish I could speak X'GBri, too, said Edna, startling me. Didn't she know?

Edna, don't you remember?

She was drawing a blank.

The hearing we just attended was not conducted in Standard. Everyone was speaking the main X'GBri dialect. Edna, you were, too.

I wasn't!

You were. I'm positive. You can't understand what I just said to this guard?

How could I? I never had that drip. I just had the pilot drip. . . .

No, you must have had more than that. Though come to think of it, I wasn't exactly sure what she had had. I remember seeing one training session, and then I was rushed off to be infected by the synthetic GodWeed. By the time I saw Edna again, she had been programmed with most of her present personality.

"I heard you speaking X'GBri," I said.

"Really?" She seemed pleased by the idea. I wasn't pleased at all. If she had the skill, she should know it. This was odd. I tried not to pass my anxiety on to Edna.

We rode through elegant streets. The few pedestrians we passed did not stare at the car. I supposed there was no point; anonymous vehicles like this one must have been quite common, if not the norm. Edna was looking out her window with fascination, crowding the guard on her side. He stoically ignored her.

I checked for Bomarigala again. Still there. This time he touched me back. He didn't say anything, but I knew he was following us in his own car. He intended to see me once we were in our respective quarters. His would be next to ours; apparently the matriarchs considered us to be associates. Funny, I wasn't sure that we were, anymore. On the other hand, I wasn't sure that we were *not*. I wondered if Bomarigala knew I was having doubts, or if he cared.

After perhaps half an hour, we drove into an underground parking lot, much like the one under the X'GBri hotel on GodWorld. We parked next to the elevators. Edna felt a pang of homesickness. She was thinking about KLse again.

"Maybe we'll see him on GodWorld," I said. She was on the verge of tears, and I wanted to distract her.

"Maybe he won't be allowed to go back there," she said, uncomforted.

"Wait and see." I took the guard's offered hand. He pulled me out of the backseat a little too energetically, but was otherwise businesslike as he surveyed the underground lot with his fellow officers. After a moment, he received the nod and escorted us to the elevators.

We rode up in silence. Edna was calming down. She was thinking about a nice, cozy bed, something to eat and drink. I encouraged those thoughts.

"I can't believe how fast it all happened," she said.

"You mean the hearing?" I said. "Probably most of it will take place without us. They just wanted to get a good look at us."

"I pictured days of being questioned," she said. "I thought they would question me as thoroughly as Voxi had."

"Maybe Voxi was supposed to do it for them." I was thinking of how he had behaved with the matriarchs, as if he had been their special agent. But apparently WWul had thought that *she* was their agent. Our part of it seemed like it had ended quickly, but I doubted that it was that simple.

When the elevator doors opened, I was struck with a feeling of déjà vu at the sight of the hall with its antiques, its high ceilings and massive doors. It was very much like the hotel; but the antiques looked older and the style must have been from an earlier age. Only the soft carpet was new; it muffled our footsteps as we walked to our quarters.

The man who had one year left to serve unlocked our door. He gave me an odd look as he stepped aside so we could enter. Alarms went off in my head, but I didn't know what else I could do but open the door. Light spilled out of the room, flashing and fracturing in my eyes, and I jumped back.

"It is safe inside," the guard said. "No one will harm you there. It is only—the glass reflecting light."

I tried to make my eyes focus on the interior of the room. I couldn't tell what was in there. I saw part of Edna's face in a far corner as she slipped past me and into the light. I followed, and was even more lost.

The entire room was lined with mirrors, ceiling to floor. The panels were not regular, but were cut in angular, jagged shapes, hung so that you could not tell which were straight on and which were turned at other angles. The ceiling was also mirrored, but the fragments were so small they reflected only tiny bits of light and color. The floor was highly polished marble.

"Beautiful," I said, hating it. My palms began to burn, just as Edna's had burned at LLna's touch; and her headache was becoming mine as well. I felt a sharp stab of fear and exhilaration at the thought of such contamination.

"The hall is well guarded," said the voice behind me. "You may visit the other human guest, but you may not take the elevator down to the street."

I turned to find him, but he had shut the door. I was confronted with another splintered reflection. I saw Edna's face and hands fluttering around in dismay, but could not find my own.

"Don't panic," I told her. "There must be a door to

the bedrooms around here somewhere. Use your hands, close your eyes if you have to."

Edna was stumbling around the room, mumbling. I couldn't understand what she was saying or thinking. I touched the front door, found that the guard had left it slightly ajar. I opened it all the way, and suddenly Bomarigala was standing there. He looked momentarily surprised, and then his eyes looked past me into the mirror maze.

"What in blazes?" he said, frowning.

"Our interior decorator was insane," I offered.

He looked at me again, his brown furrowed. "I want to talk with you," he said. "We'd better do it in my room."

He turned, assuming I would follow. I was relieved to do so, to leave the mirror maze behind. "I'll be right back, Edna," I said. She didn't answer.

"This way!" Bomarigala was calling.

I left the door open, in case Edna wanted to come out for a break. Bomarigala was at the other end of the hall, opening another door. I hurried to join him. He looked at me as I walked, openly admiring me. I wished he wouldn't just then. It made the guards think that something was going on between us. They were politely looking elsewhere, watching us from the corners of their eyes.

Bomarigala ushered me into his room and closed the door.

"I like your decorator better," I said, admiring the dark woods and subtle colors of his sitting room. "I hope they don't think they're impressing us with that monstrosity in our quarters."

"Perhaps that was not their intention at all," said Bomarigala. He was still standing, and he didn't offer me a chair either.

"What do you mean?" I asked.

He came closer, as if he were about to tell me a secret. "You have enemies here," he said. "And on OMSK."

"No kidding."

He laughed. "I'm not your enemy," he said.

"No. But with friends like you . . ."

He raised a satanic brow. "Don't you know why I

came here, Aten? I thought they were going to execute you. I threatened them on your behalf. I risked everything I have to get you back."

"To get *me* back," I snapped. "You mean to get your precious synthetic ringer, your key to the Net. I know what you intended now. We weren't meant to spy for you, you just wanted in! But the GodHeads didn't want *you,* so you found someone you thought they might accept. Edna! And they *do* accept her, Bomarigala, beyond your wildest dreams, and all the while you've been waiting and watching at your end of our link until the moment when you could ride in with her! When you could force your way in."

"Yes." He slipped off his gloves and casually tossed them onto a couch. "But it turns out the GodHeads don't mind. They think that linking the Net with a synthetic net is a good idea. We don't even need Edna anymore. Anyone who wants to can use the synthetic to interface with the Net now. And OMSK holds the patent for the human sectors."

He had shifted gears so easily, so admirably; and now he stood before me with the military bearing of one of those guards, with enough confidence and experience to impress a matriarch. I wondered if anyone there had inquired after his marital status. He seemed too perfect to be real. But he *was* real, and I knew what he was doing.

"You don't need Edna," I said, disgusted. "So you've decided not to pay her."

"I doubt she'll want pay, where she's going."

I wasn't surprised. If OMSK had words of intent carved over its proverbial front door they would read: RUTHLESSNESS, EXPEDIENCY, SAVAGERY. But I wasn't prepared to let them cheat her that easily.

"You *will* pay her what you owe her," I said. "Whether she wants it or not."

He was unruffled. "You'll be paid, Aten, you needn't worry about that."

I tried to move away from him, but he blocked me. "I was just going to sit down," I said.

He grabbed my wrist and lifted one of my burning palms. He kissed it. My heart started to pound. Any

question I had harbored as to whether Bomarigala had
been my secret lover on OMSK was now answered.

"Let the GodHeads take Edna," he said. "They can't
have *you*, Aten. You're mine."

The specter of Peterhamil rose in the back of my
mind. He seemed to be saying, *I told you so!* Bomarigala
was talking about more than romance when he said that
I was his.

"*You* made me," I said. "You're the one who designed my personality."

His eyes admired me. He looked pleased. "No one
has ever figured that out about themselves before, Aten;
no one in my long memory of miracles and monstrosities
on OMSK. But you're special. You are the sum of every
woman I've ever wanted. You even have a little of me
in you. I suppose I should be proud."

I tried to slap his beautiful face. I hadn't even framed
the thought before I was doing it, yet his hand was there
to stop mine.

"The link," he reminded me. "It's such a useful
thing."

"I'll block you out," I warned. But his eyes were
laughing at me.

"You've been programmed not to," he said. "You can
block the others out, though. Voxi hasn't had free access
for some time. He might be able to force his way in, but
he'd have a fight on his hands."

Tears were welling in my eyes. I felt almost like Edna,
not the cool, experienced agent I was supposed to be.
Was *supposed* to be; but all of that must have been false.
All of that must have been a story that he had written
for me. He towered over me like an X'GBri, dressed in
black secrets and blue threats. "Why did you do it?" I
choked. "Why did you have to make me?"

An expression of wonder crossed his face. Then pleasure. "Because you're so beautiful," he said. "I wanted
your mind to match your body."

He pulled me close and kissed me. His kiss had such
heat in it, I knew he couldn't be lying about what he
had done, why he had done it. When he was done kissing
my mouth, he kissed my face, my throat, pulling my
body tight against his.

"I made you a real person. I didn't make you love me," he whispered. "I could have done that. But I prefer the chase, Aten. I'll chase you the rest of your life if I have to."

I couldn't believe it. Bomarigala, scion of OMSK, ruthless mover and shaker, investing so much energy into such a romantic notion. Into *me*.

He opened his side of the link and let me in. He made himself as vulnerable as I was; he let me feel his need. His body loved the feel of mine; his hands couldn't decide where to rest. *Remember how it was on OMSK?* he said. *Edna didn't know how to make love. But you did, Aten. You knew very well.*

I admit I was awed by him. I had always been. He had fought his way to the top of the OMSK hierarchy, just as Voxi had fought. He was ruthless, but he had courage.

And he had made *me*.

He was peeling off my lounging clothes. I gasped, feeling my own skin through his hands. This was better than what had happened on that dark night, two years ago. It was even better than Edna and KLse had been. I fumbled at his clothes; he had to show me their X'GBri secrets. When I touched his skin, I felt how my hands felt to him. I looked into the face I had feared and saw it transformed by passion. I couldn't fathom it, I felt dizzy. I didn't know *anything*—not anything.

"You aren't the only one who was made," he said. "All of us on OMSK have been programmed at some time. *Many* times, Aten. Even me."

"And you've had your face changed," I said. "And your body. You couldn't be this beautiful by nature."

"I *am* this way by nature," he said, enormously pleased. "This is my real face, my real body. And this is yours." He pulled my suit down, exposing my breasts. His large hands covered them easily. We were both panting by then, excited by the feedback. The thought of what would happen soon and how it would feel from both sides occurred to us at the same moment. He picked me up and carried me into the bedroom.

I'm sorry, Edna, I called silently, begging her not to think I was a traitor.

*   *   *

It took us a long time to get the rest of our clothes off. What followed took even longer. It was night by the time we had finished. I lay in his arms and wished I could stay there until morning.

Of course, you can stay, he said, trying not to order me.

Edna, I reminded him.

"She will keep for one night," he said aloud.

But I couldn't hear her anymore. I called and called, and it was as if she were deeply unconscious. I couldn't imagine that anything had happened to her while I was gone; I would have felt it. But something sad and scary was beginning to boil in my stomach. I had to see for myself that she was safe.

"She's probably going crazy in that monstrous suite," I said, making myself sit up and pull away from his perfect body. He watched me, silently. I got dressed, trying not to hurry as the fear began to build.

"Aten," he asked gently, "do you ever wonder who you were before you were yourself?"

I didn't want to even think about that. "Tell me later," I said firmly. "Let's get this garbage over with first. I want things resolved, and then you can tell me anything you want. The truth, the whole truth, and nothing but the truth."

"Do you think you could stand the whole truth?" he asked. "Perhaps I should just tell you a little."

"Later," I said, and almost ran out of the room. But at the last moment I couldn't help looking at him. He was propped up on an elbow, naked except for the sheet across his legs. He took my breath away.

"I've killed to get where I am today," he told me. "But I would quit for you, Aten. I would leave OMSK."

"Really?" I asked, touching him through the link. He opened to me.

Yes, he said. And it was true. I could only shake my head in wonder.

And then I heard Edna. Faintly, as if she were very weak.

"I have to go!" I said, and ran away.

*   *   *

When I opened the door to our suite, the room was dark and silent. The darkness was a relief, but the silence was ominous. I locked the door behind me, mindful of Bomarigala's warning about enemies. The guards had seemed honorable, but I had no idea what defined the parameters of their honor.

"Edna?" I called.

I heard a sudden, strange sound, like a bird fluttering around the room, striking the surfaces of the mirrors.

"Edna, turn on the lights."

She sobbed something incoherent. The sound made my heart pound with alarm.

"Please, baby," I pleaded, as if she were a child, "turn on the light. Let's talk. You'll feel better after we've talked."

"Aten," she said, right next to my ear, "the mirrors!"

"Did you find the bedroom door?"

"No!"

I could have kicked myself. Poor Edna had been wandering inside that dreadful maze of mirrors for hours. Her headache was worse than before. I could feel it pounding at my own temples. She must have finally turned the lights off in desperation.

"Come on," I said. "I'll help you look."

And so the two of us felt mirrored walls, looking for anything that might resemble a door. Since Edna had been looking for hours, I assumed they must be very well hidden. I had even formulated a backup plan in which the two of us would ask Bomarigala to share his quarters with us. It would have been awkward, but . . .

And suddenly I found the bedroom door. "Edna," I cried triumphantly, "here!"

"Really, Aten?" She sighed like a lost soul.

"Come on," I said. "We'll get you a bath and maybe some supper. Then into a nice, soft bed, okay?"

She didn't answer, but I felt her take my hand. I led her through the door and fumbled for the lights. I found the button right next to the door.

Light dazzled my eyes, splintering and reflecting into infinity.

"Aten!" she screamed. "Aten!"

This room was mirrored, too. I saw Edna's reflection

a thousand times over, but couldn't find my own, couldn't even find myself.

"You're in the mirror!" she was screaming "You're in the mirror, not me! I can't find me!"

I saw her image flying to a thousand points and smashing. I felt searing pain in my hands, heard the smashing of the glass and Edna screaming, screaming, flying to the next mirror and smashing it, too, sobbing, "It's you Aten, not me, not me, I'm not here!" And the glass was everywhere, cutting me, reflecting fractured images of Edna outlined with my blood.

Bomarigala! I screamed down the link. *KLse! Voxi!* But I had locked the door. I needed to unlock it so they could get in and help, but Edna was flying everywhere, smashing the mirrors with my hands, screaming and crying and looking for herself, and I couldn't find me either.

I couldn't find me. And then Edna had smashed the last mirror, and we were both gone.

I couldn't move without cutting myself. I was already so cut, I couldn't imagine that there was any place left to bleed. I made myself pick up one of the big shards even though it sliced deeper into my ruined hands. I looked into the shard, and Aten's face looked back. I couldn't find mine at all. I had her face, her body, and she wasn't anywhere at all.

They had to break down the door. Glass went flying everywhere. It was a stupid design, all that glass. They found me in the broken bedroom. Bomarigala cut himself when he picked me up. He tried to hold all of the bleeding places. His face was pale and hard. He called me Aten. That's when I knew it was true. I was Aten. Aten was me. But we couldn't be anyone, because we were both made-up anyway.

"She's gone," I told him.

"She can't be," he insisted. "She's supposed to respond every time her name is called."

Aten, we called together. *Aten! Aten!* But there were only bits and pieces of me, nothing large enough to make a whole picture.

Voxi came. He tried to help Bomarigala bind my wounds. KLse wanted to come, but they wouldn't let him. He had to be restrained, I could feel him struggling at the other end of the link. He tried to talk to me, but his words didn't make any sense.

Paramedics came. They had to pry me away from Bomarigala and Voxi. Everyone ended up getting cut by all that broken glass as they tried to touch me. There were sharp bits sticking out of me. There were sharp bits inside my head.

Where's Aten? Voxi asked Bomarigala, thinking I couldn't listen in on their link.

Completely submerged, Bomarigala answered. *It shouldn't be possible.*

You shouldn't have given her two personalities! Voxi accused, grieving as he watched them trying to save my body.

We didn't plan it that way! Bomarigala snapped back, full of his own pain. *We couldn't get rid of Edna!*

Get rid of Edna. Get rid of Edna. Who wants plain old Edna? She should have died on the road to town. Don't give her any water.

The bleeding was stopped. The pain made me want to laugh. There was so much of it, it was ridiculous. I was floating on top of it, all of my emotions had drained away with my personality. With my blood. It was all over me, all over them, all over the floor.

What an extravagant mess, I thought to myself, amazed at what I had accomplished. I hadn't known I could be so successfully destructive.

I was bundled onto a stretcher. Bomarigala and Voxi insisted on coming with us as they carried me out and up to the roof, where an expensive aircraft waited to lift me off to the hospital. Seeing the anguish in their faces didn't please me. It wasn't for me, it was for Aten. And the scowls of the paramedics shamed me. They were dismayed by my injuries. And yet somehow it wasn't me, I wasn't the injured one, I wasn't participating in the scene at all. I was just standing by, wondering, *How are they going to help her? Can they fix her? They'll probably have to sedate her.*

We floated off into the ether. I felt more detached by the moment. I didn't care where we were going, when we would get there, what would happen to me when we did. As far as I was concerned, we could just float around forever, drifting from cloud to cloud.

When we landed again, and the noise and the bustle of the outside world rushed in to fetch me, I just went along with the tide. I was momentarily interested in the frantic professionalism of the emergency room staff. But they sedated me pretty quickly. Things began to look even more abstract than they already had.

It seemed to me that one moment I was surrounded by movement and sound, and the next moment I was completely alone in a dimly lit, quiet room. Where were Bomarigala and Voxi? Hadn't they just been talking to me, trying to tell me something important? I couldn't make out a word they were saying, and now they had simply vanished.

"They decided to leave you alone for the time being," someone said.

I wasn't alone in the room after all. The pale man was there, the one from my dream. He was sitting in the chair next to my bed, his legs crossed and his hands resting on one knee.

"Peterhamil," I said, without much thought.

"No," he said. "That was what Aten called me. My name is Peter Hammill. It's an Old Empire name, like yours. Peter is my first name and Hammill is my family name. We all used to have them."

"What was *my* name?" I asked him.

"Edna Hume," he replied.

"How do you know?" I wondered, almost caring.

"Because your mind was *not* wiped, Edna. It was hidden. I know this, because I was the doctor who did the hiding."

I would have laughed, but my chest hurt too much. "You're a thousand years old?"

"No. You are. I'm not even here."

"Oh." Now it made sense. I was seeing him, just as I had seen Aten all this time, thinking she was real, making a fool out of myself in front of others by talking to her and then answering myself in her voice. I was probably answering myself right now, making my voice deep so it would sound like his.

"You are," he confirmed. "I'm an artificial personality, too. Peter Hammill made me. But I'm aware of myself. I even have sort of a body sense, though not anywhere near as elaborate as Aten's was."

"Oh," I said again, thinking that now would be a lovely time for a nap. I closed my eyes.

"Edna," he called.

I cracked my eyes open again. I could still see him.

"You can't go to sleep," he said. "You can't stay here."

"Why?" I wondered, not wanting to believe it.

"Because they're going to try to get Aten back."

"Good!" That news almost made me happy.

"They're going to try to do it by submerging *you*."

That made me take notice. I almost sat up. The aborted movement reminded me how much pain I was really feeling.

"Edna isn't even supposed to exist," he said. "When they fished you out of stasis, you were supposed to be blank. They thought you would become Aten—it was far more useful for you to become her. But you haven't gone away, you've remained a separate personality."

"I like Aten," I said. "I want her back."

But did I want her back at my own expense? I tried to imagine nonexistence. Even in my shattered state, it was a scary concept.

"How come I didn't go away?" I asked.

"Because you weren't wiped."

He was giving me a headache. Of *course* I was wiped. I would have a past if I hadn't been wiped.

"Maybe you'd better start at the beginning," I decided.

"That's exactly what I intend to do," he said, uncrossing his legs and leaning forward, intently. He really looked real. I was impressed. "That's why I was created. To help you find your hidden memories. Peter Hammill was trying to help you."

"Gee," I said. "That was nice of him."

"I think it was," he agreed. "I think he did it out of kindness. But it's going to be hard, Edna. You're going to have to leave this place. It's going to be painful."

Pain was the last thing I wanted to hear about. "Couldn't we just find my memories from this comfortable bed?"

"No. You have to go home."

"To GodWorld?"

"No. Your real home. It didn't even have a name back then; and now it's just a number in the star charts."

He was crazy. I couldn't even go to the bathroom by myself and he was talking star charts. Light years.

"You can get out of that bed," he insisted.

"I can't. I'm hurt too bad."

"You *were* hurt. They've sealed up all of your wounds, you won't even have scars. Your broken ribs are healed, too. It hurts a lot, and you're weak from blood loss, but you can make it to an egg."

"An *egg*? You're crazy."

He stood up. "You have an escape program, did you know that?"

"No . . ."

"It's one of your agent programs. You can get out of this place undetected and steal an egg. You can pilot it all the way back to your homeworld."

Wow! An agent program! Like Aten's!

"But it's all lost," I remembered. "Aten is lost."

"It's *not* lost. It's submerged. I'm going to call it up for you."

Suddenly I knew I didn't want him to. It wasn't that I was just afraid of the pain, it wasn't that I was just lethargic from the medication. I didn't remember what was in those not-wiped memories, but somehow I knew for a fact I didn't want them back. I didn't want to go.

"No," I said. "I'll stay here and take what comes."

"It's not safe here," he insisted. "The matriarchs set you up, do you realize that? They put you in that maze of mirrors deliberately. They were trying to cause you to have a psychotic break. It was the only way they could thwart the GodHeads and discourage Voxi and KLse from pursuing you. They're your enemies, and they won't be satisfied with leaving you alone."

"They can't *all* be my enemies," I said, thinking of those elegant ladies, hurting at the rejection. "Someone has to be on my side."

But he was shaking his head. "I can't let you say no. I wasn't made to let you say no. I'm sorry Edna; I'm enough of a person to know I don't want you to suffer. But I'm not enough of a person to have a choice."

He leaned over my bed.

"You killed the raptor," he said.

I didn't understand. I looked into his eyes, and the

terrible eyes from my dream looked back at me. There
was pain then, the nonphysical kind that makes you want
to double over as if you've been kicked in the stomach.
But it was only brief, a promise of suffering to come;
and then I was suddenly a cool professional.

I made myself sit up. It hurt, but not enough to stop
me. I stood, waited to find my balance, and then moved
carefully to the door.

I didn't feel a moment of doubt as I crept through
that hospital, evading staff and guards. I knew things
about X'GBri technology, codes, layouts that must have
come from OMSK intelligence. Soon I was in a stolen
car, headed for a private airport nearby.

I was physically exhausted. It was nice to sit down
behind a wheel and rest, even while I was noting streets,
addresses, obeying traffic laws. It all was reminiscent of
Aten. She almost seemed like a person to me again; I
kept thinking she was in the backseat with Peter Hammill. But neither of them became solid for me. I knew
they were ghosts.

The guards at the airport challenged the car, but they
didn't make me roll down the window, and I was admitted almost instantly. The car belonged to one of the
matriarchs; she owned the airport. I drove past fancy
airships and sleek spaceships, all the way to the obscure
rear of the complex. What I wanted was there. It was
seldom used, but it was kept in tip-top condition, as were
all of the matriarch's belongings. I parked the car and
got out to look at it.

It was an egg. Human technology, but adapted for
X'GBri use. It was bigger than the one Aten and I had
used; and it was vastly superior in its capabilities. Early-
boosted technology, X'GBri know-how. I opened it with
the matriarch's private code and climbed in. I sealed it
up again.

It would be lonely in there. After all, it was just me
this time. Me and two ghosts.

Make that one and a half ghosts. I kept thinking that
I had left Aten behind at the hospital. She didn't seem
to be with me anymore.

"Will I ever get her back?" I asked Peter Hammill.

But he didn't answer. There wasn't room for both him

and the agent program. Funny, I would have thought that I had a lot more storage capability in my brain.

On the other hand, there were two entire personalities hiding in there, both submerged, both waiting to be retrieved. Edna and Aten. I had to go out and get them.

Go *in* and get them.

I had no idea how to do that. But I knew how to steal that egg. And that's what I did, lifting off without incident, buying passage with my stolen codes. My hands programmed the jump coordinates into the navigational system and I disappeared from X'GBri space. They wouldn't know I was gone until it was too late; and they wouldn't have any idea where to find me.

After all, wasn't that what I was trying to find out myself?

HOMEWORLD

I was curled in the passenger couch of the egg like an embryo, not awake, not asleep, aware of breathing, aware of warmth, aware of the powerful jump engine underneath me, at times almost feeling as if I were a part of the machinery. Outside the egg, space was folded, or warped, or was skipped over entirely; I was never quite able to grasp the concepts. The science of the Earlies was so far beyond human, it almost seemed like religion. Not that I understood Human science that well, either.

It didn't matter, as long as nothing broke down; and this pampered toy wasn't about to do that. The matriarch might never even look at it in her whole life; but if she did, it had better be gleaming and perfect.

I was grateful for it. In fact, I would have been perfectly contented to stay curled up inside, jumping from one end of the galaxy to the other, not thinking, not worrying, not looking for my past. After all, a past was such a cumbersome thing. But every time thoughts like that trickled through my sleepy mind, Peter Hammill would whisper in my ear that it just wasn't possible. He couldn't allow it. He was very sorry. I told him it was all right. I didn't want him to feel bad, especially since he would have to do it with my neurotransmitters.

I don't know how long I traveled. There was no day and night, and I didn't watch the chronometer inside the egg. But finally I was roused with alarms. It was time to drop the egg into a planet-sized gravity well.

Home. I looked at it from orbit. It looked a lot like GodWorld, but there were no storms raging. The sun was type G, not the type-F monster that powered GodWorld's superstorms. The clouds down below were mild and wispy. I couldn't see very much water. A hint of ice on a few of the highest peaks, and a trace of color that might have been mineral rather than vegetation. Even the two poles looked kind of dry.

I sighed around a painful knot in my chest. It had finally come back to that. To the water. Maybe I should try to land near one of those bodies that could be seen from orbit.

No, Peter Hammill insisted. *You have to find your old neighborhood.*

My old neighborhood? No one lived down there now. There were no transmissions vibrating through that empty air. There were no lights burning. There were only straight lines that must have been roads. Long, endless, dusty roads.

The warm ground under my bare feet.

There, said Peter Hammill, and he gave me the coordinates. I let us drop into atmosphere and pointed our butt at the ground. Gravity seized us; I fired the landing engines, and we settled down as smooth as any pilot could have done it. LLna's husbands would have been satisfied with my performance. Even Voxi would have.

For a while there was just the *tick-tick* of cooling metal. Peter Hammill wasn't talking to me now, I was completely alone. I sort of liked it that way. Outside, the sun was shining hot. It came in through the view windows and touched my face. I didn't feel compelled to go anywhere.

But thoughts were drifting around in my head. I was remembering things I had been told on OMSK. They told me I had been in stasis for a thousand years. What would be left of the colony on this world after a thousand years? Did they build for the long run?

I sat up and looked at the terminal that still displayed a tactical readout for this world. There it was in colored lights, with information about its mass, gravity, atmosphere and so on in little informational boxes. Apparently the standing water was loaded with poisonous minerals, but there was a lot of good underground water. That explained why people had built seemingly in the middle of nowhere. They must have just pumped what they needed.

But there was no name for my homeworld, at least not in the X'GBri language. There were only numbers.

"What's the world called, Daddy?"

"Shithole."

"John, don't use that kind of language with her!"

Those voices weren't in my head. Not like Aten's and KLse's had been when they used the link. But I didn't hear them with my ears, either. They were more like . . .

Memories . . .

"Peter Hammill?" I called, hoping that he would explain. But I was still alone. I was alone and I was stiff and even bored. I was on a world I had never seen before. I should look at it.

But I *had* seen it before. That was the issue, wasn't it? What a lot of work, getting all that information back. How long would it take?

Oh well.

I popped the hatch. Hot air rushed in. It wasn't uncomfortably hot; I even sort of enjoyed it. It was very dry. I didn't mind that. I climbed up and out into a vast panorama of light, heat, and rock. The sky was a vivid blue; the ground was brown in some places, red in others. Scrubby plants dotted the landscape, some of them even sporting little flowers. And there were mountains on all sides of me, jagged, tall, silent.

Wow, my own voice said inside my head, *this is kind of neat. This must be what it was like for the EggHeads in the old days.* I imagined that I was one of those prospectors, gallivanting around unknown space in my egg, looking for Early ruins, or looking for worlds on which humans could live. This world looked livable. I didn't see any reason why it should have been abandoned. I climbed out of my egg and put my feet on the ground, pretending that I was the first living human who had ever made a footprint there.

But of course, I wasn't. That became clear very quickly, when I saw what was left of the road. I walked toward it with a new feeling prickling the back of my neck. Was anyone here, still? Would they offer me harm? Or would they just annoy me with questions I didn't know how to answer anymore?

The road was partly obscured by sand and dirt. The pavement was cracked in a million places, the concrete edges and dividers had hardy weeds growing through their cracks. The road stretched from vanishing point to vanishing point, like time itself.

A thousand years. The tombs of the ancient Egyptians had survived a lot longer than that. Aten told me they still stood on earth. Didn't anything still stand here? Anything besides me?

This wasn't the road I had walked on. That road had been a dirt track, nothing more. I had felt the warm ground under my feet. Slowly I bent and took off my safety boots. I peeled off my socks and let my bare feet press into the dust. They were so tender now! But I remembered that barefoot feeling. Even if I never remembered anything else, I had that one down.

This road wasn't the one from my dream, but it would do. Before I was ready to walk down it, however, I went back into the egg. I got a safety pack and strapped it on. Now I had food and water rations. I even tucked my boots and socks into the pack, in case my feet got tired of remembering the ground.

I found something else in the egg, too. A gun. It was a projectile weapon, a very good one. It was high caliber, but I thought I might be able to shoot it without falling over. You had to give the X'GBris credit, they did like fine weapons. And they always knew how to use them. My agent program must still have been running, because I knew how to use it, too. I strapped the holster around my hips. Now I *really* felt like an EggHead.

I climbed out of the egg again and picked a horizon. I picked the one that seemed to draw me. It was the one toward which the sun was crawling. I put my feet on the road and started walking.

The temperature outside was about ninety-two degrees Fahrenheit, very pleasant. I drank my water sparingly. I didn't care when I was still thirsty after drinking. It seemed normal; I couldn't remember why the concept had ever upset me. My feet were sore at first, but they began to toughen up almost immediately.

It was dead quiet, except for the soft sounds my feet made on the road. My breathing started to sound loud to me; every burp and sneeze sounded like an explosion. But I wasn't alone.

I started to hear little scurrying sounds after I had been walking for a couple of hours. Something was running through the scrubby plants, something small and nervous. Tiny flowers waved back and forth from the passage of small bodies.

Flowers. Must be spring, I thought to myself.

"Yeah, there are two seasons on this planet. Eleven months of summer, one month of spring. Enjoy it while you can, kid."

"How come it's so hot all the time, Daddy?"

I stopped. Something had almost come, then. I could almost see a face. There had been a flash of light and color, I had almost glimpsed my surroundings. But I hadn't been looking at them, I had been looking at *him*. At someone. Daddy. He had seemed handsome, but not like Bomarigala. Which was good. That would have been too weird.

I walked until the sun had moved right into my face; and then I wished for a hat and dark glasses. I didn't think about much of anything else, until I started to get hungry. When I had sat down for some rations, I thought about where I might sleep for the night. The ground would certainly be hard. I hoped there weren't poisonous insects that came out at night. I wondered if this world supported any larger predators.

Well if it did, the alleged predators certainly would be wary of humans. And anyway, I wasn't scared. I felt all right. I wasn't even very sad about Aten. Or KLse. It was hard to think about anything much. It was sort of like being on vacation. All of your troubles are piled up on your desk, back at the office.

Finally I came to a spot where the road branched. Part of it peeled off to my right, going out to another vanishing point. I stopped and looked at it. While I was standing there, my urge to go forward turned into an urge to go right. I took the exit. The sun went from burning my nose to burning my left ear.

I walked until the sky started to streak and bruise with sunset. The mountains off to my right became redder, and purple shadows stretched across my road. It would be night soon and there was no building in which to shelter, no ruin of a house or an office. No nothing.

Bush-dotted plains to my right, bordered by the distant mountains. Bush-dotted hills to my left, struggling to turn into mountains themselves. Just as the light was dying, I found a culvert, half filled with dirt and debris from a millennium of rains and winds. It wasn't much of a shelter now; I couldn't even get my whole body into it. But it was better than nothing.

As the sun went down, the temperature began to drop drastically. I hadn't thought of that. I dug through my pack and was delighted to find a thermal blanket. I wrapped myself into a cocoon and wriggled as far into my hole as I could.

I nibbled a few of my rations, took a couple of sips of water, then just lay there and listened. The night was a lot noisier than the day. Bugs came out and called to each other. There were some squeaks and chirrups, too; and the occasional sound of tiny feet, running.

I didn't think. I just listened. Eventually, I drifted off to sleep. Just before I went over the edge, I did have one thought.

This isn't so bad.

I only woke up a couple of times during the night, once to shift position, and the other time because I thought I heard a noise. It sounded like something vibrating. It sounded like: *vvvvvvvvvvvvvvvvvVVVVVVVV OOOOOOOOOOOOOOOOOOOOOooooooooooooooorrrnn.*

I opened my eyes and listened while I was awake. But I didn't hear the sound again, so I went back to sleep. I dreamed that something giant was crawling all over the hills, looking for me. My hands burned, and I wanted to pull them out of the blanket so they could cool off; but I didn't want to move or the giant things might see me. I wished my hole were deeper.

Morning came. I opened my eyes, and there were no giant monsters, only a little bird sitting on a nearby bush, its tiny feet clutching a twig almost as delicate as its legs were. It was brown and red with a white breast. Its feathers were more like fur; it looked like a fat little puffball with two inquisitive eyes stuck somewhere near the top.

Bleep? it said.

"Bleep?" I answered back, as nearly as I could.

It hopped to another twig, but was otherwise unintimidated.

I got up slowly. I needed to go urinate, and I wanted privacy; which was foolish, considering that I was the only one around. The little bird was watching me closely. I went behind the biggest bush I could find (which wasn't very) and took off my catsuit. I took off my panties, too, not wanting to mess up anything that I couldn't wash. Then I squatted, awkwardly, and let go.

Bleep? said something behind me, almost ruining my aim (what there was of it, anyway). I looked over my shoulder and found that the puffball bird (or a near cousin) had moved to where it could see what I was doing. It was apparently fascinated. When I had finished, it jumped to the edge of the resulting muddy spot and examined it with first one eye and then the other. After that, it leapt into the mud and hopped around on it, having a lovely time.

I struggled back into my clothes. The pack contained some gum with the snappy name of TOOTH-AID, the best substitute for a toothbrush that could be packed into a small space. There were some wet wipes as well, which I used.

Bleep? said the puffball, eying the wet wipes. I put them down where he (or she) could look at them. The puffball hopped all over them. A moment later, it flew off with one of them clutched in its tiny feet. It struggled to get aloft, but managed to hold on to its burden until it was out of sight.

I climbed back onto the road, which was still empty in both directions, and began to walk again. The morning sun felt wonderful after the chilly night. In fact, except for my sunburn, I hadn't minded the heat from the day before at all. Did that mean my recurring dream wasn't from my past after all? No road, no Mr. Kyl, no gun, no off-limits water cooler guarded by cruel office people? No misery, no thirst . . .

"The whole planet is a desert," Daddy said.

"That's what I like about it," Mr. Allen replied, but Daddy didn't listen.

"People should never have come here," he said. *"If you stumble and fall, this place will soak you up like a drop of water. Just a drop of water that shouldn't even be here in the first place."*

"You're right about people not belonging here," Mr. Allen said. *"But you've got the wrong reasons."*

I still couldn't see Daddy. But I knew who Mr. Allen was. He was the guy from the dream, the one I had called *the old man*. But he wasn't really an old man. He was only about fifty years old. His face was sunburnt from years of exposure and he never smiled. But he loved the desert. He was the one who . . .

Now it was gone, like a balloon string that slips out of your hand, and you leap for it, but it's already far out of reach. I was really frustrated for a moment, but then I just let it go. Who cared? Stuff would come back to me or not. I already didn't like the sound of Daddy that much. He always seemed to be complaining. And he was wrong to call this place *shithole*. It was beautiful. I liked being there in all that hugeness, a big sky stretched over me and only mountains to keep me company. I liked the silly little puffball bird that went *bleep?* And I liked walking down that road, and I was just going to keep doing it until I got tired of it, which maybe I never would.

Up ahead, Peter Hammill beckoned. I stopped and blinked, thinking he was a bit of sun in my eyes. But the sun was burning my right ear now, it wasn't in my eyes. Peter Hammill was standing in the road, far enough ahead that I almost couldn't be sure it was him, waiting for me, waving for me to hurry. I picked up my pace, but only because I wanted a better look at him.

He disappeared while I was blinking. I looked all over for him, but he was gone. I figured it was just my brain playing tricks anyway, so I didn't worry too much about it. I got out my water and took a couple of swallows. I thought about venturing off the road, having a closer look at those mountains.

"No!" Peter Hammill called. He was back on the road again, still far ahead of me. He waved frantically. "This way!" he called, motioning for me to continue up the road.

"Wait for me this time!" I called back.

"I can't help it," he said. "I'm only self-aware some of the time. I'll try to wait for you!"

But he vanished again. I kept walking up the road anyway, because I didn't want to disappoint him. Maybe there was something to see up there if you just kept walking.

I walked all morning. When the sun was right over my head I stopped for lunch and had a few more swallows of water. It occurred to me that my water supply wasn't going to last more than a couple more days if I drank sparingly. And I wouldn't be getting enough water if I did that; if I wasn't careful, I could end up passing out in the middle of the road. I could become delirious and forget where my egg was, I could die of thirst. I felt fine at the moment, except for an occasional Peter Hammill hallucination. But that could change; and when it did change, I might be too far gone to realize it.

Tomorrow morning I would have to turn back and go get more water. That's what I would do. Having decided that, I forgot about the matter and kept putting one foot in front of the other.

Peter Hammill was up ahead again. This time he was pointing off the road, toward some mountains that were farther away. I stopped and looked at them. They would take more than a day to reach.

"I don't have enough water to get there!" I called.

"You're just going to your old neighborhood," he called back.

"Where is that? I don't see any buildings!"

"They've been gone for a thousand years!"

"Then why am I going there?" I asked.

"Because that's where it all starts!" he answered.

I felt a twinge of apprehension. I had liked walking in an empty world with an empty mind. Now it looked like something was going to happen. *Go back to the egg and get the hell out of here,* I told myself, knowing it was good advice.

"You can't go back!" Peter Hammill called. "You have to go forward!"

I planted my feet, stubbornly. "Why do I have to know what really happened?" I said. "Why can't I just make good stuff up and pretend it happened?"

"Because the truth is still there!" he insisted. "It will keep coming up at odd moments. Look at your hands!"

I did. I could still see the lines from where they had knitted my skin back together. I had lines like that all over my body.

"Broken mirrors!" he called. "That's what you've got now. And it will only get worse unless you come back and pick up the pieces!"

I sighed. I didn't feel like picking up any pieces. But Peter Hammill would keep nagging me until I did. So I walked up to his place in the road, (where he promptly vanished), and took a left turn in the direction he had been pointing. There was a road here, too, but I didn't know it until I stubbed my toe in some pot holes in the old pavement. It was covered by sand and dirt in most places.

Rough under my feet.

No, it was warm ground under my feet. When I had lived there, they hadn't paved it yet. It had been a track in the dirt; vehicles had driven down it, people had walked on it. We had played in it, getting dirty the moment we ran out the front door. Our mothers had given up on trying to keep us clean. Water was for drinking first; washing clothes and bathing was something you had to do very efficiently, and only once a day.

I watched my dusty feet as I walked. They were mine, I was sure of it, but now they looked so small. My catsuit was gone, I was wearing shorts, and my legs and knees were so dirty my skin looked mottled. I had a hole in my shorts, too; but my shirt covered it, so I didn't care. I looked up and saw the houses on both sides of the dirt road. They were dusty, too, but some people worked hard to make them look good. I saw a lady in her front yard making designs in the dirt with her rake. I stopped and looked at the designs. She glared at me until she realized I wasn't going to mess them up. I would never do a thing like that. I thought the designs were pretty.

I smiled at the lady and waved, but she had decided to ignore me; so I decided to go home. The sun was dropping down into the evening side of the sky. Supper would be soon. I saw other kids standing in their front yards, sticking around so they would hear their moms when they called. They stared at me. I didn't stare back, because those yards weren't my territory. If I had been watching *them* from *my* yard, I would have been the one who was bold.

It was a long walk. It never felt long when I was going out to play. I would wander out to my favorite empty places and pretend to have adventures for hours and hours. No one played with me. My clothes were too old and torn, and their moms said I was too dirty.

Mr. Allen was nice, though. I saw him in his yard as I passed on the way to my house. When I waved, he waved back; but I could tell he was busy. Mr. Allen and I had this understanding that when he was busy I needed to leave him alone. That was okay, as long as I knew where he was. He was the one I always took things to when they were broken; not Daddy or my brothers. He told me all kinds of interesting stuff. He showed me all the different plants that grew around there, and sometimes I remembered what he told me.

Mr. Allen really did look busy, so I hurried to my house. I had been alone all day and I was ready for company again. Everyone would be home by then. Everyone except for Daddy; he got home at odd times. Lots of times he didn't get home until all us kids were in bed. Sometimes I heard him and Mom talking in the kitchen. I never heard them talk sweet to each other, but I kept waiting for it. Moms and dads were supposed to love each other. That's how it was on the vids. Sooner or later, Mom and Daddy would start talking that way to each other and then everything would be all right again. Just like in the vids.

I found my yard. It made me dizzy to look at it; I remembered everything in it. Our broken toys, the broken barbecue, the broken waste unit, Mike's and John's spare parts for the vehicle they were trying to repair so they'd have transportation into town. They could get jobs if they could drive to town. Sometimes Mr. Allen helped them. I saw my daddy helping once or twice.

I blinked and the yard wasn't there. It was just dirt, a flat place stretching for miles toward some mountains that were more beautiful than the squalid houses could have dreamed of being. But a second later the houses were back, my yard was just like I remembered it. I thought about getting the rake and making pretty designs like the lady had made. I wondered if we even had a rake.

"Mom?" I called. She was probably in the kitchen. I heard voices in there.

"Mom?" I called again. I saw the kitchen door. It had been repaired several times, but still wanted to come off its hinges. There were several years' worth of smudges all around the doorknob, which didn't work anymore anyway. I pushed on the door and said, "Mom?"

There she was, by the sink. She was scraping old food out of a pan, getting ready to start supper. Carol was helping. Carol was a teenager, like John and Mike. I looked at Carol.

Aten looked back.

"Here it comes," she said. "I don't think you're going to like it."

Actually, Carol didn't look like Aten at all. She had brown hair, and she kind of swished when she walked. Carol liked to play music and dance when our brothers weren't home. Sometimes she showed me how to dance. But she spent a lot of time with her boyfriends; there wasn't much time for lessons.

Mom was standing with her back to me. She had red hair, like me. It hurt my heart when I looked at her. It felt like a fist was inside my chest, squeezing things.

"Mom?" I said. But it was like she couldn't even hear me.

"Shut up, stupid!" said David. He was a couple of years older than me. He was always telling me stuff I did wrong. Sometimes he helped the neighborhood boys chase me and beat me up.

"Mom, do we have a rake?" I asked, trying to ignore him.

Mike laughed. "Why would we have a rake? We don't have any grass."

Mike and John weren't mean, they just told me stuff I didn't understand. That lady had had a rake for her dirt, so why wouldn't we? Maybe it was in that huge pile of junk out back. Lots of things were in there, you just had to be patient enough to look for them.

I went through the living room, where things looked nice. That was where Mom kept her good things: art and books and furniture that had covers Mom and Carol had made on the sewing machine. I was proud of that room. I wished I could show it to the kids whose mothers said I was too dirty.

I went into the backyard. It was a bigger mess than the front. I thought I should pretty it up first, after I had found the rake. But on the other hand, the front yard was what people saw. The backyard was enclosed by a block fence, just like the other yards on our street. I should do the *front* yard first; if only I could find a rake.

I poked at the pile of junk. It was so big, my whole family could have hidden in there. That was seven people. No, eight! Eight counting the baby. The baby mostly stayed in her crib and screamed. She would give away our hiding place for sure.

I couldn't find anything that looked like a rake sticking out of the edges of that pile. I found a broken wooden pole that must have been the handle for something once. Maybe I could make nice lines with that. It would take a lot longer. . . .

I tried to make neat rows. But they just looked like ugly scratches. I looked at my ugly yard and felt like crying.

"Hey," said a voice that made my heart leap. "Eddy, what are you doing?"

"Daddy!" I cried, like he had been lost for years and just come back. He had come through the gate at the side of the house, no one else even knew he was home yet. I was the first! I went running to him and he swept me off my feet. He hugged me close and swung me around. Then he held me in the crook of his arm and smiled at me.

He was handsome in his uniform. He was an air/space officer, a captain. He looked too clean to be my daddy.

"Want to go to the starport with me?" he asked.

"Yes!" I cried. I couldn't believe my good luck. I almost never got to spend time with Daddy. I only heard his voice in the night most of the time. Sometimes he would come in and kiss me good night. I could smell men's cologne on him, and whiskey. I loved the smell.

He took me out through the side gate. I thought we were sneaking out, but he stopped at the kitchen door and stepped inside for a moment. Everyone looked at us.

"I have to run an errand at the port," he said. "Eddy's coming with me. We'll be back in a couple of hours."

No one said anything. Mom didn't even look at us.

David did though, and he looked jealous. I almost stuck my tongue out at him, but Daddy had taken me out before I could do more than consider the idea.

Daddy put me in his vehicle. It was a military vehicle; I always suspected that it could fly if Daddy pushed the right buttons. There were safety straps, but he never used them. He didn't put them on me, either; I just held on to the bar on the door as he zoomed down the street. I looked for Mr. Allen as we passed his house, so I could wave at him. He wasn't outside, so I just sat back and felt proud, seeing those kids stare at me and my military dad driving by on official business.

We raised a cloud of dust. I think Daddy was speeding. He always drove fast, like he wished the land vehicle were an airship. Or a rocket. But he slowed down when we had driven just a few blocks. He pulled up outside a house and put the brake on, leaving the engine in neutral.

"Wait here," he told me. He jumped out and strolled up to the house.

A girl met him at the door. She was Carol's age, a high school girl. I thought she would run in and call her dad, but instead she picked up a suitcase and walked back to the car with Daddy. A man came to the door and glared at their backs through the screen. I waved at him; he looked at me like I was some kind of horrible bug. A moment later he closed the door.

The girl climbed in on my side. I scooted over to the middle.

"Hi, there," she said, brightly. "What's your name?"

"Eddy," I said, preferring what Daddy called me.

"How old are you, Eddy?"

"I'm four and a half. How old are you?"

"I hope I have one like you someday," said the girl.

"You'd better not," warned Daddy.

I wondered how come the girl was in the car. I thought he would drop her off somewhere, but we drove out of the neighborhood with her, down to the dirt road I always walked down when I was going out to play. We went a lot farther than I ever did, all the way up to the main highway, which was paved. Daddy breathed a sigh of relief and sped up even more.

I sat and stared at the top of the dash, which was all that I could see from there. I wished the girl would leave so I could look out her window. She had her arm up on the back of the seat, like she was trying to be friendly with me. I looked at Dad, trying to figure out why she was there, what was happening.

His arm was on the back of the seat, too. I was only four and a half, but I knew his hand and hers must be touching. After I realized that, my mind just sort of went blank.

We drove into the city. Buildings were reflected in the glass of the front window. I watched them slide over us, wishing it was my mom in the front seat with us and not this dumb girl.

"The older kids aren't even mine," Daddy said. "I did Maggy a favor by marrying her when I did."

We pulled up at a gate. The soldier there was real friendly with Daddy. He looked at me and said, "Hello there, little lady!" He grinned at the girl.

We drove through the gate. "Look at the ships!" the girl cried. I tried, but I still couldn't see over the dash. "Oh, John!" the girl said, breathlessly. "I'm leaving this rotten world! I'm really leaving!" Their hands clasped over my head.

That's nice, I thought to myself. *Daddy's driving her to the starport so she can go away. That's nice of him.*

We parked and we all got out of the vehicle. Daddy went to the back and pulled out another bag. It was military green, just like his clothes. That was weird; I thought the girl only had one bag. Maybe Daddy had loaned her one.

They both took my hands, like we were a family. I even tried to pretend we were. Maybe if I wished hard enough, this girl would turn into my mom. We would all walk away from the dirty neighborhood where we really lived and into this clean city. We could send for the nice stuff in the living room. Just keep wishing, just close your eyes.

We went through the security/decontamination point, but the people checking IDs barely looked at the girl's. They didn't look because they could see we were obviously a family, she was obviously my mom. I would have told them it wasn't so if they had asked me, but why should they ask? Wasn't Daddy acting as if the girl was his wife?

We walked a long way, into a main terminal and then down long, long corridors, some of which had moving floors. I wanted to stop and rest, since the floors were already moving; but Daddy and the girl were still walking, like they couldn't wait to get where they were going.

And finally they did. We went into a waiting room for one of the outbound ships. Daddy sat me down in a chair, he and the girl sat on either side of me. We waited. I closed my eyes and wished some more, but the girl never turned into Mom. And now I had an unbearable urge to go to the bathroom.

After a while, people started to get up and get into a line. Daddy and the girl got up, too. I started to follow, but Daddy picked me up and put me back in the seat. "Wait here," he said. He and the girl held hands and looked into each other's eyes. She said something to him. He gazed at her the way he should have gazed at my mom, and then he pulled a few dollars out of his pocket and came back to me. He handed me the money. "Here's something in case you get hungry," he said. He grinned at me, and then he and the girl walked out the outer door together, holding hands again.

I was glad the girl was leaving. Daddy shouldn't hold her hand like that. When he came back, *I* would hold his hand; and when we got home I would take him in to see Mom. They could look at each other like he had looked at the girl.

I waited.

I waited.

I waited some more. Night fell. Lots of people came and went. The dollars started to get soggy in my hand. I still had to go to the bathroom, only worse. After a while, it started to hurt. But I couldn't get up and leave. When Daddy came back, I had to be there. I had to be there or I would never see him again.

The night passed slowly. I dozed, but my need to pee kept waking me. I started arguing with myself. I could run to the bathroom and back. Daddy had given me money to eat, so he must have expected to be away for a while. If I hurried, I could be there when he got back. Why didn't he come back? Was he outside working on a spaceship? Like he had worked on Mike and John's vehicle sometimes? And how come the girl had called Daddy "John"? That wasn't his name. His name was Daddy; Mom had said my brother John was named after her first husband.

Her second husband was named John, too, Aten said, through our link. *They must have joked about that. Marrying two men named John.*

She should have taken it as a bad omen, I said. I looked around for Aten. Maybe she could wait for my daddy while I ran to the bathroom. But she wasn't anywhere in sight. If I got up, I just knew he would come looking for me. He would come looking and I wouldn't be there, and I would never see him again.

Morning came. This would be it. He had to come back now. Where was he? At least I didn't have to pee anymore. I was hungry, my whole stomach hurt. I was beginning to think Daddy would never come back.

There was a drinking fountain near my seat, so I ran over to it and stole a few sips, watching over my shoulder for Daddy. Suddenly my need to pee came back with a vengeance. I almost ran to the bathroom then, but I couldn't make myself do it. So I went back to my seat and crossed my legs real tight. I waited all day. More people came and went. I watched them. No one looked at me. I held the dollar bills until my hand ached, afraid to let them go. My bladder was aching, too, a sharp pain that made me double over.

Hundreds of people passed before my eyes. I stopped thinking and started pretending again. Pretending was what I did all day, when I played by myself. I had been doing that for as long as I could remember, I had been walking down the road and out of town from the time I could first walk. I would wander out, wander back, wander out, wander back. Sometimes in the evening one of the older kids would read to me. They had wonderful books with pictures in them.

Night fell again. No Daddy. I knew he wasn't coming back then; but I couldn't make myself leave. I couldn't go to the bathroom. If I did that, what would I do next?

Where would I go? I had to pee so bad I was beginning to think it wouldn't matter where or when I did it. But I couldn't make myself let go, I was clenched up so tight.

Sometime near dawn, Aten walked up to me. She was wearing a flight attendant's uniform.

"He's not coming back," she said.

"I know."

"You might as well let me take you to the bathroom."

I got up and put my little hand in her grown-up one. I could hardly walk, it hurt so bad.

"Did you see that bimbo he ran off with?" I asked Aten. "God, she was younger than my big sister. That must have been illegal or something."

"Military guys could get away with anything in those days," said Aten. "They covered for each other. You saw those guys at the gate. Your dad was probably buddy-buddy with a lot of guys who were willing to look the other way for him if he did the same for them. Those military guys used to marry women and abandon them every time they were shipped to another planet."

" 'Wait here,' he told me," I said as I struggled down the hall. "What a rat. He just brought me along so he could get the girl through security. Without me, they would have wondered about her age, for sure. Can you imagine doing a thing like that to a little kid?"

"No," said Aten. "I'm sorry, Edna."

"It was years ago," I said. But it wasn't, that was the point. It was right *now*. "I had a broken heart. I sat there the whole time grieving. I suppose I started grieving the moment I saw them holding hands."

We turned into the bathroom. I cheered up considerably at the sight of all those gleaming stalls. Suddenly the bathroom was about a million times more important than Daddy had been. I was a lot gladder to see it, too.

Aten pushed a stall door open and helped me struggle out of my shorts. She had to lift me onto the pot. I thanked her and grabbed a handful of toilet paper.

"You were pretty sophisticated for a four year old," she said, averting her eyes politely.

"Yeah," I said, and was finally able to let go. It felt so good, even through the pain, that I could hardly believe I was finally able to do it. "It must have been all that time I spent on my own, wandering around. And I talked a lot to Mr. Allen. He was sort of a teacher to me."

It took a long time to get all that pee out. I didn't want to move until I was sure I had really finished. I didn't want to have that uncomfortable feeling again, ever.

"They've called your mother," Aten said. "They finally figured out you'd been abandoned."

"Took them long enough," I grunted.

"They probably didn't want to know," she said. "I bet they didn't want to have to go through all the paperwork. It must have happened a lot, you know. Kids abandoned at the starport. Hooray for the human race."

"Hooray," I agreed.

When I had finally finished, she took me to the sink and gave me as good a wash-up as she could. I was awed by the fact that she let the water run without worrying about the waste.

"The starport must have gotten their water for free," she said.

"It was still nice of her," I said, remembering the flight attendant who had been so kind to me, who had taken me to the bathroom, and then taken me home. She hadn't really looked anything like Aten.

"She just didn't want you to get her car dirty," said Aten.

"Thanks a lot."

"This was supposed to be an odyssey of truth, remember?"

"Yeah, yeah. Let's get on with the next part. I don't remember it; I'll just have to walk through it. I can't wait to go home and tell Mom that Daddy ran off with one of Carol's friends."

Aten dried my face with a paper towel. "He probably came on to Carol, too. After all, he wasn't her father—"

"Aten, too much truth ain't good for *anybody*."

"Right," she said. "Ready for the next part?"

"As ready as I'm going to be."

Aten led me out of the bathroom. By the time we got out into the hall she had turned into an extremely thin blond lady with big boobs. Her flight attendant's uniform was spotless. She smiled at me through too much makeup.

"Your mommy's waiting for you at home," she said.

I didn't answer. I knew there was worse to come.

The drive home seemed to take no time at all. The lady dropped me off right outside my house. She didn't offer to come to the door with me. She drove off as soon as I had stepped away from the car. I faced my house alone.

It was ominously quiet.

I walked slowly through the front yard, passing all those ruined projects into which Mike and John had put so much fruitless work. Now that Daddy was gone, I could see them for the piles of junk they really were.

I opened the kitchen door and peeked in. Before I saw anything, I heard something. The baby crying. She had cried before, but this sound was ominous.

"There she is," Carol said. She came and took me by the hand. She led me past Mom and John and Mike, who were all sitting at the kitchen table. Mom didn't look at me as I passed her. I was beginning to wonder if she ever had.

"He cleaned out the bank account," Mom was saying, with this voice that made me want to stop up my ears. It wasn't loud or anything, it was so quiet you could barely hear it. Mike and John had worried, grown-up looks on their teenaged faces.

Carol led me into the living room, where David was sitting. David's face was streaked with tears. He wasn't happy to see me. Carol sat me down right next to him, on the good couch. I gave her the dollar bills that were still wadded up in my fist. She looked at them blankly for a moment, then looked at me with a face full of deadly comprehension.

"I want you two to stay on the couch while we talk some things over," she said. "Okay?"

"Okay," I promised.

Carol went back into the kitchen. I sat still and tried to understand what they were talking about out there. I heard a lot of stuff that didn't make any sense. I heard John talking about how long it would be before the water was turned off. I heard Mom crying a couple of times. The older kids didn't cry with her. They tried to come up with ideas.

I wished I could come up with ideas, too. I couldn't think of any.

"It's your fault," David whispered with barely contained fury.

"Huh?" I replied.

"You were too many kids," he whispered. "If it weren't for you, he wouldn't've left."

"Nuh-uh," I said, wondering if I should try to tell him about the girl. I didn't know how to explain it. Daddy wanted the girl, so he left us. Could it really be that simple?

"Daddy—" I said, and then David was hitting me. The first blow landed on my ear, knocking my vision out along with my hearing. Then he was pounding my face and I was trying to raise my hands to protect myself. I couldn't see, my head was buzzing, David's voice was screaming somewhere in the distance.

Then suddenly the world came back with a jolt. I was on the floor; John was pulling David away from me. He tucked David under his arm and stormed out the back door with him. The door slammed behind them.

I wasn't even angry. I actually pitied my brother for the punishment he was about to get. I crawled back onto the couch and tried to be invisible.

Aten was sitting next to me. She put her arm around me.

"He cleaned out the bank account," she said.

"Yeah."

"Your mom didn't work?"

"Not yet. She got a job later."

"Would they really turn off the water?"

"They will. They duped a lot of people into settling here, and then they hit them with all sorts of extra charges. People at the top are rich, but people like us are barely surviving. I think they call it the trickle-up theory."

"You mean trickle down," she said.

"Nuh-uh."

Aten looked around at our living room. I think she liked it. That made me feel good.

"Where's the gun?" she asked, suddenly.

"What gun?"

"The one you're going to use to shoot Mr. Kyl."

Oh, *that* gun. It was an antique. It had belonged to Daddy. I wondered if he had taken it with him. Mom had hidden it in her dresser drawer after she had caught David and me playing with it. Actually, only David had played with it. He had showed me how to load it, and then he had pointed it at me. Mom had appeared out of nowhere and grabbed it away. David had run into the room he shared with John and Mike, thinking he was going to get into trouble. But I had sneaked behind Mom and watched where she had hidden it. I wanted to know where it was in case I ever needed it.

I slipped off the couch. Aten tip-toed after me. We went into Mom's room and looked in the drawer. The gun was still there, hidden under some faded linens.

"Who is Mr. Kyl, anyway?" asked Aten.

"Daddy's friend."

Mr. Kyl had come to the house a couple of times. He wore a fancy suit. He was a city person. Mom had made me stay out of sight when he visited, but I had peeked.

I heard the back door slam. I tucked the gun back into its hiding place and eased the drawer shut. I hid behind Mom's door with Aten. I could see through the crack between the door and the wall. John was dragging David into their room. David was still crying, still stubborn. I sort of admired that. I would have been too scared to be that stubborn.

"Eddy?" John called. I froze where I was. I didn't want to get punished, too. I heard John's searching through the house, calling "Eddy?" from various rooms. I scurried out from behind the door and into the kitchen.

"Here!" I cried, "I'm here!"

John looked at me for a long moment. He looked sad. He took me over to the kitchen sink and poured a tiny bit of water onto a rag. He wiped my face with the rag. Blood came off.

"I told him not to hit you again," said John.

"Thanks," I said, trying not to cry about the look he still had on his face.

"If he hits you again he knows he'll have to answer to me," said John.

"Thanks."

I looked over at Mom. She was looking at me, too. She didn't look mad. She looked scared, sad, worried, regretful. She looked like a woman whose world had just collapsed on top of her.

"I'll have to talk to Mr. Kyl," she said.

And in the next moment, she and I were in the car. *Wait a minute!* I objected. *What about supper, what about a good night's sleep? What about a pat on the back and someone to say, "That's all right, Eddy, it wasn't your fault"?* I was worn out, I couldn't take much more of this remembering stuff. I must be lying somewhere in real time right now, slowly dying of thirst.

"We have to do this," Mom said. "Mr. Kyl is the only one who can help us, now."

That sent a shiver up my spine. I knew Mr. Kyl wasn't going to do anything of the kind. I knew it even back then, when it was really happening. I knew it when I was just four and a half.

I had a feeling Mom knew it, too. But she kept driving, anyway.

We were in Mr. Allen's car. Mom had borrowed it. It was just her and me; for some reason she thought my presence would help. I didn't see how it would, but I was ready to do anything I could.

Back we went to the gleaming city. I gasped when I saw the office building where Mr. Kyl had worked. It was the one from my dream. No good would come from this.

But I climbed out of the car with Mom and walked up those spotless steps. We went into the cool, cool lobby, and Mom went through the humiliating process of trying to get one of the secretaries to tell Mr. Kyl we were there. The lady kept coming back and saying he was too busy, but Mom wouldn't take no for an answer. She had a desperation that was kind of scary. The woman kept sneering and scowling at us, yet she couldn't quite seem to summon the nerve to chase us out.

Finally we were told we could see him if we were willing to wait until he was available. The lady said it could be hours. I saw Mom wavering. I wanted to shout, "No! No, hold your ground!" But Mom said okay. She was tired. She hadn't slept since the night Daddy had driven off with me.

She was making a big mistake. She thought the woman would be shamed by her obvious weariness, by her desperation. But the woman thought we were animals. She had no shame.

We waited for hours. My legs got twitchy. I had to go to the bathroom, so I went off in search of one. I wasn't about to go through the agony of trying to hold it again. Mom had fallen into a doze on the waiting room couch. She didn't see me go.

I found a bathroom. It had a toilet in it, but no sink. There were moist towelettes for wiping your hands. I used them to wipe every bare part of my body, thinking that if I looked cleaner, Mr. Kyl might give us the emergency money we needed. But I sure wished there had been a sink in the room, because I was thirsty. Very thirsty. I tip-toed out of the bathroom and looked around the office.

I saw some people standing around a water cooler. The sight of it made my heart pound. I watched them standing there, the neat little cups in their hands. They sipped the water, like it wasn't any big deal. At home, we couldn't get a drink without asking first. I thought about the mean secretaries and the way they had treated my mom. I thought I'd better not ask them for anything.

But that cooler called to me. I watched the lovely, blue lights in the water. How it sparkled. I listened to the sound it made when it came out of the spout and into the little paper cups. I imagined how it would feel in my mouth, going down my throat.

I waited until they had all gone away, and then I stalked the cooler.

I got all the way up to it. I managed to get one of the paper cups out of the high dispenser. I put it under the

spout and pressed the button. I felt the coolness of the
water right through the cup. I brought it to my lips.

One of the secretaries wrenched it out of my hands.
She poured the water down the drain under the spout
and, balling up the paper cup with single-minded feroc-
ity, she threw it into the trash. Then she grabbed my
wrist and slapped my hand, five times, so hard that the
pain brought tears to my eyes. I gritted my teeth, refusing to scream.

The secretary yanked me from the room and thrust
me back into the waiting area. I stumbled back over to
where Mom was sitting in a daze and got back onto the
couch. My face burned so hot I could feel heat radiating
from it. I tried not to see the smirks of the other secretaries. But I let myself go ahead and hate them. I hated
them with an astonishing passion.

So far our visit to Mr. Kyl was not going too well.

"What a bunch of goddamn bitches," Aten said, from
her seat next to mine.

"Office people," I explained.

"Office people aren't like that, Edna! I've never seen
anyone act that way before. If I hadn't just seen it with
my own eyes, I wouldn't have believed it."

You mean with my *own eyes,* I almost said, but I didn't
want to hurt Aten. I didn't want her to feel miserable,
like I was feeling. Or scared, like Mom was feeling.

"Here comes Mr. Big himself," said Aten.

Mr. Kyl was sauntering into the waiting area. Mom got
painfully to her feet. He smiled a condescending smile.

"Well, Maggy," he said. "I'll bet I know why you're
here today."

"May we talk in private?" she asked. All of the secretaries were listening in.

"I'm afraid you'll have to make an appointment," he
said. "I'm booked solid today."

"I've been trying to make an appointment for three
days," she said, her voice cracking with anger and strain.
"What do you expect me to do when the water runs
out?"

"I expect you'll have to dip into your secret bank account," he said.

Mom just blinked at him. She didn't know what he

meant. "My *what*?" she said. She looked at him in disbelief, but this just increased his contempt.

"John told me all about it," he said. "You're not going
to cheat the government, Maggy. If you get thirsty
enough, you'll find the money."

He turned his back on her and started talking to his
secretaries about various appointments, like we weren't
even there anymore. My mom started crying. I wished
we could just leave. But when Mr. Kyl tried to walk past
us, my mom fell on her knees in front of him. She started
to beg him. She told him there wasn't any secret bank
account. She said please, please, my children.

"You're a lousy actress, Maggy," said Mr. Kyl, and he
walked around her.

My mom got to her feet. She took my hand and led
me back to the car. I got in on my side, she got in on
hers. She rested her head on the steering wheel and
sobbed until I thought she was going to be sick.

I didn't cry. I sat there and nursed my hate until it
was as big and bright as the sun. I reveled in it. I let it
eat me alive.

"Wow," Aten said from the backseat. "This is what
led up to it. This is why you shot him."

"Yes," I said.

"What was all that about a secret bank account?"

"My dad told everybody that my mom had money
from her previous husband's insurance, after he died.
He never believed that it got used up before she even
met him."

"Why wouldn't he believe her? Didn't she have records to show him?"

I just shrugged. I didn't know if she had shown him
any records or not. I liked to think not, because I was
pretty sure my dad hadn't meant to let us die of thirst.
He wouldn't have done that, would he? He wouldn't
have had to do it. He had left us on a planet that didn't
even have a name. He would never see us again.

"He probably didn't believe her," I said.

"Don't count on it," said Aten.

"I won't."

And then we were home again.

*   *   *

I opened my eyes. I was alone in my tiny room, in our box of a house. I was in my little bed. I had gone there because the others had wanted to be alone so they could die. I was honoring their wishes.

Mike and John had gone begging to the neighbors after the water had run out. We had run as much of it as we could into tubs, bottles, sinks, cans, every container we could think of. We had thought it would last awhile if we only used it for drinking. But it had only lasted a week. That had been—how many days ago?

Mike and John had gone begging to the neighbors. But the neighbors had chased them off with guns. There was no water to spare; every family had to think of their own first. We were dead. People averted their eyes from us, unless we came too close, and then they aimed their guns at us.

"What about Mr. Allen?" whispered Aten. "He wouldn't have said no."

"Mr. Allen's water got turned off years ago," I whispered back. "He's a survivalist. He scavenges water from the desert."

That was where Mike and John were now. Mr. Allen had taken them out to look for water. They promised Mom they would bring it back. She had stopped talking just before the water ran out, so I don't know if she believed them.

The whole planet was a desert, that's what Daddy had said. Even the cooler places. Because there wasn't hardly any water on the surface. It soaked the water up, and then it soaked people up, too.

The water is underground, Mr. Allen had said. *You just have to know where to dig.*

I had gone out back and dug until my head had ached. The water must be *way* underground. Deep, deep.

I got out of bed and went into Carol's room. Carol was curled up on her own bed. I had tried to talk to her a little while ago, but Carol couldn't talk. Her tongue was too swollen. Her eyes were dreadful; I was glad they were only half open. I think she had given us younger kids most of her own water ration, while it lasted.

I watched to see if her chest was moving up and down. I thought it was. Sort of.

I didn't put my head on Carol's chest to listen to her heart. I was afraid Carol would push me away. Or worse, that she wouldn't react at all.

Everyone had blamed me when I came back without Daddy. David had been the first; but eventually the others had started thinking that way, too. They kept staring at me when they had run out of options for the day.

I could still see Daddy's smiling face in my mind. I had never seen him look so happy. He and the girl held hands. . . .

Mom was curled up in her own room with the baby. The baby had stopped crying a long time ago. That was good, because Mom didn't pay attention to the baby anymore. It had cried for a long time, and then it just whimpered. Then it made these noises that I couldn't stand, these desperate little noises.

I didn't want to see Mom. But I made myself go into her bedroom. I didn't look at the bed where Mom and the baby were lying. I went to the dresser and pulled out the bottom drawer. I pulled aside the linens and grabbed the gun.

It was still loaded.

I took it. I went outside. I saw David out there, lying with his head next to the pipe that went into the house. He had discovered that if you put your mouth right up next to the joint, you could get a few drops. There was still a little water in the pipes. I walked past David and his pipe, out of the yard and into the dirt road.

The dirt felt so good under my feet. It rose in a cloud all around me, floating over all the little box houses. The people I passed were pretending not to see me. I walked past the lady who made designs in her yard with her rake. When she saw me, she held it in front of her like a weapon.

I didn't care. The hate was singing in my blood. It was pushing my limbs, right-left, right-left, moving me down that long road and onto the highway. It was a long walk for a little girl. It was an impossible walk for someone dying of thirst. But I had my hate to keep me going. It was more than enough.

I had seen vids on our screen before it had been disconnected. I knew about revenge. I knew about shooting the bad guy and fixing everything. I cradled that gun against my chest like a kitten and never doubted what was going to happen for a moment.

I walked forever. My tongue felt funny. Pretty soon it would start to look like Carol's. I had to get to Mr. Kyl before that happened. I had to get there. I thought about that water cooler in the office. I saw the lights sparkling in the lovely blue depths of the water. Water coming out of the faucet, water going over waterfalls, water coming out of the sky. I pictured a giant water cooler and imagined shooting a hole in its side and sucking the water out of it.

Daddy was laughing at me. His face was smug, like Mr. Kyl's. He stuffed the bills in my hands and said, "Wait here."

I walked into the city. I found Mr. Kyl's office. It was right off the main drag, I suppose I just lucked out. I walked up the steps and into the cool, cool interior, so cool it hurt. I could smell water in there. I expected to be confronted by the mean secretaries, but the office was crowded with ordinary people like my mom, all looking desperate like she had, all waiting for someone to help them out of their trouble. There was one secretary up front, a girl I had never seen before. And there was also a man I had never seen before, trying to help the people.

He was tall and thin, with a very serious expression on his face. It was the same expression I had seen on Mike and John, thousands of unhappy times; but this man was older than them. He was older than them but younger than Mom and Daddy. His suit was rumpled.

He didn't see me. The overworked secretary didn't see me. The people didn't see me. I was below eye level. I walked through them like a ghost.

I followed my nose to the smell of the water, into the inner offices. I saw the water cooler. Mr. Kyl and his secretaries were standing around it in a casual group, talking and laughing with each other. They stood there in their good clothes, acting like they had nothing to do while that nice young man and the young secretary struggled with the work load in the outer office, with the desperate people who needed help. Mr. Kyl stood there in his good suit, smiling that smile that he must have thought looked wry. It didn't look wry, it looked smug.

My heart leapt at the sight of him. I felt the gun in my hand, loaded, the safety off, and there was Mr. Kyl, my enemy, mine to kill, mine to punish. How wonderful it felt to raise it, to point it at him, to see his expression when he finally noticed me, when he finally realized what I was pointing at him. To hear the silence that fell, see the smiles slide off those hated faces, see Mr. Kyl down the sights of my gun and pull the trigger, hear the pop, and feel the kick that knocked me right off my feet.

He folded up like a piece of paper and drifted to the floor. His face was such a mixture of pain and surprise, it was almost comical; but I was too shocked to laugh. Everything seemed to be going in slow motion, and he had been screaming for several moments before I even recognized the sound as coming from a human throat. People flocked around him. I sat where I had fallen and tried to get my brain started again.

I finally remembered to pick up my gun. I started to get to my feet. Someone helped me up, took the gun from my hand. I looked up into the horrified face of the young man. His hand was gentle on mine.

"Water?" I croaked.

He led me to a chair and sat me on his lap. Someone else fetched the water, the young secretary from the outer office. She handed me the brimming cup; I couldn't believe it was in my hands. I felt the cool wetness through the paper, I never could get over that sensation.

"Drink slowly," said the young man, but he didn't have to tell me. My thirst was too big to rush. I brought the cup to my lips and took a delicate sip, barely enough to wet my lips. A few drops spilled into my mouth, where my tongue immediately absorbed them. It swelled with the contact.

But I kept sipping tiny bits at a time. While I was working at it, people were rushing in and out of the office. Some people in uniforms came and huddled over Mr. Kyl, who wasn't moving or groaning anymore.

"He's dead," I croaked.

"Why did you shoot him?" asked the young man.

I looked into his face again. He already suspected why I had done it. But I told him anyway, just let everything spill out: Daddy and the girl, the broken things in our yard, the dust and heat and the beautiful things in the living room. Daddy cleaned out the bank account, and Mom wouldn't look at me, the baby didn't even cry any-more and the neighbors chased us off with guns, and Mr. Kyl laughed when Mom begged him. And now ev-eryone was dead except me and I didn't care if I had to go to jail.

He listened to every word. He understood everything I said, even the jumbled-up stuff. He believed me. He asked the secretary to fetch me a little more water; just a little because too much would make me vomit.

He bent his head close to mine. "I'm the head of this office now," he told me. "I'm sending a relief team to your house *right now*. You'll get your water and your relief checks. Okay?"

"Okay," I said, thinking how nice he was, but it was too late. They must all be dead; my trip through the desert had taken years. But they could go and find the bodies, they would know what had happened, everyone would know the truth and that Mr. Kyl had been cruel and wrong.

At least *this* man knew. That was a triumph.

Aten came back with the second cup of water. "Are they going to arrest you?" she asked me.

I took a sip before answering her.

"They questioned me for a little while, but I was only four years old. I told them the same thing I told this nice young man. His name was Mr. Venable. He even stayed with me at the police station. He was my advo-cate. No way Mr. Kyl would have ever done something like that for anyone."

"Mr. Kyl was a sadistic prick," said Aten. "I'm glad you killed him."

I took another sip. "So am I," I confessed. "Do you think that's bad? Am I a sociopath for feeling no guilt?"

"No," said Aten, without the slightest doubt.

"*Someone* had to do something," I said, thinking about my family back home, lying near death. They had tried, but I had had an option that hadn't been open to any of them.

"You killed your first man at four years old," Aten said. "Extraordinary."

"What do you mean, my *first* man?"

But Aten was still thinking. Maybe she was trying to sort out what was mine and what was hers. Maybe she was trying to remember her own childhood. Maybe not, because then she said, "It must have been hard growing up without a family."

"I didn't grow up without a family."

"You were adopted?"

"No, I lived with my own family."

"But they're dead!"

I shook my head. I remembered now. They weren't dead. Even the baby had survived. Another day would have killed them, though.

Aten brightened. "They must have been so grateful to you for saving their lives! Imagine, a four-year-old girl taking that kind of responsibility on herself. Hooray for you, Edna!"

But she was wrong. I remembered now. They hadn't thanked me. Mike and John had gotten scholarships and moved away as soon as they could. Carol had gotten married, and she had gone offworld. David had never stopped blaming me, and the baby . . .

Her name was Katey. She had grown up with no memory of the crises. She had grown up spoiled by Mom, who had felt so guilty about almost losing her that she couldn't stop trying to make up for it. Mom had gotten a job and worked long hours, trying to pay the bills. And I . . .

"Oh well," I said. "Who cares what I did after that? I've remembered enough. I can go back to GodWorld now."

"No, Edna," said Peter Hammill. I was sitting on *his* lap now.

"Why not?" I said. "This was what my recurring dream was all about. I'm finished, I want to go away now!"

"You're not finished," he said firmly. He held me tight on his lap, as if I might try to escape. "You were older when you came to OMSK, Edna. You were in deep trouble, much deeper than this. You don't get sent to OMSK unless you're a hard case. You have to remember the rest of it."

"No," I said, as if I had a choice.

He just looked at me with sad eyes. He was compassionate, like Mr. Venable. He had seen horrors, too. But unlike Mr. Venable, he had *participated* in some of those horrors. And now the burden of it lay behind his blue eyes, across his pale brow, in the lines that framed his mouth. There were shadows on Peter Hammill, just like there were shadows on me.

On me. Killing a man at four and a half. Going home to a family who hadn't understood what I had done, hadn't understood what I had suffered because they were all so caught up in their own struggles. A family that had thought I could take care of myself, whose time and energy had been focused on their own, separate escapes.

And I . . .

I was walking down that dirt road again. But I was different now. My body was tall and strong. My skin was brown where the sun touched it. I knew the terrain around me, I had a water pouch strapped to my hip and I had a bow and quiver of arrows strapped to my back. It was a composite bow, made of bone, sinew, and horn, like the Mongols had made and used thousands of years ago, on Earth. Mr. Allen had made it for me and given it to me on my twelfth birthday.

"Now you can stop pestering me to borrow mine," he had said.

He had made twelve arrows for me, too, but they had metal shafts and synthetic feathers. I never wasted them, I still had all twelve.

I looked to those mountains to the west of my house. They had always called me, from the time I had first been able to toddle. Now I hunted in them. I grinned when I thought about my skill. But the grin was almost devoid of humor.

There was a weight on my shoulders. It was invisible. I knew it was composed of the time that I had lived, the things I had done, the things that had been done to *me*.

And the things that *hadn't* been done. But still, there was a fierce joy lying somewhere near my heart. What was it? I looked for it, and a shadow flew over me.

I looked up, and saw it. I really saw it. It cried out to me in recognition.

"No," I begged Peter Hammill. "I don't want to remember any more."

It was Raptor. My great black bird, my friend. He looked down at me from his flight and pierced me with his eyes.

Those terrible eyes.

"Why are you out here hunting?" Aten asked me. I couldn't see her anywhere, but her voice was clear.

"I don't go to school anymore," I told her.

"Why not? I thought you liked learning stuff."

"Everyone thinks I have cooties," I said, bitterly, thinking of the mothers who had told their children they couldn't play with me because I was too dirty, thinking of the bad reputation I had gotten from killing Mr. Kyl. Some people had known the justice of it: Mr. Allen, Mr. Venable, and the young secretary, some of the police. But most people thought that I made a good scapegoat. They were comfortable thinking of me as subhuman.

Subhuman; but that didn't stop some of the boys from thinking I would be fun to screw. On my knees in the dirt, and grateful for their attention.

Like hell.

"What are cooties?" asked Aten.

"Bugs," I said. "Dirty, smelly, disgusting person."

"Oh that," said Aten, dismissively. "I've gotten that way on some hard assignments. A hot shower and some pesticide wipes that problem out."

I didn't have the heart to tell her that those hard assignments had never happened. Which was too bad, because her past sounded a lot better than mine. Hell, why not pretend that her past *was* mine? If I pretended hard enough, like I had tried to do with Daddy . . .

Yeah, that had worked out real well. Forget it. I had hunting to do. I brought home meat for our table four nights a week; fed myself one hundred percent of the time now. I knew all of the edible plants, I knew how

to get water if my pouch ran out. I had too much pride
to eat Mom's food, but she didn't refuse what I brought
her. As long as I skinned and cleaned it first.

"Why do you hunt with a bow?" asked Aten.

"It's quiet," I said. "Mr. Allen taught me to be quiet."
He had taught me a lot about the desert, hunting, survival, once I was old enough to really listen. A lot of
stuff I had learned on my own. I preferred being alone
anyway, and now I spent ninety-nine percent of my time
that way.

"I'm surprised this world has any large game on it,"
said Aten.

"Depends on what you mean by large," I said. "Jacks
can weigh up to thirty pounds. That's enough meat for
a week."

"How come you have to shoot them? Couldn't you
trap them?"

"Jacks are too smart. They have opposable thumbs,
they love to undo things."

I climbed up into the foothills. The sun beat down on
me, but it didn't bother me much. I had gotten used to
the world, to rationing water, pacing myself, and resting
a lot. I knew how to hunt jacks, too. It took patience.
You had to go well into the mountains, up where their
favorite food grew. They loved roots from the Smith-
berry bush (but hated the bitter berries), and they loved
to chew on purple aloe because it had sweet water in it.
You had to go downwind of a likely looking patch of
jack food and assume a position you could hold for a
couple of hours. And then you had to stay perfectly still.
If you moved a muscle, they wouldn't come out.

For me, that meant kneeling and holding an arrow in
position, ready to shoot. I rested my bow arm on my
knee, didn't try to hold the bow up. Then I concentrated
on my breathing, trying to get oxygen to all of my muscles so they wouldn't scream so much about the immo-
bility. I also had to fight to keep from getting sleepy.

Once I was part of the landscape, all sorts of animals
came out. Puffbirds would come sit on me. Even the
raptors would come around, and they were usually too
shy of people. Too smart, too: they knew I was there
even when I wasn't moving; but if I didn't behave like

a threat, they would sometimes fly overhead. Today they didn't seem to be anywhere near. I made like a statue and waited.

Jacks were delicious. You could eat them all week without getting sick of them. There were lots of different ways to cook them. Mr. Allen had given me a whole book of recipes.

Pricklehogs were edible, too, but kind of tough. You had to cook them forever to get them into a chewable condition. They had tusks, which Mr. Allen used to make things, but it seemed like a lot of hassle to me.

Curlytails weren't bad to eat, but they were almost too small for my arrows. I could put an arrow right through a jack's heart, kill it instantly; but sometimes when I shot curlytails, the poor things would fly to pieces. I felt terrible about that, so I avoided them unless they were really big.

Of course, there were plenty of bushrats around, and they tasted pretty good. They were as small as curlytails, and a lot easier to trap if you wanted to go to that trouble; but I was the only one besides Mr. Allen who was willing to eat them. Mr. Allen and the raptors.

You look like the statue of a young hunter-goddess, said Aten. That was a fanciful thought. I was ugly, all the guys said so. But I was strong and young. It felt good to be out in the world. It was wonderful to become part of the landscape, to let the life flow in around you, to forget time and trouble. I was so good at it, when a jack trotted up to that patch of purple aloe, I didn't even get excited.

He sniffed the air. He didn't suspect me; jacks always sniff around like that. They like to make sure a place is safe before settling down to enjoy themselves. If they weren't moving, you couldn't even see them. They had dirt-colored fur, mottled so they looked just like a patch of ground if they hunkered down and tucked their stubby ears against their heads. Their eyes looked like a couple of black stones. This one was a fat old fellow, obviously wise to the ways of the world. He sniffed, inched closer, sniffed some more, looked around.

Three puffbirds were sitting on me by this time. They talked to the jack.

Bleep! they said. *Bleep!*

It perked its ears up and looked for them. It found them hopping up and down on me, but it took me for stone. I waited.

The jack began to nibble on the aloe. I would shoot soon, but for the moment I just watched him. He should enjoy his aloe a little before he hopped into my stew pot. It was only fair. He would be good, tender and juicy.

In the distance, something went *crack!*

Everything froze, ready to run. I cursed, silently. That had been the distant sound of a gun. Those damned hunters from town made noise that could be heard for miles around. They were idiots, they were creeps, and they were just plain mean. They shot at raptors every chance they got. Never hit one, of course, because the raptors were always well out of range.

The jack was very upset. Hunters from town got jacks more than they got anything else. And they were lousy shots, too; they would inflict terrible wounds instead of killing cleanly. I say if you can't do it right the first time, don't do it at all.

By that time, steam was practically coming out of my ears, I was so mad. The puffbirds were hopping around in an agitated manner and the jack was looking at me again, this time with suspicion in his eyes. I couldn't move to shoot, or I would lose him.

Crack came that damned gun again, this time farther away, but the jack jumped anyway, as if he were dodging the bullet. When he landed, he wasn't facing me anymore, he was looking elsewhere. If I made a sound, he would be off in a flash. I slowly raised my bow. I pulled the string taut and pointed the arrow at the point near his spine that would put it right through his heart.

Something landed on some nearby rocks. I didn't look to see what it was, I just reacted. In one stupid moment I pointed my arrow at it and shot. I didn't even aim properly, but I knocked the thing right off the rocks.

I didn't know what it was. The jack had already disappeared by the time I had gotten to my feet, the puffbirds had flown off, bleeping. I ran to the other side of those rocks and looked down at my prey.

It was a raptor. I had shot it through the muscle that

controlled its right wing. It looked up at me with wide, pain-filled eyes. It was panting; it gave a weak cry when it saw me. Not a frightened cry, more like a query.

Its eyes looked into mine, and a fist closed around my heart, squeezing it mercilessly. Those eyes weren't like human eyes, they didn't hide anything. They were plain, direct, fierce.

Don't try to shoot the raptors, Mr. Allen had warned me. *They're not for shooting, they're hunters, like you.*

"I didn't mean to," I told the raptor. "You startled me."

It just looked at me with those terrible eyes. Those eyes brought me to my knees. I had never felt so helpless, so sorry in all my life. It gave another weak cry.

It had come because it was curious about me. It had wanted to look at me, and I hadn't been carrying a gun, so it hadn't known I could hurt it.

I took off my shirt and wrapped it around my left arm. I presented that arm to the raptor as I sidled around to pick it up. It struck at my wrapped arm with its powerful beak, but it was too weak to do more than tear the cloth, bruise me. At full strength it could have penetrated to the bone.

I don't know how I did it, but I picked the raptor up. I didn't let it grasp my forearm with its talons; they would have gone right into my flesh. Its body was as long as my forearm, its injured wing dragged in the dust, spread out to its full length. Its wingspan was over six feet. It stopped biting when I cradled it against my body. It rested its head against me, still panting, probably in so much pain it couldn't even cry out anymore. I wept at the thought of it.

I carried it back to my neighborhood as fast as I could. I tried desperately not to jar its wounded wing, but I knew it was hurting, I knew it was fading fast. People came out into their yards and stared at me half running down the road with my strange burden, crying, my heart broken even worse than when Daddy had run away.

"Mr. Allen!" I cried as I went up his front walk. "Mr. Allen! Mr. Allen!"

He had been in his workshop. He came to the door

and gaped at me. His face went very serious and sad
when he saw the bird.

"Please fix him," I begged. "Please."

He didn't say anything. He nodded me into the shop,
and then for the next couple of hours I did my best
to assist while Mr. Allen performed an act of amateur
veterinarianism. He found a bandanna and fashioned a
makeshift hood for Raptor. Then he used his metal bit-
ers to pinch off the arrow just below the wound. I had
to hold Raptor while Mr. Allen pulled the broken shaft
out. Raptor cried out, and I tried not to sob too loud.

After that, Mr. Allen could only do his best to patch
up the wound. He stopped the bleeding and bound it
up, but he gave me one of those serious looks after it
was all done and Raptor was resting. It was the same
look he had given Michael and John when they had told
him our water had been shut off.

"He's a wild creature, Edna. He might not get his
wing strength back again, and if he doesn't, there's no
way he can hunt. And even if he heals up proper, he
should never have gotten this close to people. He'll trust
us too much."

I didn't want to believe it. I wanted Raptor to get
better, and then I wanted him to go back to his world
in the mountains and stay there for the rest of his natural days.

"We'll take care of him," I insisted. "And then we'll
send him home again."

I stroked Raptor's head, and he gave a soft cry, this
time not so full of pain. Mr. Allen just looked at me and
shook his head.

I climbed into my bedroom window. I spent as little
time at home as I could. David liked to goad me into
arguments, and sometimes they could get violent. I
would get so mad that Mom and Katey would get scared.
David knew that; he was hoping to alienate me even
further from them. As if it could go any further.

I heard Katey playing music in her room. Mom had
bought her a new music center. She had over a thousand
chips to play on it, and she liked to play it loud. It made
me long for the sound of the desert and the mountains.

She would never know how nice it was just to sit and listen to one of those silly puffbirds.

I was filthy, but that was just too bad. Mom was on one of those low-rate plans where you got only so much water for the day and then nothing came out of the faucets. Everyone else did their bathing in the morning, and my remaining siblings were so hung up on their looks that they spent twice as much time as they needed to in the shower. They probably didn't want to get painted with the same brush that had tarred me; neither of them was even willing to admit that I was their sister.

Mom just did her work, came home and did her best. I didn't bother her about anything, anymore.

I lay down on my bed and prayed for Raptor.

Just before I fell asleep, I felt Aten lying beside me.

"You shouldn't blame yourself," she said. "It was an accident. The human brain just can't process information fast enough."

I hadn't thought of it that way.

"Do you think KLse would have made a mistake like that?" I asked her.

"Maybe," she said. "The fastest information processors in the known galaxy are the Earlies. Everyone else lags way behind."

I tried to remember what the Earlies looked like. I could picture what their glyphs looked like. They had been all over LLna's GodHead robes.

"The Earlies loved to bathe," Aten teased me.

"I do, too."

"If you loved it that much, you would fight Katey and David for shower time."

"I'm sick of fighting them for everything."

And I was sick of being constantly reminded that no one was on my side about anything. No one except sometimes Mr. Allen.

No one but Raptor.

"He loved you," Aten said in a strange voice. Maybe she was beginning to suspect how much I loved the black bird. My friend who couldn't lie, couldn't change his mind, couldn't stop loving just because he had met another bird he liked better.

My friend who couldn't betray.

"I'm on your side," said Aten. "I'll never betray you either."

"Sometimes you remind me of him," I said. It was true; I wondered if I hadn't inadvertently projected Raptor's qualities onto Aten. And because she was a construct, she had absorbed them, become them. I wished I could absorb some of them myself. To be like Raptor, and Aten. Noble. Bold and undoubting.

"Are you going to cry again?" asked Aten.

I was already crying. That part of my face would be clean, anyway. I was thirsty and I couldn't do anything about it, because the faucets were dry.

"He'll get better," I said.

"Jump ahead to that part," said Aten. "Why hang around in the time when you were so worried?"

Why indeed? For some reason I was afraid to jump ahead. I knew Raptor was going to get better, but my heart was aching. Maybe because I knew I was going to have to let Raptor go when he got better. I wouldn't be able to fuss over him anymore, to feed him and help Mr. Allen recondition him for flight and hunting. We had spent months doing that, until I had forgotten how mad I was at my family, how disappointed I was in them. Raptor had become my family; and Mr. Allen, too, though I could tell it was a grudging thing for him. He hadn't wanted to let me get too close, to let Raptor come into his life either, and now he had the two of us to worry about. That wasn't the way a survivalist wanted to live. He wanted to be a hermit, a priest of the desert who didn't have to trust in the ways of fickle humans. I didn't blame him for that.

"We have to let Raptor go," I told Aten. "You're right. That's why I was afraid to jump ahead."

But I was telling Aten lies, and that was just the same as lying to myself. I was afraid of what was going to happen, and yet I was afraid of staying here, too, afraid of worrying about Raptor and feeling the guilt of having hurt him. I *had* to get past the painful part, to leap ahead to the end of things and get this whole sorry experience over with. I was tired, God only knew what was happening to my body in real time, where I was and whether I had had anything to eat or drink. I had to thrust myself into the next part.

In another moment I felt Peter Hammill lying on the other side of me, his hands folded on his chest as if he were a mummy.

"I'm sorry, Edna," he said softly. The pain in his voice filled me with dread.

"Wait," I begged, but it was too late. Time doesn't wait.

And no fair trying to skip it completely.

I woke, briefly, in the middle of the desert. I could see some concrete foundations nearby, but nothing of the houses that had rested on them. I was back in the present, in real time, and I was thirsty. I thought maybe it was over, I wouldn't have to remember anymore. I sat up and looked around.

I wasn't in my old neighborhood anymore. I had walked to what was left of the city. That was why I could see so much evidence of human habitation, even after a thousand years. There were even bits of some buildings left. Those must have been the offices or residences of important officials, institutions that people had thought would be there for the duration.

I was happy to discover that I hadn't urinated in my catsuit. I must have been taking it off when I relieved myself. It was dirty, though. I would have to see if the egg had a change of clothes in it when I got back. I got slowly to my feet. Maybe I would have even made it back to the road that would eventually lead to my egg; but then a shadow passed over me and I looked up.

I was seventeen again, dirty and cootie infested, and hunting with my bow. Raptor was flying near. He and I had become far closer than I had ever imagined. We hunted together. Mr. Allen said he had never seen anything like it.

Raptor would show me where the prey was. I would stalk it and shoot it. He would eat the first kill, as much of it as he wanted. Then he would kill something for me. At first he tried to feed it to me as if I were his mate. But I couldn't humor him in that regard, and he had finally grown accustomed to my strange ways.

I think he would have liked it if I had gone and built myself a nest near his. I think maybe part of me would have liked that, too. He didn't have a raptor mate because of me; I had usurped his affections. It seemed a small price to pay in exchange for his life, at least from my point of view. In the evening, I left him and walked back home. He would fly overhead, watching me until I was out of his territory, and then he would veer off and head for his own home.

I had thought that meant he was safe after all.

"See?" I told Mr. Allen. "He isn't tamed. He isn't going to come into town where people can get a good shot at him."

Mr. Allen would just grunt with this sort of wait-and-see look on his face.

Raptor was following prey for me. He always found it; his skills were far better than mine. But he was patient with my backward ways and my weak eyes.

I watched him circling. I looked at him and loved him and wished it could all go on forever, that what had happened wasn't going to happen after all.

Then there was a *crack* and Raptor dropped from the sky. It wasn't a hunting dive, I knew that.

They must have been watching us from a distance, those hunters from town. They must have congratulated themselves for their cleverness. No one had ever shot a raptor before. No one had that kind of trophy to show off in his living room, stuffed and posed, glass eyes glaring at its admirers.

I ran so hard my heart almost burst. But when I got close enough, I crawled. I could hear their voices then, mean and gloating, like they wanted to fight with somebody. I peeked into a gully and saw those grinning bastards holding Raptor under his wings, admiring the span. His head lolled, the life gone out of him. But his eyes saw me still. They looked at me and pierced me like arrows, until the love and life drained out of my world.

I fitted an arrow to my bow and shot the man who was holding Raptor. It pierced his throat. He was barely falling before I had shot another man through the heart. I kept shooting, while they rushed for cover, confused, uncertain where the shots were coming from, or even what was killing them until the feathered shaft was sticking out of their flesh. Some of them wasted valuable time shooting their guns in the wrong direction.

One arrow for each man and one left over. In a matter of minutes, ten men lay dead or dying. I felt dead, too, but my legs still worked, my arms still worked, my eyes had picked the killing spots with machinelike accuracy. I went to where Raptor had been dropped. He lay in a broken heap.

I straightened his cold body, tried to fold his wings, but they wouldn't stay. He must have died instantly, his eyes were clouded over already, but I didn't see them that way. I still saw them the way they had looked the day *I* had shot him. *I* did.

"What have I done?" I asked Aten. "What have I done?"

She said nothing. She could see it, too, why it had happened.

"I never should have tamed you," I told my dead friend. "I never should have helped you. It's all my fault. Why couldn't I just leave you alone?"

I heard someone else crying, weakly. For a long time I couldn't see anything but Raptor, everything else was all over anyway; I never wanted to see, think, feel, eat, sleep again. The sun could just stop shining and the world could stop turning. But eventually I heard the crying and realized it wasn't mine.

Three of the men I had shot were still alive. I had to finish them off. I still had one arrow; I wondered if I should use my hunting knife to cut their throats. I got up and went to the nearest one, tried to look at him to see what would be the best shot. But he looked back. He looked back with terrible eyes, just like Raptor's.

"Don't shoot, Edna, please don't shoot," he begged in a dreadful voice.

He had an arrow through his shoulder. I had missed vital organs, but he was bleeding to death. He hadn't even been carrying a gun. I thought I knew him; he couldn't have been much older than me.

He didn't understand why I had shot him. Not any more than Raptor had. No, that was for me alone, the burden, the understanding of it all.

"I'll get help," I told him. He just looked more confused. My voice frightened him, it sounded like sand had gotten into my throat. It sounded like the desert itself was talking with my voice.

I ran back to town. I went straight home and phoned the police. I told them everything that had happened. I told them where to find the men.

Then I hung up and waited for them to come get me. Waiting was easy. There was nothing else I wanted to do anyway.

My mom didn't visit me in jail. My brother and sister never would have anyway, but I didn't blame them for that. I didn't blame any of them.

My guards treated me like I was fragile and crazy. I grieved so hard for Raptor, it wore me out. Sometimes I wondered if you could die from grief. I kept thinking about how he had been in life, how he had glided in that big sky. I kept thinking about the days when I had been nursing him back to health. He had trusted me early.

I didn't want to eat. Sometimes I ate just to humor them. They seemed to have figured out why I had shot the men. They gave up trying to talk to me about it, though. And they never told me what people were saying on the outside about what should be done with me. I assumed people thought I should be shot myself. An eye for an eye. But if that was what they were thinking, they were the ones who owed *me* lives.

I didn't want to think about it anymore. I wished I could just stop thinking completely.

Mr. Allen came to visit once. He stood with his head down and his eyes averted. "I wish I'd never helped you," he said. "I wish I'd never taught you anything. You should have been going to dances and wearing fancy clothes like your sister. I wish I'd never even talked to you."

"Raptors' lives are short and sweet," I said, which wasn't really what I meant. I was trying to crowd my feelings into a few paltry words, and they just wouldn't fit. But he understood.

"I'm sorry, Edna," he said finally. "I'm sorry for my part of it."

"It was a good part, not a bad part," I said, and I had to turn my face away, because he was getting ready to cry and I knew he never wanted to do that. I knew he would appreciate the gesture that saved his pride. And mine.

"You're going to OMSK?" he asked, barely able to get the words out.

"That's what they say. They say they'll wipe my memories and start me over again. Maybe that's for the best."

"Never," he choked. "Never for the best. You're fine the way you are. They're the ones that did it to you. Don't know if I would have done different myself if it'd been my friend that was killed. Don't know if *anyone* would. Some things human beings just can't help!"

That was all probably true. But seven men were dead. And if they asked me if I was sorry, I didn't know what I would say. I had hated them when I killed them, even more than I had hated Mr. Kyl. Afterward I felt pity for them, but I would trade their lives in a second for Raptor's. People wouldn't understand that, how you could love a bird more than ten human beings. I was a mass murderer, and mass murderers went to OMSK. I was a hard case.

"I'll still be alive," I said.

He didn't agree, I could tell. He was thinking that only my body would still be alive. Everything that I was would be conditioned out of me. I had thought about it myself, when I wasn't thinking about Raptor. I didn't want to tell him that I liked the idea.

"I'll never forget you the way you were," he said, just before he left. "I'll never forget the way you and the bird took to each other. I wasn't sorry then, I'll tell you. It was purely wonderful. That desert loved you. I guess I loved you, too."

And then he went away, because those were things he had never said to anyone, before.

"I'll try to remember you, too," I called after him, but I was sorry I had said it. Those words probably hurt more than they helped.

A little while later, a guard brought me something to

eat. He sat and tried to talk to me while I struggled through the meal. I think he was trying to make me feel better, but I was too distracted and worn out to be good company. I didn't manage to eat much, either. I gave him the picked-over plate and he shook his head.

"I never saw a case like you before," he said. "Most people who kill act like they didn't do nothing worse than a little shoplifting. But you would starve yourself to death if I didn't come in here and fuss at you. If it was up to me, I wouldn't know what to do with you."

Then he went away, too, and I just sat and stared at the white walls.

A door opened down the hall and Aten walked in. I heard her feet going *flap-flap* on the floor. She stopped on the other side of the bars and looked at me. She looked very thoughtful.

"Mr. Allen was right," she said finally. "I think I would have done the same thing you did."

I didn't tell her that of course she would, since she was me.

"It wasn't your fault," she said.

But it was my responsibility. Hadn't I made choices all my life? Hadn't I plotted my own path? Wasn't I the master of my own disaster?

"They'll wipe me at OMSK," I said. "It'll all be over."

"But they *didn't* wipe you, remember? This is what it's all been about. You've got these memories back again."

"I don't want them."

She didn't answer that. I felt very tired then, so I lay down on my cot and closed my eyes. I could still feel Aten near. I knew she wouldn't take it personally. I just couldn't talk anymore.

A little later I opened my eyes again. I was lying on the desert floor. Peter Hammill was standing over me.

"That's all," he said.

"Thanks." I closed my eyes, but they wouldn't stay shut. I opened them again to find him patiently waiting. He had sat down next to me.

"I couldn't bring myself to wipe you," he said. "I want you to remember that. Others may have blamed you for the things that happened, and I suppose you blame yourself, too; you wouldn't be the person I've admired so much if you weren't so stern with yourself—"

"Admired," I said, chiding him for his bad judgment.

"I know more about you now than I did then," he continued. "But even then I knew you couldn't be what they said you were. And now I know you from the inside out, as it were, and I loved Raptor, too. So did Aten. We know how you feel."

"I killed seven men," I said. "They had families, they had people who loved them. Their wives must have ended up down at Mr. Venable's office, begging for aid. I know that now, and I still hate those men for what they did. I'm still guilty."

He was silent for a long moment, while we both thought about it. A thousand years had passed since the killings, and I had changed, but that only seemed to bring them into sharper relief.

"It's not that you hated those men so much," Peter Hammill said at last. "It's that you loved Raptor so much. People don't usually love that deeply, Edna. And people don't usually have an opportunity to kill those who killed their loved ones. You were right there, you had your bow, your instincts were so strong. I was right there with you, and I killed them, too. So did Aten. And now the three of us are guilty together."

"I'm sorry," I said, but he shook his head.

"I'm not. You've taken me beyond the limits of my programming. You've loaned me life. It must have been because of the GodHeads. When they touched you, they infected you, a little. Some of the GodWeed is in your blood now. It's more like a neurotransmitter, you know, than a drug that acts on neurotransmitters."

I gazed up at the millions of stars overhead. "I didn't know that," I said. "Or maybe I did and I forgot."

He didn't say anything more then. He had done what he had been designed to do. I didn't blame him for it. I was back to my miserable old self, and the grief of losing Raptor was still fresh. Only now I was looking at it with a wider lens, with more experience under my belt, and I could see everything that had gone wrong, everything that had led up to his death, my crime.

"I can't go back to GodWorld now," I said.

"You must," said Peter Hammill.

"You can't tell me that. You can't compel me. Your job has been done. I'm not innocent anymore; they won't take me this way."

He didn't answer that. He just pointed. I had to lift my head to see what he was pointing at, and that was hard. Spots swam before my eyes, making the night even harder to penetrate. But eventually I was able to make out a figure sitting on some nearby rubble. It was a figure in black robes. Red glyphs burned against the fabric like a trail of glowing insects.

"Edna," called the figure. I knew his voice.

I made myself sit up. "KLse?" I called back.

He got up and walked over to where I was sitting in the dust. He looked as tall as a mountain peak. I tried to stand up and face him, but I couldn't. I felt like I hadn't had any water or food for years. My safety pack was gone, though the gun was still strapped to my hip. My feet were bare and dirty, my hair was tangled. I was just a bigger version of the ragged little girl I used to be.

KLse pulled back his hood. His features were sharp and familiar, but his eyes had changed. They were still the same color, but now they were full of the Net. Those raptor eyes that saw all that I was, also saw more than KLse ever could have seen on his own. I withered under his gaze.

"You're a GodHead?" I said, ashamed to be in his presence.

"I *will* be a GodHead," he said.

I looked at him again. He sure looked like a God-Head to me. He was more than he had been, far more, so much so that I couldn't imagine why he would even deign to speak to me now.

"Edna, you were infected by LLna and TGri," he said. "Do you understand? The Net can find you wherever and whenever you go, from the point of infection until you die. I'm not the me you know now, I'm the me I will be in your future."

I gazed at him, drinking in the sight of him. He looked magnificent in his robes. Despite my wretchedness, I was glad to see him. I could hardly believe that such a man had ever been willing to make love to me. Now I knew

I had always seen Raptor in him, even more than I had
seen Raptor in Aten. I knew why he had moved so
quickly into that place where only Raptor used to dwell.

My heart didn't know what to do with it all.

The sky behind him began to lighten. It showed me
what was left of the ruined city. I had walked all the
way there, in the grip of my memories, and my pack was
gone. My water was gone. Dawn was coming, and with
it my death.

"Have you come to say good-bye?" I asked, glad that
I was too dry for tears.

"No!" said KLse. "I've come to tell you to come
home. Come back to GodWorld."

I shook my head. "I can't. I won't make it back to
the egg."

"We're working on that, Edna. Don't be afraid. We
won't let go of you that easily."

"No," I said. "You see what I've done. I'm not your
harmless little Edna. I should stay here where I belong."

"You have always been my concern," he said. "And
you always will be."

I could hardly believe what I was hearing. He was my
KLse, yet his face no longer went back and forth
through the extremes of X'GBri expression. He seemed
more abstract, almost as if he were half occupied with
something else. Yet he was completely aware of me,
completely focused on what I was saying. Is this what
the matriarchs had feared? Did it frighten them when
they couldn't understand a man's body language anymore? Did it hurt Voxi when his LLna looked at him
with so many people behind her, involved in a marriage
far more permanent and intimate than what he had
shared with her?

Puffbirds were bleeping at the dawn. Bushrats were
sniffing around the ruins, watching me with one eye as
they hunted for something to nibble. They couldn't see
Peter Hammill or KLse, because they weren't there.

"They can't see me," agreed KLse. "But I'm here,
Edna. I can touch you." And he did. He knelt next to
me and put a warm hand on my cheek. I leaned into it,
closed my eyes and tried to smell his skin. I thought

maybe I could, but I wasn't sure. I hoped he couldn't smell me, because I was a dusty mess.

He clicked his teeth. "I would lick you clean if I could."

"I wish you could give me water," I said.

"Can you get to some purple aloe? That would sustain you long enough to get back to the egg."

"No. That grows in the mountains. One day's walk from here, and I haven't got that much steam left." I turned my face into his palm. It didn't feel solid. Not totally. But it was real enough to make me happy, at least for the moment.

"Voxi will be surprised when he learns what you've done," said KLse. "You're not the little nothing he thought you were. You're more like Aten than he could have guessed."

"There is no Aten," I said. "She's me."

"She exists," said KLse. "She doesn't know the truth yet. Her mind is protecting her from it."

"You mean *my* mind is protecting her."

"No. That's not the case."

I sighed. I didn't want to argue with him, I didn't want him to take his hand away. But I was so confused. I had just gone back and retrieved myself. Aten wasn't here now. Bits and pieces of her had kept me company on my journey, but now where was she? And *what* was she?

"What is a mind?" I asked him. He should be the expert, now that he was in the Net. "I only have one brain, so I really only have one mind. Aten is a delusion."

"No," said KLse. "In your case, it's hard to come up with simple answers. It's hard in the Net, too, to say what a mind is, except that you always know one when you meet it. And I have met Aten."

I almost felt jealous then, which was silly considering that Aten and I were the same woman. But I also felt hopeful, because I missed her. The jealousy died before it could even take root.

"The Net is one mind and many minds," said KLse. "Many brains contribute to its existence. And yet the sprite has no brain at all, but it definitely has a mind."

"The sprite?"

"GodWeed," he said. "It's self-aware. It's aware of us. It's aware of *you,* Edna. Do you feel my hand?"

"Yes," I breathed.

"We're going to try something we never tried before. We have some ideas about travel that we've been testing. We've had some limited success. There are enough of us in the Net now that I think we can make it work."

"Travel?" I said into his palm.

"It's tricky because you're not a GodHead," he said. "But the Net has touched you. The sprite is in your blood. You have to find it, Edna."

"Help me," I begged, though I didn't really know what he was talking about.

We're still linked, he said. *Open the eyes you have inside you.*

I still had no idea what he meant, but I could feel him in there tugging at our old link. It was such a relief to have him there again. I had missed him so. I reached for him across that inner landscape, I felt his hand in mine, just as I felt it on my face. I realized it was the same thing; it had all been going on inside, but I had hallucinated the tactile responses.

Open your eyes, coaxed KLse.

I did. I saw light first, blinding light. KLse was still there, but I couldn't see him anymore. I was sprawled on the desert floor, under a sun that was far crueler than the one my homeworld circled. I knew it was crueler, yet it didn't burn me. It seemed to stop just short of that.

It was GodWorld's sun.

"Good trick," I said. "I didn't even have to use the egg to get here."

No, said KLse, *you haven't gone anywhere yet. You're in No Time. Lift your head and look around you.*

I did. It was an interesting view. Thousands of people were all around me, stretched out, like I was, on a desert floor. At the foot of each one, including me, a little plant was growing. It had a round base, sort of like a cactus, and three buds that grew on stalks.

The one at my feet started moving. It put its side buds on its hiplike base and talked to me out of the middle bud.

"Hello," it said. "So far so good!"

"Are you the sprite?" I asked.

"Yes," it said. "I'm pleased to meet you. I've never done this trick before, so I'm a little nervous."

"You're nervous?" I had never seen a nervous plant before. And I was surprised that this little fellow was so friendly, too; I had thought anything as powerful as GodWeed would be like a roaring dragon. But it really was friendly, I could feel it in my blood. It was doing this because it *liked* me. *Me,* with all of my considerable faults. That was salve for my wounded heart.

"Can you see the other people?" it asked.

"Yes." I checked to make sure it was still true.

"Those plants growing at their feet are me. I'm me, too. Don't let it confuse you too much, it makes sense when you remember that I'm a plant. Those people are all people who have been here at some time in their lives. Theoretically, this desert stretches into infinity, because a lot of people will eventually be in the Net."

"I thought this was No Time," I said, trying not to think too hard about it.

"Right," said the sprite. "That's how I know our endeavor will probably be successful. Here's how it works. I suspect that you can travel through space in this realm. You have to go to a spot where you will eventually be. I do it all the time, but I just jump from self to self. You'll be doing that, too, in a way. You'll find your other self, the one who's at the egg."

"Wait a minute," I said. "Isn't that cheating? I can't be at the egg unless I get there."

The sprite rubbed its head bud with one of its side buds, thoughtfully. "I don't think it's cheating," it said at last. "It wouldn't work if it were."

"Well, maybe it won't work."

"It will," it said confidently. "I've been all over this realm, and I know you'll be at the egg. I know we're going to talk again, too. I've seen it. But the trick is, *you* have to know it. You have to get there."

I got slowly to my feet. Despite my new perspective, I couldn't see that much farther across the desert. People still stretched as far as the eye could "see."

"Can I walk there?" I asked.

"I don't see why not," said the sprite. "If that's what

helps you visualize progress, that's what you should do. I usually just spread my pollen out on the wind and float around."

I didn't think I could spread my pollen, though it sounded rather pleasant. I moved my feet instead.

"Which way?" I asked the sprite.

"Just follow your nose," it said.

I couldn't smell anything in particular, but I assumed it meant I should follow my feelings, just like I had on my homeworld. I had found my old neighborhood that way. And I was still on my homeworld, so the feelings should still be there.

They were. I went after them.

"Good-bye," I told the sprite.

"Good-bye," it said, brightly. "But you're not really leaving me. I'm all over the place."

I started to pick my way through people. Some of them seemed to be sleeping, others were talking to their own version of the sprite. I noticed that some of the sprite plants were in full bloom, others barely had buds on them. I tried not to listen to the conversations. What I overheard didn't make a lot of sense anyway, and some of it sounded really personal.

I was so busy trying not to intrude, I tripped over someone. She yelped, and I went down right on my face. I scrambled off her, and she sat up. I wiped sand out of my eyes.

"I'm sorry," I said. "I've never done this before."

"That's okay," she answered. "What are you doing?"

I took a hard look at her. She was beautiful, one of those women with golden-brown skin, amber eyes, and black hair, like the people I had seen on GodWorld. Her hair was longer than mine, and braided. But she wasn't the only one I saw there. I could see another face, right over hers. The other face was like a friendly salamander's, except that the eyes were full of lively intelligence, and the face was so mobile that the slightest movement in it spoke volumes. Were two people occupying the same space, at a different time?

"Which one of you am I talking to?" I asked them.

"Both," they answered. "We're just one person."

"Oh," I said, thinking that I understood. "Me, too. Right now I'm Edna."

"I'm An," they said, but they meant both of them. They weren't two people at all, like Aten and me. They were one. *She* was one. And something about her was familiar.

"An—" I said. "Have we met?"

"Maybe," she said, studying me closely with both pairs of eyes. "Some people know me as Ankere. I took that name later in life."

Ankere. The one who brought the Earlies back. The one who became an Early herself. Now I remembered all that stuff, and now I understood what it had really meant.

"Nice to meet you," I said.

"But I know you," she said. "Now I remember you. I had a dream about you, once. You were the thirsty one."

"I'm still thirsty. And I hope you didn't dream me up!"

"So what are you doing?" she asked. "I didn't know people could walk here."

"I'm trying to get back to my egg. The sprite says I'm going to get there anyway, so I can do it."

Ankere looked past me, at her own sprite. "Is that true?" she asked.

"Yes," it said. "But I didn't know she would be able to talk to people. This opens up the possibilities for communication even farther. It's staggering in its implications!"

Ankere looked very happy about the prospects of improved communication. Her Early face was absolutely delighted.

"I'd better get going," I said, climbing to my feet again. "If we keep talking, I could be here forever."

"This is No Time," said the sprite. "There is no forever."

"Don't confuse her," Ankere laughed. "Go find your egg, Edna. We'll talk again."

I climbed to my feet and got my bearings. "I'll see you"—I almost said *later,* but then thought better of it— "in another part of No Time."

Ankere waved with a hand that was human and one that was webbed. The sprite waved one of its blossoms.

I picked my way across infinity. Conversations ran together in my mind. I tried even harder not to listen; now that I knew I could talk to anyone I wanted, I was worried I'd get sidetracked. I tried not to look at anyone either, because once I thought I saw KLse in the distance. He might be having his first conversation with the sprite, for all I knew, and I didn't want to mess that up.

Eventually I thought I saw an oval shape gleaming up ahead. I couldn't fix my eyes on it; it was sort of ghostlike, like an image reflected on a window through which I was looking. My nose guided me toward it.

"That's it!" called one of the sprites.

"You've made it!" called another.

"Come home," called a third. "We're waiting for you on GodWorld."

Open your eyes, said KLse.

I had thought they were already open. I was so caught up in the illusion that it took me some time to shift my perceptions and open my real eyes, the ones that looked *outside* my head.

I opened them. My egg solidified inside a real landscape. I took a step toward it and was unpleasantly surprised when gravity and inertia gripped me. It had been so easy to move through No Time. But I was complaining about nothing. I had skipped over miles of terrain, days of travel by foot; now I could certainly walk a short distance to save my life.

KLse was gone. That hurt. He was back in the future, and the KLse who lived in Real Time didn't even know where I was now. I would have to be patient and find my way back to him. And when I did, I would have to give him time to love me, just like I had done with Raptor. Only this time, it would be KLse healing *my* wounds.

I found my own prints in the dust, the ones I had made when I had ventured out days before. Other prints crossed them: little scratches in the dirt that belonged to puffbirds, the hooves of a curlytail, the prints of a jack. My mouth watered at the sight of those. But then I saw something new.

They weren't prints, they were gouges, like something heavy had been stuck into the soft ground, something sharp. But they were regular, they bisected my prints from the left and then circled around and went right up to my egg.

And the hatch was open. I stopped and looked at it. Something was in there, something just behind the shadows, looking at me. Something big. Something that made a sound.

"vvvvvvvvvvvvvvVVVVVVVVVVVOOOOOOOOOOOOO ooooooooooorrrrrrrrrn," it said. It pulled itself out of the hatch and perched halfway in and halfway out, an impossibly huge insect with dripping jaws. I gaped at it. Nothing like it had lived on this planet while I had. As far as I knew, nothing like it had lived in the universe.

I felt for my gun. It was still there, but when I started to draw it, I suddenly thought of Raptor.

Draw the gun, I told myself. *Shoot.* And I agreed with myself. But my hands just shook, I couldn't make myself do it. I couldn't make myself kill again, not anything, not even to save my life. And in the meantime, the creature had pulled its enormous bulk out of the egg and was crawling toward me on six limbs, dripping saliva as it came. I just stood there like an idiot.

Not a bug, I thought to myself, inanely. *No exoskeleton. And it's too big, couldn't move under its own weight if it were an insect.* Like any of that made a difference if it wanted to eat me, which it certainly looked like it did; yet I couldn't make myself pull the gun. The creature crowded up to me and grabbed me in its forelimbs. Its jaws encircled me and saliva dripped on my face. It tasted me with some short hairs on its mandibles.

It froze. Then it let me go and scuttled back as fast as it could.

"GodHead," it said, in perfectly understandable Standard.

I just stood there and twitched. I still wasn't thinking; I should have run for the egg, but my body had other ideas. I gazed at the thing and suddenly realized what it was.

"Vorn?" I asked it.

It didn't nod or say yes; it must have thought the question was completely irrelevant. Instead it just said, "Sorry," and crawled away. It moved very fast on those multiple limbs: I was glad I hadn't tried to run. It would have caught me, easy.

So that's what a Vorn looked like. That's the sound I had heard that first night here, when I had thought I was dreaming, and that was why humans didn't live here anymore. They had told me on OMSK about the Vorn war, told it all in past tense, because Ankere had ended all that when she had figured out how to talk to the Vorns. You couldn't just make speech sounds—you had to do it with smell and taste, too. If I hadn't had the GodHead smell on me, the Vorn might have eaten me.

The humans must have fled a Vorn invasion. I had a moment of panic, worrying about my family; then realized that the Vorns hadn't become a force in this part of the galaxy until six hundred years after my family had been dead.

Dead. Dead for a thousand years. My family dead, and Mr. Kyl dead, and seven men. Mr. Venable and Mr. Allen and Raptor. And now only Vorns lived here; but even they hadn't been that successful on this planet. I wondered why.

And then I stopped wondering. I climbed into my egg and closed up the hatch. I lay on the couch for several minutes and looked at controls, sipping water from a tube and lazily wondering if I should clean my dirty feet before I took off. The sun shined through the view windows and into my face again, and I let myself think about how much I still liked this world.

Look, Aten said, though I couldn't see her. *Look out the view windows.*

I sat up and looked. At first I didn't know what she meant, but then I saw the shapes wheeling in the sky.

The raptors are here, she said. *They survived. Your Raptor still lives, in them. See them, Edna? They don't know about people anymore. They're safe.*

My heart stopped as I watched them. But then it lurched to life again. It beat strongly, reminding me that I still lived, too. I still lived and I wanted to keep doing it. Raptor was safe now. I couldn't hurt him anymore. And he had forgiven me anyway, long ago when he had let his head rest against me as I had carried him back to town. He had forgiven me.

Rest now, Aten told me. *I'll take the egg up. You've paid your dues, Edna. And then some. Rest.*

I lay back on the couch. The sunlight was warm there. Aten couldn't pilot the ship, of course, because she didn't exist outside me. But I didn't want to tell her that. One of us knowing the truth about her past was plenty, for the time being. I couldn't even think about approaching that other issue. Not yet.

The warmth of the sunlight slowly faded. Aten must have closed the radiation shields. But she must have done it with my hand. That wasn't a good sign. I hadn't even felt her do it. My hand fell back on the couch, limply, as if it had suddenly realized to whom it belonged.

I had to rouse myself and take care of business. In another moment I would.

I closed my eyes. I didn't feel better, exactly; I just felt more at peace. I still grieved for Raptor, I still wished with all my heart that I hadn't made that first mistake when I had shot him and bound him to me. But time had passed, I had changed, the universe had rolled on, and the raptors still hunted the skies. It was enough, and I was tired now.

I was falling asleep. I knew I'd better open my eyes and get started. I shouldn't spend one more night there; who knew if the Vorn would come back? It might change its mind about eating me. I had to wake up and attend to business.

I fell asleep. Panic touched me as I went down, warning me about something that had nothing to do with the Vorn. I was in trouble, but it was too late.

I was going too far down to get up again.

Once Edna was asleep, her iron grip on me finally began to relax. I tried not to get excited as I felt it slipping away. I just waited for my chance, and then I gave her an extra sedative once she had let me go.

She went into a deep, safe sleep.

I breathed a sigh of relief. It had to happen, of course; once Peter Hammill had shown up in her psyche, the only way to get rid of the compulsion was to go back and retrieve those lost memories. She had infected me with her psychosis through our link and dragged me along. I had tried to help when I could, but I had been helpless baggage most of the time.

I stretched like a cat. It felt so good to be free! The first thing I did was use the bathroom unit. I had had to urinate for hours, just like Edna. I had suffered everything she had, the thirst, the pain of a swollen bladder, the humiliation or being rejected by her community, the pain of being abandoned by her father. . . .

If I kept thinking about it, I would get to the Raptor part and I would cry.

Poor Edna. She had suffered so much. I didn't mind that she had kidnapped me. She hadn't meant to do it. Bomarigala would have to hear about this particular side effect of the synthetic. It would certainly throw a monkey wrench into his plans. Edna's brain had controlled me, utterly. At times I had even forgotten that I existed.

I strapped us into the couch and fired the takeoff engines, blowing us out of the gravity well. Edna didn't stir once, not even when the g-forces were pressing down on us. Once we were free of the planet, I keyed a jump for GodWorld into the system. I didn't even have to calculate it; it was part of the standard programming. This egg wasn't just a fancy toy, that was for sure. It had been used for business. I hoped its owner wouldn't feel compelled to kill us for taking it.

I used wet wipes to clean myself up, then combed clean foam through my hair. Edna's homeworld was a beautiful place. I had liked it, too. But I had missed hot showers.

I didn't try to clean Edna up. I didn't want to wake her. In fact, I hoped she would stay asleep until I could talk with Bomarigala about possible solutions. I didn't want to lose my link with Edna; I had grown used to it. There had to be another solution.

I didn't rest until I was sure Edna was still under. No problem; she was out cold. I checked her vitals to make sure she wasn't *too* far under. I cared about her welfare as much as I cared about my own.

That was an interesting thing to realize. I had always cared about Edna, but her memory adventure had done something to me. I wasn't the same person anymore, either. My heart ached when I thought about Raptor, but it also sang now that I was free again. It was an odd combination. I fell asleep thinking about it.

I dreamed about No Time, but I knew I wasn't really there. In my dream, we never made it back to the egg, we just kept tripping over people.

When I woke up, the egg was signaling that we had gone into orbit around GodWorld.

I sat up in a panic. How long had I slept? My bladder told me it had been a lot longer than I should have.

Edna was still asleep. Once I had checked her vitals, I relieved myself, then searched our stores for some safety boots. I had been forced to take mine off while Edna had us both in the grip of her psychosis, and now mine were lost, too. I had always heard that schizophrenics had a habit of taking off their shoes and walking around barefoot. It was an uncomfortable thought.

And I couldn't find any safety boots. We would just have to look like weirdos until I could buy us some new ones. I didn't think we'd have to dodge any killer plants; the starports had plenty of shops for people who wanted to get decked out in safety gear before meeting the challenge of GodWorld. But I worried about the hot pavement we might encounter on our way in. A type-F star could fry bare feet pretty fast.

Traffic around GodWorld was heavy, but at least there weren't any superstorms going on. I was allowed to pilot the egg down myself. Of course, since our registration was X'GBri, we went down in an X'GBri port. I hoped we weren't about to get into more trouble than we could handle.

But no one came to greet us at the landing site. There was just the usual transport vehicle that you could rent. I popped the hatch and climbed out to survey our situation. I emerged into the blazing daylight, which completely whited out my vision. I had to go back and get some protective goggles before I could see anything.

GodWorld's sky was just as wide as the one over Edna's homeworld. I felt a pang of artificial homesickness. I looked across the shipyard and saw people walking here and there in the distance, attending to their own business. They were bundled up against the harsh light, so I couldn't see what race they were; but their height seemed un-human. No one was paying the slightest attention to us.

The transport vehicle had pulled itself up to our site automatically; it was just a few steps away. I hopped across the gap and managed to get into the transport vehicle without burning any toes. Its control board was user friendly, with simple directions in four different languages. I entered the matriarch's code into the vehicle's terminal, and it lit up like a Christmas tree. Apparently she had endless credit, anywhere she wanted it. That sort of scared me, considering that I was stealing it. But there was nothing I could do about it at the moment, so I went back to the egg. I would have to pick Edna up and carry her to the vehicle myself.

Only she wasn't there.

Her safety straps were undone, and the bathroom unit had been used again. She wouldn't have had time to get far from the egg. She didn't have goggles or protective clothing, she would be dazzled and sunburned pretty fast. I climbed out and stood up on the lip of the hatch, trying to see as far as possible. There were a lot of ships near me, people still walking back and forth taking care of business, but I didn't see Edna. She might be hiding behind one of those ships, but why would she do that? Was she afraid of me now?

"Edna!" I called at the top of my lungs, then felt like slapping myself on the head.

Edna, I called through our link. I felt the message go out, but the link didn't seem to go anywhere. I called and called to her, but my calls just seemed to fade into infinity.

She wasn't there. Our link had dissolved.

All of the strength went out of my limbs. I had to ease myself to the ground or I would have fallen. Once there, I couldn't even stay on my feet, I sat down on the tarmac. Even in the shade, the heat burned my butt through my clothing, but I didn't care. My mind hummed like a machine that's been left on long after its usefulness is over.

"Edna," I tried to call again, but my voice had no strength.

I was amazed, because I was devastated. I should just have been worried, puzzled. What was wrong with me? It was almost as bad as Edna had felt about losing Raptor.

Calm down, I told myself. *Get a grip. Say a mantra.*

So I did, until my body began to feel normal again. I was able to get up. I was able to close the egg's hatch and hop over to the vehicle. I was even able to begin to formulate a search plan. There was a limit to the number of options Edna had. She could try to contact KLse, if he was here. I was betting that was exactly what she would do.

She hadn't run away from me, she had just forgotten me. It was her psychosis. I supposed I should be grateful that I wasn't in thrall to her anymore, she hadn't dragged me along this time.

But I *missed* her so much. And now I was worried, too.

Calm down, I reminded myself. I programmed directions into the vehicle's brain and sat back. It glided onto an access road and pointed its nose toward the main port terminal. There would be coms in there, I could call KLse myself and coordinate with him.

I drove along in relative peace for about fifteen minutes before I realized that the vehicle was veering away from its path. I checked the board for malfunctions, but there weren't any. Someone else had overridden my command.

Oh-oh. Someone had recognized the matriarch's code. I wondered if I should try to jump out of the vehicle. But it was moving way too fast for that, so I was stuck. I sat back and tried to think up a good excuse for using the matriarch's code, not to mention her egg and her credit. . . .

Needless to say, nothing occurred to me. In another five minutes, the vehicle was pulling up to a small, private building, in a shaded receiving area. A group of armed men were waiting out front for me. They were wearing protective clothing, but this close I could tell they were X'GBris. No one else could be that tall. I tried not to look too scared as the door popped open and a big hand reached for me.

I took it, as if I were simply a lady being helped out of a vehicle by a gentleman. The grip seemed oddly gentle, considering that I was being arrested. He helped me out of the car and gazed down at me for several moments through his goggles. Then he pulled them off, along with part of his face mask, and I was looking up at Voxi. I gaped at him, amazed that I was actually glad to see him.

And then he hugged me so hard he almost squeezed the life out of me.

GODWORLD

I thought I would never see you again, Voxi said through our link. *I thought you were gone for good.*

I had worried my reaction was unwise; Voxi's seemed downright reckless, in comparison. But his feelings were genuine. I was so surprised by the strength of his emotions I couldn't think what to answer. I was having enough trouble just breathing. Finally he released his stranglehold and stood with his hands on my shoulders, searching my face.

"I'm glad to see you, too," I managed. It was true, though he certainly hadn't done anything to earn my regard, except perhaps be himself, I suppose. His expression was stern; anyone looking at us would have thought he hadn't liked what he had heard, but he did like it.

My life was getting more complicated, not less.

"Edna is missing," I suddenly remembered to tell him.

"Good," he said. "You're better off without her."

I wished he would stop saying that. He had said it before, when Edna and I were hurt, after the mirrors had been broken, when she could least stand to hear such a thing. Just thinking about that time made me dizzy. I shook my head, as if I could get my brain to think straight that way. All I managed to do was give myself a mild headache.

"Come inside," Voxi said. "You need protective clothing, even under the screened areas. You're not dressed for this world."

They were all looking at what was left of my pretty lounging outfit, and at my bare feet. X'GBri frowns were creasing their faces. I knew I was a sight, though I had cleaned up a little in the egg.

"I want to call KLse first," I said, and the frowns deepened.

"Why?" snapped Voxi.

"He's the first guy Edna will try to contact. I want him to be on the lookout for her. She doesn't have the right clothing either, Voxi. She doesn't even have shoes."

He scowled so hard his hybrid face almost achieved full X'GBri status. He was thinking hard, shutting me out of the link while he did it. Finally he seemed to reach some kind of peace with himself, and his face relaxed again.

"I'll call KLse," he said. "I'll take care of finding Edna. You go with my spouses to the gear shops."

He took my arm and guided me toward the entrance doors. His spouses fell in behind us.

"By the way," he said, "you're under arrest."

I laughed, nervously. He didn't join me. I thought about telling him it wasn't me, that Edna's psychosis had kidnapped me, that I had just been a helpless passenger all this time. But I didn't want him to blame Edna, not when he had promised to help find her.

"Am I going to jail?" I asked, thinking about the hug I had just received.

"You're going to the GodHeads," said Voxi.

"Edna is the one they want."

Voxi ushered me in through the automatic doors. He and his fellow spouses surveyed the area. Other X'GBris were going about their business, some singly and some in groups. A few took notice of us, but their gazes were politely disinterested. Voxi satisfied himself that it was safe to enter, and then he spared me a glance.

"You and Edna are a package deal," he said.

He gestured to one of the other husbands, who took my arm. Voxi veered off toward the coms and I was tugged along to the shops.

We went into a human-owned business. I wondered if that was to put me at ease or if the X'GBris preferred to have humans do certain things for them. I almost laughed at how studiously the clerks ignored my ragged appearance. They even offered me some wet wipes for my feet, and then some slippers to walk about in while I picked out what I needed. I doubted they would have been so courteous to me if I hadn't been accompanied by my three giant, scowling friends.

I had put on a safety suit (a very spiffy and expensive one, just to be difficult) and was looking at some safety boots when my brain suddenly tapped me on the shoulder and reminded me of something.

If KLse was on GodWorld, I could call him through the link.

I studied the boots, pretending to look for a pair that was more feminine (as if safety boots ever could be), while I felt along the link for Voxi, to see if he was monitoring me. I felt no trace of him.

I had never called someone from a long distance. I had never really thought to use the link that way before; it had just been something that made Edna and me a team, something we could use to make our job easier. Since Voxi had come along, I had been practicing shutting the thing *down,* keeping people out. I hadn't even thought to explore my limits in the other direction.

I couldn't just yank on the link. Anyone who was hooked up to it would feel me doing that. But I could spread myself out into it and just—open up. Just thinking about it was enough to make it happen, kind of like what the future KLse had told Edna to do to get to No Time. I had to open some inner eyes.

Once I had done that, I could feel all the lines stretching out into the world. I even tried to follow the one that led to Edna, but that didn't work. That was a mystery I was going to have to solve later; for now I just took a look at the structure of things.

Our little net was fragile. It might not have seemed that way to me if I hadn't been able to see what was lying beyond it. When I opened my inner lens far enough, I could see a universe around it, a structure so vast and complex that at first I didn't recognize it for what it was: the GodHead Net. It brushed against the wispy links of our synthetic net, strengthening it in some places when it formed temporary connections. Or almost formed them. Something hadn't happened yet, something I needed to do. . . .

"Try these, they're size nine," the saleswoman said, almost making me drop the threads. I dutifully sat down, put on my new socks, and shoved my foot into a boot. I tried to pay attention to how it felt when I stood up again; wouldn't want to be stuck in painful boots for the rest of my visit.

Inside, I took firmer hold of the delicate threads of the synthetic net, trying to ignore the siren song of the GodHead Net, so temptingly close.

KLse? I called.

Someone touched me back, instantly. I was even pretty sure it was KLse. But in another moment, someone else had slammed the door shut on me, nailing me down so hard I could barely contain a cry of alarm.

I looked at Voxi's spouses. They all looked back at me, knowingly.

"You've been infected by the synthetic?" I asked the one who seemed to have the most authority.

Yes, he answered through the link, and I knew he must have been the slammer. His mental presence was unmistakable. He was very strong, he almost felt like a GodHead. I narrowed my door to the link again, sadly, knowing I'd better keep those thoughts to myself.

I tugged the other boot on. They both fit well. I sighed with relief; at least my feet would feel good now.

It's good to have shoes on again, I told the slammer.

You were barefoot all this time? he asked, a flicker of curiosity reaching his face.

Edna walked barefoot when she was a little girl. She wanted to feel the ground under her feet again.

He let more curiosity trickle down the link. He paid for my things while the other two watched me. They were infected, too. They let me know, wordlessly.

As we left the shop, I asked the slammer, *What's your name?*

Why? Are you interested in me? he said.

I don't want to call you "Hey you."

You've never done that.

Okay, fine.

They surrounded me and escorted me through the

busy terminal. We stopped in front of the exit and slipped our hoods over our heads, putting on our goggles and face masks before walking out into the blazing daylight.

And into dead silence. No one was there but us. The heat was one possible reason. Afternoon had advanced since I had been in the shops, and it now felt about twenty degrees hotter. The safety clothes we were wearing weren't designed to keep us cool, but I was grateful for them as we walked across an empty parking lot. I could feel the acid fingers of that cruel light trying to pry its way around the protective fabric. It was hard to adjust to it, even with the goggles on.

I wondered just where the heck we were going, out in the middle of all that hot, bright nothingness. Then a plain van with opaqued windows pulled into the lot and stopped about ten feet from us. My escorts didn't seem alarmed at the sight of it. Voxi climbed out of the driver's side and walked around to our side. He pulled open the sliding passenger's door and climbed in. He waited for me with his hand out.

The slammer was walking around to the driver's side.

My name is KRni, he told me as he climbed behind the wheel.

I took Voxi's hand and he helped me into a seat. I couldn't tell if he had heard KRni's message to me or not. I really wondered, because KRni's command of the link was stronger than any I'd ever felt. I wondered if a challenge was on the horizon. If it was, it wouldn't necessarily involve any physical grappling. Would that be another big change for X'GBri society? Or was I simply ignorant of the full nature of their struggles for status?

Voxi sat on my left; another husband sat on my right. The fourth husband slammed the door and then settled in back, where he could look out the back window. We all pulled off our goggles and masks, safe in the filtered light from the windows.

KRni turned the air conditioning on full blast, and we pulled out of the lot and sped down the main drag, away from the starport.

We were headed into the open desert.

"Where are we going?" I asked.

"Red Springs," said Voxi.

I remembered that name. That was where TGri was supposed to be waiting for Edna, at the GodHead monastery. If my memory served me correctly, it would take a couple of days to get there by land vehicle.

"What about Edna?" I asked. "She should be coming with us. Did you call KLse?"

"That's taken care of," he said. "Don't worry about it."

His tone seemed to be saying *Don't ask about it anymore.* I didn't like the sound of it.

"She didn't have any safety clothes," I reminded him.

"She does now," he said, confidently.

"How do you know?"

"Because I took care of it myself. She's safe, and she's with people who will look after her. Let the GodHeads decide what should be done with her, Aten."

Done with her. Like she was a problem instead of a person. And how had he straightened things out so quickly? I wasn't at all sure that I should believe him. Yet I couldn't detect a lie in him.

"Am I still under arrest?" I asked.

"Yes."

The dusty road stretched into infinity ahead of us. Another vehicle passed us going the other way, buffeting us with displaced air. Voxi and my other seat companion were tense until it was out of sight.

"What happened to the matriarch's vehicle?" I asked.

"She picked it up," said Voxi.

"She's here?" I asked, alarmed.

"No. Her agents are here. Her agents are always here."

"I thought *you* were her agents." I looked at him out of the corner of my eye.

"There are agents," he said. "And then there are agents."

He was teasing me. I probed him through the link, gently, trying to bear in mind that a short while before he had hugged the breath out of me. He started, but then let me come closer.

All hell busted loose when you disappeared, he told me.

I'll bet.

Where did you go?

Edna's homeworld.

Where is that?

I gave him the coordinates. They meant nothing to him, so I tried to show him a mental picture of the place. It was easy to imagine, since we were currently driving through another desert. As I thought about it, it became easier, realer. Sharing the analog with Voxi was lending it more substance. I showed him Edna's mountains, the raptors. I showed him Mr. Allen and Mr. Venable. I showed him Edna with her bow, stalking prey.

He was impressed. And then without meaning to, I showed him the bodies of the men she had killed.

He was even more impressed.

That's how she ended up at OMSK? he asked.

Yes.

None of it was a waste, he said, with more sympathy than I'd ever seen from him. *It brought you here.*

Here. To the GodHeads. That thought gave me pause. Was the Net really so much bigger than the individual lives that it swallowed? Was it bigger than Edna's grief? If it was, I hadn't been taking it seriously enough.

When you disappeared, he said, *you almost caused a civil war. No one could believe that you had escaped by yourself, so everyone thought everyone else had kidnapped or rescued you. Feuds that have been brewing for generations almost came to a head. The GodHeads had to intervene.*

So at last they had been forced to throw their weight around. That had probably frightened the matriarchs even more.

Some of them, agreed Voxi.

Like the one whose property we stole.

Maybe.

Is your society really that unstable? I wondered.

We always had our checks and balances, our rituals and protocols. The Net is going to reorganize all that. Some think it should, some think it shouldn't, some wish the whole problem would just go away. There it is in a nutshell.

I could hear myself telling Edna, *Situations don't really*

fit very well in nutshells, do they . . . ? How long ago had I said that? Seemed like forever.

Another car buffeted us on its way past. This time I caught a glimpse of what worried Voxi. He was afraid someone would stop us before we got to the GodHeads. But he managed to keep the identity of our would-be antagonists secret.

How come you didn't tell the GodHeads to come get us? I asked.

He didn't answer that, but I caught a trickle of the truth when he automatically checked on something. He checked on KRni. Something KRni was doing. Knowing KRni's strength, I had a notion what that might be.

He's shielding us from the GodHeads, I said. *Why?*

You'll know all within a couple of days, Voxi said. *Be satisfied with that.*

Of course, I wasn't. But I kept quiet. He was right, one way or the other we were going straight to the monastery. Whatever plans Voxi had, the Net would have plans of its own. He was audacious to think he could work things his way. That was a trait humans shared with X'GBris. You could almost admire it, if it weren't such a pain in the ass.

He clicked his teeth at me. Our van continued to speed its way toward infinity.

Night fell, but we didn't stop to rest. KRni switched places with the husband who had been riding shotgun. We nibbled road rations (actually, I nibbled and they swallowed stuff whole), and we stopped a couple of times at roadside rest areas for bathroom breaks. But we weren't wasting any time. I think our average speed was one hundred mph.

How come we didn't take an airship? I asked Voxi. *We could have been there in a couple of hours.*

Only VIPs take airships to the monasteries, he said.

We're VIPs!

Exactly.

I sighed. *Look, who's after us?*

Who isn't? he said, and that was absolutely all he would say about the subject. I threw questions and accusations at him, all to no avail. I couldn't even get his surface feelings, like I had done with KLse, because KRni was throwing such a damper on us.

So it was a *boring* ride. Except for some distant mountains that never seemed to get any closer and for an occasional spiked plant growing by the side of the highway, there wasn't anything to look at. I fell asleep before the sun went down, just because there wasn't anything for my mind to do (except worry about stuff, which I didn't have the energy to do).

I drifted for a long time without dreaming about anything coherent. I don't think I was totally asleep, because I was always aware that I was riding in a van next to Voxi and his fellow spouses. A couple of times I thought I detected tight-beam messages being sent between them, but I could have just imagined that part. Once I thought I opened my eyes and saw part of the sunset. It was awe inspiring. The sun went down like a roaring, multiarmed dragon, turning the horizon molten just before it finally sank, unwillingly, below the edge of the world.

But that might have been a dream, too.

I woke up sometime during the night to find myself drooling on Voxi's arm. He had moved so that I was learning against him. I wiped my chin and adjusted my position slightly, trying to get more comfortable. I thought about asking him if I could put my head in his lap. A little flirtatious, but I was tired of sitting up for hours on end.

Voxi, someone said, warningly.

He came instantly awake. I hadn't even known he was asleep. X'GBris must be much lighter sleepers than humans. I sat up and blinked in the dim, interior lights that had come on after nightfall.

Now that we were all awake, I wasn't able to snoop on the tight-beam messages that passed between Voxi, KRni, and the husband who was driving; but the content of those messages became very clear when Voxi got up and moved to the back window. He peered out for a moment, then turned back to me.

"Superstorm," he said.

"Coming from behind us?" I asked, too dazed and tired to be completely alarmed.

Emily Devenport

"No. We're headed south; the eye of the storm is moving in a southeasterly direction. You can look at it on the weather screen if you want."

I wasn't inclined to do so. "Can we outrun it?"

"For a little while. But it will intersect our path within a couple of hours."

"And blow us right off this road?" I was feeling more alert by the moment. But Voxi shook his head.

"These vans are designed for travel in all kinds of weather. When the winds catch up with us, we'll switch to roadhugger mode. It will slow us down considerably, though."

The taxi cabs of TradeTown had taken us through a superstorm, but they had been surrounded by monolithic buildings. The winds couldn't have been nearly as strong as they would be out in the open desert. "Can we get to shelter?" I asked.

He didn't answer. He and the others were speaking aloud now, but in that X'GBri undertone that's so hard for humans to hear. I crawled over next to Voxi and looked out the window myself. I couldn't see a thing. Voxi moved back over to the middle seat and then climbed over to the front with the driver. They continued to speak in the undertone.

I sat across from KRni and watched his face. He was looking up front, an abstract expression on his face. It reminded me of the way LLna and TGri had looked, the way the future KLse would look. At that moment, I knew KRni's future for certain.

Are you going to present yourself as a candidate? I asked him.

He glanced at me. *Don't goad me,* he warned, then turned his attention back to the discussion up front.

I'm not goading you. But that storm is coming up fast, if I'm reading your expressions accurately, and there's no shelter within reach. No shelter you want to take, that is. Some big questions are looming, and you're the one who's back here with me.

Move back to your seat, then, he said, not even sparing me a glance this time. But I wasn't going anywhere. I looked past him, out the side window. This time I did see something. The stars behind him were being blotted out by some huge, black thing.

Like a giant raptor, spreading its wings. . . . KRni mused.

So he had peeked into the analog I had built with Voxi. This man was really meant for the Net. It was just a matter of time. And we were running out of time.

You can call the GodHeads, I told him.

No. Out nets aren't linked—yet.

You can call them, KRni. You're going to be a GodHead.

This time when he looked at me, he didn't look away again. We glared at each other for several moments. Then he leaned forward and whispered, "*You're* the one who's going to be a GodHead. I've got other plans. *You* call them."

But I shook my head. Edna was the one who would be a GodHead, if we could ever just find her. I didn't have access to No Time. But KRni . . .

He hadn't been touched by one. He hadn't been infected. Maybe he was right, maybe you needed that link, however tenuous, before you could play with GodHead time. Edna had been touched by LLna's and TGri's sweat.

And *I* had touched Edna.

Heat blossomed in my hands. I looked down at them, expecting them to turn red, but they were pale. I flexed them, blew on them, but the burning remained, and now I could feel it spreading up my arms. I wasn't imagining it. Just thinking about the GodHead infection was causing my body to manufacture it, bring it forth from wherever it had been hiding.

I touched KRni's hands and he started like a cat, throwing me off. He gaped at me, then looked down at his palms. He regarded them for a long moment, just as I had looked at mine, and then all expression drained from his face. He raised his eyes to mine, and I saw murder there.

I kept quiet. I didn't dare move, either, not even to lower my eyes. I watched him struggle with himself as the storm behind us howled in hot pursuit.

"Why did you do it to me?" he said, his voice barely above a whisper.

"Call them," I pleaded.

"It was not for you to decide. Not for you to change my life."

"You don't have to stay with them," I said. "You can leave. They won't force you."

His face was growing calmer by the moment, his eyes more cool and distant. Yet inside he was aching. He hid it from Voxi and the others, but not from me. I had caused it, he wanted me to feel it. And I did. But I knew what his destiny was, even if he didn't want to. I knew who my only real advocate was in the van. I was surprised now that I saw it, but I wasn't about to waste the opportunity.

"Voxi thinks he can seize control of the Net, doesn't he?" I asked. "He thinks he can make the power grab to end all power grabs."

"What he thinks is not your affair." But KRni glanced up front, where the conversation between his spouses was continuing without knowledge of what had passed between us.

"Which matriarch is he working for?" I asked, though I didn't expect an answer. I was just looking for a reaction, amusement, irritation, something to let me know I was on the right track. I got one I didn't expect. Pain. Then doubt. He frowned at me.

He leaned forward and seized my hands again.

I felt his palms burning against mine. *You know I won't be able to make myself leave the Net,* he accused. *My marriage has been destroyed. You owe me a debt, and I'm going to collect it. Believe that.*

I did. But I couldn't let him go.

Tell me, I demanded. *You're going the same place as me. Tell me why we can't risk going to one of the storm shelters.*

We don't have to go to a shelter. We can keep driving down this road. The guidance system will take us straight to Red Springs.

But his confidence lagged slightly when he said that. If I hadn't just infected him, I might not have caught it. He was strong, he didn't normally lack confidence. But something big was up, something that made him nervous. I already knew him well enough to know that it would have to be one hell of a something. So I guessed.

If we use the guidance system, will that route us through some kind of central system? Will they know where we are?

He didn't answer. That was confirmation enough.

Some of the matriarchs are mad at you . . . I began, and felt a rush of anguish from him. Suddenly I realized how naive I'd been, how ignorant.

All of the matriarchs are mad at you, I said.

He scowled at me, but his hands tightened on mine. His pride was hurt, yet he wanted me to understand. *What else?* he demanded. *You were in the audience chamber with the rest of us. You can't be completely insensitive. You have turned us upside down.*

I shook my head. *The Net has turned you upside down. Don't blame us! And you guys are the ones who perfected the synthetic in the first place.*

He shrugged. *That doesn't mean they wouldn't like to murder you with their bare hands, those women. You took what was theirs in one fell swoop, and you weren't even trying. You just waltzed in, and suddenly the God-Heads are behind you like—* he looked outside, at the raging blackness—*like a superstorm. They've courted the GodHeads, they've pleaded with them, but they've never been willing to make the sacrifice that would—*

"What are you doing?" demanded Voxi.

He had crawled back to us without making a sound, and now his voice was quiet as he confronted us, calm. Yet there we were, clasping hands, deep in a conversation that hadn't included him, the senior husband. I began to tremble, and to realize just how tolerant JKre had been with KLse and us.

KRni wasn't afraid. That scared me even more. He sat calmly reviewing his options; and since we were still linked so closely together, I had no choice but to review them right along with him. I didn't like them much.

"Are you challenging me?" Voxi asked, as if he were asking about the weather. Of course, on GodWorld, the weather was a pretty serious matter. This was a serious matter, too. To them, it was more serious than the storm, the matriarchs, the GodHeads—everything that lay out-side our cramped universe.

"Yes," KRni said, switching to their main dialect. "I'm challenging you."

He let go of my hands, and then he moved until he was between me and Voxi. That put them literally nose to nose, and I was squashed back against the rear window. I tried to peek out from behind KRni, but he was too big. I wished I was just about anyplace else in the universe at that moment.

I waited for them to fight, to crush me in that small space.

"You're not even in line to be senior," Voxi was saying.

"I don't care to be senior," KRni replied.

There was a dangerous silence. That wasn't part of the ritual. What the hell was KRni doing? Was that sup-posed to be an insult to Voxi?

"Our marriage was over the moment LLna was sucked into the Net," said KRni. "Only desperation has held us together since then."

Another silence. This one was worse than the last, if possible. I couldn't stand it, sitting there watching them fall apart like that. I drifted toward them, inside the link. I touched them. I couldn't help it, even though I knew Voxi would probably strike at me like a snake for touch-ing him when he was so angry, so vulnerable, so confused. . . .

But he didn't strike. Instead, he clutched me, held me close. *What is he doing?* he demanded. *What is he talk-ing about?*

He's going to be a GodHead, I said, wishing I didn't have to tell him. *He can't help it, Voxi.*

She's right, KRni confirmed. *But that's not all, Voxi. You know it. You've known it all along, but you haven't wanted to think about it. This what the Net has really done to us. This strange new territory.*

We'll cross that bridge when we get to it! insisted Voxi, but KRni wasn't going to have that. Not anymore.

We're crossing it now, he said. *The bridge is here.*

Voxi pushed KRni into one of the seats. He slid into the other one himself, leaving me crouched between the two of them. He didn't want to hit KRni anymore, but the battle was still raging between them. I looked up front and saw the husband who was driving trying to divide his attention between the road and the rearview mirror. The other one was in the middle seat, openly staring. He wasn't frowning; he had a resigned look on his face. His expression turned my stomach with pity, with guilt.

I wished I hadn't had to witness this. I wished I hadn't understood it so well.

If we were still married, KRni told Voxi, *we would all be with LLna now.*

Voxi bared his teeth. *So go to her. She'll still have you, I'm sure.*

But KRni shook his head, wearily. *We're individuals now, brother. We can't go back. Whether we become GodHeads or not, we're bound for the Net. There's no hierarchy in there. We're going to be autonomous.*

You would think he had just pronounced some dreadful doom. I had always thought autonomy was pretty cool. In fact, I was aiming for it myself. But it bothered them. It meant their marriage was over, they were a bunch of single guys without a clue, without a pecking order, without customs and rituals to guide them through the empty spaces in between.

Well, shit, I said, *think up some new ones!*

That startled them. It also pissed them off, but I preferred that to misery.

"You can't go back to the way things were," I said, "and you can't go home and marry someone else, be junior husbands for the rest of your lives, assuming they don't kill you outright. So go forward. Don't try to figure out the Net until you've been there!"

Voxi laughed, human-style. He didn't put much effort into it, but it broke the tension.

"We'll get there," he said. "And then we'll see."

KRni didn't argue with that. He was in complete agreement, as far as the statement went.

"Are you going to put this thing on automatic pilot, then?" I asked.

"No," said Voxi.

"We're going into a shelter?"

"No."

I looked at KRni. I didn't ask if he was going to call the GodHeads. He hadn't made up his mind to do it, and I was suddenly sure that Voxi wouldn't have it. Voxi had other ideas, and it wasn't going to be healthy to try to thwart them.

"Go back to your seat," Voxi told me. "Try to sleep."

I nodded. I started to crawl between them, to the middle of the van. I heard a soft hiss behind me and froze. I looked over my shoulder.

KRni's head had fallen forward on his chest. He was sound asleep. Voxi had a hypo in his hand. He grinned at me.

Just in case he had other ideas, he said.

Yes, Voxi had earned his position as first husband. I turned around and crawled back to my seat.

The storm overtook us in another hour. I was lying on
the middle seat with my feet in Voxi's lap when the van
suddenly lurched sideways and the interior lights
blinked. The wind slapped at us from one direction and
then another, while our driver tried to switch us over to
roadhugger mode. We slowed down to a crawl.

Voxi leaned over the front seat, between the driver
and the other husband who had joined him up front. I
glanced at KRni; he was still out cold.

I wished I could see what everyone was looking at.
They certainly couldn't see out any of the windows. It
was inky black out there, a weird darkness that shifted
and flowed like sand. If I looked at it too long, my eyes
hurt, as my brain doggedly tried to make patterns out
of the chaos.

I blinked and looked at Voxi again. I saw the blue
flicker of a screen just beyond him, on the front dash. I
suspected they were using the van's sensors to determine
our progress. I wondered if the information was reliable,
or if we were going to end up going off the road and
into a gully. I glanced back at KRni again, wondering if
I should try to move him so that he was in a more
comfortable position.

He wasn't alone back there.

I blinked again, trying to make my eyes work properly. All the other husbands were up front, so who . . .

Who was the thin blond guy who was looking at me
with such a wry expression on his face?

Hello, again, he said.

Peterhamil.

That's Peter Hammill, he said, *remember? I was the doctor who was supposed to wipe Edna on OMSK. You and I shared part-time consciousness on Homeworld.*

I glanced at Voxi; he was oblivious to our guest. And why shouldn't he be? After all, Peter Hammill was a program who had been left in Edna's memory. I wasn't sure I liked the fact that I was hallucinating him again, especially since he was supposed to have run his course. But on the other hand . . .

Where is Edna? I asked him.

Close, he said. *She'll reach Red Springs the same time we do.*

Why are you here now? I asked, hoping he wouldn't be insulted by the question. I felt sorry for him, but I didn't want him to know that. He just smiled at me.

This is GodWorld, he said. *Being so close to the Net has made me more substantial. I'm not sure why, but I intend to ask if we ever get to Red Springs. In the meantime, I feel as real as you do. I don't know if the original Peter Hammill was such a nosy fellow, but I couldn't help wondering if you were all right.*

I glanced at Voxi again. I doubted he would be looking away from the screen anytime soon, but you never knew. He probably wouldn't see Peter Hammill, but I wasn't sure of that.

I'm not sure either, admitted Peter Hammill. *But probably he can't. You might want to direct your eyes at KRni, just in case. You could always say that you're worried about him.*

I am, a little.

Peter Hammill looked across at KRni. He even touched him. I wondered if he could feel anything, or if he just imagined that he did. *He's fine,* he said, *just very deeply asleep. X'GBris are tough fellows.*

That was true, even if I couldn't trust the rest of his diagnosis. He looked at me again, as if he sensed my suspicions. But he didn't seem to take them personally. If anything, he was looking at *me* with compassion. That made me uncomfortable. The last time he had looked at me that way had been back at WWul's hotel suite, when he had warned me that I had been programmed.

Didn't you say you were born on Celestine? he asked me.

Yes, I agreed, sure of that, at least.

I've heard that's a beautiful world.

It was. In fact, it was incredibly beautiful. It was like fabled Olympus. I hadn't thought about it in years. How could you forget a place like that? After all this was over, when things had been straightened out and I had been paid, I should go back there and take a long vacation. Visit old friends, family, go home . . .

Home. I tried to picture it and couldn't. I tried to think of the names of those old friends, old school chums and neighbors, tried to picture even one relative.

Couldn't.

Well, maybe one. I could picture my mother, Kirito. She had been tall, with red hair.

No, wait, that was Edna's mother. Damn, I had been totally infected by her memories. I wondered if I'd ever get them sorted out again. I sighed and rubbed my head. I felt a touch on my shoulder and looked up to see Voxi, his half-human face softened with a distracted sort of concern. I smiled at him, touched by the rare display. He nodded and turned back to his screen.

I peeked at Peter Hammill again. Still there. He waved at me.

Bomarigala admitted he's tampered with my personality, I said, before he could say it for me, *with my memories.*

Yes, he said, *that's what we did on OMSK.*

I don't think I'll be working for them again, I decided.

He cocked his head, as if he were looking into a space beyond me, something I couldn't see. He nodded at what he found there. *I don't think that issue is going to come up again, ever.*

What do you mean?

He didn't answer.

What were you looking at, just then?

He cocked his head again, but this time he was looking at me. *It's odd to be almost a person,* he said. *You feel as if you've got large chunks cut out of your life, but you don't always realize they're missing until someone points them out to you. For instance, I was just wondering where I was born. The original Peter Hammill didn't program that into me, because he didn't think it would be necessary. I was just supposed to prod poor Edna and then evaporate. I wasn't even supposed to know myself.*

Yet you do, I said, sneaking a cautious look at Voxi's back.

I do, he agreed. *Maybe even as well as you do.*

Except for a few crucial facts about your past, I reminded him. He didn't take offense. He didn't look scared either, or worried by the superstorm. I wondered then, did he depend upon my brain for his survival as much as he did Edna's? If something happened to me, would he be diminished?

Yes, he said, startling me. He was tuned in to me as well as Edna had been. That should have made me nervous, but I had grown accustomed to Peter Hammill on Edna's homeworld. And he had such a pleasant, intelligent face.

What happened to the original Peter Hammill? I asked him.

I haven't been able to get near any kind of library terminal, he said. *I was hoping that once you and Edna entered the Net, I could go off on my own and do some digging.*

Go off on his own—that was an intriguing thought. In the Net, maybe he wouldn't need our brains to make him real. And if that were the case, many artificial people could live there. People created by real brains, but not dependent upon them once some sort of critical mass was reached.

I wish you luck, he said. *I'd like to know what you come up with.*

Luck to all of us, said Peter Hammill. *The stakes are high, Aten. But if we can just get to Red Springs—*

There was a dull thud, and the van lurched to a halt.

The men were cursing, so I didn't say *What the hell was that?* though I was certainly biting my tongue. Wind and sand still buffeted the vehicle, and now the screen was dead. The driver hit it a couple of times, peevishly, but it stayed dead.

I glanced back at Peter Hammill, but he was gone, cut

off in midsentence. KRni was still sound asleep, so I pressed myself next to Voxi in an effort to see what was going on up front. I needn't have bothered, nothing but a lot of cursing was going on. Voxi didn't even notice my body pressed against his.

I tugged at his sleeve. He threw me an impatient look.

"Did we hit something or did something hit *us*," I asked him.

He frowned, but seemed inclined to tell me the truth. "Hard to say. If it's the latter, we'll know soon enough."

I felt him sending a tight-beam message to the others, and then he climbed behind my seat and fiddled with a storage locker. In another moment he was handing guns and body armor to his spouses. I got armor, too, but no gun. Voxi and the driver strapped armor onto KRni's inert form, no small task. Then they pulled some special goggles out of the locker and put them on. I didn't get a pair of those, either.

"What are those for?" I asked, suddenly worried that we might have to go out into the sand and wind. Or worse—that they would go out and leave me there with no clue.

"Infrared," said Voxi. That put butterflies in my stomach. If they were going to try to see heat signatures with those in a superstorm, they were going to be relying mostly on instinct when they aimed their guns. Of course, our alleged assailants would have the same problem.

I hoped.

In the meantime, no one was hammering at the door to our van, which suited me just fine because I still couldn't see anything out there.

I struggled into my armor, then Voxi made me lie on the floor. He made sure KRni was down, too. I thought that was kind of sweet, certainly a good indication of Voxi's capacity for fidelity. I lay on my stomach and sighed, trying not to go stir-crazy. We could have been having supper in Red Springs by now if we had taken a flier. Even a shelter would have been preferable to where we were now, since we could have walked around in that.

I sighed again. I closed my eyes and wished I could fall asleep. *Wake me when we get there,* I told Voxi.

Amazingly, I really did fall asleep.

I woke some time later. It might have been five minutes or five hours; it was still dark and stormy outside. The van rocked and creaked, but otherwise seemed to be holding its position. I picked my head up and tried to find everybody. KRni was still on the floor in back, but I couldn't see the others. Were they asleep? That didn't make sense, at least one would be on guard. Maybe they just didn't want their heads near the windows.

Voxi? I called cautiously.

Here.

Where are you?

He touched my ankle. He was lying between the front and middle seats. The other two must have been crouched down up front, then.

How long has it been since the thump? I asked.

A little over two hours.

So we probably just hit something, right?

He didn't say yes. He was alert, and his weapon was in his hand. *Do you have weapons training?* he asked me.

Just the standard, I said. *I learned to shoot on a range. I've used beam and projectile weapons, but almost never in the field.*

I should think an agent for OMSK would be more accustomed to combat, he said, with curiosity.

Not at all. Most of the time I'm more of a bonded courier than any kind of soldier. I'm much more adept at staying out of scuffles than winning them.

He touched my ankle again, let his free hand rest there. *I want you to stay out of this one. I want you to lie flat with your arms over your head. Don't move unless I tell you to, and then go only where I say you should.*

No problem, I said. The padded armor went from my neck all the way to my wrists and ankles. Not the most comfortable stuff in the world, and I really had to wonder how Voxi and the others managed to move in theirs. But they seemed accustomed to it. I supposed I was just a weakling human.

I could feel the weight of Voxi's hand on my ankle, though the leather of my boot made it impossible to feel anything else. It was still comforting. I suddenly wished that my feet were bare again, so he could touch my skin. I imagined how it would feel as his fingers explored the sensitive, tender soles. My thoughts must have been leaking, because I felt him moving closer inside the link, trying to see what I was fantasizing about. I showed him, and he gave my ankle a squeeze.

We'll have our time, he promised. *I have my own ideas about what we can do.* And he showed them to me. I wished he hadn't, because now I *really* wanted out of that van, out of that storm, and into a nice, private hotel room with Voxi, just the two of us. At that moment I didn't care about the GodHeads, about the matriarchs, about the killer plants and the murderous sun of God-World; I even managed to stop worrying about Edna for a while. I just wanted Voxi.

Even thoughts of Bomarigala didn't discourage me. I hadn't thought about him on Homeworld at all, and I had only brought him up to Peter Hammill in connection to my alleged conditioning.

He wants to marry you, said Voxi. My thoughts weren't very well guarded at all.

How do you know? I asked.

He told me.

He didn't tell me.

He's OMSK, said Voxi. *He won't tell you anything until you've earned the information, twice over.*

Marry Bomarigala. That was a strange thought. He had been great in bed, but I wondered what it would be like to belong to the man. Because that would be the situation. He had made me, he knew me better than anyone, he knew things about me I didn't know myself. I could imagine what it would be like, always contending with him, always trying to figure out his angle, always being on the alert.

It was kind of exciting.

You enjoy being pursued, said Voxi, without malice. *Typical female.*

I'm not used to being so popular, I said.

Then you've been running with the wrong crowd.

I thought about the other men I'd been involved with. Or rather, I *tried* to think about them. I couldn't picture even one of them. I had vivid memories of KLse, Voxi, and Bomarigala, but not of anyone else. I thought harder—this was ridiculous! Of course there had been other men. There had been . . .

I saw my dirty old street on Homeworld, heard the boys calling me *ugly* as I walked out of town. . . .

Damn. That was another memory of Edna's. It looked like I was going to have to go to Bomarigala for help, one way or the other. Edna had leaked into me so much that some of my own memories were submerged now. I knew I had been with other men. I just didn't know who they were. That could be awkward if I ever ran into any of them.

Oh well. In the meantime, here we were. Stuck, and it was beginning to get stuffy, too, because now that our engine was off we couldn't run the air conditioner.

Voxi's attention was already back where it belonged, on the outside world that presumably might want to get in. I didn't disturb him again. I tried to listen for danger myself, but the sound of the storm only hypnotized me.

What would I do if I were by myself? Probably I would wait until daylight, hoping there would be more visibility. I might be able to determine if I was still on the road. If I could see even a foot ahead of me, I might—

I felt Voxi tense.

Outside, the storm howled. I waited for him to relax again. He didn't.

I waited, too. I relaxed my muscles and took deep breaths, getting oxygen into my blood. I flexed and stretched my legs, then my arms. I was wondering if I should repeat the whole process when suddenly there was a loud *SNAP* at the door, and then it opened. The storm came screaming in, dragging the van several feet across the road as it filled the cabin. I had jammed my eyes shut and buried my face in my arms as soon as the door had cracked open, but flashes of light were burning right through my closed lids—the kind small explosions or gunfire would make. I couldn't get a clean breath of air and I wasn't sure I was hearing what I thought I was: faint thuds under the sound of the wind.

I tried to tune in to the link, but then had to shut it down in self-defense. It made the storm seem mild in comparison. I could only do what Voxi had ordered me, keep my head down and try to be invisible. Weapons were being fired, and I didn't want to test my body armor.

Someone grabbed my ankle and pulled. I tried to dig my fingers into the carpet, but I was dragged right out into the storm.

The winds of a superstorm average about 150 miles per hour. That little fact popped up from my memory as the wind tried to tear me right out of my assailant's grasp. My nose and ears immediately filled up with sand; I had to clamp my hand over my mouth and try to breath through gritted teeth. He jammed me tight against his body and broke into a staggering run, crouched over at an impossible angle. That was when I knew he was X'GBri. No human could have made progress against a wind like that.

I didn't struggle, not in that gale. If I had broken loose, I would have suffocated within minutes. Instead I just prayed that we were going somewhere where there wasn't any wind or sand. Somewhere where it was warmer, because after the sun had gone down, the temperature had gone with it. While I was at it, I also prayed that Voxi and his spouses weren't dead, and that I wasn't being dragged off to my own execution.

I could have prayed for a lot of other stuff, too, but I thought I'd better keep it simple.

My assailant stopped suddenly, and I was being handed to someone else, someone who was crouched inside a shelter that cut off some of the wind. I was dragged across a floor, and then someone was pulling a mask and goggles over my face.

So you can breathe, said a familiar voice, through the link. *Can you see me yet?*

KLse. He was the one who had grabbed me and run with me through the storm. I had sent him a message down the link from the starport, and now he had effected a rescue. He and WWul and the others were now trying to kill Voxi and his spouses.

And I cared about them all.

I blinked my eyes, painfully. The grit was making me tear up, and I couldn't wipe them with anything. After a moment I could catch glimpses of things. We were parked with our other side to the wind, but sand was still gusting in through the door. KLse and GDro were there, dividing their attention between me and the darkness.

In another moment WWul and STra loomed out of the storm, carrying JKre between them. JKre's head was down, and he had to be dragged into the van. MRnu brought up the rear, firing his rifle as he covered the others. He jumped in, and the door was slammed shut.

MRnu scrambled up front. I heard the engine starting and felt us lurch forward; apparently WWul and her husbands didn't worry about being located when they tapped in to traffic control. I watched WWul and STra straighten JKre's limbs, tenderly. He had a wound in his throat, above the body armor. No one tried to patch it.

I pulled off my mask and goggles. Tears were flowing freely now, and not because of the sand. JKre looked for me, and seemed happy to find me.

"Aten," he whispered, "I want to know something about human marriage."

I could barely hear him. He was bubbling a little as he tried to speak, so I moved closer to make it easier for him.

"What is it?" I asked, hoping he wouldn't notice I was crying for him.

"A man has his wife all to himself—yes?"

"He's supposed to, yes."

"And—" he coughed, his body tight with the effort not to tear anything loose. He gasped for a moment, his eyes unfocused, and then he saw me again. "If another man sleeps with her, he kills that man, yes?"

"Yes," I said.

"Good," said JKre. And then he died.

Funny thing happens when X'GBris die. Their hair deflates. You don't realize how alive it is until it becomes perfectly still, as still as human hair. JKre's hair settled around his face. His eyes became cloudy, and his mouth hung open slightly as his jaw muscles ceased to function. I gazed down at him, tasting grit in my mouth as I tried to swallow.

"He was your advocate," WWul said, in a tone of voice that most humans would describe as calm. They would say that she was an unfeeling monster, that X'GBris must not feel grief like humans did. But I knew better. I couldn't bring myself to look directly at her.

They didn't try to close JKre's eyes, or close his mouth, or cover him. But WWul and STra sat touching him, despite the fact that his body must already be cooling. GDro sat nearby, as if awaiting orders.

KLse's hands were gently tugging me away from them. He pulled me up onto a seat and started to dab at my face with wet wipes. I stared at my knees and wished I could stop crying. It seemed rude to me, rude and presumptuous. After all, JKre was their spouse, not mine; I hardly knew him. Yet my heart felt crushed, and when I dared to think of Voxi and his spouses, my mind skittered away from the subject, back to JKre and his dead hair.

Everything whirled about in my head until all I could see in my mind's eye was raptors wheeling in the sky of another world.

What have I done? That was the thought that had occurred to Edna when the hunter had begged her not to kill him. I thought I knew how she had felt then, but I hadn't known at all. Not until now. And how could it have happened? How could I have been so careless with their lives? Before this case, I never would have acted so impulsively. But since my trip with Edna to her homeworld, I hadn't been myself. I had been disoriented, forgetful, unprofessional. One little call for help had started all this. And I hadn't even needed help, not really. Edna was the one who needed help. Edna was lost, and Voxi hadn't been willing to let me talk to KLse, because he had a hidden agenda, and ambitions, and if he was dead I didn't know if I could forgive myself. . . .

Around and around went the raptors.

KLse managed to get my face pretty clean. He made me blow my nose into a tissue, and when I did that, some of the dust came out of my ears, too. He cleaned them gently, patiently, working with single-minded concentration. When he was done with my skin, he started on my hair; but that was a lot harder. He brushed and brushed, struggling with tangles and grit. My mind slowly emptied, and found a comfortable numb place to be.

My gaze drifted to STra. He was scowling so hard it looked like his face would freeze like that forever. I looked at WWul and KLse and GDro; their faces were trying to frown, too. But it was as if all of the strength had gone out of the muscles, and they could only achieve a sickly imitation of a scowl.

Why did you come for me? I asked KLse, not as an accusation, but because I could see that they regretted the price they had paid.

Because you are my concern, he said, and for a moment I saw a shadow of the man he would become. The GodHead. He had been moved by compassion to rescue me, but there was more than that. He sensed his future, maybe even mine, too. But he was sending on a tight beam, and refusing to look at me as he did. He didn't want the others to know we were talking.

He was your advocate, WWul had said when JKre died. I hadn't thought about what she could have meant. JKre my advocate? After he had tried to kill me? But that had been an act of passion, of rage. Edna and I had pushed him beyond the bounds of his tolerance. Yet apparently he had still been on my side of things, when push came to shove. Whatever side that was. I wasn't sure, anymore.

Did you kill them? I asked, trying not to seem concerned about it. KLse would still hate Voxi, I was sure. I didn't want to push him the way I had pushed JKre.

I don't know, he said. *My job was to get to you. That was all I thought about, to get you back to our van.*

His feelings were right there for me to read if I wanted to, but I couldn't make myself do it. I've heard that a burden shared is lighter.

Bunch of nonsense.

Where are we going now? I asked KLse.

Back to TradeTown.

Not to the monastery?

Regret flooded across the link to me, along with frustration and loss. That was it, then. KLse and I didn't have a vote, and our advocate was dead. WWul probably hated the GodHeads more than ever. She probably would do anything in her power to thwart them.

KLse pulled broken hair out of the brush, then beat it on his knee to free the dust. He made it look like that was all he was thinking about. *A fleet is on its way here,* he said. *They're going to try to destabilize GodWorld's sun.*

I didn't ask who. The awe he felt when he said *They* spoke of the matriarchs. They were taking their revenge. I was glad that my own face was still so incapable of expression. If WWul knew that KLse was warning me . . .

The GodHeads will stop them, I said. *They swatted OMSK aside like a fly.*

OMSK isn't as talented with Early technology as we are, he said, and an icy finger crawled up my spine.

A fleet. The X'GBris never gathered a whole fleet to do anything, did they? Not that my faulty memory could verify. They were masters of espionage, of cold war, of short and vicious attacks. But not a full-fledged war. And again that talk of a sun-killer. Officially, no such weapon existed. But at that moment I didn't doubt that it did.

The Earlies won't let them do it, even if the GodHeads can't stop it, I said, hoping that was really true. I had never met an Early or talked with one, except for Ankere in No Time, but Edna had been the one to do the talking, and she had been too single-minded to get to know anyone there.

KLse was curious about that line of thought. He was hopeful, too, that I was right about the Earlies. It occurred to me that here was someone who would actually answer my questions for a change.

KLse, is Voxi considered an outlaw now?

Yes, he said, with a surprising lack of bitterness at the mention of his adversary. There was even a note of admiration in what he said next: *He wants to overthrow the matriarchy. He thinks the Net will do it. X'GBris would become autonomous, they could make their own*

*deals with anyone they wanted without going through old
channels. He'll be executed if they get their hands on him.*

How come you guys didn't try to kill him?

Because JKre and I agreed with him.

WWul had gone along with that, despite the fact that
the Net would threaten her own authority over her husbands. I stole another glance at her. She hadn't moved
from her vigil. She definitely regretted her decision now.
I was surprised she didn't want to wring my neck.

She thinks you're a helpless victim, said KLse.

Do you? I demanded, my pride hurt.

He hesitated before answering, and I got madder until
the emotion drained my energy levels down to the numb
zone again. He thought about it a little longer, then finally said, *Not helpless.*

I'm no victim, I said, without much conviction. *If anyone was a victim, it was Edna. And speaking of Edna,
do you know where she is now? Is she all right?*

She's all right, he soothed.

Where is she?

He sighed, wearily. His hands continued to brush and
clean my hair, but I could see he was drained, actually
tired. I had never seen an X'GBri in that state before.

KLse?

Yes, he said. *She's sleeping now, Aten. She's drugged,
but in a safe place.*

Why did you drug her?

I didn't, he said, and I felt a pang of guilt. I was the
one who had drugged Edna, in the egg. I must have
given her too much. She had been so wrung out by her
memories on Homeworld. She hadn't had the strength
to fight off a sedative.

Are you tired? he asked me, hopefully. He didn't want
to answer any more questions.

I was incredibly tired, but I wasn't sleepy. I would
close my eyes through, to please him.

Lie down with your head in my lap, he said. *You're
safe now; no one here wants to hurt you.*

I did as he asked. Their van had different seating arrangements than Voxi's; the seats were bolted against
the three walls in the passenger section, facing each
other. That seemed a very X'GBri concept; humans

would have been uncomfortable facing each other for hours on end. I wasn't too thrilled about the prospect myself, and it would be a relief to at least pretend to be asleep. If I had had to face WWul much longer she might have seen my shame, my grief, my anxiety.

And my fervent desire that she and the matriarchs fail utterly in their plans to destroy GodWorld.

Our culture will change forever if they fail, said Voxi.

I know, I said, and wished that I could feel sorry about that.

I couldn't help taking one last, long look at JKre. Then I turned my eyes away from his cooling body and jammed them shut.

Grief isn't alleviated by the handling of the body, the managing of the details of its disposal. That's just something you have to do because you don't want the wolves to eat your loved one. On GodWorld, it's the plants that are likely to do the eating if a body is left out in the open. No one was willing to let that happen to JKre.

We drove into TradeTown sometime around late afternoon, the superstorm still raging around us. WWul and STra weren't touching JKre anymore by that time, but WWul had stretched herself out next to him, and when I had awakened in the dim, storm-haunted morning, I had found her looking at him as she lay there. I didn't try to fathom the expression on her face.

As soon as we had pulled into the underground parking lot of our hotel, MRnu notified the proprietors that we had a body that needed funeral arrangements. Since TradeTown was governed by humans, that meant a coroner would also stop by, though the police would have no jurisdiction over X'GBri matters. The police only got involved if humans were implicated. Or dead. I could have complicated matters if I'd cared to, but I made it clear that I was nothing more than a friend of the family.

It was the least I could do.

We waited at the van. We all stood outside; WWul's vigil was over. All of us were still wearing our armor, still dusty from the storm. Theirs had burn and impact marks on it.

I tried to imitate the stance of the X'GBris, to show respect. Things didn't look any better just because it was morning. I hadn't gotten used to the fact that JKre was dead yet, so every time I had awakened during the night, I had remembered it all over again, and it was almost like finding it out for the first time.

Brains sure are pesky things. I was beginning to understand why Edna had thought that being wiped wasn't so bad.

An augmented hotel manager arrived first, a young man who was obviously uncomfortable with the unfamiliar terrain of X'GBri grief; but he made a valiant effort to read the situation. He didn't fail too miserably. WWul told him exactly what she wanted done, and he used his Net interface to call the right people.

I watched him while he communed with the Net. He looked a lot more self-assured when his mind was in there than when he was trying to talk with WWul. His face would become calm, almost happy when he interfaced; his eyes would move as if he was reading something. Then he would ask WWul something more, and the discomfort would be back.

She was in no frame of mind to humor him. And I couldn't help either, because I didn't know anything about X'GBri customs for body disposal. They turned out to be surprisingly simple. There would be no service, no viewing of the body. It would be destroyed in a plasma furnace as soon as the coroner had had a look at it.

Maybe WWul had stared at JKre so long because she was trying to fix his face in her memory. Would that work? I doubted it would for me. I couldn't even remember my own mother's face. I was forgetting JKre's face already. I found myself caught between wishing the coroner would hurry up and hoping he would never get there at all.

She finally showed up about forty-five minutes later. She was all business when she was examining the body, not allowing herself to show any compassion until she was sure everything was on the up and up. WWul told her the truth about what happened. The coroner looked at me for a long moment, then went in to look at the body.

I know what she was thinking. She was thinking that

humans shouldn't meddle in X'GBri affairs. I couldn't agree with her more.

I heard her voice inside the van. She was talking into a recorder, talking about JKre's body. When she came out again, she looked WWul squarely in the face and told her that she had given official permission for the body to be transported to a place of disposal.

The meat wagon showed up five minutes later. I stood aside and let the men with the gurney go in to get JKre. They were human, but WWul didn't seem to care who carried the body. When they came out with JKre, his face and body covered, I started to cry again, and I just could have kicked myself. I don't know how anyone else reacted to the sight of him being carried off that way, because I couldn't even see straight.

I stood there with my head down and my mouth shut while WWul talked again with the coroner and the driver of the ambulance. I couldn't concentrate on what they were saying. I was struggling so hard with myself, I didn't even know they had all left until I felt KLse's hand on my arm. He was trying to steer me into the elevator. I went with him.

On the ride up, everyone stared at me. This didn't help me one bit. But they weren't human, I kept telling myself that. I had my instincts and they had theirs. Slowly, I got ahold of myself. I even raised my eyes and looked at WWul.

"Don't be afraid," she said. "You're safe now."

She didn't have the benefit of a link with a human to tell her what my tears meant. She thought I was just frightened. I felt like a viper, like a poisonous insect. I felt like one of those GodWorld plants that lures you with the smell of water when you're dying of thirst, then shoots spikes at you.

Don't let her suspect your feelings of guilt, KLse warned me. *She'll wonder if you have a good reason for feeling that way.*

I do, I said.

No. No, you don't, my poor Aten, my brave friend.

I wished he wouldn't say things like that. It made me want to cry again. I kept my eyes on WWul, because I realized that she needed me to. That was why the coro-

ner had looked at her so directly, wise woman that she
was. The hotel manager had offended her when he had
kept looking away. And now that she had reassured me,
she expected me to show my respect with a direct,
open gaze.

So I did. But my face only baffled her, I'm sure. She
had never seen human grief before. She stared in open
amazement, and I can only hope that the spectacle diverted her from her own grief for a little while.

The elevator doors opened onto a massive, X'GBri-
style hallway. We walked on the soft carpet, WWul leading the way with STra, KLse and I in the middle, the
others bringing up the rear. WWul walked almost to the
end, quite a long distance in such a massive place, and
finally knocked on a door.

There was a long pause while I wondered who was in
there. Wasn't this WWul's suite? Were we supposed to
meet someone now? I sure as hell hoped it wasn't one
or more of the matriarchs.

Bomarigala opened the door.

He was wearing blue and black again, trousers and a
tunic that looked vaguely military, official. He looked at
our faces, schooling his own like the pro he was, and
stepped back so we could enter.

We all filed into the room and he closed the door
behind us. WWul had moved to the center of the room,
where a chair awaited her. I realized that that must be
one of the central concepts of X'GBri interior design,
the wife chair. She sat, and the husbands arranged themselves around her. Bomarigala came to stand next to me,
facing them.

"You have lost a spouse," he said. "Is that so?"

"That is so," confirmed WWul.

"I regret your loss," he said formally.

"Your regret is noted."

"And did Voxi also suffer casualties among his
spouses?" asked Bomarigala. "I sincerely hope that he
did."

"I can't be sure," said WWul. "We fought in chaotic
circumstances. It is astonishing that our casualties were
not higher."

The whole scene was starting to make me dizzy. Bomarigala was doing exactly what was called for under the circumstances; WWul appreciated his perfect grasp of protocol. Yet he was only being polite; and I, who felt her loss so keenly myself, could do nothing but stand there like a zombie.

"I have been in touch with the various security forces," said Bomarigala, meaning, I assumed, those that belonged to the matriarchs, to OMSK, and possibly even to GodWorld. "Voxi's location is still a mystery. It's possible that he has managed to contact the GodHeads."

"It's possible that he is dead," said WWul, flatly, and I could see that she was voting for that possibility. "But if he is not, he certainly will have found a way to disappear by now. His execution will have to wait for a better day."

I tried not to twitch. I was thinking about the fleet that was on its way. I didn't try to touch Bomarigala through the link, ask him if he knew about it. I didn't trust my own ability to keep a straight face; and anyway, first things first.

"Our endeavor has cost us dearly," said WWul. "JKre was a first husband."

STra was still frowning. I wondered if he was glad his rival was dead, or if it was really that simple.

"I owe you a debt," said Bomarigala.

"Yes," said WWul, and for the first time I thought I could hear something close to human sadness in her voice. She had just demanded a concession from Bomarigala, a master of OMSK, and he had agreed to pay her. That was the acknowledgment of her loss she had been waiting for, the only expression of sympathy she really wanted from him. A favor owed.

Someday she would try to collect the favor, and she expected him to pay it. But I wondered if he would.

Nothing was said for a long moment. I swayed on my feet. WWul's eyes darted in my direction.

"Take her now," she said. "She is tired."

Bomarigala looked at me, his eyes burning briefly with triumph. I was a bit humbled by it. I looked at WWul, tried to say something, anything.

She had sat in a chair just like that when Edna and I had first walked into her life. Her husbands had stood around her, a complete family. She had been so proud and self-assured. Edna and I had blown into her life like a superstorm. Yet somehow she didn't seem to realize that I was to blame.

"Good-bye," I croaked.

She nodded. I turned away with Bomarigala.

"Wait," said KLse.

We froze. I knew what he was going to say. I made myself face them again. KLse looked into my eyes, confirming that I was still his friend. Then he turned to WWul. "I cannot stay," he said.

For a human, the death of a spouse and divorce are the two hardest things to cope with, the two most painful things. They were both happening to WWul at once. She gazed at him, thunderstruck.

"No," she said.

KLse's body was rigid, his face twisted into a dreadful knot of anguish. "Yes," he said, his voice breaking with emotion. "I do not wish it, but I have no choice."

"Choice!" screamed WWul, almost coming out of her chair. Only STra restrained her. "All the time you talk of choice! I am your *wife*!"

KLse had to swallow several times before he could speak again. "You and I stand on opposite sides of a rift," he said at last.

"The Net!" cried WWul. "Say it aloud, KLse. You want the Net, you've been seduced by it! You don't care about marriage, and you will throw me away for that obscenity!"

Every word stabbed him. He treasured WWul; divorcing her was like cutting off one of his own limbs. He would never get over her loss, no matter who else he loved, no matter what he became. But he couldn't stand with her, behind that invading fleet.

"I divorce you," he said.

WWul's face drained of expression. The other husbands looked shocked, too, but less so. Maybe they had suspected they would lose KLse from the moment he had been infected with the synthetic. Maybe that had been the big argument in the family before JKre died.

"I'm leaving with them," said KLse. I felt dizzy again, with the strain of it all, the impossible pain these aliens were feeling. I wished I had never stuck my big fat nose into their marriage. I wished I was just an interested observer, like Bomarigala.

"You are divorced," WWul said, so softly I could barely hear her.

KLse flinched as if he had been struck. Then he squared his shoulders and began to turn away.

"You're an enemy now, KLse!" WWul cried. "I will fight you like an enemy."

He hung his head at that. Then he nodded, painfully. He moved clumsily to the door and waited there for us to join him, his back to us.

WWul stared at him in disbelief; then slowly her eyes found mine. I waited for her to finally see my guilt, but that wasn't what she saw.

"You have suffered," she said. "I regret that."

I shook my head in disbelief. "I'm sorry," I said to her.

She frowned, and I said it again. "I'm sorry."

And then Bomarigala's hand was on my shoulder. He guided me to the door. KLse opened it, and the three of us left together.

The door closed firmly behind us.

I wanted to take KLse's hand in the hallway, to comfort him, but he didn't want me to. It wasn't until we got on the elevator again that I realized that he wouldn't do that when another man was present. It implied a challenge. KLse didn't know where I stood with Bomarigala, or where I stood with him. We rode back down to the parking garage.

"This way," Bomarigala said, taking my arm again. But KLse wasn't following us. I stopped and gazed at him with dismay. "Aren't you coming?" I asked.

He shook his head.

"Why not?"

"I'm going to the GodHeads," he said.

I had already known that. I had thought that was where we *all* were going. But Bomarigala apparently had other ideas. He squeezed my arm, trying to nudge me back into motion. I tried to say something to KLse, to make the connection that would keep us together. But my brain couldn't come up with anything.

I touched him through the link. He touched me back, but still no coherent words were exchanged. He knew how I felt, and I knew how he felt, but we couldn't find a conclusion to the conversation. Finally he turned away and disappeared among the rows of parked vehicles.

I watched him go, ignoring the squeeze on my arm until I couldn't see him anymore. He wasn't rejecting me, he was going to the GodHeads. It was hard for him to be without a family. I needed to do something, but I wasn't to the place where I could do it yet. That was the problem. I needed to get there.

Finally I gave in to Bomarigala and let him lead me to his vehicle. It was another nondescript van, identical to the one Voxi had procured. I climbed up front with Bomarigala. He drove us out of the garage and into the superstorm.

I wondered how KLse was going to get around. Divorced, he probably didn't even have access to credit anymore. I prayed he wouldn't try to just walk out into this maelstrom. I tried to touch him through the link again.

He was there, but he wasn't communicating.

"Leave him alone," Bomarigala said. "You'll never understand X'GBri psychology. Not completely."

"I bet they do in the Net," I said.

"Maybe you're right."

I looked at him. He was magnificent, as usual. His black hair was shining and clean. His body supported his clothes, rather than being confined by them. I turned so I could look at him instead of the superstorm.

He had linked up with traffic control, so his hands weren't even on the steering wheel. He was monitoring various readouts, glancing up at me from time to time. His eyes admired me, which was vaguely surprising to me. I was so dusty and exhausted.

Just a dirty little girl in rags . . .

My self-image was beginning to feel like Edna's. I couldn't let that happen. When I saw her again, I would work to change hers into mine. We would both be happier that way.

"Where are we going?" I asked.

"To my hotel."

"I know that. I mean, where are we going? What's going to happen?"

He gave me a long, hard once-over, not admiring, but measuring. "Back to OMSK," he said, finally.

"What about the fleet?"

He grinned, and I knew he was remembering his own failed attempt to hurt GodWorld, the message the Earlies had sent him. I don't know if the memory stung, but it certainly seemed to give him perspective. "If they succeed, we don't want to be anywhere near the destruction. But I doubt they'll succeed. They're desperate, and desperation never breeds triumph."

"Bomarigala, I don't want to go back to OMSK."

He was watching his controls again. "It's your job," he said.

"I want to do something else now."

"Like what?"

I looked out at the muddy, swirling light. *They should have called this place "Wrath of GodWorld."*

"I don't know," I said. "I'll think about it. I'll go to Celestine and take a long vacation."

"No one lives on Celestine," said Bomarigala. "They're still rebuilding from the Vorn war. It will be decades before people are allowed back there. Why would you want to go there?"

I didn't answer. Now that he had said it, I knew it was true. Celestine had been invaded, destroyed. I had never lived there, I had no family there, my mother had never been there.

"Did you make my mother up?" I asked him.

He frowned. My manner was disturbing him. He seemed disappointed in me.

"Kirito," I prompted. "Was she a real woman, or someone you made up?"

"She was real," he said. "She was *my* mother."

That hurt. Kirito had been my pride, my background. She was a war hero, an officer, beautiful and brave.

"Who was my mother?" I asked him.

"I don't know," he admitted. "I don't care about that. I care about you as you are. When we get back to OMSK, I can rid you of any doubts you've ever had, Aten. I can clean up the damage Edna did."

I felt a moment of longing for that, for the forgetfulness of a wipe. No grief, no loss, no wheeling raptors. "Where is Edna?" I asked him. "She's coming, too, right?"

"No," He said, with finality. "Edna is not your concern any longer. She's been paid for her time and taken off the payroll. I'll assign you to another case as soon as we get home."

There was something wrong with that. I tried to reason out what it could be, but that was like standing on shifting sand. We drove into a yawning darkness, and the sand fell away from us. We had pulled into the entrance of a parking garage.

We went deep. I wondered if this place was fortified enough to withstand an attack from orbit. It wouldn't survive the explosion of a sun, of course. Nothing could do that. Sand and rock and concrete would melt, vaporize—everything would just fall away from you and you would float in blackness. Or you would if you hadn't been reduced to atoms in the wake of that first shock wave. You wouldn't even know it; you wouldn't know anything at all.

What was it like, being dead? Was JKre anywhere at all, as JKre? Was he a soul, or a beam of energy, or just a fading memory in my mind? Was he with Raptor now, the two of them waiting for me?

Ankere was in the Net. She had died a couple of decades ago, but she was still in No Time with the GodWeed sprite. She could even have new conversations with people. In a way, she had answered the conundrum for me. When Ankere wasn't in No Time, the past was where she existed. She couldn't travel back to the past if it wasn't there anymore. So JKre was still somewhere. I just couldn't see him anymore.

"We're here," said Bomarigala, and he turned off the engine.

We climbed out of the van. This new place was much like the one we had just left, but it was built on a human scale. We were back on home ground. I felt comforted by that, but also homesick for KLse and Voxi's world. I guess there's just no pleasing some people.

We rode up in a human-sized elevator, into a hallway

that was elegant enough, though somewhat lacking in a true grasp of aesthetics. I suppose I had been spoiled by my exposure to X'GBri design, so subtle yet so profound in its effect. I think we humans do best when we're just being our plain old selves, not trying to look fancy.

Bomarigala sure was good at it, though. He was a cut above. And I . . .

I looked at myself in the hall mirrors. I was beautiful, even dusty, even bundled up in padded armor. That was sort of a nice thing to know, after everything that had happened. In fact, now that I thought about it, I hadn't seen my own reflection for a long time. I had seen Edna's, but not mine. Such a dizzy, dizzy thought.

"I'm so tired," I told Bomarigala as he opened the door to his suite.

"I know," he said, and he sounded tired himself. We went inside. He closed the door behind us, and then he gathered me into his arms and squeezed me tight, holding me against him like I was a long-lost treasure. I enjoyed the feeling. He valued me, Bomarigala. Master of OMSK. I had been worth risks. When he kissed me, I enjoyed that, too, but I was not aroused. My mind kept drifting back to KLse, alone in the storm.

"I thought I would never see you again," Bomarigala said, giving me shivers. He led me into my room and I sat on the edge of my bed. I thought how nice it was that he was giving me my own space instead of expecting me to share his. *He wants to marry you,* Voxi had said. If he did, he was going to treat me very carefully for a long time to come.

He watched me. He was troubled, though not hurt by my weariness. He was troubled on levels that had more to do with Edna than with me.

"She didn't hurt me," I told him. "Edna would rather die than hurt me."

"She doesn't have to die," he said. "No one wants her to die. Just to go away."

I frowned. "What about the GodHeads, then? How will you find another candidate?"

"Voxi's taking care of that."

A weight lifted off my heart. I closed my eyes and almost fell asleep sitting up. I caught myself before I could fall over. Bomarigala had moved close. He took my hands in his, almost anxiously.

"You need rest," he said. "And something to eat."

"Where is Voxi now?" I asked.

He sat down next to me. I turned so I could see his face, and waited for him to fill in the blanks.

"My team found him just after WWul's," he said. "Voxi had wanted to take you into the Net with him, that was our only disagreement. I hooked him into our traffic control, off the main grid. He arrived safely in Red Springs this morning."

I tried to be happy about that good news, but I was too profoundly disappointed at the way things had been timed. "How come you didn't want me to go in?" I asked. "That was what you hired me for."

"You aren't yourself," he said. "Edna screwed you up."

"No, she didn't," I protested, weakly.

"We couldn't screen her properly after we found her. God only knows why she was really at OMSK. We had to go with what we had. It turned out to be a mistake."

He didn't know Edna was a mass murderer. If I had been a good agent, I would have told him, right there. But I wasn't a good agent anymore.

He touched my hair. "Even dirty, it's beautiful," he said. He took a great handful of it and pulled it back from my face. He kissed my cheek.

"If WWul demands payment of your debt—" I began.

"I was being polite," he said. "I'll pay if it's convenient to do so. Maybe even if it's not. But that debt may be void, soon."

It wouldn't be void unless WWul was dead.

"Don't kill her," I begged.

He shrugged. "I have no plans to. That wasn't what I meant."

I sighed. I wondered if there was anything else we should talk about before I let go of everything. Surely I was forgetting something.

"Stop worrying about it," said Bomarigala. "Stop grieving, Aten. It isn't your affair, and he wasn't your husband. From what I could see, he wasn't even your friend."

Emily Devenport

I didn't tell him that term was irrelevant in this case.

"The quality of your life is about to get much better," he was saying. "You and I make a good team. Think about it. You have time."

He got up and walked confidently out of the room. I continued to sit on the edge of my bed. I tugged half-heartedly at the throat of my armor, but it was too much trouble to take it off just then. The lights of the superstorm were leaking in through the gauze covering four different sets of windows. They swirled about the room with restless energy. I watched them, attentively.

I don't know how much time had gone by when KLse slipped into the room. I wasn't surprised to see him. I realized that I had been waiting. I smiled at him.

"He's in the shower," KLse said, quietly. "We can go now."

I stood and brushed ineffectually at my armor. "I didn't get a chance to wash off the grit," I teased.

He grinned at me. "After all the work I did, you're still not satisfied? Demanding woman."

I took his hand then. A troublesome thought occurred to me. "He said he could read Edna and me anytime, through the link. He said we're conditioned against blocking him out."

"You can't block him," said KLse. "But I can. KRni isn't the only one who can slam doors."

I hugged him. He hugged me back, fiercely. But a moment later we were hurrying out the door, down the hall and into the elevator. We didn't have much time.

KLse had stolen a van. He had followed Bomarigala and me back to our hotel, and then simply waited for me to be alone. I should have known he wouldn't be a lost little lamb. After all, X'GBris were *dangerous* when they weren't married, not *helpless*.

We aimed ourselves down the long highway toward Red Springs. Our vehicle cut a wedge through the storm, hugging the road. Together we watched our progress on the blue screen. Or we slept, or ate emergency rations, or used the cramped privy built into the uncomfortable little closet in the back.

Sometimes we held hands. Once KLse held me close while I slept, and I felt better than I had in days. Maybe years.

Day turned to night, then to day again, and the storm never paused, never stopped to stretch and yawn. It raged as if it thought it lived on a gas giant instead of an earth-normal planet. A couple of times it got so bad we had to stop and dig in for a few hours. But mostly we moved steadily forward. Neither of us expected to be stopped this time.

We tried to call Voxi through the link. KLse helped me focus until we could both see our net in its fragile entirety. We touched Voxi, but he was too faraway to talk to. Maybe he knew we were coming. Maybe he thought we were in trouble—I hoped not. I didn't want anyone else to get killed for me.

"We'll try again later," KLse promised. And we did, when we were almost to Red Springs. But that time something else was going on. That time all the lines were busy.

"The fleet?" guessed KLse. I thought it was a good guess.

A short while later we got a message on our screen: WELCOME TO RED SPRINGS.

"We must be right in the middle of it," I said. "Where's the city?" The storm had obliterated all signs of life. But I supposed they were used to it.

KLse was typing our names and asking permission to come in.

VOXI WAS WORRIED ABOUT YOU, they sent back.

I took over the keyboard. I WAS WORRIED ABOUT HIM, TOO, I typed. CAN YOU GUIDE US TO THE MONASTERY?

YOU'RE ALREADY ON OUR GRID. ARRIVAL TIME FIFTEEN MINUTES. HAVE YOU EATEN? IT'S PAST SUPPER TIME, BUT WE'LL RUSTLE SOMETHING UP FOR YOU.

THANKS, I typed. They seemed awfully friendly for GodHeads. TGri had been so intense, so imposing, he had seemed too full of the Net to relate to people on an everyday level.

"Maybe that wasn't a GodHead who was talking to us," said KLse. "Maybe that was support staff."

Neither of us had much of an idea of what to expect. I had sort of thought they might be like Catholic monks, living in giant stone fortresses, but spending most of their time communing with the Net instead of praying to God. But they had to eat and sleep, had to exercise, take time off, all of the things their bodies would require, didn't they? I sure hoped so.

I had seen pictures of them the way they had used to be, before Ankere brought the Earlies back to help them get the Net established. They had been filthy, wild-haired, and their eyes had burned with a lunacy that was really a weird sort of accelerated sanity. They had existed with a different perception of time from the rest of the universe, not the linear one most of us think of as normal; and they hadn't been able to find a way to let anyone else know what they knew or see what they saw. That was why people had called them GodHeads, because they had been perceived as drug addicts, wretches who gave up their lives to eat GodWeed. They had raved like religious fanatics, no one had understood them. They had forgotten to bathe, eat, sleep.

That's why they had infected Ankere. Not because they had wanted her to be one of them, but because they had seen what she was going to do someday. They had seen who she was going to find. They knew she was going to find someone who could help them: The Earlies, those people who had left glyphs hinting of a vastly superior technology all over the ruins of their abandoned cities. Everyone else had thought the Earlies were dead; but the GodHeads knew that the Earlies had just moved to a new neighborhood.

The GodHeads knew that the Earlies loved to communicate, *lived* to communicate, and that if anyone could help them sort out their Net, the Earlies could.

And the Earlies had helped them. But I wasn't sure how. I didn't know what technology had been used to turn the GodHeads into the imposing group they had become, into people like LLna and TGri. And I wasn't able to imagine what we were about to see, what the monastery would be like, what Red Springs itself was like, or even how big it was.

KLse was nervous, too. He had doubts he wouldn't let me see. I didn't pry, just stretched my legs and tried to look forward to supper.

My first hint of what was to come came through the passenger's window. I had been peering through, thinking that I had glimpsed light and movement somewhere out in the sand-infested darkness. I was just beginning to think my brain had made it all up when something burst into my field of vision. It was red, or maybe gold, or maybe a bunch of colors in between the two. It was an embryo that hatched into a tadpole, which grew into a salamander, then shrunk back into an embryo. It did that several times, and then it turned sideways and vanished.

It was replaced by a million miniature pictures, all in rows, like words, all moving in their own way, all demanding my attention. My eyes darted back and forth, trying to take them all in before the van had moved out of range.

Glyphs, KLse said, and the image of the salamander

materialized in my mind's eye again. It seemed to wink at me. It was the Early glyph for "glyph," which also meant "information." I knew that because I had received a drip for Early glyphs on OMSK; but not the comprehensive language course, just a general overview. I knew their history and could read a few. But my brain didn't know that. It tried to drink them all in, thirstily. I couldn't make myself look away.

"How are they . . ." I slurred, thinking that the God-Heads were somehow projecting the glyphs to us through our link, right into our brains. But then I could see the solid walls upon which the glyphs were carved, and I realized that we had entered a compound. Glyphs were written across every available surface. They burned in the darkness as if they were made of light. But I knew they weren't.

My own visual cortex was causing the effect. Early glyphs don't glow on walls, they glow inside your head. It was maddening, because I understood just enough to enthrall me. I wished I had asked for a comprehensive language drip, but there hadn't been any particular reason for me to have one at the time. OMSK never does anything for anyone when there's no profit involved.

KLse shook me, gently, but he couldn't shake me loose from the compulsion. "It's not bothering me as much," he said. "Can you close your eyes?"

No, I sent. But I was starting not to mind. I was getting used to it.

We pulled into a tunnel and went down into their parking structure. The walls were still covered; I stopped expecting them to be bare. I hoped our dinner plates wouldn't be covered, too. I could imagine myself mopping up my gravy with a piece of bread and having a salamander wink at me through the mashed potatoes.

"This is weird," I said to KLse, and felt proud of myself that the words weren't slurred this time. Definite improvement. "Do you think it's part of the GodHead conditioning?"

"I was wondering that myself," he said. "But I'm not having the same reaction. Maybe it's a test."

The thought disappointed him. He was wondering if he had flunked.

"Maybe you're not *supposed* to have a reaction," I said. "If anyone has flunked, it's probably me."

I couldn't tell him I already knew he was going to make the grade, that Edna had talked to his future self. I didn't want to jinx it. I thought they would probably still want Edna, too; but I didn't know if they wanted me or not. Or if I wanted them. If they were willing to invite me in, I would take a look around, but I wouldn't necessarily stay.

The underground garage was huge, but only about half full of vehicles. Most of them were the same sort that KLse and I were in; a few seemed like they might belong to visitors. Our van pulled into a slot, and shut itself down.

No one was in sight.

KLse and I climbed out. It was cold down there, and dead silent—if you didn't count the mental chatter of all those glyphs. We looked around, trying to determine which way to go. We could see everything clearly down there, yet the lighting was dim, the colors subtle—except for the glyphs, and I wasn't sure they were any particular color anyway.

"Does that bother you?" I asked KLse, who had been following my train of thought.

"No," he said. "It makes me feel curious."

"Ah hah!" I said. "Another test. You pass."

He clicked his teeth. We began to walk out into the wide aisle between the cars, our boots going *tap-tap-tap* in the hollow silence. I tried to look at the architecture under the chattering glyphs; I sort of thought it might be Early influenced. My eyes were just beginning to adjust to the illusory movement on the walls when I caught a glimpse of real movement.

Something was crossing the aisle, farther down. I started to call, then got a better look at what was moving.

It was a couple hundred feet from us, but I could see it was huge. I could also see that it had several limbs, and glistening jaws. It stopped and looked in our direction. When it turned its head, I saw red fire trace itself up and down a black-painted carapace. GodHead glyphs. After all, you could hardly get a conventional GodHead tunic onto a Vorn body.

The Vorn looked at us for another moment, then continued on its own way again.

"Should we call him back again?" I asked.

"Her," said KLse. "The males are only about half that size. I think if she was our guide, she would have said so."

"Down here!" called a deep voice. KLse and I looked toward the far end of the aisle. Two tall figures were approaching us, these with only two legs apiece. They wore GodHead tunics. KLse and I went to meet them. When they got a little closer, I recognized TGri and LLna.

I was glad it was them and not Voxi or one of his spouses. KLse couldn't be trusted around them just yet. And vice-versa, I'm sure. LLna and TGri knew that even better than I did. I was glad to see them. And what became apparent to me as they got closer and closer to us, was that they were very, very glad to see *us*.

We met in the middle, and regarded each other for a long moment. I had forgotten how pale TGri's eyes were. Like the eyes of a blind man, but those eyes saw too well.

"This was the thing you had to do," he said.

He could have meant a lot of things, but I wanted to be sure. "You mean that this is what I had to do before our net could be as strong as yours," I said.

"Yes," said TGri.

"How come you couldn't just tell me that?"

He clicked his teeth. It was a startling sight, humor in that forbidding face. "We can't just look at the future and then tell everyone what to do," he said. "If we did, we would screw it all up."

Hah! I thought. *Tell that to the future KLse who rescued us on Homeworld!*

But he wasn't lying to me. He was a GodHead, and I wasn't, and the truth was still too strange for me. I was going to have to take the next step before we could even have a decent conversation.

"So what's for supper?" I asked.

"Come upstairs," said LLna. She was giving KLse long looks, telling him things with her demeanor that I couldn't read as well. He was a newly divorced male, and she a female, and this was unfamiliar terrain for him. He seemed to feel comforted by whatever was passing between them.

LLna and TGri led us back down the aisle and under a wide arch. From there we got into an elevator, and even that was covered in glyphs. My eyes darted here and there, but my brain wasn't trying to figure it all out anymore. It was sort of like being in a room full of people with a vid going in one corner; you're talking to people, but your gaze keeps returning to the screen.

My eyes were equally interested in TGri and LLna. Their presence was disturbing, glad as I was to see them. They made me feel jumpy, as if they might move in sudden, devastating ways at any moment. It wasn't their body language that gave me that feeling; their bodies held no more tension than one would normally see in X'GBris. But I could sense activity going on, right under my eyes. I knew they were busy, even while they were talking to me. And what was more troubling, though more subtle, was the way they smiled. They both had an odor that my nose couldn't define, and their eyes . . .

That was the one thing about GodHeads that hadn't changed since Ankere's time.

"You guys get a lot of visitors here?" I asked, thinking of the vehicles downstairs.

"Scientists," said LLna. "Anthropologists, archaeologists, psychologists, neurologists, physicists, mathematicians, astronomers, engineers, chemists, pharmacologists. Reporters. An occasional politician."

"Family?" I asked.

"Not often," she said, her eyes glowing with a storm of information.

Her hair was beautifully coifed. *Who combs your hair for you now, LLna?* I wondered. *Did you find another lover here while your husbands were gone?*

How I wanted to ask her how she was getting along with Voxi and the others now that they were back. I was hoping she hadn't lost any of them in the battle with WWul's husbands. She wasn't glaring at KLse, didn't seem to be angry with him; or me, for that matter. But even if she hadn't been a GodHead, I couldn't have been certain.

We got off the elevator and entered a hallway that made me glad we had two guides. It reminded me of a painting by a Pre-Empire artist, M.C. Escher, who loved to distort time and space. The hallway had no ceiling, and I could see stairways, rooms, alcoves, open courts. They weren't quite twisting into each other, but the

Early glyphs that covered them made it seem like they
might if you gave them half a chance. We saw several
people going about their business, all in GodHead tunics
except for the Vorns.

LLna and TGri moved quickly down the hallway.
KLse kept up with them easily, but I had to follow at a
near run. I tried to make sense of what was around me.
I looked up and thought I saw a salamander dangling
his webbed toes in a pool. He waved at me.

We went through another archway, into a big, comfortable room with a normal ceiling. It was warm, despite its size, and the glyphs that covered its walls were
of a more relaxed, homely nature. The floor was dark,
polished wood, covered here and there with thick
X'GBri carpets. Comfortable chairs of many different
sizes stood alone or in small groupings.

Bookshelves were full of hard copies, anomalies in a
place where surely text of any language and type could
be flashed before the mind's eye at the whim of a God-
Head; yet these were not dusty with disuse, and many
volumes lay on tables with bookmarks in them. It
seemed that even here, some people preferred to hold
a book in their hands and read printed words.

*When information comes at you faster than the speed
of light,* said KLse, *maybe it's nice to slow down once in
a while.*

LLna and TGri showed no sign whether they knew
we were using our link. They led us to a small grouping
of chairs in a corner, under a painting of some dancing
bears in a forest. Somehow, the bears managed not to
clash with the glyphs. I didn't know what weed the bears
had all eaten, but it certainly wasn't GodWeed.

We sank into our chairs. Trays had been set in front of
KLse's and mine, and on those trays were covered dishes.
Mine contained salmon on pasta, with asparagus and dijon
sauce. KLse's contained an equally tasty X'GBri dish. The
food was so good that I was halfway through it before I
remembered to say something very important. I looked at
LLna, who was watching me serenely.

"I don't know where Edna is," I said.

"She's here," answered LLna.

I didn't believe her. I wasn't alarmed about that, exactly. It just didn't make sense. I felt for Edna along our link, and got the same, unsatisfactory result I'd been getting since we had arrived on GodWorld.

"When did she get here?" I asked, trying not to sound like I knew she was lying.

"A little while ago," said LLna. She seemed unruffled.

I ate three more bites of my salmon. I wanted to enjoy it a little longer before they gave me the run-around.

When I had eaten enough, I put my utensils down, wiped my mouth with the napkin, and said, "When can I see her?"

"When you find her in the desert," said TGri.

I studied him. I remembered what he had said the first time he had laid eyes on Edna. He had come to the mall specifically to find her, and he had said, "Tell them at Red Springs that TGri wants you to walk in the desert."

"Why do we have to go into the desert?" I asked him.

"To eat the GodWeed," he replied. "You must walk until you find a living plant, and then you must pick and eat a bud from one of its stalks."

"Don't you have any here?" I said. I should have thought they had a gardenful.

"GodWeed thrives under the most difficult conditions, in competition with some very dangerous plants," said TGri. "The plant itself cannot be tamed."

That was funny, considering what a friendly little thing the sprite was. I couldn't imagine it battling killer plants. But it must have been tough to survive all those years without human cultivation. And if it was tough, maybe that was why it liked Edna, who had walked miles so she could shoot Mr. Kyl for hurting her family, and hunted alone in the desert for food and water.

Edna, who had killed the men who killed Raptor.

I wondered if TGri and LLna already knew what KLse did not.

"Edna had a psychotic break on O'KHro," I said. "She had a program in her head that made her go home, to the place she was born. Some doctor from OMSK put it there a thousand years ago. She was sent to OMSK for committing mass murder."

KLse was astonished. But TGri and LLna were not. They already knew everything I was telling them.

"That's why they wiped her," KLse was saying. "Of course. I knew it had to be something serious to get her to OMSK." He looked at LLna, and I could see he dreaded the answer to the question he had to ask her next.

"Will you still take her?"

"Edna is always welcome," said LLna. She glanced at me, and I could have sworn I saw a flash of humor in her eyes. "The sprite likes her," she said. "That's all that really counts."

"Why can't I see her now?" I demanded. I missed Edna terribly. Talking about her only made me realize that more. But LLna was shaking her head, human-style.

"You will only reactivate the psychosis that hurt you both so terribly on O'KHro," she said. "Those broken mirrors . . ."

"Just hide the mirrors," I joked, lamely.

She lifted a large, graceful hand and pointed to her temple. "The mirrors are in here," she said.

I couldn't argue about that. I remembered too well what it had been like to be in thrall to Edna's psychosis, to be completely unable to act on my own volition. There had been times when I had almost forgotten my own existence, as if I had been so drunk that I had just blacked out. There were large chunks of time after Edna's breakdown that I didn't even remember, like most of the time at the hospital and most of the time in the egg on the way to Homeworld.

Shithole, her dad had called that world. I could still hear him saying it, but I couldn't remember my own mother's voice.

"KLse and you will go together," TGri said, his voice almost soft, almost kind in the human-style. I stared at him, trying to fathom what he was. He knew what I was thinking, though he wasn't reading my mind or listening in on our link. He was reading my face, my body. There were humans in the Net with him, he must have known them better than he knew his own family.

"KLse should go with Edna," I said.

TGri's eyes looked into me and past me. "Edna will have a companion," he said.

I wanted to ask him who, but a group of people came

into the room, talking loudly and enthusiastically about something. I wasn't quite sure what it was they were discussing, but I assumed from their demeanor and their lack of robes that they were some of the scientists LLna had mentioned earlier. They glanced in our direction briefly, but looked away quickly with a touch of embarrassment. They must have realized we were candidates.

They definitely *weren't* candidates, these humans in the casual clothes who were discussing things that I could only partially follow. What wonders the GodHeads were revealing to them, I could only guess. They fetched their own suppers and settled down in chairs in another corner, still happily arguing with each other between bites.

"You must be tired," LLna told me. "You must want a shower."

I was tired. But I was beginning to wonder if showers weren't totally pointless. After all, we were going out into the desert soon.

How Edna would have laughed if she could have heard that!

"How long must we wait before we can venture outside?" I asked TGri.

"The storm will abate by midmorning," he said. I didn't ask him how he knew.

"I'm up for a shower," I said. "I just hope the walls in my bedroom don't talk all night long."

They clicked their teeth at me. We stood and left the newcomers to their supper and their conversation. Some of them watched us go, polite curiosity in their eyes.

I was feeling pretty curious myself. Watching LLna's graceful back, I wondered whom she was sleeping with tonight. Had she and Voxi made up? Would she sleep with any of the other husbands if Voxi was still being stubborn? Had she known that he would try to take control of the Net? How I wished I could get her alone and ask her. But even if I had been alone with LLna, I doubted that I would have the gall to pry into her personal life that way.

No, I would just have to ask Voxi the next time I saw him.

As we walked through the various halls and levels on

our way to the visitors' quarters, I began to wonder if one had to be a GodHead to understand the layout of the monastery. Or an Early. If this was the way they all saw the universe, no wonder they had had so much trouble communicating with ordinary people. I rather liked it, though. It had a fantastical, dreamlike quality. I half expected the people in the hallways would float past us rather than walk.

Our room was in an X'GBri quarter; and it was *one* room, with one bed. I was glad for that, because I had been planning to ask KLse if I could join him anyway. For his part, he didn't seem disturbed at the prospect.

"You'll be called for breakfast," said TGri. "But not at the crack of dawn. You'll find that everyone here keeps their own hours. We have that luxury."

LLna was waiting at the door. As always, both LLna and TGri had a half-preoccupied look about them. I tried to imagine what they would have looked like in the old days, before the Earlies had come.

A moment later, I wished I hadn't. The mental image was almost too much for me.

I turned away from them and sat on the bed. "Good night," I said, my eyes on my feet. "Thank you for allowing us to come."

"Good night," said TGri. "By this time tomorrow evening, you're going to understand why we did."

I watched their legs as they left. KLse shut the door behind them.

"Who's first for the shower?" he asked.

I didn't see any reason why we had to take turns. We could save a lot of time if we shared. He caught my thought and seemed to agree.

It wasn't that I was feeling terribly amorous. It was just that I was so glad to see him. We went into the bathroom without another word and inspected the facilities. In here, the Early influence was plainer than ever. The Earlies dearly loved to bathe. There was a tub, a small pool with a waterfall, and a large shower.

I needed to wash my hair, so we opted for the shower. KLse had to help me take off the padded armor. Underneath, my safety suit was almost pristine, if somewhat

rumpled and sweaty. We put it into a cleaner, along with
KLse's clothes, and we laid our boots side by side.

His body was just as wonderful as I had remembered,
though my memories had been filtered through Edna's
adoration. I hoped she wouldn't mind that I was there
with him, and that he was enjoying looking at me, too.
He didn't try to make love to me, though his erections
came and went. He scrubbed my back, and I scrubbed
his, and he went to towel himself off while I took extra
time to rinse my mop of hair.

After I had brushed my teeth (X'GBri teeth only require a rinse), we put on the briefs that had been left
for us and crawled into bed together. KLse put his arms
around me and I rested my head on his shoulder. He
kissed me, and for a moment it looked like we might
make love after all. The moment was so sweet, it almost
took the rest of the pain from my heart.

But sleep was creeping up on us. I cuddled against
him, feeling small and dainty in his arms. I drifted off
to sleep without knowing it.

The salamander was growing and shrinking before my
eyes again. I watched it without much thought, but after
a while the repetition started to drive me nuts.

"Can't you do something else?" I asked it.

It stopped, midshift, and looked at me. "Sure," it said.
"How about this?"

It turned into Ankere.

"Actually," she said, "I prefer to be called An. Ankere is just a fancy name."

It seemed to me that I had heard her say that before.
And I couldn't remember eating GodWeed, so I shouldn't
even be in No Time.

"You're dreaming," said An. "I'm not really here."

"How do you know that?" I wondered. For someone
who didn't really exist, she seemed to have a lot of
self-confidence.

"You just seem to have that sort of mind," said An.
"Watch."

And she shifted into Peter Hammill. "Hello," he said.
"I *do* really exist. Sort of."

I felt KLse's shoulder under my cheek. I could hear

him breathing, too, which was a comfort. But I also seemed to be standing somewhere, and Peter Hammill looked as real as he always did.

"Don't you ever dream?" I asked him.

"Yes," he said, "but I don't think I can sort my dreams out from yours at this point. After all, it's your brain that's sleeping, and your subconscious from which the dreams are drawing their substance."

I snuggled against KLse. "Do you miss having your own dreams?" I asked Peter Hammill.

He shrugged. "Not really. You can't miss what you never had."

His face began to take on amphibian qualities. It looked like the salamander was about to perform an encore.

"How come you keep doing that?" I asked what was left of Peter Hammill.

"I'm not doing it," said the salamander. "Your brain is."

"Why? My brain is tired, it needs to count sheep or something."

I wished I hadn't said that, because now a line of salamanders were jumping over a fence. "Because," they said, each picking a word in his turn, "your brain is being rewired. You looked at an infection glyph."

Oh great. That's what had happened to Ankere a century ago. That was how she had become an Early. Now I was going to be an Early, too.

"No, you aren't," said the salamanders. "You're just adjusting to the glyphs."

"Good," I said.

"Besides," the last one in line said, pausing before he made his jump, "you're already too many people."

He jumped over the fence, then hurried down the hill and out of sight.

Good, I thought. *I'm too many people, so I don't have to be another one. What a relief.*

It made sense to me while I was dreaming. But when I woke up in the morning and remembered it, I almost didn't want to get out of bed.

I felt normal in the morning, once I was up and around. I was nervous of course, but I didn't feel like my brain had been rewired. When I looked in the mirror, I didn't see an Early looking back at me.

KLse and I put on safety suits. Mine was the expensive one Voxi had bought me. I don't know where KLse got his. I was surprised to see that it was black. He folded away his grey clothes as if he never expected to see them again.

"Did you have weird dreams?" I asked him.

"I had sad dreams," he said, and I was sorry I had asked. I had almost forgotten how miserable he must feel about his divorce. He looked rested, though. He looked like his usual, vigorous self. And at breakfast, he ate like a horse. I did, too. They made us eat that way.

"You're going to need twice as much fuel as usual," LLna told us. "Eat until you're full, and then eat some more."

"Drink, too," added TGri, pushing a pitcher of tea toward us.

Great, I thought. *It's always fun to piss in the desert.* But instead of attracting funny little birds that went *bleep?*, we would probably be assailed by moisture-seeking roots from carnivorous plants.

We were back in that big, comfortable room. Overhead, the bears were still dancing in their painting, but the scene seemed brighter. It was as if the morning light had crept through the maze of the monastery and into that frame to light their forest. They were having such a good time dancing around and picnicking. The scene couldn't possibly have been farther from the reality we were about to face.

Or from the X'GBri GodHeads in their stern tunics, who sat facing us with pale, unblinking eyes.

"Do you like that painting?" I asked LLna, pointing to the bears.

"Very much," she said. She seemed amused that I would ask. Probably she guessed how curious I was about more personal aspects of her life.

"But it's not anything like an X'GBri painting," I ventured.

"That disturbed me at first," she said. "But it was like a great adventure, this painting. I couldn't imagine why anyone would tell a story that had never happened, *could* never happen. It took me a long time to realize that the painting makes the story true. Once I knew that, I couldn't get enough of it."

She grinned a fierce X'GBri grin, shocking me. "So you see?" she said. "Now I have the key to your human hearts."

"You certainly have the key to human heartburn," I said, and stuffed the last bite of my strawberry waffle into my mouth. I was so full I couldn't help belching. But my X'GBri companions didn't seem to mind.

LLna and TGri looked downright happy. Or maybe excited was a better word. It was a bit unnerving, or possibly flattering, I couldn't decide which. Did they act this way every time a new candidate showed up? If this had been a horror vid, they would have been vampires waiting to add two new victims to the fold. But I didn't think they were vampires. I just wondered what the hell I was doing here. After all, I wasn't working for OMSK any more. If KLse hadn't wanted me with him, if I hadn't wanted to see Edna again, would I be sitting here now?

I gazed at the painting again. The bears seemed to wink and grin at me.

Bomarigala had a lot to do with why I was there. He had done more than just give me a personality that pleased him. He had set me up to do this. When he had come out of the shower to find himself alone, he ought to have known that he had only himself to blame.

And if I ate GodWeed that morning, I would blame the salamander from my dream. His crack about how I was already too many people had piqued my curiosity.

"The storm is over," said TGri.

KLse tensed. I had to remind myself that I knew he was going to make it into the Net; I was the one with the unknown future. I tried to imagine myself in GodHead clothes. If that was all you were allowed to wear, maybe it was for the best if you *didn't* make it in.

We stood and made our way out of the room, which had become a little crowded. Someone had moved more tables and benches in to accommodate the big breakfast crowd. There were a few regular people, like us; but most were GodHeads, and I marveled at seeing so many of them in one place together. The presence of that many GodHeads filled the room with an odd tension, like that of an electrical storm. We wove our way through them, and I knew without a doubt that they knew who we were and what we were going to do. They might have even known what was going to come of it.

KLse and I were led through the maze of the monastery. As we were approaching a wide, brightly lit archway, I felt the first wave of heat. The desert was out there, and we hadn't even been given any goggles. We went out into the naked light.

I blinked furiously and tried to see where we were going. Someone had taken my arm and was nudging me toward a group of shadows, which turned out to be more GodHeads. Goggles were pressed into my hands. I put them on with relief.

These new GodHeads were human. Their hair was long, like X'GBri hair, but not the wild, tangled mess I remembered from the history vids. They were three men and one woman, of varying ages. Some of them smiled at us and some didn't; but all seemed to be watching us with anticipation.

And with naked eyes. They didn't have goggles on. TGri and LLna didn't either.

"I'm Baga," said one of the humans, a fellow who might have been middle-aged. When he moved, I saw a glitter of bio-metal at his temple. He was an augmented GodHead, one of the people who linked the Net with lesser nets. He extended a water pouch for each of us, and gave us hunting knives with sheaths that strapped to our hips. "Once you find the GodWeed, eat one of the buds. From there, you'll know what to do."

"How do we find the GodWeed?" I asked him.

"TGri's already touched you," he said. "And you touch KLse. Your blood will tell you."

"Oh," I said, feeling a little annoyed. I supposed it made sense that GodWeed had to grow in the wild, but that didn't mean they couldn't go out and harvest a stash of buds for initiates. That would have been nice and convenient. But no, they were going to make us go out and find it the hard way. I looked at KLse, who looked back at me. He was ready. I supposed I was, too.

But damn, it was hot. Even in that little courtyard, which had some thin shade from a few trees that had leaves so skinny they looked more like twigs. You couldn't tell that there had just been a superstorm, you could never believe that anything could blot out that monster of a sun. But the GodHeads weren't even sweating in those thick tunics. They gestured toward the gate, which led out into the biggest, widest wasteland I had ever seen in my life. I couldn't see a damned thing growing for miles.

"See you later," I told the GodHeads. They seemed certain that I would. I tried to take heart from that.

KLse and I pulled our hoods up and walked through the gate, into the desert.

I couldn't resist glancing back. The GodHeads were still watching us. Through the goggles, the glyphs on their tunics still looked red. They were an impressive group, even the shorter humans. They seemed bigger than their physical selves. Was it an illusion they were projecting? In the Net, what was the difference between illusion and reality?

I turned back to the desert and tried to watch where my feet were going.

It wasn't like Edna's desert, not really. Her sun had been milder, and the plants and animals far more abundant. Yet I began to feel at home as I walked in God-World's desert. We were going toward some distant mountains, and they called to me. I hoped Edna was being called in the same direction.

KLse and I set a relaxed, steady pace. We tried to drink sparingly from our water pouches. We had no idea how long we would be out there. Those mountains never seemed to get closer. I started to feel a little light-headed within the first hour. KLse felt fine, but we stopped to rest, anyway. He made me squat in his shadow to give me a break from the sun.

"Isn't it getting to you?" I asked.

"Not yet," he said.

"I hope Edna is holding up okay."

"We would know if she was in trouble," he said confidently.

"I'll bet she likes it here," I said. "I'll bet it reminds her of home. She used to hunt with a bow and arrow."

He shifted on his haunches, trying to get comfortable. "Who did she kill?" he asked.

"You mean the first time or the second time?" I asked, knowing he meant both. "She shot a man when she was just four and a half."

"Why?" he said, taking a small swig of water.

"He made her mother beg for money. Then he wouldn't give it to her."

"Good reason to kill a man," said KLse. He capped his water pouch and stood again. "Look," he said, pointing with his chin.

There was a tree growing out in the middle of nowhere. Amazingly, it had shade. We stared at it for a long moment.

"Seed storms," said KLse.

That was what would happen to us if we went near that tree. It had an extensive sensory root system, and if we set it off, the tree would shower us with seeds that would pierce our skin and then bore their way inside. Once there, they would begin to grow. Doctors could cut and cut to get them out, but if even a few cells remained, they would begin to grow again. Even drugs couldn't wipe them out completely.

We made a wide detour around the tree.

The sun was directly overhead before we saw another sign of life. Or rather we heard it. The heat was beating up into our faces off the hot sand by then, blasting us from all directions, and then we heard the sound of water.

We looked around. It sounded like a stream, a clear cold little stream with sparkling water, splashing on wet stones.

"Take a sip of water," KLse ordered me. I obeyed. It helped, a little. We looked again for the Tempter plant.

It was hard to find. You have to look for little sprouts of grass. The main body of the plant is underground. That's the part that makes the noise, making it look like there might be water under the sand. After all, how else could the grass be growing there? Grass that was so green and tender, so full of moisture. We followed the sound, cautiously, and walked up a gently sloping dune.

On the other side was a whole patch of Tempters.

They looked so harmless. They looked like a little patch of grass struggling to survive out in the middle of an inferno. We weren't fooled by them, but we couldn't walk away from them. They weren't growing alone out there.

There was a clump of GodWeed right next to them.

KLse was considering the situation. The GodWeed wasn't surrounded by the Tempters. They curved around it in a rough U, as if they were trying to encroach on its territory. Or maybe the opposite was happening, because the GodWeed looked very hardy. It had several handsome buds on it.

"This is what we came to find," said KLse. He began to move cautiously toward the GodWeed.

"Look out," I warned. "You don't know how big the plants are underground."

He seemed determined to take the lead. I didn't argue, but I drew my knife in case I might need to cut him out of a trap. From what I had heard, it wasn't easy to get away from a Tempter once one had grabbed you, but I was certainly going to do my damnedest.

KLse was taking cautious steps, feeling the ground with his boot before putting his weight down, then waiting to see if there was any kind of reaction. He kept as far away from the grass as he could. I was just beginning to think he was going to make it when I saw a tiny stirring of dirt about two feet behind him, in ground he had already tested.

"KLse . . ." I warned, and then the ground gave way right underneath him.

He immediately sank almost up to his knees. I screamed and dove forward, ready to plunge my knife into the green maw that was clasping both of his legs with thorny lips. I had taken three running steps when KLse pointed his right wrist at the Tempter, flexing his hand out of the way. He gripped his right forearm with his left hand, and a blast of heat and light exploded at his feet.

Green stuff gushed up from the ground. KLse sat down on the edge of the hole and pulled his legs out, unharmed. He got to his feet and looked at the destruction with fascination.

I had stopped short, almost falling on my face in the process. "Are concealed weapons allowed on this trip?" I asked.

"They didn't say they weren't," said KLse.

I laughed, weakly. I watched him edge around the pit and resume his cautious advance. Apparently he was inclined to save ammunition.

A few minutes later, he was bending over the GodWeed. He cut two fat buds from their stalks, and edged his way back again. I didn't breathe easy until he was standing next to me.

"Let's get far away from here," he said. "Let's get out in the middle of nowhere." He didn't want to be next to any dangerous plants when we ate those buds. We had no idea how they were going to affect us.

We walked toward the mountains for another hour or so. By then, the heat was really beginning to feel like it was going to kill us. Finally we saw some rocks in the distance and decided to make for them, hoping they would harbor no plants. We both needed to sit in the shade for a while.

The rocks were uninhabited. We fell into their meager shadows and took out our buds.

"Sip some more water first," said KLse.

I did, but I was wondering if I shouldn't save mine until *after* I ate the bud. It probably was going to taste terrible. KLse took his out and swallowed it whole. That X'GBri gullet of his would grind it down.

But the buds were as big as plums, covered in a tough fiber. I tried to bite into mine, and couldn't do anything more than get my teeth stuck. I pried it out again, and attacked it with my knife, managing to cut it into four parts. I could see its inner structure then. It was pulpy and contained seeds and a fibrous mass. I began to chew the first quarter.

It was dreadful. I chewed until I got it into a swallowable state, and then choked it down. I didn't feel like going on from there, but I forced myself to eat the second quarter, too. I had swallowed that one and was in the middle of the third when KLse began to vomit.

He had been watching me with amused sympathy when a look of terrible distress twisted his features. Then he bent over double and began to retch.

"KLse!" I cried, horrified. I bent over him, helplessly, trying to see into his poor face. He tried to ward me off, and in a moment I could see why. The stuff he was bringing up was smoking. His bile was highly corrosive, and he didn't want me to touch it. He was careful not to get any of it on himself or to let it dribble onto his chin.

He vomited up the entire contents of his stomach (which by that time was nothing but liquid), gasping for air in between retches. I looked for the GodWeed bud, thinking that the poor guy would have to wash it off and swallow it again. But it wasn't in the mess. Either it was staying put for some reason, or it had already been dissolved and absorbed. And once *my* stomach had broken down the bud I had swallowed . . .

I looked at the last quarter, wondering if I should try to throw up the ones I had already eaten. I could feel them sitting in my stomach like a lump.

"Eat it," gasped KLse.

"Huh?" I said. He had turned a sickly color, and looked like he might start vomiting again.

"Eat it," he said again. "This is why they made us eat that big breakfast."

"Wonderful," I said, and I reluctantly pushed the last quarter into my mouth. I chewed it as long as I could stand it, and then I swallowed it.

KLse had begun to retch again. He coughed up what was left of the water in his stomach, and then dry-heaved for a while. I sat with my hand on his back, trying to be a comforting presence since I couldn't do anything else. I waited for my own convulsions to begin, but they never did. Instead, I got a queasy feeling that slowly abated, until I simply felt . . .

Well, I suppose drugged is the word. But not like any drug I had ever experienced before. I didn't feel woozy or sleepy; I didn't feel speeded up or paranoid. I felt relaxed, alert, and didn't know at first how my perceptions had been altered. Poor KLse stopped retching. He rinsed his mouth out, and then I made him lie down with his head in my lap. He took his goggles off with shaky hands. The light didn't seem to bother him.

"I'm not miserable," he assured me. "It's not the way you usually feel when you vomit."

"How come I'm not vomiting?" I wondered.

"I don't know," he said. "I guess everyone is different. Do you feel anything happening?"

"Yes. I guess so."

"Just wait," he promised.

So we did. We waited until the sun started to go down. I took my own goggles off and wiped my grimy face. It wasn't until then that I noticed something interesting.

"I'm not hot anymore," I said. "Look, I'm not even sweating."

He hadn't been sweating in the first place, at least not that I had been able to tell. I looked into his eyes, waiting to see that GodHead glare, but his eyes were just sort of bloodshot. It was a pretty sight. X'GBri blood looked purple when it was still in their veins.

"When do you think it happens?" I asked him.

"I don't know," he said. "Maybe it's already happened and we're just not used to it yet."

"Your eyes look normal," I said.

"Your eyes look beautiful."

He was staring at me in that direct, X'GBri fashion. It made me feel good. His hair was tickling my hands. I wondered if his hair could feel me.

"Yes," he said. "But not as well as my skin."

He was close inside the link. In fact, he was so close,

I hadn't even known it. "Let's look at our net," I suggested. "Let's see how it's changed."

"Okay," he agreed. We clasped mental hands and looked at our net. But it was gone. Something else had taken its place, something that swelled inside our heads and stretched out into the void beyond the stars. We soared with it, trying to find its end, until it twisted back on itself and took us home again.

And it was morning.

"Oops," I said. The entire night had passed while we hadn't been looking. Little brown birds were perched on the rocks above us now, watching us with sharp eyes. They knew exactly what we were. I got the feeling they were waiting to see if we would do anything useful.

"Did you see it?" asked KLse, in wonder.

"Yes," I said, misunderstanding him.

"We've linked the Nets," he said. "We did it. We're the bridge."

"Wait—" I looked again. There it was. I had thought our little net was gone, but it had become stronger. It had woven itself into the complexity of the GodHead Net.

"Okay," I said. "Now what?"

"Now," KLse said, "it's time to pass out." And his eyes turned up in his head.

Frantically I clawed the cap off my water pouch. I splashed his face and called his name. The little brown birds squawked at me. They didn't see what all the fuss was about.

KLse sighed and turned his head in my lap.

"Don't worry, Aten," he said. "I'm not dying." And then he went limp.

I felt for his pulse. It was steady. His body temperature didn't seem to have altered much either. I sat back against the rocks, his head still in my lap, and tried to take stock of my own situation. My stomach still seemed to be working on the bud. Obviously I didn't have those powerful X'GBri acids to work for me. Everything that was happening to KLse might happen to me, too, once my slow digestion got its job done. So I tried to relax. In fact, I closed my eyes, sure that when I opened them

again I probably wouldn't feel much different than I was
already feeling.

We were drifting on the wind, KLse and I. We were
seeping into underground water. Birds and other animals
ate us and crapped us out again. We made war with
other plants and tricked them into spreading us along
with their own seeds. It was a very satisfying job, and
the perks were great.

We were dipping our webbed toes into delightful
pools. We were a living glyph, pure information. We
couldn't wait to spread it around, pass it on. We went
from egg to tadpole to adult, and back again.

"It's happening," said the salamander. "You're coming in, and you're going to bring the universe with you."

"Is there room?" we wondered.

"There's room," promised the salamander. "Look."

We opened our eyes.

I knew I was in for trouble as soon as I was ushered
into Bomarigala's office. He had on his poker face. His
very beautiful, expensive poker face, I might add. It always took my breath away.

"Aten," he said, pronouncing the name carefully, reminding me how much lower I was in status and syllables
than he. "I have an important assignment for you. Probably the most important assignment you will ever have
in your life."

"Yes, sir," I said, as neutrally as I could, but he
laughed, showing me most of his white teeth.

"Yes, you're going to hate it. But you are uniquely
qualified for this job. You are the only agent I have
whose personality is strong enough to survive the Net
intact."

"Now wait a minute!" I cried. "Who do you think
you're kidding? Is that what you said to Rena? Is that
what you said to Andera and Kori? Now they're all
GodHeads. I guess you *like* giving all your best agents
to the enemy."

Bomarigala let me get all the way through that speech
without interrupting. That should have told me some-

thing right there. He would have cut me off at the knees if he hadn't been amused by what I was saying.

"None of those esteemed individuals would ever have dared to speak to me with that tone," he said. "You have only proven my point."

I nailed my cool back down and said, "At your service, sir."

"Yes," he said. "You are." He got up, moving as lithely as a big cat, and walked around his desk. I tried not to flinch. I kept still until he had walked past me. Then I got up and followed him. I kept one step behind him, my eyes on the curtain of hair that fell down his back. So black it was nearly blue.

I had no idea where we were going. I never did, not until it was too late. I had known it would be like that when I signed on at OMSK. Sacrifices for enormous gain.

We got on a lift and moved in toward the center of the complex, in toward the medical levels. I had spent a lot of time there, lately. I had received several drips. I had learned several new, useful skills in the space of a few short weeks. Even if they never paid me another cent, I was still ahead of the game.

I felt Bomarigala's eyes on me. I glanced at him, caught him checking me out. He had come into my room a couple of weeks before, just before my drips. He had made love to me. He had been very good, but I didn't remember my own performance. He hadn't done it again, so I assumed he had just been curious. I was curious about a lot of things myself. The drips had taught me so much.

We got off the lift and entered forbidden territory. You didn't walk those spotless corridors unless you were a top-level tech, a special agent, or Bomarigala. I seemed to remember being wheeled in, once. I had been sedated and strapped down. I had looked at the lights and the walls in wonder. I had looked at Bomarigala.

He took me into a training room. It contained one station with two chairs on either side of it. Bomarigala gestured me toward one seat and he sat in the other. He played his fingers across the keypad and a stimulator emerged from the table. He trained it on me and began to flash lights into my eyes.

At first I tried not to look. But I was quickly snared.

"What is your name?" asked Bomarigala.

"Aten."

"How are you employed?"

"I'm a special agent for OMSK. I've worked for this facility for ten years."

"What is your mother's name?"

"Kirito," I said, proudly. My mother was a war hero. She had died earning her last syllable.

"Who is Edna?" he asked.

I didn't know.

"Who is Edna? Where does she come from?"

"I never heard of her," I said.

"You're extraordinarily beautiful," said Bomarigala.

"Of course."

"We've perfected the synthetic." He did something to the light, making me blink. "Do you believe that?"

"Yes."

"Your contacts on GodWorld are X'GBris. WWul and her husbands. One of the husbands is already infected. His name is KLse."

"Kelsy?"

"Close enough. In a moment I'm going to inject you with the synthetic."

"Yes."

"You'll be going to GodWorld in an egg. Do you feel confident about this?"

"Of course." I smiled. One of my new skills was piloting. I was thrilled about that.

"You'll eat GodWeed," said Bomarigala. "You'll enter the Net. But you won't stay there. Take a look around, see how it works, and then report back. Of course you'll do that."

"Of course I will," I agreed.

"No, you won't," said the sprite.

"Huh?" I looked at Bomarigala. He hadn't heard the sprite. He was injecting me with the synthetic. The sprite was looking over his shoulder. It waved at me with one of its buds.

"You don't have to leave unless *you* want to," said

the sprite. "He can't tell you what to do in here." It watched Bomarigala inject me with the synthetic. It was fascinated.

"That's all," said Bomarigala. "You're ready to go."

"Yes, sir," I said, trying not to giggle. The sprite looked so funny bending over his shoulder like that. Bomarigala took me down to the docks and stuffed me into an egg. I blasted away from OMSK and floated to GodWorld. I popped the egg and climbed out onto the sand, where the sprite was waiting.

"Are you mad at me?" I asked the sprite.

"No," it said. "It's not your fault. And besides, Bomarigala programmed you to come here. He did us a favor, accidentally. Now we can have a good look at the synthetic sprite."

"The *synthetic* sprite?" I asked. I blinked, and suddenly I was lying in the desert of No Time. The sprite was growing at my feet. It pointed at something over my head. I looked and saw another sprite. But the new sprite just sat there.

"This is how the Net works," said the GodHead sprite. "No Time is where all the information is exchanged, through chemical messages. I'm the one who delivers all of the messages. I deliver them to myself, in No Time. See? See everyone who's here?"

I did. I lifted my head and saw people and GodHead sprites stretching into infinity.

"I talk to all of the versions of myself in No Time," said the sprite. "Very much like the way plants communicate with each other in Real Time. But I have become aware of strangers here. I didn't realize that the strangers look just like me, so I couldn't find them. It wasn't until I tried to talk to a synthetic sprite that I realized what it was. You see, the synthetic sprite isn't self-aware, like I am. It's just a machine. And that's great."

"It is?" I said, trying to follow it all.

"Yes. This is how people can join the Net without becoming GodHeads. Previously, we had to mechanically augment GodHeads to link up with augmented outsiders. That was how we were earning a living, linking up stock markets and thousands of other kinds of communication/information nets. It worked all right, but

there were a lot of people both inside and outside the
Net who weren't satisfied with the slow rate of information exchange. Especially scientists. Scientists don't mind
talking to each other at a slow rate, but it's hard for
them to talk to the Earlies that way."

My head was spinning. The sprite paused and looked
at me with concern.

"It's hard to get used to, at first," it said. "Don't
worry, you're not sick or anything."

"Is KLse all right?" I asked.

"He's fine. He's progressing faster because he's already absorbed one hundred percent of me."

"I'm still working on it," I said. "I'm just a little confused. It seems like a lot has happened since I landed
the egg here. There was somebody else with me."

"Edna," said the sprite.

Of course, Edna! How could I have forgotten her? I
had to chalk it down to GodWeed.

"Don't forget the infection glyph you were exposed
to," said the sprite.

"Yeah," I said. "What's with all the glyphs around
this joint, anyway?"

"The Earlies brought them along when they joined
the Net," said the sprite.

"You have Earlies in here?"

"All of the Earlies," said the sprite.

I wondered if I had heard it right. It was telling me
that every single Early in the universe was a GodHead.
That was a little hard to absorb.

"That was how they solved our first problem," said
the sprite. "They have no trouble switching back and
forth between linear and nonlinear time. They anchored
us in Real Time. And their glyphs make it even easier
for me to exchange information with myself. They pack
more information into a code than even I could with my
chemical code. Of course, to make that change I had to
become an Early myself. I had to look at an infection
glyph."

"Uh-huh," I said.

"But most people who look at infection glyphs don't
respond to them at all, and most people don't become
GodHeads. So scientists who *aren't* GodHeads have had

to exchange information with the Earlies at a fairly slow rate. Because they can't receive as fast as the Earlies can send, if you catch my drift."

"In this case I do," I said. After all, it took years for humans to get all of the information that's packed into just a few Early glyphs. It was probably pretty frustrating to work at such a slow rate.

"Now you've solved our problem," said the sprite. "The synthetic sprite isn't self-aware, but now that it's linked up with us, it exchanges information as well as I do."

I thought I was starting to get the drift. But I had to ask a question.

"How come everyone couldn't just become God-Heads?" I asked.

"Well," it said, "most people don't want to. It's kind of a demanding life. But the main reason is that I just don't *like* everyone. You see, this is *my* life. I don't want *everyone* in it."

"I can understand that. So what now? Am I a God-Head? I don't exactly feel like an agent of faster-than-light information exchange right now."

"You won't yet," said the sprite.

"What do I still have to do?" I wondered.

"Talk to Edna," it said, and pointed to someone who was lying a few feet away.

I sat up. Edna was lying there. She had two sprites with her, one at her head and one at her feet. I crawled over to her and looked down into her sleeping face.

She looked so peaceful. It was almost a shame to wake her. But it had to happen. I touched her shoulder, gently. She sighed. And then she woke up.

The sun had been shining on my face. Aten had closed the radiation filter; she had done it with my hand. Now the sun was blasting into my face again. It felt kind of good, but it made me wonder what was going on. I opened my eyes.

I was out of the egg. My first thought was that the Vorn had dragged me out and taken me to its sandy nest. I was propped up against some rocks, and when I tried to move I noticed that someone was lying with her head in my lap.

His head. It was KLse. The future KLse, dressed all in black. I touched him. He mumbled something to me and opened his eyes.

The Net gazed up at me.

"Edna," he said.

"You came and got me after all," I said, my heart bursting at the sight of him.

"No," he said. "Aten brought you here. Aten came with me into the desert."

Aten. It seemed she had used more than my hand. I had felt her near. She had touched my shoulder just a moment before, but now she was nowhere in sight. There was nothing but sand and light, forever.

"Where are we?" I asked him.

"GodWorld."

I should have known. The sun that burned down on us wasn't the sun of my homeworld. But it wasn't burning me, despite its intensity.

"How did I get here?" I asked him, thinking that perhaps Aten had brought me back through No Time.

"The matriarch's egg," he said. "Don't you remember any of it?"

I remembered Raptor. And Daddy, and Mr. Allen, and I remembered killing seven men. If more had happened to me since, I wasn't so sure I wanted to know it.

"Am I in trouble?" I asked.

He clicked his teeth at me. "You're an astonishing woman," he said. "Both of you."

I was surprised that he knew about Aten and me. A moment later, I knew how ridiculous I was. Of course he knew; everyone knew but Aten. Everyone had seen me talking to myself, taking on my different roles. It was funny now, but I doubted Aten would feel that way when she found out. I should have told her the truth when I had the chance. Now here I was, stranded in the desert, and KLse looked so weak. I felt odd myself. My stomach was working. Aten must have eaten recently.

I stroked KLse's brow. He liked that. He was glad to see me again. He had known which one I was, instantly. Did Aten change my face so much when she was behind it?

It was kind of spooky knowing that someone else had been walking around in my body. But if it had to be someone, at least it had been Aten. I was glad that she had found KLse. But what else had she done? I felt light-headed. Maybe from thirst. But no, I didn't feel like drinking from my water pouch. What was going on in my stomach? What was going on in my blood?

What was going on in my brain? Something about the link? KLse was in the Net now, I could see that. Maybe I could feel it through him. I touched the threads of our link.

I felt it inside me. The Net. My heart started to pound, and that just spread it more quickly through my body.

We ate GodWeed? I asked KLse.

Yes, he said. *Where is Aten now?*

"Here," I said, touching my head.

"No," said KLse. "Not just there. She's in the Net now. She must have found you there."

I was tempted to think he had lost his senses, but deep down I knew he was right. Deep down where the GodWeed was dissolving in my gut.

"Do you think I could find her again?" I asked. "Do you think I could see her?"

"Yes," he said. "Just like you can see the sprite. It only exists inside the Net, but it's a real person."

That was reassuring. But where did it leave us? KLse was still looking sick, and I doubted Aten would just walk up to us if we stayed put. So what next?

"Who's that?" asked KLse. He had turned his head toward the open desert. I squinted in that direction myself and thought I saw something moving.

"Is someone coming to get us?" I wondered. "From the monastery? That would be nice."

But as this person came closer, we could see that he wasn't wearing a GodHead tunic. He was human, pale skinned, sandy haired. He waved at us.

"For heaven's sake," I said. "It's Peter Hammill."

Peter Hammill walked the rest of the way to our shelter of rocks and then squatted down next to us. He looked at KLse with some concern, like a doctor would.

"Your body is adjusting to the GodWeed," he said. "It happens that way for one out of four X'GBris."

"How do you know?" I asked him.

"I've been poking around in the Net," he said. "I've found out a great deal, already. For instance, I know what happened to the real Peter Hammill."

"He went to prison," said KLse.

"Ah," said Peter Hammill, "you're almost all of the way in. Good. You'll be feeling better soon."

"Peter Hammill went to prison?" I asked, beginning to feel like a real slowpoke. "Why?"

"Lots of reasons, actually," said Peter Hammill. "He was convicted as a dissident and sent to a heavy-world prison. He died there. Poor fellow was really trying to help you, Edna; but apparently he helped a few people too many. They never found out about you, though. They can't touch you, now; not in here."

That was a relief, but I felt terrible about the man who had risked everything to help me. "I'm so sorry," I said.

"Me, too," said Peter Hammill. "I'm very much like he was, and I'm sure I couldn't stand a heavy-world prison. It only took him two years to die there. But I'm glad to be here now, Edna, and I have you to thank for that. If your mind hadn't been so elastic, Aten and I would have perished long ago."

I didn't know what to say. You're welcome, my pleasure? Now what the heck are we supposed to do!

"Can we go back to the monastery?" I asked him. "KLse needs to rest."

"Yes and no," said Peter Hammill. "You see, we're not really here. The three of us are in an analog of GodWorld. Your bodies are still resting under the rocks, you're perfectly all right. But until you've completely assimilated the GodWeed, this hallucination will continue."

"In that case," said KLse, "I can get up and walk around if I want to."

He got to his feet. He looked unsteady and his color was still too pale, but he stayed upright. He reached down and helped me up, too.

"Funny," he said, "This feels just like my real body. I'll have to remind myself that I don't have to pass out if I don't want to."

I put my arm around him, trying to steady him. It must have looked silly, he was so much bigger than me. But it made me feel better, and he allowed it.

"Shall we go watch the space battle?" asked Peter Hammill.

We looked at him. "Space battle?" I asked.

"The X'GBri fleet," he said. "They've entered human space. All allied forces were ordered not to intercept them, but the invaders must be itching for a fight. They've attacked three colonies on their way here, and local ships were forced to engage them. There have been casualties."

"How many X'GBri ships are there?" asked KLse.

"Two thousand," said Peter Hammill.

KLse was silent. He didn't look surprised. Personally, I found it all hard to imagine. Space wars had been make-believe stuff you saw on the vid, when I was a kid. In fact, it all sounded kind of exciting.

"How can we watch it?" I asked. "Do we have to walk somewhere?"

"Let's see if the sprite will let us watch in the main theater," said Peter Hammill.

And a moment later we were standing among the stars.

There were people all around us in the darkness, so many I was surprised we weren't crushed in the crowd; yet I couldn't actually see any of them. I could see the stars, I could see planets, and most of all I could see ships, thousands of them. I knew they were warships, though I had never seen their like before. They all had pointy things jutting from their snouts, as if they intended to duel by stabbing each other. I didn't know if those pointy things were weapons or communications arrays, but the overall effect was an aggressive one. They were above, below, and around us, magnified, the space around them distorted by the theater so we could see them all.

I felt something stir next to me, not KLse or Peter. I looked down and saw the sprite. It pointed with one of its stalks and said, "Wow, look at the sunkiller!"

The sunkiller floated in the middle of the X'GBri fleet; it was ten times bigger than the largest of the ships that escorted it. It was the biggest, weirdest, most fabulous gizmo I had ever seen in my life. I couldn't even tell which part of it was the weapon and which part the jump engine; my training in egg piloting hadn't covered warships and doomsday devices.

"It's a lot more impressive than the one Bomarigala made," said the sprite. "A lot sneakier, too. None of my agents were even aware it existed."

"Are they bringing it *here*?" I asked, horrified.

"They're in our outer system," said the sprite, "just beyond the orbit of our seventh planet. See it there, the gas giant with the pretty rings? But they won't get any closer. The Earlies are going to move them."

The allied ships were hanging back, trying not to engage the X'GBri fleet; but they were in a tough situation. The X'GBri ships were attacking everything in sight, including other X'GBri ships that were apparently siding with the allies. I saw the allied ships winking in and out, trying to harass the invaders without actually engaging them. But some of them were taking heavy hits, and I doubted that strategy was going to work much longer.

"Didn't the Earlies help you out the last time this happened?" I asked. "Where are they this time?"

"Coming," said the sprite. "They have to gather a lot of ships, and even for the Earlies that takes time. At least, it does in Real Time."

"Can they destroy the X'GBri ships?"

"Heavens, no," said the sprite. "They wouldn't do that. Earlies never hurt anyone, they just move them."

"*Move* them?"

"To a remote part of the galaxy. They'll move them so far away it'll take them years to get back again. And when they do get back, if they attack us, we'll move them again, until they just get sick of it."

They didn't look like they were sick of it just yet. I had to admit, it was fascinating to watch them. They were firing beams and globs of light at each other, torpedoes and particle beams, I suppose. Sometimes the lights were red or white; sometimes they were deep blue; and you could never see what good they could possibly do until they actually connected with something. Sometimes they seemed to distort the image of a ship, twist it out of sound, and sometimes they seemed to coalesce into bubbles when they encountered their target. I finally realized that I was seeing the effects of explosions against shields. But sometimes ships shuddered under those impacts, and bits of metal peeled off, spilling ice crystals in their wake.

"The Earlies better get here soon," I said.

"They will," said the sprite. "They know I've got friends on those allied ships. Ah! Here they are."

I blinked. It looked as if the images we had been watching were being distorted by some kind of interference, like you might see on an elaborate vid screen. Thousands of dots broke up the picture. They became lines, and the lines stretched themselves out into flat, two-dimensional images of ships. The images fluttered again, and the ships became three-dimensional.

They were each as big as the sunkiller. The X'GBri ships had begun to fire on them as soon as they had resolved themselves into lives; but the energy all seemed to twist harmlessly off around some unseen corner. The allied ships winked out of space, leaving just the Earlies and the invading X'GBris, who stopped firing at them. The X'GBri ships seemed to stretch like taffy. I blinked; that had to be an optical illusion.

"They're going to try to jump," said the sprite. "They'll never make it."

I watched the sunkiller. Would they leave it or try to take it with them? It hung there like a sun-eating god, waiting for its sacrifice. The X'GBri fleet had parted to let it through, as if they thought they could still deploy it, despite the Early ships. I thought I saw a blue fire dancing around its superstructure—it was going to fire. I held my breath, wondering if it would hurt to die in a supernova.

And then it was gone. It became two-dimensional, turned into a line, turned into a dot, and then winked out. A moment later, the X'GBri fleet did the same.

"Are they going to be all right?" I asked the sprite. I was glad they weren't going to smash our sun, but I felt a little bad for them, too.

"They'll be fine," it said. "They'll be really mad, but they'll have a chance to cool off on the way back to known space."

"How long will it take them to get back here?"

"Twenty years," said the sprite.

I felt KLse flinching as if he had been struck. I held on to him, but he didn't fall.

What's wrong? I asked him, trying to see him in the darkness.

WWul was on one of those ships, he said.

I was thunderstruck. WWul attacking GodWorld? Didn't she know KLse was here?

Yes, he said, and that one word contained everything I needed to know about what had happened to KLse's marriage. It was over. And as much as I loved him, it was not something I could celebrate.

I wished Aten were there. She might have known what to say. For all I knew, she was standing there in the theater with us, but I would never find her there. I had been tempted to shout her name, but I hadn't been able to work up the nerve.

The sprite tapped me on the ankle. "Excuse me," it said. "Someone here would like to talk to you."

Aten! She was there, after all! But I couldn't see anything but stars.

"Close your eyes," said the sprite. "Then open them again."

I shut out the stars. When I opened my eyes again, I saw the light of No Time.

But KLse and Peter Hammill hadn't come with me. One moment my arms had been around KLse, and the next they were empty.

"Oh no!" I said, "I can't lose him again, not now!"

"You haven't lost him," said the sprite. It was growing at my feet. All around us, people were stretched as far as the eye could see, all communing with their own versions of the sprite.

"KLse is still lying with his head in your lap," said the sprite. "In here, there are millions of versions of him, all talking with me."

I looked around me. I saw lots of people, but not KLse. Still, it made sense. Everyone who was there seemed to be alone, one person for each sprite. Though I saw one person who had *two* sprites nearby, one at his head and one at his feet.

"Remember how you traveled through space here?" asked the sprite. "That was a breakthrough. You've given us all sorts of ideas about how we can improve communication here. Usually, I'm the one who delivers all of the messages, but when you tripped over An, you were able to talk directly to her."

"I remember," I said.

"Here she is again," said the sprite, and it pointed to a lady who was sitting up, not far from us. She was beautiful and golden skinned, with long black hair. When she smiled and waved, the Early inside her was easier to see.

"If you don't mind," said the sprite, "we'd like to try it again. I've told An what your situation is. She'd like to help you find Aten."

"Don't *you* know where Aten is?" I asked.

"Yes," it admitted. "I know where lots of Atens are. But we're trying an experiment here. Will you help us?"

I couldn't say no. Not after everything the sprite had done to help me. I didn't even want to say no, because I was curious myself.

"I'll try," I said.

"Good. You should be able to walk over to An without any trouble. But from there, the two of you should try to avoid any versions of yourself. We don't want to cause any nasty time loops. They have a habit of pinching themselves off."

That didn't sound like the sort of pinch that just stung a little bit. "I'll avoid myself," I promised, but wondered why that didn't mean I should avoid Aten, too.

"Here we go!" said the sprite.

I got up and aimed myself at An. I resisted the urge to say good-bye to the sprite, since no matter where I was in No Time, the sprite would be there, too. An smiled at me, encouragingly. It was an odd smile. It seemed to say more than just, *Hello, I like you, you're doing fine.* It was the Early in her face, transforming simple gestures into complex ones.

"Can you hear me?" I called, though we were only about ten feet away from each other.

"Yes," said An. She stood up to meet me. In another moment, we were standing side by side. I was surprised to see how much shorter than me she was. At least a head shorter.

"So far so good!" said the sprite growing at our feet. "Now you have to do the same thing you did on Homeworld. You have to follow your instincts to Aten."

"Okay," I said, and tried to tune in to them. But my instincts must have been on vacation, because I didn't get any impressions of Aten at all.

"Let me help," said An. I felt her tugging on the link, the old one I had had with KLse, Voxi, and Aten. It was still there, but now it was much stronger.

Let's follow the thread that leads to Aten, said An. As soon as I heard her voice in my head, an image exploded behind my eyes. It looked like a salamander, going from egg, to tadpole, to adult, then back again. It stopped in the middle of its transformation, winked at me, and then turned sideways and disappeared, much in the same fashion the X'GBri fleet had just disappeared.

An's hand was on my shoulder, steadying me. "Don't let that bother you," she said. "That was an infection glyph. We exposed you to it because we thought it might integrate you with Aten and Peter Hammill. But you just became more separate. It will sort itself out of your system once the GodWeed has finished its work."

I was shocked. Aten had warned me about the infection glyphs. But apparently she had encountered one herself, recently, and looked at it with my eyes. Now it was in my brain, and I would just have to trust that I wasn't about to turn into yet another person.

"Why did you want us to disappear into each other?" I asked.

"We didn't," said An. "Not exactly. We thought you *needed* to come together. We didn't know you were all so well-defined."

Of course, they must have thought I was crazy. *We* were crazy. They had tried to cure us, but we were incurable.

"I know how you feel," said An, and I believed her. Somehow, when she said things I knew she meant them. After all, she was an Early; and they loved information, not *mis*-information.

She touched the link again, and this time there were no hallucinations. We looked at the thread that led to Aten. It seemed to stretch into infinity.

"Ah-hah," said An. "This is going to be a long journey. But every step in here amounts to miles in Real Time. Come on."

She started to walk, following the thread. I followed, too. We began to pick our way between people and GodWeed sprites. Some of the people seemed familiar, but I tried to ignore them once I determined they weren't Aten.

We looked at the thread, periodically. It stretched and twisted off into the distance. "Will we ever get there?" I asked An.

"We have all the time in the world," she said.

That was true, it wasn't like we were wasting time. There wasn't any time. I couldn't even feel how long it had been since we had begun. I wasn't bored, I wasn't tired, I wasn't thirsty. I kept looking.

Edna, someone called. I stopped dead. That wasn't Aten's voice, and it wasn't An's. It was male, but it wasn't KLse's, either.

It's Voxi. I'm still with you.

How long have you been here? I demanded.

With you? Since before you ate the GodWeed.

An had stopped. She was waiting patiently, trying not to look too hard at the people around us.

How are you going to tell Aten the truth? he asked.

I don't know, I said, impatiently. *I'll cross that stream when I get to it.*

Bad approach, he said.

I tried not to get mad at him. *How would you do it?* I asked.

Carefully, he said.

"Great." I motioned to An, and we began to pick our way across infinity again. I hoped Voxi would butt out, but he was still there with me. He watched us without comment for a long time.

When did you become a GodHead? I asked, trying not to be irked at the prospect.

I didn't, he said. *KRni did. One of my spouses.*

You bum, I said. *Everyone else is doing your work for you.*

I could almost hear his teeth clicking. *It's worked out well,* he said. *And now that the matriarchs are out of the way for the next twenty years, we can build the Net we should have had all along.*

Apparently I had missed a lot when Aten had run off with my body. Like an entire political coup. Voxi's hopes for the synthetic had panned out. That was nice for him, possibly nice for his entire race; but I still had these personal problems that weren't getting any better. And they weren't little, bitty problems, either, they were great big ones. For all I knew, being in the Net was just going to magnify them.

"Oh!" said An, and she stopped. She waited for me to catch up to her, and she pointed.

I saw Aten, sitting up and talking to a GodWeed sprite. The sprite pointed one of its buds at someone else, and Aten turned away from us to look at this new person.

It was me. But not the me I was now; it was another me, who seemed to be sleeping. Aten got up and made her way over to that other me.

"Hurry," said An. "She's about to talk to the you who doesn't know as much as the you you are now."

I picked my way over to Aten, An just behind me. I tried not to trip over anyone; for all I knew, there were other versions of me lying around there as well. Aten was leaning over the sleeping me as we came up behind her. She touched the sleeping me on the shoulder and I opened my eyes. I hid behind Aten before I could see me.

"Where'd she go?" I heard Aten say.

"It's not a good idea for people to talk to earlier versions of themselves in No Time," the sprite said.

"Huh?" said Aten.

I couldn't help peeking. The sleeping me had disappeared. Aten was kneeling on the ground, talking to my sprite. I touched Aten on the shoulder, and she jumped like a cat. Her eyes focused on me, and she laughed with relief.

"Edna!" she cried. "There you are! Where have you been?"

"Watching the space battle," I said, looking closely at her face. She was the Aten I had seen in those first days, when I had thought she was a real person. She didn't look that much like me, except for her size and coloring. Had my face changed when Aten had taken her turns? Is this what others had seen in my own face?

"The X'GBri fleet," Aten was saying, looking worried. "What's happening?"

"It's already over," I said. "The Earlies moved the invading fleet to a remote part of the galaxy. The sprite says it'll take them twenty years to get back again."

Aten was trying to take it in. She was also looking at me so fondly, she was making me feel shy. She put her hands on my shoulders, as if to reassure herself that I was real.

"When you disappeared from the egg," she said, "I was so worried about you. I pictured you stumbling around in the fierce ultraviolet, getting burned. But you don't look burned at all. What happened?"

"I don't remember," I said, honestly.

"You don't remember anything?"

An and the sprite were watching us, quietly. They were waiting for me to tell Aten the truth about herself, but I wasn't quite sure how to approach the subject. How do you tell someone that they don't exist outside the confines of your skull? And why should they believe you? I couldn't even prove it to Aten, because in No Time she had her own body.

"I didn't know what was going on until I woke up in the desert with KLse's head in my lap," I said. "The GodWeed was already in my stomach."

The smile faded from Aten's face. A scary sort of blankness was taking it place. The implication of what I had just told her suddenly came home to me. *She* had been the one with KLse's head in her lap. *She* had just eaten the GodWeed. I hadn't thought about what I was saying.

"Aten," I began to say, and then couldn't figure out how to continue. We stared at each other blankly for an endless time.

And then something swooped down on Aten from the sky. It grabbed her and tore her away from me, flying off like a raptor. At the last moment I grabbed at her ankle, managed to catch it, and I was lifted too. I felt someone else grab *my* ankle. I looked down and saw An hanging there, just as I was hanging, and the ground rapidly diminishing below us. The sprite waved at me with one of its buds, as if I had just taken off on a scheduled flight.

I looked up, past Aten's body. The raptor wasn't a bird at all. It was Peter Hammill.

What the hell are you doing? I called down the link to him.

You can't tell her in No Time, he sent back on a tight beam.

Why not?

Can you imagine what a psychotic break would be like in here? he said. *You think the first time was bad, all those shattered mirrors?*

Well how is this an improvement on that situation? I asked, still hanging on for dear life. My hand was already sore, and I had An's weight dragging me down as well. I didn't know if we could actually get hurt inside an analog, or No Time, or wherever the hell we were at that point, and I didn't want to find out the hard way.

I didn't mean for this to happen, said Peter Hammill. *I just meant to get Aten away before she could hear more than she could stand to hear. I didn't know I could fly, and now I don't know how to stop.*

Do you at least know where we're going? I said.

No. Look down. I can't tell where we are now, can you?

I looked. The endless field of people from No Time had disappeared. Below us was a white something, not a blank nothingness, but a shifting something, almost like sand. An was looking at it, too.

That looks familiar she said, on a wide beam so that we could all hear her.

Should we try to land on it? asked Peter Hammill.

No! warned An. *I think that's time. You can get buried there. I wonder if Shifty City is down there . . . ?*

Shifty City? we all asked at once.

A city in the middle of time, said An. *I've visited it twice, by accident. You can get things done there, but it's dangerous.*

We'll avoid it, then, said Peter Hammill.

We flew on for some time. I was pleased to discover that my hand didn't get any more tired than it already was, so I could hold on without too much trouble. But it sure wasn't any fun being dragged across the sky like that.

Hey, Peter Hammill, it suddenly occurred to me to ask, *how are you flying?*

What do you mean? he said.

How are you doing it? You don't have wings. Are you just thinking yourself through the air?

He was silent for a long moment. And then suddenly we began to fall.

I wish you hadn't asked me that! he said on the way down. *I don't know how I was doing it!*

We all tumbled to the ground, still holding on to each other's ankles. Blue sky and white sand swirled together in my head, making me dizzy and aggravating the feeling of elevator drop in my stomach, until suddenly we were all sprawled on the ground.

By then we had let go of our various ankles. We sat up and blinked at each other.

"That didn't hurt," said Aten. "I thought it was going to hurt."

"I hoped it wouldn't," said An. "I tried to think positively."

"Where are we?" asked Peter Hammill.

We looked around us. The white sands had gone; now we were surrounded by an ordinary desert, with scrubby bushes, and ordinary, un-sandy dirt. Some little birds hopped off one of the bushes, fixing us with their bright, curious gazes, and said, *Bleep?*

"Homeworld," I said. "After all that fuss and muss, we just ended up back on Homeworld."

Aten had squatted and was brushing at the ground with her hands, uncovering something. "This is too level," she said. "I think we're on a road of some kind."

We all squatted next to her. In another moment, she had uncovered pavement.

"It's my road," I said.

"Are we stuck in your dream?" wondered Aten.

I stood and gazed off at the horizon, turning 360 degrees. I easily found my old mountains. I even saw raptors riding the thermals above them. But there was something ethereal about them; I could almost see the sky through them. The whole landscape had that quality. *Almost* real. I thought for a moment, and then pointed.

"That way," I said. "That's where the city is."

Without discussion, we all began to walk. It felt like the right thing to do. But when we had gone a short distance, I wondered, "Will I have to shoot Mr. Kyl again?"

"I'd be happy to shoot him for you, if you'd rather," said An. "I feel I've come to know him so well."

I remembered, she had said that she had dreamed she was me once. She must have seen what Mr. Kyl had done. That thought gave me some satisfaction.

"I don't really want to shoot him anymore," I said. "But I'd like to tell him what a rat he was, to his face."

"Not that it would make a dent in his smug exterior," Aten said. "But I'd like to tell him a few things, myself."

I wondered if we were going to see anyone at all. There was something strange about my homeworld, now. Something had changed, though I couldn't see what it was. Yet still, I felt that even the world had noticed the change, even those eons-old mountains had taken note.

We walked for a long time, and the sun moved across the sky. I loved the feel of it on my skin, just as I had loved it all those years ago when I was still almost innocent, when I had hunted and dreamed. As we walked, something began to appear in the distance ahead of us, over the curve of the world.

It was a city. But as we got closer, I could see it was far grander than any city I had ever seen on Homeworld, possibly even grander than the cities of O'KHro and GodWorld, if that could be possible.

"That's not Shifty City, is it?" Aten asked.

"Definitely not," An assured her.

" 'We're off to see the Wizard,' " sang Peter Hammill, " 'the wonderful Wizard of Oz . . .' "

The city steadily grew in our sight. We walked until the long shadows of distant mountains began to creep across our path. I gazed at the distant structures, admiring their lines, feeling that awe I had felt in TradeTown, with KLse at my side. . . .

I could almost feel him there now. . . .

My stomach tied itself in a knot, and my head filled with yellow sand. I lost all feeling in my body then, and didn't even know if I was still standing. Then suddenly it returned, and I felt too much. I began to retch.

"Edna!" Aten was calling. She was holding my hand. An had taken the other one, and they were trying to get me to look at them. I could see them, but they seemed very remote from me. I was standing in the road with them, but I was crouched over, too, and someone was holding my head as I vomited.

"One out of twenty humans vomits when the GodWeed has dissolved in their stomachs," KLse was saying, right into my ear. I felt his warm breath on my skin, his beloved hands soothing the wet hair back from my brow.

"Edna!" came Aten's voice again, anxiously.

"I'm vomiting in Real Time," I told her.

I felt her hand in mine. I felt An's hand, too. KLse made me put my head in his lap.

"Your body is safe with me," he said. "Go where you must, Edna."

And then I was standing on the road again. I couldn't see or feel KLse at all, but it comforted me to know he was still there, still close. He must have known where I was going. I wished he had told *me*.

An and Aten didn't let go of my hands until they were sure I was really back. "I'm not sure what's going to happen," said An, "but I have a feeling you're supposed to be here, Edna. The rest of us might wander around aimlessly without you."

I felt steadier, then. The world seemed a little less ethereal, though it still had that strangeness.

"I feel different, too," said Aten. "You and I must have eaten GodWeed at about the same time, Edna. I think it's completely dissolved now."

I tried not to look unhappy as the prospect of telling her the truth once again loomed before me. I turned my face toward the city, dodging Peter Hammill's attempts to catch my eye. And then I noticed something.

"What's moving there?" I asked.

Everyone looked. Something was crawling all over the buildings.

"Bugs?" guessed Aten. "Maybe we shouldn't get too close."

An shaded her eyes. "Wait a minute," she said. "Those aren't bugs. Those are glyphs!"

"Early glyphs?" asked Aten, with some trepidation. I got sort of a queasy feeling, myself. If there were infection glyphs waiting for us there, I wasn't so sure I wanted to go to the city after all.

"There's only one way to find out," said An, and she charged ahead, down the road. The rest of us followed her; but I was telling myself that if it got too weird, I wouldn't go any closer than I had to. I exchanged glances with Aten, and I could tell she felt the same way. But Peter Hammill didn't. He looked excited. He matched pace with An, and we brought up the rear.

Soon we could see that they really were glyphs. They were "crawling" over every possible surface, calling to us. My doubts vanished, and I picked up my pace, pulled by the siren song of my own curiosity.

At last we had reached the outskirts. An stopped suddenly, and we almost bumped into her. Peter Hammill went a few more steps down the road, and then he stopped, too.

"Those aren't Early glyphs," said An, her tone somewhere between astonishment and excitement. "What are they?"

What indeed? We started walking again, slower this time, following the winding road through the center of the silent city. No one came to greet us, no one watched us from the windows. Yet those glyphs were trying to tell us something, they were positively shouting to us. They danced and sang in a language we could almost, but not quite, grasp. Yet it seemed so familiar, like we *ought* to know it, and if we just looked long enough, we would remember.

I had become so focused on what my eyes were seeing that I forgot about the huge silence that reigned in that city, until suddenly I heard a wonderful sound. It was the sound of splashing water.

"A tempter," warned An.

"We don't have Tempters on this planet," I said. "That's real water."

The sound made me glad. It told me that I could stop trying to decipher glyphs for a moment and go find the source of the water. I followed my ears, and then my nose as the wet smell drifted on the light breeze. The others followed me, trustingly. We rounded a corner, found ourselves in a lovely little courtyard. It was shaded by desert trees, and at its center a little pool was nestled among some smooth stones.

An Early was sitting at its edge, dangling its feet in the water. It looked up at us and smiled. It was not a simple smile.

"Mother!" cried An. "What are you doing here?"

"Trying to help," said Mother. She didn't look much like An, but in a way she *did* look like her. Their mannerisms were similarly complex. It wasn't until that moment that I really understood what the history books had meant when they said that Ankere had become an Early. She had seemed so human to me, because that was what I had wanted to see. But now that she was talking to Mother, I knew how she had changed.

An took off her shoes and went to dangle her feet as well. The rest of us hung back, me out of shyness, Aten out of uncertainty, and Peter Hammill for reasons I couldn't guess. An splashed happily for a moment, then grinned at Mother.

"Those glyphs aren't Early glyphs," she said. "They're an artifact of *our* distant future."

"That's my theory, too," said Mother.

"And I suppose we'll leave them for the same reasons you left them."

"I suppose you will," agreed Mother.

They both seemed satisfied with that conclusion, but I hadn't quite kept up with them. Aten was a little faster.

"Why will we leave?" she asked. "And where will we go?"

Mother spread ripples across the surface of the pool and then watched the patterns merging and breaking. "Some day you'll know it's time to move on," she said. "Just as we did. And so you will leave, just as we did. You'll go where you want to go."

"But all you did was move to the other side of the galaxy," said Aten, stubbornly.

"Did we?" asked Mother, impishly.

I thought about the way the Early ships had looked when they arrived in Real Time, how they had been flat and two dimensional. Where had they been? Where had they really come from?

"The other side of the galaxy is for you," said Mother. "To poke around in for a while. When you've seen it all, you will want to go elsewhere. You'll leave information behind you, for the new ones. And when they seek you out, they'll teach you things you hadn't imagined they could teach."

Peter Hammill knelt at the side of the pool and looked into its depths. "We've taught you something?" he asked. "That's hard to imagine."

"Seeing is believing," said Mother. "I know *you're*

real, Peter Hammill. I have made infection programs like the one An was exposed to, and I have seen machines achieve personalities of sorts; but I have never seen someone quite like you before."

Peter Hammill was pleased, but Aten's curiosity still wasn't satisfied. "Why are you so eager to spread information around?" she demanded. "The X'GBris were ready to kill you! You've given information to your enemies."

Mother splashed again, watched the ripples. "The more our enemies know," said Mother, "the less inclined they are to be our enemies."

"Why?" pleaded Aten.

"Because knowledge is power," said Mother. "The rest is illusion."

I drifted closer to the pool. The water had become still, mirrorlike. I looked at my reflection. It was the same old me, looking back. I was relieved to see that.

"Aten," said Mother. "Come look in the pool."

"Why?" asked Aten, suspiciously.

"Because you're the last one here with something to learn. You're not afraid of the truth, Aten. You're a brave woman."

"Bomarigala programmed me that way," said Aten. But she went to the pool. She looked in. "Edna," she said, "you're in the way. I can't see myself."

My throat closed up so tight I couldn't answer her. I looked up at her, miserably, and watched the truth slowly dawn in her face. She saw, and she crumbled.

"No," was all she said. And then she flew off, like Raptor. She spread black wings and streaked into the sky, away from me.

"Aten!" I cried. "Don't leave me! How will I get along without you? You're part of me! Come back!"

I watched her wheeling in the sky. I knew then that I couldn't stand it if she went away. Daddy had gone, my brothers and sisters had gone, Raptor and Mr. Allen had gone, and they had all taken little bits of me with them. But Aten was my pride, my confidence. Aten was me. I couldn't lose her and survive.

"Come back," I whispered.

And she heard me. She dropped out of the sky. She became Aten again, and she hung her head.

"It's hard," she said, her voice cracking with the same tears I was shedding myself. I took her hands and held them tight.

"In here," I said, "you're you. With a body of your own, just like Peter Hammill. It doesn't matter if someone else made you. You're the one who gets to make you from now on."

Aten looked at me, long and hard. She was trying to find herself there. I think she did, a little. But we weren't twins. Our personalities had gone their own ways, and now the Net was setting us like concrete. We were individuals.

Autonomous, said Voxi, through the link. *All of us.*

We heard splashing. Mother had lowered herself into the pool. She gave a sigh of such rich, marvelous contentment, we couldn't help but be delighted by it.

"And now," said Mother, "the three of you must go have some words with the sprite. It wants to thank you."

"For what?" asked Aten, though she no longer seemed suspicious or defiant.

"For teaching us something," said Mother, and she winked at us.

The city blinked out around us. No Time blinked in. Peter Hammill, Aten, and I were lying with three sprites at our feet. We sat up.

"Hello!" said my sprite. "Did that seem fast? We're getting better at moving people around in here."

"It seemed instantaneous," I assured it, hoping that this meant we wouldn't have to go stumbling around in No Time anymore, trying to avoid ourselves.

"Now that you're in," asked my sprite, "are there any loose ends you want to tie up?"

In. We were GodHeads now, the three of us. Even Aten and Peter Hammill, who both lived inside my skull. What was KLse seeing as he looked into my eyes in Real Time?

"I've got something I'd like to tie up," said Aten. She sat up. "Or rather, some*one* I'd like to tie up."

"I can guess who that is," said the sprite.

So could I. Bomarigala.

"What is your name?" Bomarigala had asked me.

"Aten," I had answered, believing it.

"How are you employed?"

"I'm a special agent for OMSK," I had said, remembering years of service that had never really happened.

"What is your mother's name?"

"Kirito," I had said, the cruelest lie of all.

He had flashed lights into my eyes, and he had asked, "Who is Edna?"

"I am," I said now, knowing that he could hear me through the link, that he had probably been listening in for some time. I felt him there. He wasn't afraid.

I was Edna, I said. *And you thought she was beautiful, so you seduced her and then you decided to remake her. But it didn't work out the way you planned, Bomarigala.*

That's an understatement he said. *I didn't know that Edna was still intact. If I had, I would have wiped her properly.*

Thanks a lot, said Edna, and I was proud to hear the anger in her voice. She wasn't meek anymore, now that she had remembered she could kill to protect what she loved.

I could imagine the expression on Bomarigala's face. He wasn't angry. He rose to challenges; he didn't deny the truth. He simply stood firm, and if you tried to get him to budge, you were just going to bruise yourself. But I wasn't afraid of bruises.

I don't work for you anymore, I said. *You have my official resignation.*

I have no choice but to accept it, he admitted. But why

THE BEST IN SCIENCE FICTION
AND FANTASY

☐ **LARISSA by Emily Devenport.** Hook is a mean, backwater mining planet where the alien Q'rin rule. Taking the wrong side can get you killed and humans have little hope for escape. Larissa is a young woman with a talent for sports and knives. She's beating the aliens at their own harsh game until someone dies.   (452763—$4.99)

☐ **STARSEA INVADERS: SECOND CONTACT by G. Harry Stine.** Captain Corry discovers that the U.S.S. *Shenandoah* is at last going to be allowed to track down the alien invaders who are based beneath the sea—invaders who had long preyed upon Earth and its people—and this time they were going to bring one of the creatures back alive!   (453441—$4.99)

☐ **MUTANT CHRONICLES: *The Apostle of Insanity* Trilogy: *IN LUNACY* by William F. Wu.** It was a time to conquer all fears and stand up against the tidal wave of the Dark Symmetry. Battles rage across our solar system as mankind and the Legions of Darkness fight for supremacy of the kingdom of Sol. But though there is unity against the common enemy, the five MegaCorporations that rule the worlds are fighting among themselves. The struggle for survival goes on.   (453174—$4.99)

*Prices slightly higher in Canada   **RCF9X**

Buy them at your local bookstore or use this convenient coupon for ordering.

PENGUIN USA
P.O. Box 999 — Dept. #17109
Bergenfield, New Jersey 07621

Please send me the books I have checked above.
I am enclosing $ ———————— (please add $2.00 to cover postage and handling). Send check or money order (no cash or C.O.D.'s) or charge by Mastercard or VISA (with a $15.00 minimum). Prices and numbers are subject to change without notice.

Card # ————————————————————— Exp. Date ——————————
Signature ——————————————————————————————————————
Name ——
Address —————————————————————————————————————
City ——————————————— State ——————— Zip Code ——————

For faster service when ordering by credit card call 1-800-253-6476

Allow a minimum of 4-6 weeks for delivery. This offer is subject to change without notice.

ENCHANTING REALMS

☐ **SCORPIANNE by Emily Devenport.** Lucy finds herself with a new identity on a new world at the brink of rebellion. Even here, she cannot escape the nightmare memories of the assassin who strikes without being seen, the one who has sworn Lucy's death, the stalker she knows only by the name Scorpianne.
(453182—$4.99)

☐ **THE EYE OF THE HUNTER by Dennis L. McKiernan.** From the best-selling author of *The Iron Tower* trilogy and *The Silver Call* duology—a new epic of Mithgar. The comet known as the Eye of the Hunter is riding through Mithgar's skies again, bringing with it destruction and the much dreaded master, Baron Stoke.
(452682—$6.99)

☐ **FORTRESS ON THE SUN by Paul Cook.** When a lethal illness strikes his people, Ian Hutchings demands aid from their captors on Earth. Receiving only a denial that such illness exists, Hutchings has no choice but to find his own answers. As time runs out, the prisoners uncover one astonishing clue after another in a conspiracy of stunning proportions. "Highly inventive and engaging.'"—Robert J. Sawyer, Nebula Award-winning author of *Starplex.*
(452262—$5.99)

☐ **THE ARCHITECTURE OF DESIRE by Mary Gentle.** Discover a time and a place ruled by the Hermetic magic of the Renaissance, by secret, almost forgotten Masonic rites, a land divided between the royalists loyal to Queen Carola and the soldiers who follow the Protector-General Olivia in this magnificent sequel to *Rats and Gargoyles.*
(453530—$4.99)

Prices slightly higher in Canada.

Buy them at your local bookstore or use this convenient coupon for ordering.

again. She was still his concern. I knew where they would sleep that night. And I . . .

I wouldn't mind being Voxi's pillow friend for the night. In fact, the prospect was almost enough to make me forget how hungry I was.

The sun was setting as we entered the back gate of the monastery. No one waited for us there; they knew we were coming. They were holding supper for us. The walls of the courtyard were turning red in the dying light, and it became beautiful, not the desolate, heat-blasted place it had seemed before. I stopped, thinking of that other courtyard, the one with the pool and the Early, the one where the light of truth had crept into my consciousness.

As the others went through the door, I turned and watched the last of the light setting the horizon on fire. *Aten,* he had said. *It was what they called their sun.* I would keep it. It was mine. It was the name by which the universe would come to know me. And that knowledge was power, just as the Early had said.

And the rest was illusion.

I turned away from the sunset, and went to find my friends.

its shade so long ago, centuries ago. They had no power to tempt us now.

As we climbed the low hills outside of Red Springs, Edna seemed to get stronger. Soon she was able to walk on her own. She held KLse's hand until the monastery was in sight; but then she came and held mine, walking next to me.

"Is it all really true, Aten?" she asked. "The drips, the jumps, the Net? Have we really done it? I'm not just having another delusion, another—" She searched for words, and I thought of all those broken mirrors we had left on O'KHro. "Another psychotic break," she said, finally.

"I think it's all really true," I said. "But if we're just dreaming it, I think we're so good at it, it's just as good as true. That's an improvement, considering where we came from. Don't you think?"

"Yes," she said, and seemed relieved. She squeezed my hand. "And I can't wait to prove it by eating a huge meal."

"Wait until you see the bears in the dining room," I said. "I think you'll like them."

She didn't ask me what the bears were doing there. She trusted that she would find out soon. She was still herself, not me at all. I would have demanded to know everything before I saw it. But Edna loved surprises. I was glad to know there were some nice ones waiting.

Aten, Voxi said. *I had felt him close, all the way home. I had enjoyed knowing he was there. I'm hooked up to the Net, too.*

I know that, I teased.

I can see you. I'll be able to feel you, too.

Really? I said. *But won't you be sleeping with LLna, tonight?*

It's not my turn.

I almost laughed out loud. It looked as if Voxi's marriage wasn't in jeopardy after all. Not even by me. But that was okay with me. I didn't want to ever witness another breakup like the one KLse and WWul had suffered.

I glanced at Edna and KLse. He was holding her hand,

"It's really true," she said. "The Net made you real?!"

"I feel real," I assured her. "I feel as real as I ever did, and I think that's pretty damned real."

KLse helped Edna get to her feet. She was weak, but her weakness wasn't echoed in my own limbs. I still felt close to her in our link; the link that persisted despite the fact that we were also GodHeads. It was delightful to know that it still survived, that extra dimension.

You are the ones who will replace the augmented God-Heads, said a familiar voice in my head. Voxi. Waiting for us at the monastery. *You're the big hookup, now.*

At last, I said. *Real job security.*

The sun was low in the sky, settling into late afternoon. My stomach growled, as if it were really hungry. I didn't try to work out how that could be happening. Maybe I was still living in Edna's head, despite appearances. Or maybe I was living in a bigger head now, the one that dreamed the Net, the one that shared so many living, breathing bodies.

It sang inside my blood. It was like the glyphs that had covered the city from the future, except that I could understand it. I could hear *all* of it, or just small parts of it if I preferred. I knew what the stock markets were doing, what weather systems were developing on various planets; I knew the status of thousands of experiments that were being conducted, or symphonies that were being composed. I knew how the Earlies had moved the sunkiller, and *where* they had moved it; and I knew why An had recognized the strange glyphs that had chattered at us from those walls of the future. My brain was talking to itself, and to the Net, with the same kind of code. It was the roots of a new language, one that would grow from the minds of many races instead of just one. Someday we would all get there. But for now, there was only one place I wanted to be.

"Let's go home," I said.

We left our little shelter of rocks and turned our feet homeward. We didn't need to ask each other where that was; we could have found it in a superstorm. Edna leaned on KLse as we walked past the Tempters, and that lone tree that had tried to lure KLse and me into plant, so I didn't understand that for a long time; but the Earlies are so fond of their comforts. Once they became GodHeads, things really changed around here, you can bet on that!"

"Good-bye," I told the sprite.

"See you later," it assured me.

The light of the Real Time poured down on us. I blinked, thinking that I had taken over Edna's body again. She must have been slumbering inside me again. But in another moment I saw her, lying with her head in KLse's lap. The two of them were wearing their safety suits—no, that was *my* safety suit Edna had on. I looked down at my own body. I was wearing a GodHead tunic. Peter Hammill stood a few feet away. He was looking down at his own tunic-clad body in wonder.

"I have a body," he said. "I can feel my own body." I could feel mine, too. And when KLse looked at us, he could see us. *Really* see us.

"Anyone linked to the Net will be able to see you," he said. "And hear you, and feel you, just like anyone else. Pretty soon, that's going to include a lot of people."

He bent over Edna and tenderly stroked her face until she opened her eyes. She saw him, and she was so glad she almost broke my heart. I watched KLse closely, to see if he appreciated her reaction. I discovered that appreciation was too mild a description.

Peter Hammill put an arm around me and leaned close.

"At last," he said, and I heartily agreed.

I wondered where KLse had been while the rest of us had been chasing through time. Instantly I knew he had been on Homeworld, rescuing Edna and me. For him, that sad and tender moment had just occurred, and now Edna was back with him in Real Time.

"Your eyes don't look—*stormy* anymore," she said. "They don't look—you know—so wild."

"Yours look normal to me, too," said KLse. "I think it's because we're looking *out* of the Net now, instead of into it."

"Are you all right?" I asked Edna. She looked up and was amazed to find me there.

just like it. For the first time since I had found out the truth about myself, I felt truly comforted. I *did* exist, I was real. I wasn't going to unravel or go into oblivion at the flicker of electrochemical lightning.

In fact, I wasn't going to go into oblivion at all, like poor JKrie had. I was part of the Net now. I would be like An, whose real body had died a century ago; yet there she had been in the city from the future, exchanging theories with Mother, asking new questions.

That was wonderful.

"We've started something good here," said the sprite. "GodHeads like you will link our Net with people who are infected with the synthetic. Some day that could be the universe! No more mechanical augmentation, no more struggling to translate, no more time lags. This is the best thing to happen to us since An brought back the Earlies. Thank you."

"But we did it unwittingly," said Edna. "Voxi and Bomarigala made the synthetic, they're the ones that got things going. We just happened to be the unwitting messengers."

The sprite put two of its buds on its hips, an almost comical sight. But I liked it very much then; I wasn't inclined to laugh.

"I know those two got things started," it told Edna. "But *you* are the one who taught us the real possibilities, Edna. You showed me that GodHeads could move through No Time, could talk to each other. *You* were the one who was three people in one. You don't have the nonlinear grasp of time that KLse does, but you are strong, you are flexible, and really that's the reason that all of this turned out as well as it did. And I like you. I'm glad to have you as a friend. I thank you for that, too."

"I'm the one who should be thanking you," said Edna, but she was pleased. She had finally been made to see her true value. She wiped a tear from her eye, and she looked at me. She was still my Edna, but that hurt, uncertain quality was gone from her face.

"And now," said the sprite, "it's supper time. Your body has been through a lot, and you'd better go take care of it. That was one of the things the Earlies helped us to become aware of, the demands of bodies. I'm a

Shouldn't he? He had what he was after, and more. *We hold the patent to the synthetic for the human worlds,* he said. *Voxi owns the X'GBri patent. We have all become fabulously wealthy.*

Maybe you have enough money to buy another Aten, I said.

That made a dent. I didn't need to remind him that he had almost quit OMSK for me. Or at least, he had considered it. Circumstances had made him see the light. But he still would have liked to have taken me back with him, and fixed me up the way he liked me. Make me the Aten of his dreams.

Why did you name me Aten? I asked him, since he didn't seem inclined to trade insults with me.

It's an ancient word, he said, *from a civilization long dead. It was the name of a god.*

Not a goddess? I said.

It was their word for the sun, said Bomarigala, and I knew then what he had lost. I knew how he had paid for his sins against us, and he knew it, too. *See you in the Net,* he promised, and then I felt him go. I didn't chase him. I had to be satisfied with my victory, such as it was.

"He wasn't telling you the whole story," said the sprite. "It's true that OMSK and Voxi own their respective rights to make the synthetic, just as other races have been granted the rights to make their own version of it. But we own the Net. We *are* the Net, and we're about to get a lot richer than them. Which doesn't mean that we're not going to make Bomarigala pay you what he promised he would when he hired you for this job."

"Hah?" I said, "Make them pay *both* of us." Meaning both me and Edna.

"Hah?" said the sprite. "We'll make them pay *all three* of you?" Meaning Peter Hammill, too.

Peter Hammill sat up, smiling ruefully. "Can I spend money?" he asked. "Imaginary creature that I am?"

"Sure," said the sprite. "After all, *I* do. I'm just like you. I don't have a body either. I couldn't exist without the GodHeads."

I hadn't thought of it that way, but it was right. Maybe that was why it had decided that it liked us. We were